Praise for *Wiv[es]*

"A wickedly funny look at the upper crust."
—*Parade*

"Delectable. . . . Delightful."
—*Vogue*

"Sykes gives Kevin Kwan a run for his money in this saga of obscene wealth, designer outfits, miniature dog breeds, and over-the-top landscaping set in Oxfordshire, a rural area of vast estates now mostly in the hands of the nouveau riche. . . . You'll dive in and never look back."
—*Kirkus Reviews* (starred review)

"Full of sly commentary. . . . An escapist, dishy read."
—*Booklist*

"Sweetly eviscerates the foibles of England's wealthy and fashionable Cotswolds set. . . . Sykes . . . has a Nancy-Mitfordesque ability to skewer a scene like an outsider while still providing the detail that only an insider, or at least near insider, could offer."
—Amanda Taub, *New York Times*

"Fun . . . will delight Sykes's fans."
—*Library Journal*

"A forensically well-observed narrative. . . . A shiny satirette of country living."
—*The Times* (London)

"A comedy of manners with an emphasis on the comedy. . . . Sykes's madcap fare is always more than just a good time, it's a nuanced look inside a specific world, where even the most humorous happenings can tell us something meaningful."

—*Town and Country*

"*Wives Like Us* may be set in the most gorgeous English manor house, but I'd happily sleep in the shed if it meant I could tag along with these marvelous characters."

—Jenny Jackson, *New York Times* bestselling author of *Pineapple Street*

"Made me laugh so hard I actually knocked over my lamp. Can a book be so wickedly smart, so effortless, so chic and hilarious that you would stumble through the night to find a new lightbulb just so you can keep reading way past your bedtime? In a word, yes."

—Kevin Kwan, *New York Times* bestselling author of *Lies and Weddings* and *Crazy Rich Asians*

"I absolutely adored *Wives Like Us*."

—Daisy Buchanan

WIVES LIKE US

ALSO BY PLUM SYKES

Party Girls Die in Pearls
The Debutante Divorcée
Bergdorf Blondes

WIVES LIKE US

A Novel

PLUM SYKES

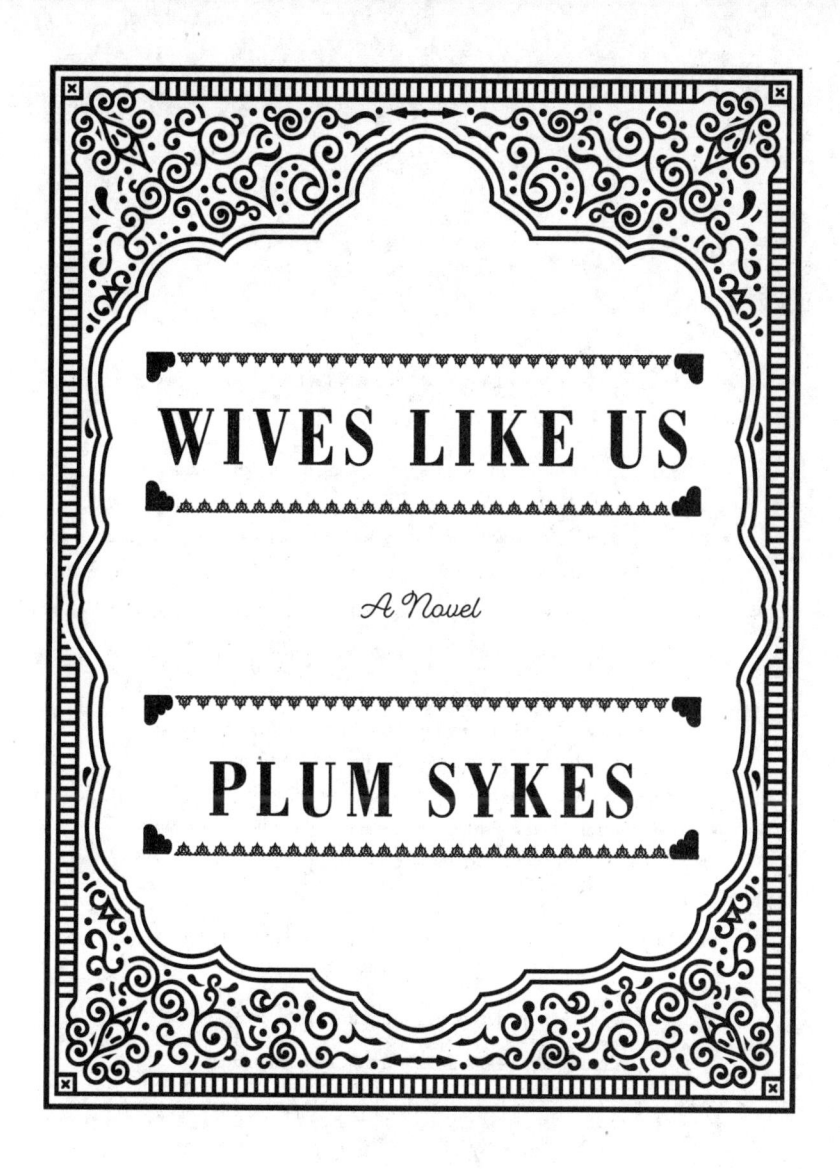

HARPER ● PERENNIAL

NEW YORK ● LONDON ● TORONTO ● SYDNEY ● NEW DELHI ● AUCKLAND

HARPER PERENNIAL

This is a work of fiction. Names, characters, places, and incidents are products of the author's imagination or are used fictitiously and are not to be construed as real. Any resemblance to actual events, locales, organizations, or persons, living or dead, is entirely coincidental.

A hardcover edition of this book was published in 2024 by Harper, an imprint of HarperCollins Publishers.

WIVES LIKE US. Copyright © 2024 by Plum Sykes. All rights reserved. Printed in the United States of America. No part of this book may be used or reproduced in any manner whatsoever without written permission except in the case of brief quotations embodied in critical articles and reviews. For information, address HarperCollins Publishers, 195 Broadway, New York, NY 10007.

HarperCollins books may be purchased for educational, business, or sales promotional use. For information, please email the Special Markets Department at SPsales@harpercollins.com.

Invitation design by Phillip Beresford, 2024

FIRST HARPER PERENNIAL EDITION PUBLISHED 2025.

Library of Congress Cataloging-in-Publication Data has been applied for.

ISBN 978-0-06-242912-4 (pbk.)

25 26 27 28 29 LBC 5 4 3 2 1

For Tess and Ursula

WIVES LIKE US

I

Ian Palmer (thirty-six, looked thirty-two due to daily application of Elemis Man "*Le Tinte*" moisturiser to face and neck) was snoozing like a cherub. The Executive Butler to one Augusta—"Tata"—Hawkins was slap bang in the middle of that delicious dream he sometimes had in which his prince had come. He had just reached the moment where Charming arrives, glass loafer in hand, and is about to pop it onto his butter-soft tootsie, when the theme from *Psycho* interrupted his reverie.

"*EEEEE-EEEEE-EEEEE-EEEEEEEEEEEE!!!*" screeched the violin strings from the iPhone next to Ian's bed, and he jerked upright from his starched linen pillow. That blood-curdling ringtone meant only one thing: Mrs. Hawkins was awake. It wasn't even 5.30 a.m. and this was not usual procedure. In Ian's experience, Mrs. H. rarely saw in the sunrise without the help of certain substances occasionally available at some of the wilder parties in the area.

Still, a butler of Ian's calibre could handle any demand at any hour. He fumbled hurriedly for his glasses (tortoiseshell Tom Fords which gave him that Colin Firth in *A Single Man* look), took a deep inhale as per his online *pranayama* class, then slowly breathed out. He pressed the green button to answer the call.

"We're up early, Mrs. Hawkins," he cooed in the liquid caramel tones he had perfected for work.

An exuberant shriek reverberated down the line. "Ian! Finally. I've met her. The glamorous American who's moved into Great Bottom Park—*the* Selby Fairfax."

Ian could barely contain his elation. But he did of course, as per his role. Ian's USP was his ability to maintain a cool as glacial as the interior of an Asprey's ice bucket.

"Congratulations, Mrs. Hawkins," he purred.

"There's more—"

"Do tell, Mrs. H."

"She's coming to dinner a week from today. There's not a moment to lose."

"Preparations must begin in earnest," Ian agreed solemnly.

"Oh, Ian, you are *the best*. I wouldn't know where to begin with this event without you."

A man like Ian was a rare commodity. When it came to staff, everyone in Oxfordshire—that rose-strewn English county in the Cotswolds where the action takes place—wanted "an Ian," as they put it. He was, in butling terms, a minor celebrity. Not only had he graduated *summa cum laude* from the Greycoats' Butler Institute in Mayfair, he had completed his training as under-butler in Mr. Valentino's household in Rome. It was there, among the marble columns, gilt fringing and scarlet ballgowns, that Ian's taste and skills had been carefully moulded.

Ian took the "executive" in "Executive Butler" seriously. He was a driver, a concierge, a fixer and a friend to Tata. Possessed of the even disposition required to satisfy the unpredictable whims of The Rich, Ian had forged a glittering career doing just that. Whether his boss desired an exquisite *melanzane alla parmigiana* for lunch, a discreet last-minute delivery of cocaine for a dinner party, or advice on what to keep or return from the latest Net-A-Porter haul, Ian made it his business to fulfil every request with effortless ease. As a result, when Tata was confounded and didn't know what to do, the default position—"Ask Ian"—resolved most problems. Even now, when Ian was suffering his own agonising heartbreak, he undertook never, ever to let down his employer. He was as important as a husband—often, more so.

"Breakfast conference, my room?" Tata continued.

"I'll be there in a jiffy," Ian replied. "May I bring you a tray?"

"Yes please . . ." she said. "I'd die for a macchiato, Ian. In one of those new silver lacquer cups that just arrived from Tiffany. You know the ones I mean?"

"Indeed." Of course he did. Ian knew Mrs. Hawkins's china collection as well as the back streets of nearby Chipping Norton, where he'd grown up.

"And a little grilled halloumi with fresh parsley and those crunchy Welsh salt flakes sprinkled on the top."

"The 'Halen Môn' salt?"

"Exactly. God, you must think I'm a fusspot."

"Not *at all*, Mrs. Hawkins." Ian took it upon himself never to appear judgemental. After all, butlers couldn't afford to be critical of the one-percenters who kept people like him employed. "I'll bring a tray to your room as soon as it's ready."

"Then we'll discuss *everything*."

"*Pronto*," said Ian in his immaculate Italian and rang off.

A few moments later, as Ian dashed about his bedroom, pulling on pinstriped trousers, a neatly pressed white shirt, charcoal-grey jacket and navy tie, then throwing a nubbly natural-linen apron over the ensemble, he felt perkier than he had in weeks. The reason? Within the butling universe, one's boss's social status was immediately, and in parallel, conferred upon their staff. For reasons which will soon become clear, Tata Hawkins had recently fallen far in the hierarchy of Oxfordshire, which had meant Ian's position had taken a tumble. He'd tried not to mind, but the social slide had been humiliating. But now that the new chatelaine of Great Bottom Park was paying a visit—goodness! Mrs. H. was on her way up again, and Ian would be too. He just needed to make sure Tata didn't put a foot wrong. His help was, as per *ush*, critical.

Ian slid on a pair of c.1993 Gucci loafers in toffee-hued suede— he saved his tips to pay for his treasured collection of retro Italian shoes—gently closed the door to his bedroom, and made his way downstairs and out of the Annexe. He then lolloped at a gentle canter across the gravel to the Old Coach House next door, praying that the party-planning extravaganza he was about to embark on with Mrs. Hawkins would distract him from the ghastly loss he'd suffered a few weeks ago. Although he was *of course* far too professional to let his boss ever see his pain, it had been a struggle. But this morning, things seemed rosier. The sun was shining and it was already early May, that glorious time in England when the old man's beard is frothing along the hedgerows and the newborn lambs are gadding giddily in the fields. It was impossible in this splendid weather to remain mired in abject despair, however grisly things had been. The blue skies and radiant sunshine were, Ian felt, a sign of better things to come. Ian's dream may have been cut short, but no matter, his prince would return, he was sure, crystal footwear in hand, some other summer's night.

2

Let us rewind by twenty-four hours: only yesterday, at eleven o'clock on Sunday morning, Ian could be found tending to a nervous Mrs. Hawkins (thirty-nine, but "officially" aged thirty-eight) and her overexcited eight-year-old daughter Minty at the annual village fete, which was taking place in the grounds of their home, the Monkton Bottom Manor estate. Ian had suggested that Mrs. H. establish base camp in the "Tuliperie" for the day, and there await the arrival of two of her closest friends, Sophie Thompson and Fernanda Ovington-Williams. The sun-dappled spot was far enough away from the tents and marquees to feel private, but close enough to see exactly who was coming and going. It was a blissful little paradise, with drifts of yellow and white parrot tulips planted in long grass, and was bordered by low yew hedging, with each corner anchored by the sweep of a laburnum tree. A round table had been positioned in a mown circle in the centre and laid up for lunch with a Portuguese linen tablecloth embroidered with snowdrops, those cabbage-shaped Bordallo Pinheiro plates everyone was mad about, bamboo-handled cutlery, Czechoslovakian crystal tumblers and tiny bud vases (of differing shapes and heights, of course) filled with stalks of late-blooming narcissi. Four whitewashed wicker chairs had been placed around the table, which was shaded by a yellow-and-white striped parasol trimmed with tiny white pom-poms that trembled occasionally in the breeze.

From the outside, the casual observer would have witnessed a scene appropriate for a carefully curated Instagram post. After all, here was a very attractive woman and her charming daughter being waited on by a dashingly handsome butler standing a little distance away (never so close as to intrude, never too far away to help— or to miss a single word of conversation). Tata was no slouch in the appearance department. She had a petite, toned figure, snappy cheekbones, pillowy lips and lightly sun-kissed skin (like most of her friends, she had usually "just got back" from a fabulous trip abroad). Her hair, thick as a horse's tail and regularly balayaged to a gleaming caramel, swirled generously about her shoulders. Clothes-wise, she was always pulled together, but in an expensively sexy way. Today her slim legs were swathed in skinny cream trousers, her shoulders were draped in a Bottega Veneta calfskin jacket, and her feet were clad in platform-heeled gold sandals.

Ian used the phrase "Country Bling" to describe Tata's aesthetic when he was briefing personal shoppers on her behalf (which was often). Today his boss had veered rather more towards Bling. But clothes were only a small part of the battle: Ian had learned over the years that for women like Tata a crucial weapon in their social armoury was jewellery, and it was worn on every possible occasion, however impractical it seemed. To that end, today Tata had gobstopper-sized diamond studs in her ears and a snake-shaped pair of La Maison de Couture pavé diamond cuffs curled around each wrist. She had justified buying the cuffs to Ian because the script on the box said they'd been made by a progressive women's collective in Egypt, and she *loved* doing things for charity. Ian tactfully agreed that purchasing the items was indeed a "noble gesture."

"Look! There's Iola and Gloria," cried Minty, pointing at two schoolfriends lining up at a vintage Airstream trailer a few yards away selling home-made ice cream. Though her friends were in shorts and T-shirts, Tata's long-suffering daughter was dressed as a junior royal in a puff-sleeved, cream piqué smocked dress, lace-edged socks and Mary Jane shoes, courtesy of the Marie-Chantal boutique in London's Walton Street. Her ginger hair was arranged in two long plaits tied with oyster-coloured satin bows at each end.

"Can I go with them, Mummy?"

"Course," said Tata.

"Wait a sec and I'll find your purse," added Ian.

As usual, the butler was bearing a monogrammed Paravel duffel bag which contained everything the Hawkins ladies might need today, as well as masses of things they might not. He set it down on the ground and soon produced a little purse made of raffia, which he handed to her. "Your pocket money's inside."

"Thank you," said Minty before she dashed away.

Tata watched as her daughter skipped towards her friends, then Ian pulled out one of the wicker chairs and she sat down at the table. But all was not well: a cloud of pain seemed to envelop her as she regarded the beautiful lunch setting before her.

"Tablescape heaven, isn't it?" she declared wistfully, dropping her trash-bag-sized gold Balenciaga carryall on the ground, where it landed with a thud.

"Absolutely," the butler agreed. Then he added with a rueful look, "But then, I wouldn't expect anything less. It was all your idea."

"Oh, *don't*," said Tata with a sigh, regarding Ian glumly. "Have you brought my Vogues?" she asked him.

"Indeed," said Ian. He sprang to his boss's side with a slim packet of the "healthy" cigarettes that all the mummies smoked when their kids weren't looking. Tata removed one and Ian offered her a light.

"I'm still giving up. Soon . . ." she said, inhaling, then pouting sorrowfully as a plume of smoke exited her lips. "This is unbearable, Ian."

"Things *will* get better," replied Ian, praying that his words would make it so.

He was just placing an ashtray down in front of Tata when something caught her eye and she exclaimed, "Oh SHIT! There's those Pennybacker-Hoare sisters. Please God, don't let them see me," she continued, donning an enormous pair of sunglasses and shrinking into her chair. "They're so mean."

Alas, Ian realised with a heavy heart, the Lady Anne Duffield (née Pennybacker-Hoare, thirty-eight, already mother to a football-team-sized brood) and the Lady Cecily Pennybacker-Hoare (thirty-two, single, and determined to remain so until a suitable hunting-fishing-shooting type came along), were among today's fete-goers. They were scions of the Duke of Stow, who was head of the most aristocratic family in the Cotswolds, the exquisite stretch of hills that swept through Oxfordshire and Gloucestershire, and where everyone wanted to live. Dressed in the uniform of pumps, floral skirts and frilly collared blouses favoured by old-school aristocrats, the two women were standing under the shade of a large oak tree.

"Look at them, gossiping in that awful way they do," Tata said.

Ian watched with dismay as he saw the Lady Cecily, her eyes firmly locked on the Tuliperie, whisper something in the ear of the Lady Anne, prompting an expression of contempt to cross her sister's visage. This was followed by a too-loud peal of laughter, likely designed to be heard by Tata. They then stalked off in the opposite direction.

"Presumably they'll have already broadcast the Hawkins family drama to the entire county. Oh God. This is all so embarrassing."

"No one will take the slightest notice," Ian reassured Tata, as he bustled about the table tweaking the place settings here and there.

Ian wasn't being entirely truthful. The sisters, the grandest, richest and most powerful of the Old Cotswold Lot in Oxfordshire, were the sworn enemy of the New Cotswold Lot. In their view, these HNW arrivistes, of which the Hawkins were the naffest, had swanned in and committed crimes so hateful—such as mowing the grass verges beside their houses, installing electric gates or "rewilding" perfectly good agricultural land that once produced food for the populace—that they would do anything to make their lives difficult. The Lady Anne and the Lady Cecily lived to disparage, judge, and exclude: their dream was to banish Tata and her like and reclaim the countryside for the Original Toffs (them) who so clearly deserved it.

"They treat me like I'm a leper," said Tata gloomily, pushing her sunglasses up on her head. "Now they'll be even worse."

Tata's expression broke Ian's heart. He would have described Mrs. H. as being at the bottom of her socks, if she'd ever deigned to wear them. (She didn't. She had properly sexy ankles and liked to show them off.) But Ian was not surprised by her low mood. The scenario in which Tata had suddenly found herself was enough to leave anyone at the bottom of their metaphorical sock drawer.

Ian could hardly bear to think of it as he pootled around, pouring iced water into the tumblers on the table and flicking the odd bee off a napkin, but only a month ago Tata had been mistress of all she could see. She had been living in Monkton Bottom Manor, the brand-new, fourteen-bedroom, dual-kitchen, six-sitting-room country "seat" she and her husband Bryan had built for themselves a decade ago, and which loomed majestically behind the Tuliperie, high on the hill, for all to see and admire (or deplore, if you were a Pennybacker-Hoare). Funded by the IPO of Bryan's electrical business Plugs'n'Stuff, a corporation which spewed cash (and carbon) like smoke from a steam train, the Manor was constructed of the finest local stone and had been built in the style of a huge, aristocratic Queen Anne mansion (but with underfloor heating, triple glazing, and three-bar water pressure, thank God). Tata and Bryan (fifty-three, but looked sixty-two due to that common affliction, "business-dinner bloat") had relocated here from London a decade ago, and their daughter Minty was born a couple of years later. Much to the envy of various other staff, Ian had resided in the Dovecot, a quaint Tudor cottage which was located just beyond the east wing of the main house. With its thatched roof, foxglove-filled garden, wobbly rendered walls, and resident flock of white doves, no butler could have asked for plusher quarters for himself or his collection of Gucci loafers.

The situation was pretty swell for all concerned. The Hawkinses' property—all sixteen hundred acres of it—was situated in the very heart of the parish of Monkton Bottom, which was a convenient two-hour whizz up the motorway from London. Along with the neighbouring villages of Little Bottom, Middle Bottom, and Great Bottom, this slice of Arcadian countryside, nestled between Chipping Norton in the east and Stow-on-the-Wold ten miles to the west, was *the* real-estate sweet spot, and money-soaked families escaping town had annexed Oxfordshire's dwellings from the rural folk who once inhabited them, extending cottages into farmhouses, farmhouses into manor houses, and manor houses into, well, palaces.

The Hawkinses were the prime example of this model. The Rich Husbands toiled (as Bryan often complained to Ian) at the coalface four days a week in swanky office suites in London, building cash mountains which were rapidly eroded by school fees, horses, holidays, housekeepers, nannies, gardeners, tutors, and masseurs, as well as left-field experts like cold-water swimming coaches, shamans, or equine behavioural specialists. The Rich Wives quietly dropped the careers they had briefly enjoyed in order to commit to their true vocation as modern Ladies of the Manor or "Country Princesses." (A small minority, aware of the optics, assuaged their guilt by dabbling in "hobby" jobs: work-from-home businesses involving ethical diamonds, up-cycled baby cashmere, or online wellness—anything whose commitment level didn't interfere with weekday exercise classes or social engagements.)

For Ian, employment with such a family was ideal. Mrs. H. was quite literally Queen of the Bottoms, and, as a result, Ian was Crown Prince. Tata was good to him and there was a vast staff at his disposal to keep things running smoothly at the Manor. She made up for the odd tantrum and endless demands with vast tips, long holidays, and the turning of a blind eye to occasional visits from occasional boyfriends. Country life suited Ian: having had some wild partying years in his early youth, he now avoided drugs and alcohol at all costs. Instead of falling off the wagon on a Friday night, he could usually be found sipping China tea with the widows in the village, by whom he was universally adored.

But Ian felt for Tata. Her seemingly charmed existence came with absurd pressures: he had observed the social mores of Rich Wife-land for long enough to know that its inhabitants were generally so flush with cash that they existed in a parallel universe, untouched by the concerns of most mortals. With no worries about electricity bills or food prices, healthcare or job security, the Rich Wives were left with oodles of time to obsess about appearances. Whether it was one's house, one's hair, or one's horses, a state of perfection had to be maintained at all times. It was aesthetic and social torture.

Ian would see Tata and her friends scrolling through Instagram and witness their self-esteem collapsing as they analysed snaps of their neighbours' exquisitely edited existences. There were the imposing Cotswold stone houses, bathed in honey-coloured light; there were the perfectly framed views through (Grade I* listed) sash windows of dreamy (filtered) sunsets onto stunning parkland; there were the faux-rustic kitchens, artfully photographed to show off gleaming oak tables laden with pelargoniums and peonies; there were the handbags (Céline, Chanel, Hermès) that crept into multiple posts, signifying that these women may not live in London any more, *but country turnips they were not*. Whether it was creating fashionable new flavours of home-made jam ("home-made" roughly translated to made at home, by the housekeeper), picnicking beneath pink cherry blossoms with a gaggle of stunning children, or divorcing another husband, everything the Country Princesses did was news: other women wanted to read about them, dress like them, be them. This was swiftly followed by a desire to judge them, criticise them and, if possible, hate them, which made them feel miles better about not being one of them after all.

※

To return to our tale of woe. As mentioned, only a month ago, Tata, Bryan, and eight-year-old Minty had been living in harmony at

Monkton Bottom Manor. And then one day there had been a god-awful argument (that Ian had accidentally overheard every single word of) about a mysterious jewellery receipt that Tata had found in a drawer in Bryan's work-from-home office when she was looking for her passport.

Bryan insisted the bill was "nothing," but seemed unable to explain how he had spent thousands of pounds at a jeweller's in Mayfair without a bangle, bauble, or bracelet to show for it. His ludicrous excuse, that he'd bought a retirement gift for his accountant, had made Tata suspicious. After all, Tata reasoned to Ian, Gertrude Appleby, the employee in question, did not have anywhere to flaunt valuable gems. Plus, Bryan had been acting so suspiciously lately, which was unlike him: phone calls had been abruptly ended when she walked into a room; screens had swiftly locked when she glanced over her husband's shoulder. What did Bryan *really* do those three nights a week he was at the house in London without her? Could he possibly have met someone? Why was that bill hidden in his stationery drawer at all? Tata knew enough grisly stories of Rich Wives whose husbands had a girlfriend in town to be worried. "He's keeping a secret from me," she'd told Ian. "I can feel it."

Convinced that the receipt was evidence of an extramarital escapade, Tata had confronted Bryan with it and flounced out of Monkton Bottom Manor at the beginning of April, dragging Minty with her. She had installed herself in another property on the estate—the Old Coach House, a pretty six-bedroom dwelling she'd renovated for guests a few years ago, which was situated in a patch of lowland right at the other end of the Hawkinses' land. But it was so far from the main manor house—a fifteen-minute drive by road, and even longer on the rough grass tracks through the fields—that Ian had, to his secret horror, been forced to evacuate his beloved Dovecot and move into the Annexe which adjoined it. It was a grim sort of exile for him and reminded him of an uncomfortable stay at a youth hostel in Wales on a school trip when he was twelve.

Tata had simply intended to give Bryan a shock and teach him a lesson, and had expected that within twenty-four hours of her departure he'd be begging her, on bended knee, to come home. After all, he could never survive on his own: Bryan understood business but was about as socially sophisticated as a baby badger. But Tata had made a grave error of judgement. Bryan was not the squillionaire CEO of Plugs'n'Stuff for nothing. He was a proud man with an Everest-sized ego which had been severely wounded. How *could* his wife think such things of him? Bryan moaned to Ian. How *could* she accuse him of having an affair?! He had never been spoken to like that in his life and was deeply offended by Tata's accusation. It was, Bryan insisted, *her* duty to come to *him* on bended knee, apologise, and beg him to allow her to come home. He'd decided to sulk at the Manor for as long as it took, no compromises.

Ian was stuck in the middle. He was witnessing a couple at an impasse, each too stubborn to budge. It alarmed Ian that he and Tata had barely glimpsed Bryan over the past couple of weeks unless he was collecting Minty, and even then the couple had barely exchanged more than a few icy words. The child had been told that she and Mummy were staying in the Coach House because the Big House was being redecorated. (Minty fell for this: the Manor was *always* being redecorated.)

And so it was that today Tata found herself in the undignified position of being a mere guest at the fete she usually hosted in the grounds of her home, and which she had spent months personally curating. She was mortified, not least because Bryan had seemingly handed the running of the event over to a certain Charlene Potts, more of whom later.

"If those Pennybacker-Hoare sisters have got anything to do with it, the entire county will think Bryan and I are about to get divorced." Tata visibly shuddered as she sipped at her iced water. "Honestly, if it wasn't for Minty I wouldn't have dreamed of showing up today," she went on. "But she loves the fete."

"You're a tremendous mother, Mrs. H.," Ian replied. "You never let her down."

"I'd do anything for her." Tata plucked a tulip from the grass. "I feel so guilty about what I've put you both through these last few weeks," she went on, twirling the flower limply.

"I'm fine, Mrs. H.—"

"Demoting you from the Dovecot to the Annexe. Most butlers would be on the hunt for another position already—"

"I am doing no such thing. I'm devoted to your family. And the Annexe is very . . ." Ian paused, searching for a diplomatic term ". . . pleasant."

That was, if a cold and dingy slice of a converted cart shed facing due north could be defined as pleasant. The Annexe, Ian often thought when he returned to its grim environs each evening, would be best suited for an Eskimo. But the icy draughts were not the worst thing about it. No, for Ian the tragic reality was that it lacked the space to store his large collection of Gucci loafers, which had had to be abandoned at the Dovecot for now. He couldn't possibly entertain there, either. It only had a tiny galley to cook in, a bit of a comedown after the roomy kitchen at the Dovecot which was kept toasty by an open fire and an Aga. As if that wasn't miserable enough, Ian had been run ragged doing absolutely everything for Tata and Minty: the team of staff at the Manor, which included a house manager, housekeeper, chef, laundress, maids, cleaners, and gardeners among others, was not at his immediate disposal while he was so far away from base.

"We need to be back here, at the Manor," said Tata with a little tremble of her lip. "I can't take it any more."

"Agreed. Now, listen carefully, Mrs. Hawkins," Ian said in a low voice. "When you see Bryan here today, I advise: all smiles. Be your breeziest and most friendly."

"But he's humiliated me—" began Tata.

"You need a strategy and this is the right thing. I promise. He worships you. Just be your wonderful self and he'll remember what an extraordinary woman you are. Now is not the time for pride. It's the time for humility and love. And you look *gorgeous*."

Ian waited as Tata stubbed out the last of her cigarette and pondered her plight. Eventually she turned to him and said, resigned, "You win. I'll do whatever it takes to get Bryan back."

"Good decision," the butler replied.

Tata looked at her watch. "Eleven-thirty!" she grumbled. "Where are the girls? If I'd known Soph and Fernanda were going to be so behind, I'd have been half an hour late too. By the way, there's something I forgot to tell you. It's about my birthday."

"June the fourth, if I recall correctly."

"You're so sweet to remember," Tata cooed. "Anyway, here's the thing. If we're not back in the Manor by then, and Bryan doesn't get to throw me a *fabulous* surprise birthday party . . . well, he'd literally never forgive me. The marriage would be finished. You see, it's a big one."

"It is?" Ian raised his eyebrows, feigning surprise. His boss liked him to keep up the pretence that he had no idea she was soon to be forty.

"Yes," said Tata, and sighed. "Thirty-nine."

"A milestone, Mrs. Hawkins," said Ian. "You'll be home by then, I promise."

3

Moments later, as Ian zipped through the fete-goers towards the posh Portaloos discreetly located near the car park, he soon realised that the Pennybacker-Hoare sisters had already set to work. Beastly little bubbles of banter floated past his ears:

"Anne Duffield says Tata Hawkins has moved out under a cloud—"

"She's been banished to some crummy house on the estate—"

"D-word on the cards?"

The lavatories were housed in a thatched "stable" that had been temporarily erected for the fete by a trendy loo company, rustic-restrooms.com. Ian proceeded up the steps to the gents, dashed in, had a pee, then trotted out again. To his relief, by the time he emerged the crowd had moved on from the Hawkinses' marriage and was discussing their next topic: the aforementioned Mrs. Selby Fairfax. Newly arrived in the village but so far unseen, she was just as delicious a subject as Tata. As Ian made his way back to the Tuliperie, stories about the mysterious Mrs. Fairfax bounced about like a ping-pong ball:

"The marriage broke down after the husband went on a trip to Peru and took ayahuasca. Some trendy shaman told him to Find His Truth—"

"Which was that he was gay—"

"She's from some wealthy East Coast family—"

"He left her for the kids' surfing instructor—"

"He's one of those disruptor types. Made a pile of money revolutionising the global sneaker business—"

"My kids won't wear anything else. You photograph your foot, the SneakersDirect app works out your exact size and the shoes come by post twenty-four hours later."

The whispers went on, and on, and on. As if the arrival of a terrifically beautiful, terrifically successful American divorcée and her two daughters wasn't enough to cope with, everyone knew that Selby Fairfax had landed the grandest, most aristocratic estate in the area. Great Bottom Park was the dreamiest country property you could imagine, the kind of place that triggered agonising bouts of House Lust, that peculiarly Cotswolds affliction. And no wonder: aside from its farms and cottages, stables and paddocks, and thousands of acres of parkland, the jewel at the centre of this bucolic crown was a wildly romantic Elizabethan mansion which sat nestled in its own valley, the heavenly treat that greeted the visitor who had ventured along the mile-long drive. With its gables and spires, its forest of chimneys, the ramble of courtyards and wings, its obelisks and ogees, the house was the sort of dwelling that many a hedge-funder, pop star, and online squillionaire had tried to buy over the years. But the late Lady Maud Bottom, the childless widow who had lived at the house alone for many decades, had always refused to sell. And yet right after her death, an American interloper had swanned in and bagged it, and no one could understand how or why.

Still, if one couldn't buy the big house, one could befriend the owner in order to secure invitations to it, and, indirectly, a sprinkling of the aristocratic fairy dust such invitations conferred on visitors. But try as they might, the great and good of the Bottoms had got precisely nowhere with Selby Fairfax since she'd arrived three weeks ago. Except for the Fairfax girls attending the first few days of term at Stow Hall School last week, it appeared that the family of three had mostly remained ensconced behind the miles of dry stone walls surrounding the estate. The only thing anyone knew for sure was that the air was as thick with rumour about Selby Fairfax as it was with the grass pollen that was wreaking havoc with everyone's allergies that spring.

"Mrs. Hawkins, look, here comes Mrs. Ovington-Williams," said Ian, who was now back at the Tuliperie.

"At last." Tata jumped up from her chair, waving excitedly at the remarkably beautiful woman approaching them, her children in tow.

Fernanda Ovington-Williams (real age a mystery, suspected to be mid-forties) gestured at Tata and Ian as she wove her way through the other fete-goers towards them. Every time Ian saw the half-Venezuelan, half-Swedish heiress, he was struck by her alluring good looks. Absurdly rich, she was a jet-setting fashion goddess who was all about style and extravagance. Her five children only added to her powerful aura and as a clan they exuded beauty, money, and superb genes. They soon strode through an entrance in the yew hedge into the Tuliperie, their two fluffy white South American sheepdogs alongside them.

"Wow, you look amazeballs, darling," Tata told Fernanda, kissing her hello. "Hi, kids," she added, blowing kisses to the twins, Federico and Henrik (sixteen), daughters Isabelli (fourteen) and Carlotta (twelve), and the youngest boy, Luca (eight).

Ian couldn't help noticing that young Luca had a nasty black eye. The skin on the left side of his face had turned blue and looked swollen and painful.

"No, *you* look stunning," Fernanda was saying, in her international lilt, kissing Tata back. (The accepted form of greeting in Rich Wifeland, Ian had discovered early in his tenure with the Hawkins family, was for one wife to tell another that she looked better than her.)

"Is this Phoebe?" asked Tata, scrutinising Fernanda's tiered denim dress.

Fernanda shook her head. "Actually, it's from my new secret person," she said, then continued, in a whisper, "Don't tell a soul or everyone will go there, but it's Sabine Parentis. She interned for Helmut Lang. She's got a tiny atelier in Zurich. It takes weeks to get a piece, but it's custom."

Better get on to Sabine Parentis, Ian silently mused. Anything Fernanda had, Tata wanted: Fernanda was the acknowledged queen of The Secret List, a catalogue of everything from top dermatologists and dressmakers to nail technicians and hair colourists which she only shared with loyal friends. There was, though, another Fernanda list—The Secret List at the Heart of The Secret List—which she guarded so jealously that even her own daughters had never seen it.

Ian noted that today, as ever, Fernanda looked cool in a wildly expensive way. She had properly nailed the look known as Hippie Deluxe, pairing the beautifully cut dress with flat black leather Hermès riding boots. Her glossy brown hair was tied with a large navy velvet ribbon in a low, loose ponytail that tumbled halfway down her back, and an understated black suede Métier bag was slung from shoulder to hip by a clunky tortoiseshell chain. (The designer cross-body handbag, Ian had noticed, had recently become the de rigueur accessory for country mummies: they reasoned that it was "super-practical," as the diagonal strap meant a mother had her hands free to grab a pony, child, or dog, in the event that a member of the domestic staff was unavailable to do so.) Fernanda's hands were adorned by chunky cocktail rings and several articulated sapphire bracelets which were stacked in elegant piles on each of her wrists. Dear me, sighed Ian to himself, when he spotted them. Mrs. H. would be upset: nothing troubled her more than to be out-bangled by her friends.

As if they were mocking him, Fernanda's bracelets made a tinkling sound as she waved at Ian, saying, "Hi, honey! So great to see you."

"Good morning, Mrs. Oving—" Ian started.

Before he could go on, Fernanda's youngest son sprung up onto Ian's back like a monkey, hugging him so tight round the neck he could barely breathe.

"Hey, sweetie, I know you love Ian, but don't strangle him," Fernanda warned the child.

"It's fine," said Ian, meaning it. He adored kids, especially little Luca.

"Ian, I'm sad today," said Luca.

"Oh no, why?" asked Ian.

Luca replied wistfully, "Jean-Pierre has left. He was my friend. Kind of."

"The manny," added Fernanda, looking peeved. "Walked out last night. He said he's scared of the house."

"*I'm* scared of the house," Luca chimed in.

Ian tended to agree with Jean-Pierre and Luca. Whenever Ian dropped Tata off at Middle Bottom Abbey, the Gothic pile a few miles away that Fernanda's husband Michael had inherited when he was just twenty-one, he rather got the creeps. The couple had painted the former convent completely white inside and filled it with contemporary art. Ian had almost had heart failure the time he was washing his hands after visiting the cloakroom and was greeted by a hologram of a naked Kate Moss.

"Can you be my manny today, Ian? You're more fun than Jean-Pierre anyway," pleaded the little boy.

"Luca, Ian's really busy," Fernanda told her son.

Graciously, Ian said, "Luca, how about you be my under-butler and help me get brunch for the mummies, okay?"

"Deal," said Luca, clasping Ian's neck ever tighter.

"Hey, Mom, we're going to go find the ring for the dog show," Isabelli told Fernanda, leading the family's dogs away followed by her sister Carlotta. The sisters, dressed in the obligatory teen uniform of tiny crop top, enormous baggy jeans, wedge sneakers, and miles of necklaces and bangles, sloped off together chattering excitedly.

"Henrik and I are headed to the micro-brewery," added Federico with a grin.

Fernanda narrowed her eyes mock-suspiciously at her two oldest sons, as she replied, "Okay, just one beer, though. You've got homework later."

"Yeah . . . sure, Mom," Henrik said unconvincingly.

"Hey, boys, can you guys keep an eye out for Minty? Bring her back with you later?" Tata called out to the twins. "She's been gone for ages."

"Sure," said Henrik. "We'll find her."

Fernanda and Tata watched as the twins sauntered off towards a quaint 1980s horsebox that had been converted to house the micro-brewery. Ian pulled out a chair for Fernanda and she sat down next to Tata, hanging her bag over the back of it and tossing a set of Range Rover keys on the table. Having deposited Luca on the ground, Ian then filled a water glass for Mrs. Ovington-Williams and was about to offer to go and fetch the two ladies something to eat when Sophie Thompson (an honest thirty-six) arrived.

"Perfect timing, Mrs. Thompson," said Ian as she walked into the Tuliperie. "I was going to suggest getting some brunch for you all."

"Sounds heavenly," said Sophie. Her eight-year-old son Eddie, who had a black Labrador on a lead at his side, was with her.

"Can I go find my friends?" asked Eddie.

"Sure," said Sophie.

The little boy ran off with his dog and Ian took Sophie's basket from her as she sat down. Ian was fond of Sophie. She lived at the Rectory in Great Bottom and was married to an ambitious Tory MP. Her father, an obscure Yorkshire aristocrat, had endowed her with lashings of blue blood but little else. She struggled to keep up with her friends financially, but her charm and social cachet meant she was invited everywhere. A true English rose, she had porcelain skin, a smattering of delicate freckles, and soft curls of auburn hair that brushed her shoulders. As ever, her make-up was minimal today—she had a dewy complexion that demanded no adornments except a dash of mascara and a dramatic matte red lip—and she was wearing a simple shirtwaist of pistachio gingham and flat cream brogues. As far as Ian was concerned, she looked like a character from a Nancy Mitford novel. Of the three friends, he always thought, Sophie was the classiest, Fernanda the coolest, and if Tata was not the most real or intellectual, she was certainly the canniest operator.

"Soph! God, you look *sooo* pretty," Fernanda declared. "Love the dress."

"Ssshhhh. *You* look *exquisite*," Sophie replied, as expected. "Tats, *wow*, that jacket is gorgeous. Why do you always look *sooooo* divine?"

"Stop," Tata told her friend. "You literally could have just walked out of the Gabriela look book. It is Gabriela Hearst, isn't it?"

"Nope. Really old Zara. Zara was so genius when you could only get it in that one shop they had in Madrid," Sophie replied, looking pleased with herself.

"You're *so clever* with all your bargains, Soph," said Tata. "I mean, you'd never know. God, I wish I had the class to get away with cheap stuff."

"Thanks," replied Sophie flatly.

Sensing a froideur, Ian leaped into the void. "Now, who's hungry? Luca and I are off to the Daylesford pagoda, aren't we?" he said, winking at the boy.

Sophie's expression lightened. Ian had that effect on people.

"Ooh, well, if they're doing the blackcurrant and pomegranate elixir," she said, "I'd love one."

~≈~

A few moments later, Ian made his way through the throng with Luca clutching his hand tightly.

"I'm gutted about Boris," said Luca as they walked. "I'll never forget him."

"Nor me," said Ian, a pang shooting through his heart as he was reminded of his beloved. He wondered if he'd ever get over him. "But he's happy in heaven, I promise," he added, trying to reassure the little boy.

"Can we get a donkey ride?" asked Luca.

"The donkeys aren't here this time." A ripple of nostalgia swept over Ian. Visiting the Monkton Bottom fete with his parents, Sally and Donald, a quiet couple who had run a newsagent's in Chipping Norton, had been the highlight of his childhood summers. Back then, the fete had been a simple affair which took place on the village green. But after the Hawkinses had built themselves the Manor, they offered their grounds for the occasion. The fete had soon evolved into a high-octane social and commercial event: instead of the aforementioned donkey rides, there were trips in Bryan's helicopter over the estate; the local Women's Institute tent selling Victoria sponges and Swiss rolls had been replaced with Violet Bakery hawking quince galettes and rose-water madeleines from a 1950s-style shepherd's hut; the fifty-pence tombola stall had been usurped by an organic distillery selling custom gin. Never had a village fete been so curated, or so devoid of actual villagers. The Sallys and Donalds of this world no longer felt comfortable there: it was too expensive and the fete-goers consisted of the media-finance-fashion crowd who'd decamped from London full-time, or weekenders who flitted in and out of Oxfordshire depending on their diaries.

Ian and Luca soon reached the Daylesford Farm Shop pagoda, the most lavish version of a "farm shop" one could imagine: hay bales were draped with pure-white sheep fleeces to sit on; drinks were served in iced silvery goblets; the ceiling inside was festooned with elaborate garlands of hops and giant daisies; and huge vases of cherry blossoms were dotted around the tent.

Ian approached the bleached-oak counter and ordered croissants, healthy snacks, fruit salads, coffees, and juices for Tata and her friends, then he and Luca sat on two hessian-covered bar stools as they awaited the food and drink. England, Ian reflected as he took in the busy scene, was a different place now. The amateurish, scruffy charm of the countryside was slowly vanishing. It was the kind of place people spent as much on a picnic basket as they used to spend on a pony. (£850, to be precise, for the monogrammed Matilda Goad & Co. wicker hamper that no self-respecting Country Princess would be without this summer.)

It wasn't long before Luca and Ian were walking back to the tulip garden with trays of delicious goodies.

"Ooh, look!" chirruped Luca suddenly, pointing to the lake that had been dug a few years ago below the house. A little wooden vessel was moored from a jetty at the edge of the water and a flock of white swans glided majestically across the glass-like surface. "Can we go in the rowboat?"

Ian didn't have the heart to tell the boy that the boat was about as watertight as a matchbox. It was purely decorative and had been placed in the water to add "interest" to the lake. Tata and her friends would admire it while they indulged in their weekly wild swim, an event which was usually followed by a long wallow in the wood-fired cedar hot tub (imported at vast expense from Norway) situated on the bank. Like much else about Monkton Bottom Manor, the boat was fake.

"Maybe another day," lied Ian. "Maybe another day."

⌇⌇

Ian and Luca were soon laying out the delicious food and drink onto the table for the three mummies. After he'd wolfed down a chocolate muffin, Luca crept onto his mother's lap, where he sucked his thumb and snoozed, and Ian stationed himself a little distance away from the ladies and reorganised the contents of the Paravel holdall, while keeping a close ear on the conversation.

"Mmmm, Ian, Luca, thank you," said Sophie, popping a cacao-and-coconut date ball in her mouth before turning to Tata with a concerned look. "Any word from Bryan yet?"

"No. But I have a plan," said Tata. "To be precise, Ian has a plan and I'm going along with it."

"Husbands," sighed Fernanda. "So complicated."

"Speaking of which," Tata mused. "If Selby Fairfax's husband was as rich as everyone's saying, why on earth would she have carried on working through the marriage?"

"If you were one of the most talented garden designers in the world, would you stop working because your husband had made money?" Sophie replied.

"Yes!" blurted Tata, collapsing with laughter. (She had never intended to work a minute longer than she'd had to, and she hadn't: she'd quit her PR gig the day she'd become engaged to Bryan.)

"I loved my job at *House and Garden*. Sometimes I wish I still worked," Sophie said, sounding regretful.

"You do work," Fernanda insisted. She picked up a rose *macaron* and regarded it as though it were the enemy, then put it back on the plate. "Those hand-blocked chintzes you make are so pretty."

"It's hardly a career," said Sophie dubiously.

"And you do all that amazing charity stuff for those underprivileged kids," Tata reminded her.

"The goat sanctuary is Hugh's thing," Sophie objected. "He raises all the money. I just organise getting the children there and taking them round."

"Exactly. Hugh gets the credit, you do the hard slog. Everyone knows that," said Fernanda. Like most people in the Bottoms, Ian included, Fernanda didn't have much time for Sophie's husband. She stifled a yawn. "God, I'm shattered."

"Why, sweetie?" asked Tata.

Ian wondered how Fernanda could *ever* be shattered. She had a rotating army of top-notch Filipino housekeepers so large that she never needed to make a bed or sweep a floor. It was rumoured that she'd never even been into her own kitchen.

"Husband drama," said Fernanda. "Michael called from the set in LA at two a.m. last night, freaking about some edit or something, then I couldn't go back to sleep because I was worrying about—" She stopped and gestured at Luca from above his head, mouthing the words "problems at school."

"What happened to his eye?" asked Tata in a whisper.

"Archie Duffield. Went for him on the cricket field," Fernanda replied.

"No!" gasped Sophie.

"Like mother, like son." Fernanda shook her head. "I'm not surprised the older Duffield boy's been kicked out of Eton."

"What?" cried Tata and Sophie in unison.

"Didn't you hear? Edgar, the fifteen-year-old, burned his housemaster's tailcoat as a protest against upper-class privilege," said Fernanda. "He's at the comprehensive school in Chipping Norton now."

"Bit of a comedown for Anne," said Tata, looking pleased.

"That woman's the pits," went on Fernanda. "She's saying Luca provoked her son and that it's Luca's fault he's got a black eye."

"I'm sorry. Poor him. School can be so hard," said Sophie, then yawned herself.

"Are you tired too?" asked Tata sympathetically.

"I'm used to it," Sophie replied. "But last night . . . God, Hugh had me up for hours—"

"Don't tell me you actually had sex?" A look of mock-alarm crossed Tata's face.

Sophie looked downcast.

"Sorry, Soph," Tata said. "Didn't mean—"

"No. No, I'm fine, honestly," Sophie insisted, a little too brightly. "Hugh's phone rang in the middle of the night. It was his special adviser, Davinia. *Again*. He went off downstairs and I could hear him talking to her for ages. Couldn't sleep a wink after that."

Fernanda looked at her quizzically. "Why the hell is she giving her boss all this special advice so late on a Saturday night?"

"He said it was 'government business,'" Sophie replied. "But anyway, while I was lying there, a dreadful thought came into my head."

Fernanda cupped her hands over her son's ears and went on, "You don't think he and Davini—"

Sophie cut her off. "No. Hugh couldn't possibly be having a . . . *thing* with his SPAD. He's an MP. However pretty and clever Davinia is, believe me, my husband would never risk his career like that. Or our marriage."

"What was keeping you awake, then?" asked Tata, picking at a bowl of fruit salad drizzled with local heather honey.

"I know it's completely pathetic, but I was upset about Selby Fairfax. She's my closest neighbour and I dropped off a tin of my home-made florentines at Great Bottom Park last week, with a note inviting her for tea . . ." Her voice faltered, forlorn. "And . . . well, I haven't heard a squeak."

"Soph darling, you're *way* too nice," Fernanda told her friend. "At times, I wonder if your niceness almost counts as a character flaw in the modern world."

Sophie had to laugh. "I can't help it. I was brought up to be nice. Do As You Would Be Done By and all that. But when other people aren't nice back, I'm disappointed."

Tata nodded at her. "I get it. I spent a fortune on three of those Vladimir Kanevsky porcelain tree peonies, and had Ian drop them at Great Bottom Park two weeks ago. There was a little card asking Selby and her kids over for a swim, or a play on the zip wire with Minty—and—zilch. I haven't heard a thing. Not a call, not a thank-you note, not even a text with a smiley-face emoji."

"I don't know why she wouldn't want to be friends with wives like us," Sophie commiserated.

"She will," Fernanda said, confident as ever. "I mean, who else is she going to be friends with around here? It's just a matter of time. She can't hide away forever."

"I don't mean to interrupt," said Ian, starting to clear away the remains of the brunch, "but apparently Mrs. Fairfax may have finally started to emerge from her seclusion."

"Ian, why didn't you say before?" said Tata excitedly.

"I just overheard someone mention it in the pagoda," he said, as he bustled about the table, removing dirty plates and refolding the napkins. "Apparently a local nanny saw Mrs. Fairfax dropping her two girls, Violet and Tess, on Friday morning at Stow Hall School. From what I can gather, she was head to toe in new-season Khaite."

Tata turned to her friends, an eyebrow raised, and said, "Looks like we're going to have to up our game, girls. No more sweatpants and sneakers for the school run."

"You never do the school run, Tata," Fernanda said tartly.

"It's a metaphor, Fernanda."

Before Fernanda could come up with a suitable riposte, Isabelli and Carlotta had returned to the table, with Minty and Eddie and various animals following.

"Mom, the dog show starts in five minutes. I'm going to enter The Dog the Judge Would Most Like To Take Home," said Carlotta with an animated smile. "Can you come watch?"

"Course, darling," said Fernanda.

"Eddie, are you going to enter too?" asked Sophie.

"I fancy the dog showjumping," he replied. "There's a proper course and everything."

"Bet you'll come first," said Tata.

"Wish we had a dog, Mummy," complained Minty. "Aw, this is so heavy," she went on. She had a huge, glossy turquoise shopping bag looped over her left arm.

"What's that?" Tata asked her daughter.

Minty showed her mother the bag, which had the word TALLULAHSWIM emblazoned in gold lettering all over it.

"OMG, I *love* TallulahSwim bikinis. They're so awesome," Isabelli said. "I didn't know they made kids' ones."

"Darling, what on earth have you been buying?" Tata sounded incredulous.

"I didn't *buy* it, Mummy. Charlene gave it to me. She said it's a present from Tallulah."

"Who's Tallulah?" asked Tata.

Minty smiled sweetly. "She's Daddy's new friend."

4

Minty might as well have dropped a bomb on the little party. Tata was dumbstruck. Fernanda and Sophie froze. Even Ian was mute. The children sensibly took advantage of the grown-ups' shock and dashed off in a group towards the showing arena for the dogs, except for Luca, who had finally fallen asleep on his mother's lap. As soon as they were out of earshot, Tata turned to Ian and her friends.

"Could Bryan be seeing someone—" she started, whitening.

"Course not," Fernanda insisted.

"He adores you," Sophie said.

"I'm sure there's nothing in it," Ian concurred.

The butler remained outwardly calm, but inside his heart plummeted like a stone. This was not normal protocol in a household he was running: he took pride in knowing everything about the sex lives of his employers, but clearly his usual line of intelligence (Charlene Potts, Bryan, and Tata's new PA) was malfunctioning. Ian had never thought Bryan would go so far as finding himself a girlfriend during this mini-separation from his wife. But bikini entrepreneuresses with names like Tallulah can be alluring. A chill crept down Ian's spine as he wondered if this woman was the intended recipient of the jewellery for which Tata had found the receipt.

"She's probably wearing that jewellery now." Tata bit her lip. "Oh Christ, what if she's here with Bryan and there's an awful scene?"

"You're catastrophising," said Fernanda. "Bryan with someone named Tallulah? I can't see it. I just can't. Okay? Calm down. Here. Have one of these gummies that Michael FedEx-ed me from LA. You'll feel better." She opened her bag and revealed a Ziploc bag filled with dusty-looking jelly squares.

Tata shook her head and dabbed at a tear. "I can't be stoned looking after Minty."

"'Kay," replied Fernanda. She popped one of the lumps in her mouth and chewed it. "Don't tell the kids."

"Ladies, may I suggest a round of chilled Whispering Angel?" asked Ian, in need of an excuse to step away and dial Charlene.

"Mmmm . . . yes . . . good idea," chorused the trio, perking up at the thought of a glass of the shimmering pink rosé from Provençe. It was drunk from summer's beginning to summer's end by the Country Princesses, who then de-puffed their faces with a mini-detox at the Lanserhof as soon as their children had returned to school every September.

"Right. Two ticks and I'll be back."

Ian skedaddled towards a pale pink tent a short distance away. Extravagant planters bursting with cerise peonies adorned the entrance and the inside was furnished with loungey sofas upholstered in pink-and-white striped linen, gilt side tables, and antique Persian rugs. An army of absurdly handsome waiters dressed in black uniforms with pink aprons were tending to guests, and as Ian walked up to the bar to order a bottle of wine, his eye was caught by the poetic beauty of one who was a dead ringer for Timothée Chalamet. His heart stopped a beat. Perhaps, thought Ian to himself for a tiny moment, the Whispering Angel tent was the sort of place a man like him might find his Prince Charming. But Ian caught himself. What was he thinking? He'd only just lost his soulmate. Timothée Chalamets and Princes Charming were out of the question during this bleak period of mourning.

"What can I get you, sir?" the beautiful waiter asked.

"Something to calm down three ladies in a terrible tizzy, please," Ian replied.

"Sounds like a double magnum to me."

"Good idea," said Ian. "Three glasses as well, please, and I'll take it to them on a tray."

"Course."

While Timothée bustled around sorting out the order, Ian rested his back against the bar and speed-dialled Charlene.

"Wherefore art thou, my beloved?" he asked as soon as she picked up.

"Morning, Ian love," said Charlene. No one else in Charlene's universe addressed her as though she was a character from a Shakespeare play, and Ian's florid language made her feel special. "I'm in Mr. Hawkins's office up at the house. This fete business is driving me round the bend. All that noise and all these people. If only Mrs. Hawkins was in charge today."

"Indeed," Ian agreed.

"Anyway, I need to get back to Cheyanne at the piggery. She's had twelve piglets and the littlest one is very poorly. Needs bottle-feeding every few hours."

"Charlene, I am sorry to hear that. Now, lend me your ear. Mrs. H. thinks that Mr. H. has got a lady friend, a Miss Tallulah. You'd have told me if that were the case, wouldn't you?"

"Crikey, news travels."

Ian was more than mildly irritated. "Charlene, during your training, I thought I'd made it abundantly clear that *all* news relating to Mr. H.'s personal life has to travel to me immediately so that it can travel to Mrs. H. in a timely fashion."

"Sorry. I forgot that bit."

"Clearly," said Ian.

"Anyway, when she moved in—" Charlene began.

"Moved in?!" Ian was appalled.

"Yes. When she moved in, Mr. Hawkins told me he helps young business folk and that she was a start-up person. I think she looks like that Kardashian one who's all over TikTok."

"I think you mean Kendall Jenner," said Ian. A hard knot was starting to form in the pit of his stomach. Bryan had indeed mentored young people and allowed them to stay at the Manor, but they were mostly geeky tech types, and usually men. A swimsuit tycooness with supermodel looks was a different proposition.

"Don't tell me he's bringing this Tallulah to the fete today?"

"Oh no. Definitely not."

"Phew. Mrs. H. would have had a conniption—"

"Don't worry at all. They've gone to Venice."

Ian emitted a pained howl, not unlike the squeal of a puppy whose tail has been squashed in a car door. Bryan had never even taken his own dear wife to the most romantic city in the world, and now—ugh! It was too much to bear. Taking a large gulp of air to calm himself, he said, "Brief me. Details, dear, details."

"Mr. H. asked me to book two tickets to Venice, one for him and one for a Miss Tallulah de Sanchez. They left on Friday morning."

"But Mr. H. is allergic to culture. The only thing he'll travel for is golf."

"He did ask me to book a special baggage thingy for his clubs—"

Ian had heard enough. "Charlene, listen to me very carefully," he interrupted.

"Yes."

"You are not to utter a word of our conversation, a word about Venice, a word about Mr. Hawkins, or a word about this Tallulah de Something to another soul."

"Right."

"That's why there's a non-disclosure agreement in all our staff contracts. It means we forget everything we see and hear in the Hawkins household as soon as we have seen and heard it."

"I see."

"When are they getting back?"

"Who?"

"Mr. H. and Tallulah."

"I don't know what you're talking about," said Charlene obediently.

"Charlene, the non-disclosure agreement does not include keeping critical Hawkins-related intelligence from me."

"If you say so."

"I do. The NDA allows you to tell *me* everything and no one else anything at all." A white lie, Ian told himself, was surely justifiable for the greater good of the Hawkins family.

"They get back tomorrow night."

"Thank you, Charlene. Not a word."

"About what?"

"That's the spirit. Send a smooch to the piggies for me."

With that, Ian hung up, half-pirouetted round to the bar, took the tray, and staggered back to the tulip garden beneath the weight of the double magnum of Whispering Angel.

∞

Professional despair was the emotional state that best described Ian by the time he reached the Tuliperie with the rosé. Of course, he was too well trained ever to allow his expression to belie his true feelings, but he couldn't help but worry that a hot girlfriend for Bryan was a major complication. A new mistress at the Manor—well, that would be The End. Ian's heart sank further as he poured the women's wine. They were on their phones, riveted by Tallulah de Sanchez's social media accounts.

"Two million followers? And she's got a blue tick!!!"

"Bryan does *not* like women who have had too much work done—"

"There's no way that waist is real. She's had ribs removed—"

"All that lip filler. So tacky—"

"She's not twenty-five, she's *at least* thirty-five—"

Luca woke from his doze and looked over Fernanda's shoulder at her screen. "Is she a model?" he asked, inflicting a little more pain. "Pretty lady."

All Ian could think was that damage limitation was the first port of call. And that meant keeping Tata calm. If she got hysterical, Bryan would be putty in this Tallulah's hands.

"Excuse me, Mrs. Hawkins, but I have just had word from Charlene," said Ian in his smoothest tones, "that Mr. Hawkins is in fact not attending today."

"Why?" asked Tata, taking a large glug of her wine and looking worried.

Ian, naturally, was prepared. "Mr. Hawkins is the keynote speaker at an international symposium of sustainable plug manufacturers in an industrial plant in northern Italy. Charlene says it was a last-minute invitation."

"Oh" was all Tata said. She looked forlorn. "But what about this Tallulah person?"

"Charlene has absolutely no recollection of anyone named Tallulah." This was true, of course, as long as his colleague stuck to the NDA.

Tata stood up, stretched, and said, "Girls, I need a break. I'm going to go down to the lake and have a walk."

Ian could tell that Tata was clearly upset but was trying to hide it. As he handed her her bag he said in a low tone, "I'll slope off now. See you in the morning, Mrs. Hawkins."

Tata looked despondent. "Ian, you're not leaving me *now*?" she said, taking her glass of rosé from the table.

"If you remember, we discussed me having this afternoon off. I've got the, um . . ." Ian's lip wobbled, and he found himself having to hold back tears. (After all, Executive Butlers don't weep on the job.) "As I was saying, well, Boris's funeral is this afternoon. I need to go and prepare. I am sorry to be unavailable."

Tata's face reddened. "How could I have forgotten about Boris?! Here I am worrying about some idiotic influencer, and you're suffering actual grief. I'm so sorry. I just wish I could have come to the service with you. I bet it will be incredible. Go, Ian. We'll be fine."

"Thank you, Mrs. Hawkins," he said.

As he set off, Ian glanced around and took in the sight of Monkton Bottom Manor and its gardens, which Boris had so loved. Remembering the times they had strolled here together broke his heart. He didn't know how he was going to cope with the burial. The only solution was to arm himself with a cache of those silk Charvet handkerchiefs the French Ambassador had given him during a posting in Paris. At least his weeping would be elegant.

5

That Sunday afternoon, two weep-a-thons commenced in the Bottoms.

Let us fly first, swift as the swallows that flocked in the azure skies that summer, to St. Mary's of All the Angels, the solid Norman church that has stood at the heart of the village of Great Bottom since 1157. It was here that Ian, surrounded by close family and friends, soaked through those Charvet handkerchiefs as he bid a final farewell to his beloved. The service was a hell of a tear-jerker, but Ian was eternally grateful to the Reverend Gavin Pilkington, the vicar at Great Bottom, who had known Boris well for the past few years. He delivered a fine eulogy, capturing the essence of Boris's extraordinary spirit better than Ian could have imagined. (The Church of England around the Bottoms attracted a high class of clergyman, due to the prime real estate that came with the job.) Ian was particularly touched by Reverend Gav's reference to Boris's gentle way with the elderly widows who so loved their weekly visits.

As the funeral party processed from the church into the graveyard, Ian could not have been prouder of Boris's final resting place. Reverend Gav had obtained a special dispensation from the Archbishop of Canterbury, no less, to have Ian's loved one buried in a prime plot opposite the Earls of Bottom, the aristocratic family who had built Great Bottom Park.

But there was no getting away from it. Boris was gone, and Ian was a lonelier man. At least, he comforted himself as he left the churchyard later that afternoon, Boris was at rest in the tip-top spot in the graveyard—the front row, if you will, at the runway show of the dead. Ian had commissioned an exquisite headstone: he would come back soon and plant white camellia bushes on the grave so that Boris was always in the company of fragrant blooms. After all, there was nothing he had loved more than a delicious scent.

Weep-a-thon no. 2 was taking place almost simultaneously, at the edge of the lake below the formal gardens of Monkton Bottom Manor. Here we find Tata, rosé in hand, sitting on an elaborate wrought-iron bench, tears streaming down her face, staring miserably at the flock of swans she'd never been able to tame (exactly as everyone had warned her when she'd purchased them). Today had been a total fail, as far as she was concerned. Even if Charlene had told Ian that she'd never heard of this Tallulah, hadn't Minty said that Charlene had given her the TallulahSwim bag? It was highly suspicious: Minty wasn't the kind of kid who made things up. Who on earth was Tallulah? Why was Bryan at a plug-socket symposium on a Sunday—in Italy, of all places? He never went to those things any more, and everything was made in China anyway. If only Ian hadn't had to leave early today! But he was in mourning, and Tata wanted to respect his grief.

Tata decided she'd go home as soon as she could find Minty and drag her off the bouncy castle or wherever she was. In the meantime, she decided to do a little meditation to calm herself: Yogi Rupert, the lovely Vipassana expert who instructed her every week, had taught her various chants to fall back on in anxious moments. She put her wine glass on the ground, crossed her legs on the bench, squeezed her thumbs and forefingers together, snapped her eyes shut, and hoped her tears would cease if she practised her prayers.

"*Om bhur bhuvas svaha,*" she began. (As far as she recalled, this meant something like, "Dear God, in whatever form you take, may all my wildest dreams come true.") The sound of the water lapping at the banks of the lake soothed her somewhat. Tata felt a light summer breeze brush at her cheek. The bubbling call of a cuckoo lifted her spirits. Her breathing slowed.

"*Bhargo dheyvasya—*"

"Mo-ooom. *I don't care.*" A distraught girl's voice interrupted Tata's meditation. The accent was American. Still, Tata kept her eyes shut and tried to concentrate on the soft wind and the words in her mind. "*Dheyvasya dhimahih—*"

"I just want to go back to New York for the summer vacation. See my friends, Dad, the dogs—"

"Your father's away right now," a woman's voice replied, also American. "I'm not sure he'll even be back there this summer."

"What about the dogs? I can't believe he's leaving them for so long—"

"I'm sure the housekeeper's taking good care of them."

"I need to go back and check on them."

Tata could sense the voices coming closer. She kept her eyes shut, but her mind wandered.

"You're fourteen. You can't go back to the city alone. What about making friends here?"

"Why would I want random English friends when I've got a bunch of friends in New York I've known since I started at City and Country?"

"Because—"

"Leave me alone," shouted the girl furiously.

"Violet," the woman called out.

Violet, Tata repeated to herself. *Violet.* That was definitely the name of one of the Fairfax girls. That meant that the other voice must belong to *the* Selby Fairfax. Tata wasn't sure how to play it. Whether to introduce herself to the starry new neighbour now, or wait for a more opportune moment when the starry new neighbour was not in a scream-up with her teenager, and Tata's eye make-up was flawless. On balance, she decided to continue meditating and "let the universe decide," as Rupert would have said.

"*Savitri. Gayatri. Savitri. Gayatri. Sav*—"

Someone sat down on the bench next to Tata, and an American voice whispered, "I'm so sorry to intrude."

The universe, it seemed, had decided that Tata's chanting session was over. Grateful her tear-stains were half-covered by her sunglasses, Tata opened her eyes.

"No problem," she replied, turning to look at the woman next to her, who was no doubt *the* Selby Fairfax. (Tata, like every other woman in the Bottoms, had pored over endless pictures of her in magazines and on social media.) She took in every detail: Selby had porcelain skin, high cheekbones, a delicate nose, generous bow lips, and dark, glossy hair that fell in a choppy, rock'n'roll bob to her chin. Her wide-apart, almond-shaped eyes had striking irises that were the kind of blue-black tone you find in a set of watercolour paints. They were framed by thick lashes and beautifully groomed eyebrows. She had a lean, athletic body, and was dressed with utter simplicity in an immaculate long-sleeved white tee, dark jeans, and those tan Hermès sliders that were impossible to get hold of unless you were a top-tier client. The only glitz Tata could detect was a gold Rolex on Selby's left wrist. How someone could exude so much glamour with so little bling was a mystery to Tata.

The two women sat in silence for a few moments before Selby opened her (to-die-for) "old" Céline bag and retrieved a small pair of binoculars. She peered through them towards the lake.

"Those swans are like something from another world," she declared. The accent was East Coast, Tata noted, and Selby's voice was direct and clear as a bell. "So graceful. They're my favourite birds."

Tata couldn't believe it: Selby Fairfax liked swans. She *adored* swans. Here was An Opportunity. Dreary thoughts of Italian plug-socket conferences and bikini entrepreneuresses swiftly receded.

"It's my flock," said Tata proudly. "I've even managed to breed a few from eggs."

"Wow. So this is your place?" Selby asked, looking around.

Tata nodded. "Yup."

"Well, how about that! A swan lady! I'd love to have swans. One day, one day . . ."

"They're such romantic birds."

"With a famously low divorce rate of three per cent," Selby laughed, putting the binoculars on her lap and turning to Tata. "If only human beings were as sensible." She paused for a moment and added, "Apologies for the screaming match I just had with my *awful* teenager." She gestured towards the jetty, where Violet was now sitting hunched in a heap, sulkily kicking at the top of the water with her sneakers.

"Are you okay?" Tata asked.

"To be honest, I'm feeling horribly lonely and sad." Selby offered her a wry smile. "Or horribly anxious and insecure, depending on the day."

"I'm sorry," said Tata. It pained her to think that this perfect specimen of female was suffering. "Want to talk?"

"Where to begin? Moving out of our home . . . moving to a new country. Divorce. An ex-husband who's either off finding his truth, saving the world, or screwing around, depending on his mood. New schools. Distraught kids." Selby threw her hands in the air and looked up at the heavens as if asking for help. Then she added, "Sorry, that's far too much information from a stranger—"

"No, no, not at all. It's refreshing to hear someone actually being honest."

Selby grinned mischievously. "I'm a New Yorker. We tell it how it is, however shitty it is."

"Sometimes I wish the British were more like that," Tata replied. "We all pretend. The Stiff Upper Lip lives on, still."

"Oh God." Selby sounded as appalled as she was amused.

Tata briefly lifted her sunglasses so that Selby could see her swollen eyes. "Bad day my end too."

"Anything I can do?"

Tata shook her head.

"If you're sure," Selby replied. "And thank you, you've made me feel better knowing I'm not the only total loser around here."

They both laughed, and then Selby said, "Forgive me. I haven't introduced myself. I'm Selby Fairfax. Just moved in."

She offered her hand and Tata shook it. "Lovely to meet you, Selby," Tata said, trying to sound nonchalant. "I'm Tata. Tata Hawkins."

"Tata, nice to meet you . . . wait, I know your name . . ." Selby broke off.

Tata felt herself puff with pride. Selby knew *her*?

"Have we met somewhere?" Selby asked, her brow creasing.

"I don't think so," Tata replied; then, feigning ignorance, said, "Where have you moved to?"

Selby smiled. "Great Bottom Park. Do you know it?"

"Yes, of course . . . I mean, I don't *know* it know it, I've never been inside or anything, but of course I know exactly which house it is. I hear it's incredibly beautiful."

Something Tata didn't recognise passed over Selby's face. "It *is* beautiful. It's a dream . . . and falling down." She emitted a bemused sigh. "What was I thinking? Moving from New York City to a giant, dilapidated English country house?"

"So why did you buy the place?" Tata was on tenterhooks.

"Actually, I didn't *buy* Great Bottom Park," said Selby. "It was left to me."

"Your parents left you that place?" Tata was confused. She didn't think Lady Maud had any direct descendants.

"Actually, I don't have any parents. I'm an orphan," replied Selby matter-of-factly.

"What?"

"Yup. I've even got a fairy godmother."

Tata was intrigued. "Go on," she begged.

"My parents died when I wasn't even two—"

"Oh no," said Tata sorrowfully. "That's hard."

Selby nodded. "I got lucky, though. I lived with my Fairfax grandparents on their horse farm down in Virginia. They were awesome, the best . . ." She paused and looked nostalgic for a moment, then went on, "Then I went off to the Rhode Island School of Design, met my husband—I mean, former husband—Doug, who was at MIT. We got married, lived in New York, everything was great, two girls, busy careers, and then everything exploded a year ago. Doug fell in love with someone else, and . . ." Selby looked desperately sad. "He was gone. I mean *really* gone. A lot of fallout, a lot of gossip. I was so hurt, so humiliated, the girls were devastated."

"I can't imagine," said Tata, even though she already knew every detail from the rumour mill.

"It was awful—I hated being in New York, single. I couldn't go anywhere without someone asking me about Doug, or his latest *f-ing* boyfriend. I've burst into tears in literally every restaurant in Manhattan."

"Sounds grim," said Tata.

"I was desperate to get out. And that's exactly when my fairy godmother came along."

"In a puff of smoke?" Tata joked.

"Actually, she died. My grandfather was a distant cousin of Lady Maud," Selby went on. "She used to come to Virginia and stay on the farm, and we would visit her at Great Bottom Park when I was a child. Cousin Maud was wonderful, the most amazing horticulturalist, and she'd created incredible gardens. It all inspired me to train as a landscape architect." Selby smiled fondly. "After she died, I got a letter out of the blue saying she'd left me the house and the estate."

"That's nuts. So Lady Maud is your fairy godmother?" Tata could hardly believe her ears.

"I know. But it came at the right time for me and the girls. New York felt toxic. It wasn't just the divorce. The value system there is crazy," said Selby. "Violet was getting invited to birthday parties on private islands, modelling agents were trying to sign her in the street after school, kids were taking Tess on trips on their parents' jets. I wanted the girls out, so it seemed perfect timing to come here ... Tata—wait!" she exclaimed.

"What?" said Tata.

"I'm so embarrassed." Selby looked mortified. "I *do* know you. I mean, I know your name. You're the neighbour who sent me the incredible porcelain peonies. I'm sorry I haven't replied. Why didn't you say anything?"

Now it was Tata's turn to be mortified. But she could work any situation to her advantage. She had not become the highest-earning PR girl at Freuds in London by the time she was twenty-five for nothing. Smiling as coolly as she could, she said, "Hey, it's nothing. I didn't want to make you feel awkward."

"I've been meaning to reply to your note. It's just, it's been crazy—moving, my work, the kids. I've barely left the house until today. Couldn't face it."

At this point, Tata decided to just go for it. "Why don't you come over for dinner?" she asked.

Selby hesitated for a moment, leaving Tata quivering with anticipation. Finally she said, "That's so generous of you. I'd love it. Can't wait to see the house—"

"Actually, there's some ... um ... renovations going on here ... so ... I'm 'camping' at the Old Coach House at the other end of the estate for a few weeks. I'll send you a dropped pin. It's a bit tricky to find."

"Sure."

"Great. Come a week tomorrow at seven-thirty. I'll do a super-casual dinner in the kitchen," said Tata. " 'Kitchen Sups,' as we say here in England."

Selby picked up her bag and stood to go but before she left she turned to Tata and said, "You've made my week. My first invitation and my first English friend—I can't believe it."

Nor, dear reader, could Tata.

6

May I take you back to that glorious summer's morning where we began our tale? If you recall, it was moments after 6 a.m. on the Monday following the fete and our hero, Ian Palmer, was lolloping towards the Old Coach House with a spring in his step, his boss having just imparted the thrilling news that Selby Fairfax was to dine there.

Besides providing a welcome distraction from his grief, Selby's imminent visit signalled a glimmer of hope—the hope that Tata (and Ian) would soon be back at the Manor. Ian understood Bryan: like many self-made moguls he suffered from permanent status anxiety. The minute Bryan got wind of the news that his wife was socialising with the starriest new neighbour in the Bottoms—well, that would be more than enough to have him bending that knee and showering Mrs. H. with those missing jewels. Ian would be out of the igloo and back in the Dovecot before you could say Greycoats' Butler of the Year Award. Maybe, thought Ian, his glasses misting up, once he was home in his darling cottage, with all that space, another Boris might even come along.

There was a time for grieving, Ian told himself as he opened the back door of the Old Coach House, and there was a time for party-planning, and never the twain should meet. Today he would force himself to concentrate on the latter, and he would be all the better for it. Ian stepped over the threshold into the back hall and tripped lightly towards the staff kitchen. The Old Coach House, like many of its neighbours, boasted two kitchens. There was generally a "back" kitchen where food was prepared by staff, and a "front" or "Marie Antoinette" kitchen, where at most a muffin was toasted or a button pressed on a Nespresso machine. This was where the family would dine so that they could feel as though they were eating informally "in the kitchen," like normal people who didn't have household staff.

Once in the back kitchen, Ian charged up the coffee machine, ground some beans and set the grill pan warming. The room was luxuriously kitted out—Lacanche oven, slate countertop, gas hobs, Sub-Zero fridges, and freezers galore—everything a top chef could wish for when catering a party. Ian sliced the halloumi, grilled it on both sides, then laid it out in the shape of a Japanese fan on one of Mrs. H.'s new Giambattista Valli scalloped-edge porcelain plates. He drizzled the cheese with a little of that marvellous olive oil he'd picked up at Clarke's last time he'd been in town, sprinkled it with fresh parsley and the flaky sea salt Mrs. H. loved, and set it on a glossy black tray laid with a crisp white linen cloth, napkin, and silver. The Tiffany lacquer cup was soon full of coffee, to which Ian added milky froth. He quickly polished his *Single Man* glasses, swooped back his hair, picked up the tray, delicately kicked open the swing door leading to the back staircase and made his way up to Mrs. Hawkins's boudoir.

"Knock knock," Ian called out gaily as he rapped on Tata's bedroom door.

"Come in, Ian," she called back.

He sallied forth into the sprawling suite to find his boss already propped up on a pillow in her 1960s four-poster bed, which was most notable for the giant gold palm trees that anchored each corner. The bed, she had once told Ian, reminded her of being on one of the four-person-sized waterside loungers at Nikki Beach in Ibiza, her "happy place." It was made up with layer upon layer of Sophie Conran's heavy white linens and Tata was wearing a cream satin dressing gown with a narrow mink trim on the lapels and her hair fell about her shoulders, unbrushed but alluring nonetheless.

"Already hard at work party-planning," Tata chirped, her voice sing-song and light as she jabbed furiously at her iPad.

"I can see, Mrs. H." Ian replied, setting the tray on a bedside table.

"Mmmm! Thank you," Tata said, lifting the macchiato and taking a sip. "You make the most wonderful coffee."

"In my next life, I plan to be a barista on the Via della Spiga in Milan," said Ian drolly. He walked over to the windows and drew back the moss-green silk velvet curtains at each one so that the morning sun bathed the room in shafts of golden light.

"Don't you think it's looking fab in here now Sebastian's finally hung the Brickell?" said Tata, glancing over at the enormous watercolour on the far wall, an image of three half-naked men intertwined on an unmade bed.

"It looks . . ." Ian coughed, choosing his words carefully ". . . very fashionable."

The bedroom was not exactly to Ian's tastes, but he was careful never to impose his own aesthetic opinion on an employer. Ian was a disciple of the late Robert Kime's old-school elegance, and found the trendily luxe decor at the Old Coach House a little too "Nouveau Cotswolds." Nevertheless Tata adored the way Sebastian Bingham, the interior decorator that all the cool fashion and film people used, had redesigned it a couple of years ago. Like the rest of the house (originally intended as extremely generous guest accommodation in case the Manor was overflowing), the main bedroom had been done up rather like a boutique hotel suite in Berlin or Istanbul: there was an ebonised floor, panelled white walls, that palm-tree bed, and a mid-century chaise longue, upholstered in orange suede, sat in front of the fireplace. The house might have been large and glamorous, but to Ian's eye it didn't feel like a cosy country retreat.

"Was the funeral bearable?" Tata asked, a solemn look on her face, before popping a piece of halloumi in her mouth.

Ian dropped his eyes, a little saddened. "Reverend Gav did a splendid job. Thank you for asking."

"I wish I could have come. We all adored Boris."

Ian looked sombre. "You're very kind to say so, Mrs. H."

"Would it cheer you up if I give you the full lowdown about what happened with Selby Fairfax yesterday?"

"It would indeed," said Ian, perking up. He was determined not to blub in front of his employer.

Tata had soon filled him in on the tale of Selby the orphan, her fairy godmother, and the inheritance.

"Goodness me," said Ian. "I hope Lady Maud left her all the money too. The house needs a fortune spent on it."

Privately, he was slightly miffed. Lady Maud was one of the widows Ian and Boris had dutifully visited on a regular basis over the years, and as much as he hated to admit it, Ian had expected a tiny nod in her will. His friend Graeme, another Greycoats alumnus, had been so adored by a widow in his local village that she had left him her house and dog-grooming business in Tunbridge Wells. Maud hadn't bequeathed Ian so much as a diamond brooch or a silver teapot.

"Anyway, we were sitting by the lake, chatting—Selby has a fabulous sense of humour, by the way, very dry—and I just came out with it and invited her for a Kitchen Supper here next Monday," Tata explained.

"Goodness," said Ian, his mind whirring. "There's an awful lot to do between now and then."

"Totes, and the guest list is critical. We've got to deliver the best Kitchen Sups crowd in the Cotswolds. You know what I mean—a super-fun, super-exclusive, super-intimate group. Such a shame Meghan's gone. Her loss!" Tata gabbled excitedly. "Sophie better make sure Hugh can get away from Number Ten that night. He's such a snob but, you know, he's a name, and maybe Jemima Khan will come. She's only down the road . . . I'll ask Fernanda to get

Michael to bring a cool actor . . . and there's that pop star from Blur who makes cheese now, what about him?"

"A wonderful mix," Ian told her.

"Selby Fairfax will be forever grateful to me for introducing her to absolutely everyone she needs to know in one fell swoop. I'll literally *make* her social life for her and she'll make me her best friend. Bryan will be so jealous he'll curdle like a bowl of sour cream. He'll be begging me to come back to the Manor before you know it."

"Exactly what I was thinking," Ian agreed. But he was also well aware that cementing a proper friendship with a woman like Selby Fairfax would demand more than a few intros to ageing pop stars and local politicians: Ian was already dreaming up a more sophisticated strategy, a grander plan.

"*Merci*. Would you be a doll and run the bath please?"

"With Olverum?" Ian asked as he made his way through to Tata's bathroom. He had introduced his boss to the divine Italian alpine bath essence that everyone in Gstaad used après-ski and she was hooked.

"Mmmmm!" she called back.

"Very good, Mrs. H." Ian turned on the waterfall tap at the edge of Tata's tank-like sunken Japanese bath and added lashings of bath oil. The room was soon perfumed with the clean scent of the Swiss pine forests. He heard her call from the bedroom, "While the bath's filling, I've got a few ideas to run past you."

Ian scooted back into the bedroom, retrieved a small Moleskine notebook and mechanical silver pencil from his top pocket, and stood to attention. "Fire away."

Tata purred with joy. She was in her element. "I don't want this Kitchen Supper to get, you know, out of hand, or be a big production or anything, but perhaps it should be a bit more fun than that thing everyone does where they try and pretend to be really relaxed and you end up eating a stodgy shepherd's pie and revolting apple crumble by the Aga."

"Your kitchen doesn't have an Aga, Mrs. Hawkins."

"I'm not being literal, Ian."

"Of course," he replied.

"What I mean is, I don't want the dinner to be too . . . 'country.' " She wrinkled her nose. "For a woman like Selby Fairfax, it would be a shame to serve shepherd's pie."

"A terrible shame," Ian agreed.

"Why don't we hire the Cat and Custard Pot to cater?"

Ian pondered a moment, then said, "Marvellous idea. They do everything for the Duchess-in-Waiting at Blenheim Palace."

"And maybe that girl Willa Widdle-Cobbit's free to create a concept for the table? She does the flowers for all the posh weddings."

"I can certainly look into Willow Corbett-Winder."

"Or what about the Flowerbx girl who used to work for Tom Ford? Her roses look like works of art. Whitney Something-Something?"

"I believe you mean Whitney Bromberg Hawkings. Queen of the single stem," he said. "I've got a direct number for her."

"Of course you have," Tata said, smiling gratefully. "Right. I'll call Charlene. She needs to get over here and start hand-calligraphing the invites. There's no way an event this important is going Paperless Post. Can you get on to the flowers and the food this morning?"

"Absolutely," said Ian, dashing back into the bathroom to turn off the taps.

"Fab," she called after him. "If this dinner's going to be all over Instagram, which it has to be so that Bryan sees it, everything needs to be perfect."

―――∞―――

Moments later, as Ian descended the back stairs with Tata's breakfast tray, he allowed himself to dream a little. Who knew, if Mrs. H. ingratiated herself successfully enough with Mrs. Fairfax, and the two women were soon in and out of each other's houses all the time, which meant Ian would be in and out of Great Bottom Park all the time, well . . . maybe Mrs. Fairfax would take such a liking to him that she would try to poach him! In Ian's years with the Hawkinses, this sort of thing was standard procedure: more than a few of Mrs. H.'s so-called friends had quietly tried to hire him away after a weekend at the Manor. So far, he'd always turned them down. (No one had offered accommodation for his Guccis that compared with the Dovecot.) But Great Bottom Park was a different matter.

Ian entered the kitchen and put the tray down on the countertop, ready for the housekeeper to wash up later. How *would* one resist a poaching attempt from the chatelaine of such a house, were it to happen? How could he resist getting his hands on the silver dip at Great Bottom Park, bringing in an incredible team and running the place like it was Claridge's? It would be a personal triumph to oust the late Lady Maud's octogenarian butler—Mr. Goodsen, always so patronising when Ian ran into him at the post office—from the charming Lodge House, a perfect example of English Renaissance architecture in miniature, move in and do it up in the style of Veere Grenney's famous folly in Suffolk.

As he dialled Charlene's number, Ian chided himself for his traitorous thoughts. Although running a grand pile had always been his dream, Mrs. H. had been good to him. He could never let her down. And anyway, a woman of Selby Fairfax's quality was far too classy to attempt a tacky move like a staff poach from a friend—because Tata *would* be her friend, and soon. Ian elected, sensibly, to consign his fantasy of houses greater than Monkton Bottom Manor to the back of his mind. Just as he did so, Charlene picked up.

"Whither art thou, fair Charlene?" he asked.

"In the piggery. One of the piglets has got a nasal infection, poor love. Pus everywhere." Ian could hear a lot of snuffling and oinking going on in the background. "Bit early, isn't it?" she said.

"Not for Mrs. Hawkins. She's having a party. Get ready for no days off for a week."

7

In whatever household he was employed, Ian always kept a box of Kleenex in the back kitchen. He'd found over the years that other domestic staff used him, literally, as a shoulder to cry on, and it had wreaked havoc with too many of his jackets. That Monday afternoon, had he not had a box of tissues at the ready, camouflaged in one of those glorious Flora Soames covers decorated with her famous dahlia print wallpaper, his lapel would have been completely destroyed by the snot and tears of Charlene Potts.

He was happily buffing a golden Thomas Goode sugar bowl when Charlene knocked at the kitchen window at about four o'clock. He was shocked by her appearance: she usually resembled a fresh-faced dairymaid from a Thomas Hardy novel, but today the poor girl looked like she'd been dragged through a hedge backwards. Her fair locks were scraped into a greasy ponytail, her skin was blotchy, and her eyes were raw. Ian darted to the back door and let her in.

"Petal, what is going on?" he asked, ushering her inside.

"I don't know what to do," started Charlene as she entered the kitchen. Dressed in green cord dungarees, muck-strewn wellies, and a T-shirt, she did not, Ian noted with some dismay, look very professional.

"I'll make us a cup of tea and you can spill the beans," Ian reassured her.

Charlene managed a grateful smile.

"Sit down, sweet pea." Ian directed her into a little slip-covered armchair next to the dishwasher, upon which was positioned the beautiful box of Kleenex. She grabbed a tissue and dabbed her eyes.

"It's just, Mrs. H., she rang this morning, after you did, and she said she wants me to caliphate—or something—a load of invitations-*hic-hic-hic*. With some kind of fancy fountain pen-*ugh-gghhh!* She wants them all done tonight! I can only write with a biro," she gabbled, becoming more and more distraught. "And I've got the piglets to look after."

Alas, Ian thought to himself as he filled the kettle and flicked it on. This was what happened when you hired an agricultural worker as a professional PA. One problem was that the candidate pool of director-level PAs in the countryside was virtually non-existent, the other was that despite their wealth, the Hawkinses had a tendency to cut corners (Bryan was a bottom-line kind of guy, after all), which meant they often ended up employing completely inappropriate people to fill the many vacancies in their household. Charlene was no exception.

The trouble with Miss Potts was that she was not actually a personal assistant at all. Even she would admit that she didn't know the first thing about looking after the schedules of rich families, or things like Google Calendar or Excel or any of the online apps Mr. and Mrs. Hawkins asked her to use and she struggled valiantly with but usually gave up on, causing chaos in her employers' diaries. No, Charlene, who lived on a tenanted forty-five-acre smallholding on the edge of the Great Bottom estate with her parents and five brothers, was a pig farmeress by birth. The Potts family were, as it happens, perhaps the greatest dynasty of pig farmers in the Bottoms (it was between them and the O'Neills of Little Bottom) and had worked the land on their tenancy for five generations. Unfortunately, pigs' trotters and streaky bacon were no longer the gold mine they had been in the 1880s, when the first Mr. Potts had started out. So, like so many of the local farm girls and lads, Charlene had been forced to sell out, so to speak, to the Rich Wife set. She and her peers could just about afford to farm if they worked another job almost full-time.

Only a few months ago, Charlene had pinned a postcard in the village shop in Great Bottom, offering her services as a personal assistant, nanny, driver, groom, laundress—whatever role anyone needed, none of which she had any qualifications for. She had found herself inundated with offers from wealthy local families, the most attractive of which had been the one from Mr. and Mrs. Hawkins, who did not require early-morning starts. If she rose at five, this allowed Charlene a couple of hours in the morning to help tend the pigs with her brothers before beginning work at the Manor at nine. She'd recently delivered her favourite sow, Cheyanne (named after a beloved contestant on *Love Island*), of twelve pink piglets, one of which, as we already know, was a runt who was struggling to survive.

"I think I'll h-h-have to qu-qu-quit," sobbed Charlene, twisting the tissue in her fingers. "Honestly, it's easier delivering twelve piglets than delivering a dinner party. Maybe I'm better off mooning over Cheyanne and her babies in the sty, even if I am flat broke."

Ian was agitated. If Charlene left now, there would be no one at all to help him with the Kitchen Sups. Inexperienced and virtually useless as Charlene was, at least she was a body who could do some of the less complex chores required. It would be impossible to find another decent PA around here at such short notice. In fact, thought Ian to himself, it would be impossible to find another *hopeless* PA around here at such short notice. Charlene was far better than nothing. She'd only been in the job a few months, she had a good heart, and Ian was convinced she was trainable.

The kettle was soon boiled. Ian sprinkled a teaspoon of Fortnum & Mason afternoon tea leaves (he'd been against teabags even before he knew they contributed to climate change) into a small silver teapot and poured in the boiling water. He took two china cups and saucers from the cupboard and set them on the side while he waited for the tea to brew.

"Listen, dear. You need this job, or you won't be able to afford the pigs."

"True," Charlene admitted. Her salary barely covered the animals' food and vet bills as it was. "But I don't know. It's so hard working for these rich folk. I just want you back at the Manor. It's awful without you, and Mrs. H., and little Minty."

"Charlene, please hang in there. We will be back sooner than you can imagine," said Ian as he poured two cups of tea. He handed one to Charlene and then put on his HR hat. "You know, Mrs. Hawkins values you immensely, and Mr. Hawkins sees you as a potential mentee on his entrepreneurship programme." (This wasn't strictly true—yet—but Charlene would need something to hold on to.)

As she sipped her tea, Charlene's face brightened. "That would be grand. But what about the pigs?"

"That's just it, Charlene," said Ian, thinking on his feet. "This is *about* the pigs. People like you are the future of pork, bacon, food, farming in this country. The Hawkinses could help you build a real business around your farm. You, my dear, are a pig tycooness in the making."

"Goodness," was all that the awestruck Charlene could respond.

"But for now, you and I need to work together. You are the key to the Manor, quite literally."

"What?"

"Imagine that you are a heroine of the French Resistance. You, Charlene, must resist the occupation of the Manor by this Tallulah and her bikinis."

Charlene looked intrigued. "She's after Mr. Hawkins, you know."

"Of course she is!" Ian agreed. "And not for his physique, that's for sure. Now, let's have some of the lemon Madeira cake I made earlier and discuss strategy."

"I do like your cakes." Charlene cheered up as she tucked into the pale yellow sponge.

"Right, let me take the calligraphy off your hands. I can write those invitations in a jiffy, and what's more, I will enjoy it thoroughly. I hand-calligraphed every invitation when I worked with the Grand Duchess in Luxembourg on her daughter's coming-out ball."

"Ooh, you are posh," she said. "I've got the cards and envelopes in the car."

"Wonderful. I'll write them tonight and drop them round to all the guests tomorrow. There's no time to post them," Ian said as he cut himself a skinny sliver of cake.

"There's something else," he continued after taking a bite, deciding that the time had come to articulate his full vision to Charlene. "I have grander plans for this party than simply a wildly fun night." Here he paused for dramatic effect. "I plan to find Mrs. Fairfax a divine new husband."

"Ooh, goodness," said Charlene. "How would you know who she wants to marry?"

"What about a charming billionaire?"

"Know one?" Charlene asked, eyebrows raised. She screwed up her pile of wet tissues and threw them away. She seemed to have recovered, to Ian's relief.

He smiled knowingly. "Naturally. The obvious candidate is Antoni Grigorivich."

"Who?" asked Charlene, a baffled look on her face.

"The Polish chap who bought Little Bottom Priory off Sir Reggie and Lady Caroline Backhouse last year. I have it on good information—from his personal valet, in fact—that Mr. Grigorivich is disembarking his Falcon 2000 at Farnborough airport tomorrow afternoon and then installing himself and a full staff for his very first summer at the Priory. He's just the right type. Owns a stable of leisurewear brands with factories in Eastern Europe. Swans around the Mediterranean on a mega-yacht called the *Galina*."

"Sounds fancy," said Charlene.

Ian's wheels were turning. "Of course, it can't look like an obvious set-up. A dinner with a single billionaire and a pile of married couples would be very peculiar. Mrs. H. requires a balanced guest list, and Selby Fairfax needs to feel there are *heaps* of men to choose from."

"What about that Wing Commander Freddie Naylor-Pitt bloke?" Charlene suggested. "He's quite posh. Lives down at Meadow's Leap. I heard he's back on leave from Ukraine."

"Freddie's a marvellous idea," Ian congratulated her. "I'm rather keen on Tom Meade-Featherstonehaugh too. Not a pot to piss in, as they say, but more than makes up for that in the brains department. He's a brilliant equine surgeon."

"Ooh, Tom," Charlene said, swooning. "He's as good-looking as that James Norton on *Happy Valley*. I wonder if he likes pigs as much as he likes horses?" she added wistfully.

"Charlene, we are not husband-hunting for you. Mrs. F. gets first dibs. And by the way, this is the moment at which a professional PA such as yourself whisks out a notebook and pen and starts scribbling down names."

At this, the young woman looked lost. Sensing an imminent meltdown, Ian opened one of the kitchen cupboards and handed Charlene a notepad and pen.

"Thanks. Not sure how to spell all these names but I'll try," she said, writing down the first three.

Ian, now in full swing, leaned against the countertop and loosened his tie. "I wonder if Vere Osborne should be on the list?"

Mr. Osborne was Mrs. Fairfax's immediate neighbour. When he wasn't working in London, he lived at Great Bottom Home Farm which bordered Great Bottom Park.

"That poor bloke who lost his fiancée a few years back?" Charlene asked.

Ian sighed. "It was tragic. He's still single after all this time."

"All right, sounds like he should be invited," said Charlene, noting down the name.

"Let's add Wills Corrick. He's finally separated. And Charlie Holmes's divorce has just come through."

Charlene was mesmerised. "How do you know all this, Ian?"

"The widows, dear, keep me informed," Ian told her. "I don't think we are going to have any problems finding Selby's Prince

Charming. After all those divorces during Covid, honestly, there are more than enough ex-husbands to go around. There was a plague, Charlene, and now, thankfully, there is a plague of ex-husbands."

The young woman's face was full of admiration. "If it ever goes wrong with the Hawkinses, and you *ever* want another job," she told him, "the Young Farmers could do with someone like you. We're after someone to organise the Christmas party."

"It's a wonderful offer," replied Ian graciously. "But I'm hardly qualified for a position of such magnitude." He was only half-joking. "But to be serious, your job tomorrow after you've given Mr. Hawkins a little time to recover from his Venice trip, is to let it slip—seemingly *by accident but within his earshot*—that you feel terribly torn, terribly disloyal because Mrs. H. has asked you to help organise a party for Mrs. Selby Fairfax, who you are sure he wants to meet, and you don't know where your loyalties lie."

Charlene grimaced. "I can't do that! He'll hit the roof."

"For the greater good of the Monkton Bottom Manor community, you must have courage. Talk about the party in a very loud voice to one of the maids, and say how much you wish Mr. and Mrs. H. were still together so he could attend."

"All right," she said reluctantly.

"There's just one more thing," Ian went on. If he was going to put the dagger in, he might as well do it properly. "Let Miss Tallulah know how fabulous and exclusive the party's going to be, and that she's not invited either."

8

Surprise callers to the Rectory were not something that Sophie Thompson encouraged. She laboured tirelessly to furnish an image of effortless domestic perfection, which could only be achieved with huge amounts of time, preparation, and warning. Unexpected visitors were a nightmare: what if they were to see, say, an ugly grey dustbin outside awaiting collection, or a man in grubby overalls unblocking a gutter on the front of the pretty stone house? Country Princesses never had rubbish, or blocked gutters, and it was a betrayal of their tribe's ethos to admit to such dull domestic concerns.

At ten o'clock on Tuesday morning Sophie was still in her pyjamas, which felt like a luxury. She had, for once, persuaded Hugh to do the school run. He'd dropped Eddie off and then returned to his home office at the back of the house where he would be on Zoom calls all morning before disappearing up to London after lunch. Sophie was going to get out her block prints and chintzes and work on a new design this morning which she'd post on Instagram as soon as it was ready. She wasn't even going to bother to change. Bliss.

So when she heard a vehicle pull into the drive, and Hugh's two black Labradors started barking, Sophie pottered from the kitchen where she had been washing up breakfast, along the airy front hall. She opened the door expecting to see no one more exciting than the Amazon delivery man.

"Have I got the best surprise for you!"

Tata was standing on Sophie's front doorstep, bubbling with excitement, holding a large cream envelope in her hand. She was immaculately put together in a white broderie anglaise sundress and low-heeled sandals, and a delicate Rosa de la Cruz necklace sparkling with miniature amethysts and diamonds twinkled against her tanned décolleté. Behind her, Tata's brand-new, hybrid four-wheel-drive Bentley Bentayga (number plate: BUNN1E) was purring in the driveway. Sophie still couldn't make up her mind whether the car was cool or completely ridiculous. Ian gave Sophie a polite wave from the driver's seat.

"Tata, hi," said Sophie. "Sorry, I'm not even dressed." How she wished she was not wearing her oldest, fuzziest Cath Kidston pyjamas and a revolting pair of tangerine Crocs right now.

"Hey, don't worry," said Tata. "Can I grab a coffee? I have got so much to tell you."

"Course," said Sophie, curious. "Would Ian like something?"

Tata beckoned to Ian to join them. He turned off the engine, emerged from the car, and the three of them walked inside.

"I'm so sorry the kitchen looks *such* a mess," Sophie said as she led Ian and Tata indoors.

She gestured round the completely immaculate room, which she had decorated with Edward Bulmer's "Cerulean Blue," that shade that had been so in when they moved to the country five years ago. The huge inglenook fireplace at one end of the kitchen wasn't dancing with flames, to Sophie's bitter regret: even though it was early May, no self-respecting Country Princess ever entertained in a room with an unlit fireplace. Thankfully it was mostly hidden by the Victorian pine table, which was piled high with swatches and sketches. At the other end of the kitchen were acres of marble worktop, a pale blue Aga, and the pale blue Smeg refrigerator she had persuaded Hugh to buy for her birthday last year. Though she knew it wasn't the mess she proclaimed it to be, Sophie was secretly dissatisfied with her kitchen situation. Of course, she would never have said so. She didn't want to sound ungrateful. There were people in the world who didn't even have a kitchen, let alone a pale blue Aga and a matching Smeg. But still, the kitchen at the Rectory looked like all the other country kitchens on Instagram: the faux-ikat lampshades from OKA; the squashy George Smith sofa under the window; the horsey Munnings prints on the walls—every Sloane Ranger in Oxfordshire had these things. How she loathed them now. In her fantasies she'd hire Rose Uniacke to redecorate the room in a palette of over-priced ivory-hued paint.

"On the contrary, it looks delightful in here, Mrs. Thompson," Ian reassured Sophie. And then, as if by magic, he went on, "Do let me get your fire going. I need a chore."

Sophie smiled gratefully at Ian, who went to the fireplace and started laying it.

"Aren't you going to open it?" Tata said, pointing at the envelope she'd handed her friend. She tossed her bag on the table and drew out a chair.

"Sorry. Yes," said Sophie, tearing open the envelope and retrieving a stiff cream card. She read the words on it out loud:

> *Tata Hawkins*
> *requests the pleasure of your company at*
> *an intimate 'Kitchen Supper' in honour of*
> *Selby Fairfax*
>
> *7.30pm, Monday 10 May*
> *The Old Coach House, Monkton Bottom*
>
> R.S.V.P.

"Such a coup!" Sophie exclaimed. "How on earth did you pull this one off?" She perched the card in pride of place on the kitchen mantelpiece and then started brewing a pot of coffee on the Aga.

"You won't *believe it*, Soph," Tata started, her eyes widening. "I met Selby by the lake on Sunday. We *totally* bonded and I invited her over—and she accepted. Told me everything. Maud was a distant cousin, left her the whole estate."

Sophie was intrigued. "*That's* how she got the house? Wow."

"She's *so* cool, *so* nice. But one thing, you've got to *promise* to get Hugh to come to the dinner. Got to have even numbers."

"He'll be there with bells on," Sophie said. "He's been going on and on about that house. Hugh's had Big House envy his whole life, ever since some great-great-great-grandfather gambled away the family estate in Scotland."

"The heart bleeds," Tata replied with an eye roll.

"He's ridiculous," laughed Sophie, handing Tata and Ian each a coffee in miniature Emma Bridgewater espresso mugs painted with dachshunds.

"Such pretty mugs, thank you," said Ian.

"Eddie gave them to me for my last birthday," Sophie replied, making a space on the table for the cups. "I've always wanted a sausage dog, but Hugh won't let me. He says he's got to have two Labradors for shooting," she went on, "and he can't look after a third dog. In reality, he doesn't look after *any* dog."

Tata made a face at Sophie. "I don't know why you put up with it—"

"Ssshhh, he might hear you," Sophie scolded her friend. "He's in his study. Hugh can be adorable when he wants to be, and he's so clever."

Both of these things were true. Sophie's husband had been educated at Eton and Cambridge, and he'd swept her off her feet when they'd met in their early twenties. He had a Prince William look about him and he'd seemed dashingly romantic—he used to take her for champagne at 5H, lunches at Le Caprice, and weekends in Paris. She couldn't deny that he'd been a bit pompous from the start, though she'd thought he'd change for the better as he got older. In fact he'd only become more arrogant with each passing year, especially since he'd landed a powerful government job—not that she'd admit any of this to Tata.

"It's amazing he's even here today. Usually I barely see him in the week," Sophie went on, at which point both Labradors padded over and lay at her feet. "You can't help but love them," she sighed, rubbing the dogs affectionately on their heads.

"Why is he home now?" Tata asked.

"Weekly Cabinet meeting's on Zoom as the PM's in Washington. I can't disturb him. I'll tell him about the supper for Selby later."

Sophie then sat down at the kitchen table with her own coffee. The fire was soon flickering away and Ian perched on the fender while she and Tata chatted.

"What's the dress code for Monday?" Sophie asked.

"Oh, God, no dress code," laughed Tata. "It's only a Kitchen Sups. Super-duper casual."

"I see," said Sophie grimly.

A "no dress code" dress code was the worst of all possible worlds. Confusingly, this meant there *was* a dress code, but one that was so terrifically subtle that it required intense application to the problem to achieve any sort of success. The so-called "super-duper casual" evening uniform required to attend Kitchen Suppers was an oxymoron: one had to dress (and act) for such events as though one wasn't trying at all, yet still look unbelievably glam and fashionable.

"Old-fashioned black tie was so much easier," Sophie went on wistfully. "Remember the days when you could just bung on a ballgown and be done with it—"

"Fucking FUCK OFF!" came a yell from outside.

"What on earth was that?" cried Tata nervously as Ian instinctively sprung to his feet.

Sophie said nothing, but her face was clouded with worry.

"What's going on?" Ian asked.

"You fucking bribing TORY CUNT!"

Sophie shuddered. "Ugh!" Without a word of explanation to her guests, she banged her little mug down on the table, dashed through to the boot room, threw one of Hugh's old Barbour jackets over her pyjamas as she ran along the hall, and swiftly let herself out of the front door.

∞

For a few moments, Ian and Tata looked at each other in stunned silence.

"So weird," she said. "I mean, what on earth—"

"Bloo-oo-oody liar!" came another screech from outside.

Tata had turned pale. "There's some total freak out there."

"Mrs. Hawkins, take that large iron poker from the fireplace," Ian commanded ever-so-politely, "and follow me."

Tata darted over to the fireplace, grabbed the poker and followed Ian out of the kitchen and along the hallway. The front door had been left wide open and the pair stepped gingerly out. From the relative safety of the Rectory's gracious Georgian porch, they found themselves witnessing a peculiar scene: on the slope of the grassy bank opposite, a man dressed in a purple tie-dyed T-shirt and filthy trousers was swaying as though drunk. He had a bottle of whisky in one hand and was gesticulating violently at Sophie, who was standing on the verge closest to the house, looking rather forlorn in her pyjamas and the old Barbour. She was trying to calm the man, hands out in front of her, but every time she tried to speak, he yelled again.

"Give me the poker, Mrs. H.," Ian said quietly, "and then return to the kitchen. We don't want you getting hurt."

He took the tool from his boss, who gratefully retreated inside, then he walked determinedly out to the lane, daintily holding the fire iron up in front of him as though he were about to commence a fencing match. He noticed that menacing clouds had gathered overhead, and there was suddenly a chill in the air.

"Hugh Thompson is a cunt-chewing shii-iii—t!" the man screamed.

"No!" Sophie cried out as Ian appeared at her side with the poker. "Please stop. You need help," she said to the man.

Her words were met with aggressive shouting. "You can fuck off with your scumbag Tory 'help.' There isn't anywhere to get any help since *he* closed the hospital." The man took a long swig of his whisky and then, for good measure, added, "Your husband is a lying, bribing tosser."

"Sophie, go and get Hugh," Ian told her.

She shook her head. "I can't. He's on a Zoom with Number Ten."

It was Ian's turn to shake his head. Leaving one's wife alone to deal with a drunken, abusive man in the lane—well, that was a politician for you. Ian would need to call on all his diplomatic skills to talk him down.

"Sir," he said politely, dropping the poker to the ground and taking a step towards the verge. "May I have a quiet word?"

Perhaps surprised by Ian's respectful manner, the man calmed a little, then said, "'Bout what?"

"The state of the nation," replied Ian.

"Piss off!!!"

The man lurched in Ian's direction, but as he did so he tripped, dropped the whisky bottle, and tumbled head over heels down the bank and into the road, where he lay motionless, his eyes shut. Sophie gasped. Ian, meanwhile, coolly picked up the poker and walked into the middle of the lane where the man lay and gently prodded him with it. He responded with a loud snore.

Just then, from the direction of the village, Ian and Sophie heard the sound of footsteps, and they turned to see a woman running towards them in exercise gear.

As she got closer, Sophie said, "Is that who I think it is?"

Ian peered at the approaching figure. "If you mean Mrs. Selby Fairfax, then, yes, it is she."

"Oh no," Sophie wailed. "I don't want to meet her looking like this. She'll think I'm some barmy country bumpkin."

"Mrs. Thompson, you always look wonderful, whatever you're wearing," Ian reassured her.

Simultaneously, he noted Mrs. Fairfax's ten-out-of-ten running look: her slim but athletic physique was clad in sleek navy-and-white camouflage yoga tights, a sleeveless matching hoodie, white baseball cap, and navy sneakers with a thick white sole.

"But, I mean—"

Sophie didn't get to finish. Selby Fairfax was already upon them, and skidded to an abrupt stop when she saw the carnage in the lane.

"My God, what happened?" she asked, peering down at the body. "Should someone call an ambulance?"

"Na!" came a furious exclamation from the ground.

"I thought he had passed out," said Sophie.

"Does he have anywhere to go?" Selby whispered.

Sophie replied in a low voice, "I think he's homeless. His ex-girlfriend and baby are in a safe house locally. He's known as Jacko Whisky."

Selby looked concerned. "Can we get him to a shelter or—"

"You lot can fucking fuck off with your fucking shelters!!" Jacko yelled back. Then, somehow, he rolled to one side, crawled onto all fours, staggered to his feet, and lumbered off towards the village. "I'm goin' to the pub!!!" he shouted as he wobbled away.

The trio, flabbergasted, watched until the man was just a speck in the distance. A few plump drops of rain plopped down onto the lane, and a gust of cold wind shook the trees overhead. The sky had turned a threatening blue-black colour.

"Are you both okay?" Selby asked Sophie and Ian.

"Marvellous, thank you," Ian replied, ever-cheerful despite the circumstances.

"A little shaken, but I'm fine," said Sophie. She chewed at her lip nervously. "I'm *almost* used to Jacko Whisky by now. He appears every few weeks outside our house, shouts about the government for a while, then disappears again."

"What a nightmare." Selby then put her hand out to Sophie and said, "By the way, I'm Selby, your new neighbour."

"Lovely to meet you. I'm Sophie Thompson. I live here," she said, shaking Selby's hand and then gesturing behind her at the Rectory.

"The almond florentines in a beautiful tin?"

Sophie laughed. "That's me!"

"I hope you can forgive me for not getting back to you. I'm one of those horrible rude Americans that get so much bad press. Deservedly. And you are?" she asked, turning to Ian.

"Ian Palmer," he said, shaking Selby's hand. "I work for Tata Hawkins and her husband Bryan. I'm their Executive Butler."

"Very grand," Selby remarked, an eyebrow raised in amusement. "It's really nice of Tata to invite me to supper next week."

"She's in the house," said Sophie, then added, "Why don't you come in and we can all have a cup of tea?"

"I'd love to but . . ." Selby glanced at her watch. "I've got meetings soon and I've still got a mile to run back home. Another time?"

"Sure," said Sophie, just as a rumble of thunder echoed across the land like a gigantic drum roll. Within moments rain was pelting down.

"Mrs. Fairfax," said Ian. "Hop into the Bentley and get out of the wet while I go and fetch Mrs. Hawkins. I *insist* on driving you home."

~

Let us briefly revisit the pale blue kitchen at the Rectory, where, despite the unpleasant interlude with Jacko Whisky, Sophie was feeling ebullient: she had finally met the starry new neighbour, and her husband would be ecstatic. She was about to get going on her block-printing designs, when Hugh (forty-five, looked fifty-five due to balding pate, glasses, and a penchant for a double-breasted Savile

Row suit whatever the occasion) sauntered in and put his briefcase by the kitchen door.

"I thought you were on a Zoom with Number Ten?" said Sophie.

"Finished early," said Hugh, peering into the bread bin by the Aga. "Where are the *pains au chocolat*?"

"Wherever you left them," said Sophie. Why did Hugh always ask her where everything was in the kitchen? She didn't ask him about the location of her goat yoghurt or special Ottolenghi granola. "Anyway, you won't *believe* who I met in the lane just now."

"I think I will. I heard the whole thing. Jacko bloody Whisky again—"

"You heard it?" Sophie smarted as she began laying out fabric swatches. "Why didn't you come and help?"

"Had to finish up the Health Reform Bill proposals, darling. Davinia would not be best pleased if I neglected that." Hugh put a slice of bread in the toaster, turned it on and then propped himself at the breakfast bar and began tapping away at his phone.

What Sophie wanted to say was, the fuck does it matter what Davinia thinks, when your wife is being verbally abused by a drunk and could have been hurt? She was too mild-mannered to speak like that to her husband, so she just said politely, "Try again." She grabbed a set square and tailor's chalk and marked out a design on a piece of fabric. "You won't *believe* it."

"I'm sure I won't," her husband drawled, not bothering to look up from the phone. Hugh had always been distracted, but he'd seemed even more absent since he'd become a Cabinet Minister about a year ago, around the time he'd been forced to close down the local hospital that Jacko Whisky was so (rightfully, she believed) upset about.

"Selby Fairfax."

Hugh ripped his attention from his phone and stared at his wife.

"Well, why didn't you say?" he retorted crossly. "You know I've earmarked her as a potential donor to the Foundation . . . Oh, God, you're not saying she was out there with that freak?"

"I was in the lane with Ian, trying to deal with him, and she was on a run. She kindly stopped to help and—well—it all went from there, really. We had a gorgeous chat, actually. We're going to meet up."

"Why *on earth* didn't you come and get me?" Hugh huffed.

"Because Davinia wouldn't have liked it if you hadn't finished up your proposals on the Health Bill, would she?"

Hugh ignored Sophie's tone. "Do make sure to introduce me when you can," he sniffed, going over to the fridge and taking out some butter.

"Actually, darling," she went on, ignoring her husband's dig at her, "that's all arranged. Tata's throwing a dinner for her next week. Invitation on the mantelpiece. Three-line whip that you're there."

Hugh virtually ran to the fireplace and inspected the invitation. "That's an RSVP yes," he said, sounding satisfied. "It'll be good to meet Selby and get her support for the Foundation. I'm sure a woman of her means wouldn't be able to resist the idea of helping underprivileged children spend a day at a goat paradise in the countryside, away from their awful lives in the inner cities."

"Maybe wait for your second meeting with her before tapping her for cash, darling?" Sophie suggested.

"Hmm, perhaps." The toast was ready and Hugh took it out of the machine and spread it with butter and Marmite. "Pop my office an email with the date, will you?" he said and then took a bite.

"It's on the tenth of May. Next Monday night. I'm sure *you* can pop it in your diary, *yourself*, now," she replied.

"All right, all right, no need to get all feminist about it."

Sophie simply ignored this and said, "Listen, Hugh, that Jacko guy, he's really starting to scare me. He's saying the most terrible things about you. I sometimes think he'll get violent, break into the house or—"

"He's just a harmless old soak," Hugh said dismissively. "Don't worry about it."

"What about getting your protection officers on it? Can't they do something?"

He pursed his lips. "Look, Soph, I can't be seen to abuse precious government resources. My protection officers are there to protect *me*, not my wife and child and four-million-quid house."

"Right," said Sophie curtly.

"Just tell the bloody drunk to bugger off if he comes back again."

Sophie was about to answer when she heard the crunch of tyres on the gravel outside.

Almost simultaneously, Hugh's mobile phone started to vibrate on the table, and he answered it, saying, "Davinia? You're here? I'll be out in five minutes." He hung up and then said, "The ministerial car's here to pick me up."

"Why is Davinia in it?"

"Sorry, *darling*," said Hugh in a syrupy voice, "but Lord Garborough is insisting on a face-to-face meeting this afternoon about the hospital crisis and Davinia wants to brainstorm on the journey to London. You know what these special advisers are like. Bloody bores. Do far too much work, if you ask me."

Sophie sighed but didn't say anything. There was no point. Hugh picked up his briefcase and came over and pecked her on the top of her head, saying, "See you Friday night. I'll try and get home early."

"So you'll be back for Eddie's sports day on Saturday?"

"Wouldn't miss it for the world. Right, Davinia's going to have my guts for garters if I don't get out there pdq. Bye, darling."

Sophie returned to her swatch of fabric and the tailor's chalk, but she couldn't focus. Davinia. What a ridiculous name.

9

Thank the lord, thought Ian as he motored from the Rectory to Great Bottom Park, that he had valeted the interior of the golden Bentayga only yesterday. The car was always immaculate for Mrs. H., but now that Mrs. Fairfax was installed on the roomy back seat as well, it reminded him that upholding high standards of presentation was never a waste of effort.

As Ian drove, wipers on overdrive, the rain streaked across the windscreen in horizontal shafts. Eventually he turned the car between a pair of crumbling, castellated lodge houses which guarded the entrance to Great Bottom Park. He could do little but inch the vehicle slowly up the bumpy drive which had long ago lost its gravelled surface and was now worn to the hard, rocky stone below. Whenever he and Boris had driven up here to see Lady Maud, they had quickly found themselves enveloped by an atmosphere of romance and today was no different: in places the drive was little more than a track covered in velvety green moss, in others it was camouflaged by brambles sprawling from the hedges, or shadowed by tunnels of enormous, waxy-leafed rhododendron trees and their voluptuous, blood-red flower heads. Ian did not like affectation, but he was a bookish sort, and now and again a literary moment descended upon him. Entranced, he couldn't help but utter the immortal line, "*Last night I dreamt I went to Manderley again.*"

"Huh?" asked Tata from behind.

"This place," Ian sighed. "It's poetic. It always reminds me of the house in *Rebecca*. Manderley."

"Oh right, of *course*," said Tata, who'd found over the years that her attention span was more suited to memes than novels. She'd google it later.

"Such a great book," said Selby. "But unfortunately this place looks a bit too Manderley right now. Everything's half falling down—the only building that's in a decent state of repair is the stable block."

As the car purred towards the house, Ian found himself agreeing with Selby. He had not visited the estate since Lady Maud's death, and considerable decay had set in during the ensuing year. Where there was dry stone wall edging the fields, areas had collapsed; the barns and cottages they passed were strangled with tree ivy and had lost the glass in their windows; the parkland was thick with nettles and a herd of deer, startled by the car, shot across the track; even a pair of beautiful stone urns, presumably once majestically sited on opposite sides of the drive, were now lopsided where the ground had given way beneath the plinths.

Eventually, Ian swept the car round a generous bend and a long allée of sentry-like yew trees led the eye towards the house itself. The ancient seat where the Earls of Bottom had planted their bottoms for hundreds of years did not disappoint: the building consisted of an elaborate central block of pale stone, flanked by curved wings on each side which wrapped like elegant arms around an open courtyard, and the enchanting Elizabethan facade was punctuated by mullioned windows and laced with loops of heavy white wisteria blossom. Ian soon pulled up outside the grand arched porch.

"I feel like I'm Lady Mary arriving at Downton Abbey," Tata said, mesmerised by the sight ahead of her: even in the pouring rain it was sublime.

"And I feel like one of those crazy ladies in *Grey Gardens* every time I get back here. When you see the Grand Canyon-sized crack in the ceiling of the Great Hall, you'll think I'm nuts to have taken this place on. But it's just . . . it's so dreamy, isn't it?" Selby gazed through the damp windscreen at the splendid edifice. She then quickly checked the time, and said, "I've got a few minutes till I have to meet the estate manager. Why don't you both come in?"

~~~

Would it be *very* wrong to take a shot for Instagram? wondered Tata as she followed Selby into the house. The answer of course was yes, and Ian would have been furious with her. If *only* her five thousand or so "friends"—if only *Bryan*—could see her now, strolling beneath the crevasse-like fracture in the ceiling of the Great Hall (Selby had not been exaggerating) and along the echoing corridors of Great Bottom Park behind her new friend Selby Fairfax. Imagine how many "likes" she would get. She might even pick up a few new followers. But she pushed such superficial thoughts aside—for now. The trio soon arrived at a tall oak door framed by simply carved stone.

"Come on in," said Selby, pushing it open.

"Oh—" started Tata. She had hoped to be ushered into a grand drawing room, or at the very least a gilded, mirrored breakfast room, where a liveried footman would be waiting with a silver tray of tea. Instead of being transported into an episode of *Bridgerton*, though, she found herself following Selby down a steep flight of stone steps into an antiquated, dungeon-like kitchen.

Tata took in every dusty detail of the huge old room. It was a time-warp, in completely the wrong way. The whitewashed walls were hung with everything from hunting trophies to copper pots and pans, used plastic shopping bags and dusty bunches of dried flowers. The few high windows let in only a glimpse of sky, and ugly yellow Formica cabinets and cupboards looked like they must have been installed in the 1960s. The countertops were made of a dull, industrial stainless steel and an ancient cream Aga (that seemed to be emitting almost no heat) sat against an enormous beamed chimney stack at the far end. A shabby electric oven had been installed next to it, presumably to cover for when it broke down, which

Tata imagined would be frequently. It looked as though whoever had been running the kitchen during Lady Maud's reign had added various cheap freezers and refrigerators, which contributed to the chaotic feel. The middle of the kitchen was dominated by a long oak refectory table surrounded by pine chairs and piled high with yellowing newspapers, unopened mail, mugs, schoolbooks, and even a taxidermy rabbit in a glass case. Tata was rather afraid: she wondered if she would catch something if she touched a surface. She looked nervously at Ian.

The butler stepped into the void immediately. "How extraordinary," he said diplomatically to their hostess, "to still be able to use the original Elizabethan kitchen. Marvellous."

"The kids think it's like something from *The Addams Family*," Selby said, taking her phone from her pocket and putting it on the table. "I promised them I'd fix it up—but I'm not going to. I'm starting to like it."

"It's got bags of character," agreed Ian.

Just then, two black-and-white Jack Russell terriers tore into the room and rushed over to Selby, jumping up on her.

"Oi! Down, you two!" came a stern voice, then a moment later an eccentric-looking woman appeared at the doorway, holding a mop in one hand and a bucket in the other. Probably in her sixties, she resembled an ageing punk rocker and was dressed in a neon boiler suit with a pink apron tied over it and had a pair of Marigold rubber gloves on her hands. Her ears were studded all the way up with spikes and rings, and her short hair was a violent shade of lilac. It had been combed into a tuft on the top of her head.

"Good heavens, Mrs. Fairfax. I didn't know you had guests," said the woman in a thick Oxfordshire accent, looking flustered as she made her way into the room. "I was just feeding the chickens. I'll put the kettle on."

Selby thanked her, then said to Tata and Ian, "This is our wonderful housekeeper, Doreen Hunnigan. Doreen, this is Mrs. Hawkins and her butler Ian."

"I know Ian," Doreen replied, beaming at him. "Her Ladyship adored him and his visits, she did, with poor dear Boris. Mrs. Hawkins, lovely to meet you," she said, flicking on the kettle. "Mrs. Fairfax inherited me and my other half Alan, with everything else. We live in the attic flat at the top o' the house. Alan's the gardener-handyman-groundsman here."

"Great to meet you," said Tata, who was slightly confused by Selby's staff arrangements. Most of the people in big houses she knew round here had large teams at their beck and call, and anyway, she'd never seen anyone who looked less like a housekeeper than Doreen.

"Why don't I bring the tea into the morning room for you all, Mrs. Fairfax?" Doreen asked, putting out a tray. "I could have made a cake if I'd known."

"That would be lovel—" Tata started, her spirits soaring. The "morning room" sounded so aristocratic! So grand! Her *Bridgerton* moment was within reach.

Her hopes were dashed almost immediately.

"I wish, but I've got literally fifteen minutes before I meet William Ostler at the estate office," said Selby. "Let's just stay here. But, Tata, I *promise* to invite you for tea and Doreen's cake another day, *not* in the kitchen."

The Hawkins spirits soared again, and the Palmer spirits in equal measure: things were looking up. Doreen had soon made a pot of tea, poured it for everyone, and the group was perched round the overflowing table chit-chatting about this and that when Selby's phone vibrated. "Sorry," she said, tapping the screen to check the message.

Tata noticed Selby's expression suddenly change.

"It's from Doug," she said, stony-faced, her eyes scanning rapidly.

"Your ex?" asked Tata.

"Yup." Selby nodded. "First message in ages . . ." Looking perplexed, she said, "Do you mind if I read it out?"

The Palmer–Hawkins spirits took flight like a lark ascending. Selby Fairfax was going to share an intimate message from her estranged husband—well! All Ian and Tata could do was smile surreptitiously at each other: the inner circle was within reach.

Tata nodded her head vigorously at her new friend. "We're all ears."

Selby took a long breath and eventually said, "Here goes. *Dear Selby, hope you're okay. I'm thinking of coming over this summer to see the girls and bringing the dogs for them as I'd promised. I wouldn't invite Kirk. What do you think? Very best, Doug.*" She sniffed, irritated, and then continued, "What am I supposed to say to that?"

"I guess the children must be missing him," said Tata.

Selby looked downcast. "After all this time . . . yes, course they are, but they're really confused. Instead of being with them he's just spent months on his latest truth-finding escapade with the Himba tribe in Africa."

"Talk about a midlife crisis," Tata remarked.

"Exactly," said Selby. She had a jaded look on her face.

"If it's not being too forward, may I make a suggestion?" Ian asked politely.

"Er—" Selby seemed unsure.

But Tata reassured her. "Ian might as well be a family therapist," she said. "He's navigated so many difficult situations with couples in his career."

"Too true," Ian replied. "And I've learned a few things which are sometimes useful."

Selby looked interested. "Go on."

"Listen to your children, Mrs. Fairfax. They miss their dad. Invite Doug to visit, but make sure there are strict boundaries: a time to arrive and a time to leave; build up to longer if it's a success. At the end of the day, he's the girls' father and they need to see him, however uncomfortable it may be for you."

"You make it sound so simple," said Selby.

"It is if you can keep your emotions out of it."

Selby got up and paced round the table, a frown furrowing her brow. Finally she said, "I'm still so angry with him but I know you're right, Ian. There's no other option. I've got to suck it up for the girls' sake. Okay, I'm writing back, here goes." She tapped on her phone for a few seconds and then read out the message. "*Dear Doug, great to hear from you. Definitely plan on a visit, and I'll send some dates later this week, very best Selby.*"

"Well done," Tata told her.

"I'd honestly rather stick rusty pins in my eyes than see that man but I'm going to do my part—"

"Mom!" came a voice from the corridor. "Mo-o-om!"

Selby spun towards the doorway. "What on earth is Violet doing home from school now?"

The party was soon to find out. Violet, a lanky fourteen-year-old, appeared at the entrance to the kitchen, one arm looped around the neck of a young man in his twenties, who looked, Ian couldn't help but notice, exactly like Brenton Thwaites. (The only reason Ian was so familiar with the actor was because he had watched *Maleficent*, the Angelina Jolie masterpiece starring Mr. Thwaites and Lily Collins, many times with Minty.) Supported by this exquisite youth, Violet soon started to limp her way down the stairs. She had white-blonde curls that almost reached her waist, the freckled skin and wide eyes of a Victorian doll and was dressed in the Stow Hall School uniform of a gingham dress, cream blazer, and straw boater.

"What's happened?" asked Selby, rushing to her daughter and helping her down the last of the steps and into a chair.

"It's my leg," said Violet after she had sat down. "I've done something to it."

Selby turned to the young man. "Josh, what's going on?"

"Absolutely nothing to worry about, Mrs. Fairfax. Apparently Violet slipped in the Marble Corridor and twisted her ankle."

"Ouch," said Doreen.

While they were talking, Ian caught Tata's eye, looked at Josh, then looked back at Tata and mouthed, "Swoon." Tata mouthed back, "Kitchen Sups," to which Ian responded with a stealthy thumbs-up. Meanwhile Josh was saying, "School said they tried calling you, but couldn't get an answer, so Violet rang me and I popped in to get her. It's no bother."

"Thanks for coming, Josh," said Violet, bestowing a lingering look on the young man. He was dressed in white riding breeches, black boots, and a caramel-coloured terry-towelling polo shirt. It was impossible to be immune to his beauty.

"Oh, darling, I am sorry about that," said Selby, looking stricken. "The reception here can be terrible."

"That's okay, Mom." Violet tried to lift her foot. "Oooww. It hurts."

"In that case, Vi, Doreen can see you up to bed—"

"But Josh said I could hang out in the tack room."

Selby looked at the young man, eyebrows raised quizzically. "Josh, that is very kind of you, but bed is the place for people who are too sick to be at school, wouldn't you agree?"

Josh shrugged knowingly, and Doreen helped Violet out of the room, the two terriers scampering after them.

As soon as they had gone, Selby laughed and said, "Teenagers!" Then she glanced at Josh and said to Ian and Tata, "Sorry, I didn't introduce you. This is our fantastic competition groom, Josh Hall." After Ian and Tata had said hello, Selby grinned at Josh and said, "Looks like you've got a lovestruck girl on your hands."

"I doubt it." Josh looked bashful and waved a hand in the air as if to bat away the embarrassing remark.

"If I may be so bold, Josh, are you free on Monday night—" Tata started.

"Um, I guess. Why?"

"I'd love to invite you to the little Kitchen Supper I'm doing for Selby at mine—"

"Er . . ." Josh began. Ian thought he looked about as keen to spend an evening with Tata and her friends as he did to fall off his horse and shatter his pelvis in six places. "Only if you'd like me to come, Mrs. Fairfax? I can drive you there if it helps."

"Great! The Old Coach House, seven-thirty p.m.," said Tata

before Selby could speak. "It's casual—come in your riding clothes, whatever, doesn't matter." She got up from her seat. "Right, Ian, we need to get a move on if we're going to deliver the rest of the invitations."

"Of course. The Dower House at Little Bottom next?"

Tata nodded. As she and Ian were leaving, she said, "Bye, Selby. Maybe see you Saturday at the school sports day?"

"Can't wait. The girls are really excited."

~⌘~

After Ian and Tata had left, Josh said to Selby, "Mrs. Fairfax, just wondered, would you mind if I knocked off a bit early today?"

"Of course, as long as all the horses are exercised and mucked out, it's totally fine by me," said Selby. "Why?"

He looked slightly embarrassed, then said, "It's a Zoom go-see for a fashion designer's ad campaign."

"I thought you were too cute to be a stable lad," she joked. "Now I know the truth."

"It's just a bit of extra cash on the side. I probably won't even get a call-back."

"I bet you will," said Selby. "See you later." She took a crimson sweater from the back of one of the kitchen chairs, put it on, and picked up her things to leave. "I feel a bit chilly with all that rain earlier. That's better," she added, pulling the sleeves low over her wrists.

"I'll be getting on, then." Josh headed towards the door, but just before he reached the steps leading up to it, he turned and looked back at Selby in a different way. "I hope you don't mind me saying," he said, "but that colour really suits you."

"I don't mind at all," Selby said, bemused.

With that, Josh mumbled something unintelligible, blushed a shade of crimson darker than his employer's sweater and dashed from the room.

10

As Ian and Tata crawled back down the drive from Great Bottom Park at the pace of a sleepy caterpillar, three miles due south in the walled garden of the Dower House at Little Bottom, Lady Caroline Backhouse was kneeling on a red plastic gardening cushion that she had bought in 1986, gamely attacking a length of Japanese knotweed that was choking the roses in one of her many herbaceous borders.

Lady Caroline (seventy-eight, looked sixty-eight due to all that country air, plus a drop of sweet sherry each morning at eleven) was the epitome of the British type known as a "Good Sort." She always dressed, summer or winter, in a version of a look which could be described as "the Late Queen Relaxing at Balmoral" and today she was clad in beige wool-flannel trousers, sensible brown brogues, thorn-proof gloves, a Fair Isle twinset she'd bought decades ago on a sailing holiday to the Hebrides, and a hooded mackintosh to protect her from the rain. A pillar of the community, Lady Caroline was chair of the local Women's Institute, a magistrate, a prison visitor, church warden, district commissioner of the Pony Club, wife to Sir Reggie Backhouse (eighty-two, as far as he could recall), and mother to two daughters. The Honourable Charlotte (thirty-seven) had married "well," as her mother liked to put it, to a Scottish lord with an enormous grouse moor, while the Honourable Arabella (forty) was not yet wed—but more of that later.

Until recently, Lady Caroline and Sir Reggie had lived at Little Bottom Priory, which had been the seat of the Backhouse family for hundreds of years. But, as the couple had become older and faced spiralling costs, they had deigned to sell the family pile to "that peculiar Polish chap," as Lady Caroline referred to Antoni Grigorivich, the fashion tycoon who had bought it and barely set foot on its grounds since. It was quite a comedown for Lady Caroline to move into the Dower House (with its scant six bedrooms) after being chatelaine of such a grand residence throughout her marriage, but she was too sensible to complain. Anyway, she had much to be grateful for, she reminded herself as she tugged the vicious vine from the damp ground. The Dower House, a fine example of Regency architecture, was situated on the edge of the estate they adored, but they no longer had to worry about the costs of the fencing, the walling, or the staff. True, they couldn't have twenty for dinner at the drop of a hat, but their home's elegant cosiness more than made up for the square footage they'd sacrificed.

"Looks like it might turn into a nice day, Caro," Sir Reggie called out as he wandered onto the stone terrace with a copy of *The Times* under one arm and two mugs of instant coffee in his hands. Dressed in worn red cords, a navy Husky jacket and green wellies, he glanced up at the breaking clouds through which a few patches of blue sky could be seen. As he put the mugs on the wooden garden table and sat down on the rather damp bench, three black cocker spaniels that had followed him out lay down obediently at his feet.

Reggie patted the empty spot on the bench next to him. "Breather, poppet?"

"Two ticks," she called from beneath a rose bush. Eventually Lady Caroline heaved herself up from the ground and marched onto the terrace. She plopped onto the bench next to her husband and removed her gardening gloves. "Nice walk?" she asked, taking a glug of her coffee.

"Wet but marvellous. The bluebells and ragged robin are out in the copse," Sir Reggie replied, opening the newspaper and scanning the headlines. "Huh. That's peculiar."

"What is?" remarked Lady Caroline.

"Hugh Thompson. Look here," said Sir Reggie, showing his wife the page he was reading. "He was asking questions last week in the House of Commons about reducing the tax on heavy vehicles."

"*Very* peculiar seeing as he's the Health Minister," agreed Lady Caroline, putting on her spectacles and peering through them at the article. "Surely he's got enough to do trying to keep hospitals open without getting involved in transport."

"Never thought much of him. Think even less of him after the hospital closed. Useless, like all politicians."

"I'm sure he's just doing his best. Now, let me have a look at the television section, please."

Reggie handed his wife the requested pages and turned to the crossword. Breeze, birdsong, and a puzzle, thought Reggie to himself—perfect peace. Until the sound of a car's engine marred the moment.

"Who could that be?" exclaimed Lady Caroline, standing up. They weren't expecting visitors today.

The couple trotted through the clematis-covered entrance at the side of the walled garden and out to the north front of the house. From the oval-shaped drive, which was shaded by magnificent cedar trees, they could see beyond the park railings exactly who was coming and going along the track.

"It's that *ghastly* car belonging to that *ghastly* woman," declared Lady Caroline, seeing Tata's Bentayga heading towards them.

"Calm down, poppet, it's only a Bentley," Reggie teased. He rather envied the luxurious vehicle, not that he'd have dreamed of letting his wife know. Lady Caroline only approved of twenty-year-old Volvo estate cars or similar.

"I think it's simply ghastly to swan around the country lanes in a golden car like you're Cleopatra."

"You think everything's ghastly, dear," Sir Reggie reminded his wife, patting her hand kindly.

"That's because everything *is*."

Like many of her class and generation, Caroline Backhouse's list of Ghastly Things was sweeping. Most upsetting were mobile phones, gluten-free diets, leggings, puffer jackets, and canine crossbreeds (the Labradoodle, in particular). Ghastly People included the nouveau riche who'd "ruined" Oxfordshire, the uber-rich Euros who'd "ruined" London, the man from Facebook, and the man from Amazon, but top of her official Kill List were the "Antis" (protesters who wanted fox-hunting banned). The short but happy catalogue of Not Ghastly Things included farmers, horses, NHS nurses, and anyone who'd made their money before 1925.

The couple watched as the Bentley crunched its way onto the gravel in front of the house. When she saw who was at the wheel, Lady Caroline couldn't help but smile. True, he did belong to the ghastly Mrs. Hawkins, but even Caroline was not immune to the allure of Ian Palmer. Like every woman in Oxfordshire, she wished Ian was hers. His egg mayonnaise sandwiches were something else, and he was always up to date with the latest article in *Horse and Hound*. She was amazed at Tata's ability to hang on to him.

"Good day, Lady Caroline," said Ian, springing from the vehicle with the lightness of a grasshopper. "Hello, Sir Reggie."

"Do hope we're not interrupting," said Tata, as Ian helped her out of the car. "But I wanted to give you both this personally." She handed Lady Caroline an envelope.

"Go on, poppet, open it," Sir Reggie urged her.

Lady Caroline did so and looked at the card inside. An invitation for a Kitchen Supper to meet Selby Fairfax! Crikey! But a hand-calligraphed "stiffie" for a shepherd's pie by the Aga seemed dreadfully common. Sir Reggie peered over his wife's shoulder at the card, which was so grand it reminded him of the invitation they had received to King Charles's coronation. (Caroline was old chums with Queen Camilla—they'd spent many a happy day out with the Duke of Beaufort's hunt back in the 1980s.)

"Sounds jolly," he declared. Then he looked forlornly at Ian and Tata and said, "Shame we can't come."

"You can't?" said Tata, taken aback. "Why not?"

Reggie puffed his cheeks out. "Caro's very strict about these things. She's always said that going out in the week in the country is ghastly, as is going out at the weekend in the city. We attend hunt balls or shooting dinners at weekends here, and occasionally go to the theatre or the opera during the week in London," he explained matter-of-factly before turning to his wife. "At least that's the general idea, isn't it, dear?"

"Quite right," she said. "But there's the *very* odd occasion when I make an exception. It sounds as if Mrs. Fairfax has had a horrid divorce. We really should go to her welcome dinner. To be kind."

"Well, if you are completely sure you can manage," Reggie told his wife.

"More than, dear. We must acquaint ourselves with Mrs. Fairfax as soon as possible. Besides us being supportive of her during a difficult time, we need her backing for the Summer Terrier Show." She then turned to Tata and said, "It's the qualifier for Crufts and it's always held at Great Bottom Park. Goodness knows what would happen to the terrier breeds in the future without it. We must make this exception to our usual social arrangements, Reggie, for the greater good of the terrier community."

Equally, thought Lady Caroline to herself, it would be quite out of kilter locally if Tata and all her nouveau riche friends were on familiar terms with the area's newest chatelaine and the Backhouse family were not.

"Good point, Caro," Reggie said, perking up. Being allowed to go to Tata's would certainly improve his Monday night, not least because Mrs. Hawkins always seemed to dress as a nightclub hostess for her parties. "We'll look forward to it. Lots of people coming?"

Tata smiled. "About twenty, I think."

"Ooh!" said Lady Caroline, her eyes lighting up. "Any single men?"

"Poppet!" Sir Reggie exclaimed, reddening and regarding his wife with amazement.

"Not for *me*, you silly thing," she said, giving Reggie a soft thwack on the arm. "I'm thinking of Bels."

"Bels?" asked Tata.

"Our daughter, Arabella. If you could squeeze in another guest, I know she'd love to pop up from London for the evening," Lady Caroline went on. "You see, she's in dire need of fixing up with a husband."

"On it," said Ian. "I've got the ideal man in mind."

11

By midday on Tuesday, the rickety old Land Rover that Lady Maud had owned since 1962 could be seen bumping along the back track from the main house to the estate office, Selby at the wheel. You could say that Mrs. Fairfax was less focused than usual on her day ahead—in fact, she felt giddier than a drunk duckling. It wasn't just the beauty of the sun suddenly glancing through the velvety green of the trees after the earlier downpour, the soft drifts of cow parsley puffing along the grass verges, or the adorable glimpse of a bunny rabbit's white tail disappearing into the meadows that had lifted her mood, although they had something to do with Selby's delight. No. Annoyingly enough, she mused, it was a man. Or, in this particular case, a boy.

Although she was not the pity-party type, the feelings of inadequacy, gloom, desperation, and insecurity that Selby had so freely shared with Tata a few days earlier at the lake were horribly real. If we are to delve a little deeper, it would be fair to say that post-marriage, post-children, and post-divorce, Selby had at times felt empty, quite literally. She was empty of joy, energy, optimism—even femininity. On the one occasion she had opened herself up to the possibility of a new relationship, a few months ago, she had been badly burned (dinner, sex, and a disappearing act on the man's part). After this mishap, she had staked her emotional tentpoles in a new position: Beyond Unavailable. She even had a well-rehearsed response to those overfamiliar (rude) people who asked her if she'd ever marry again. "The only thing I'll hitch myself to in the future," she'd tell them, "is a sailboat."

Then an innocent little compliment walked in the door, like it had this morning, and all those good intentions about only ever getting involved with an inanimate floating object walked straight out of it. *That colour really suits you.* A few words from the stable lad—admittedly a stunning one—who was twenty years her junior, and Selby had melted quicker than a marshmallow on a toasting fork. Still, that compliment had taken her mind off the stress of Doug's out-of-the-blue message. His rare attempts at contact usually made her feel highly anxious, but less so today. She'd send him some dates later in the week, though she doubted he'd really schlep all the way to England.

Selby eventually pulled up at the estate office, a grand title for the humble stone barn in question. There was a heap of rusting barbed wire and rotten fence posts piled up in front of it, and a dusty Subaru and an ancient-looking red tractor were parked side by side on a bare patch of earth. Still, thought Selby, it wouldn't take much to do up the little building. Lady Maud had left plenty of money with her bequest for such things. It would be gorgeous if the trash was cleared away, the stonework restored, and a climbing jasmine planted on the outside wall.

She grabbed her tote bag full of papers from the passenger seat and exited the vehicle. As she approached the barn, she noticed a window was open, through which raised voices were drifting out.

"That damn American," she heard a man's voice saying in a local accent. "She'll kill all the livestock on the farm if she's not careful—"

Selby stopped in her tracks.

"Look here, Arthur, I'm sure there's a simple explanation," said a voice she recognised as that of William Ostler, the estate manager. "Have you checked the pipes for leaks?"

"Of course we have," the man who seemed to be Arthur retorted angrily. "I know when a neighbour's been stealing water.

Mr. Osborne's in a right lather. Says she's one of those spoiled rich Yanks. They come over here and don't know the first thing about the countryside."

Selby winced. She wasn't sure what to do. Should she linger outside until the man had left, or boldly announce herself?

"Look, I'm sure you'll find she's a perfectly reasonable woman—"

"There ain't nothing reasonable about a sudden drought at Great Bottom Home Farm," came the furious reply.

"What?" William sounded worried now.

"She's drained the shared spring. There ain't a drop of water left in the borehole, the troughs are almost dry, and we ain't got enough water to feed the cows that are in the barn. Mr. Osborne's hopping mad having this happen while he's calving."

"I can assure you that Mrs. Fairfax couldn't possibly have used all the water. As far as I know, there's only her family and the Hunnigans in the house, so it's just a few baths, the laundry and the washing-up. No one ever visits. It's sad, really—the family doesn't seem to have a friend in the world."

Selby smarted. Did the people round here really see her and the girls that way? Thank goodness she was going to Tata Hawkins's supper party on Monday. She clearly needed to start meeting people, for all of their sakes.

"That's neither here nor there," retorted Arthur. "Mr. Osborne wants an explanation before he loses any livestock. Says she's probably put in an Olympic swimming pool or something. And right in the middle of calving. It's just not right."

Selby watched in amazement as the office door flew open, and a young lad dressed in mud-spattered overalls dashed out, leaped up on to the old tractor and roared off in a rush, seemingly without noticing her standing there. Seconds later, William Ostler (sixty-five, looked seventy-five, due to whiskery face and uniform of moleskin plus fours, checked shirt, and tweed tie) appeared. He was so embarrassed he could barely speak.

"Eh-umm, Mrs. Fairfax, I'm sorry about that," he stuttered.

Selby flashed a knowing smile at the estate manager and shook his hand. "Hey, don't worry. It's true we don't have any friends," she said. Then she added, "Yet."

William was taken aback. Most women he knew would have been sobbing into a lace handkerchief at this point. Thank goodness his new boss wasn't the emotional type.

"At your service, Mrs. F. Do come in," he said, leading the way back inside the barn.

Work, thought Selby, as she followed William through a low-beamed doorway and into the chilly interior, was not a thing of which much took place in the "estate office," which couldn't have been less suited to being an office. The limewashed walls and narrow windows were clouded by cobwebs, and a clunky wooden desk was positioned in the centre of the room upon which sat an old-fashioned rotary phone, a grimy electric typewriter, and piles of yellowing files and papers that had curled at the edges with age. Logs smouldered gently in a cast-iron wood-burner and the two old armchairs next to it were occupied by William's three snoozing whippets. Wisps of dog hair were trodden into a small rug in front of the hearth, and within seconds Selby was sneezing uncontrollably.

"Sorry!" she laughed, holding a handkerchief up to her face. "Allergies."

"Don't worry yourself, Mrs. Fairfax. Now, can I make you a cuppa?" he offered, as he poured boiling water into a teapot.

"Thank you, but I'm just fine," said Selby. The grubby sink, kettle and cups in a corner were not exactly inviting. "Just had tea with Mrs. Hawkins and her butler Ian. They stopped in for a visit. Sorry I didn't have time to change," she added, looking down at her running gear. "So, who was that young lad just now?"

William shook his head as he poured himself a cup of tea. "Everyone calls him Angry Arthur. Runs Great Bottom Home Farm next door for Vere Osborne, who's in London part of the time, see, working. Today, he was having a rant about the water. He's always having a rant about something, mind. Sit down, won't you?"

"Thank you. What's happened?" said Selby, taking a seat on a scuffed white plastic chair by William's desk.

William positioned himself in the chair facing Selby and took a gulp of tea before he spoke. "He says we're stealing their water. There's a shared spring, you see, that feeds this estate and Mr. Osborne's farm, which was once part of the estate. Lady Maud sold it to him ten years ago. Anyway, Arthur says their well is dry and apparently Osborne's seething."

"Could it be our fault?" asked Selby, concerned.

"I can't imagine so—you'd have to fill a lake to drain the spring. They've probably got a leak in the underground pipe somewhere and haven't found it yet. Happens all the time. Let's just pray they sort it. They're calving and the cows need a lot of water to keep producing enough milk."

"Well, if you're sure there's nothing we can do—"

"I am," interrupted William, and she noticed him checking his watch.

"Am I holding you up?" she asked.

"No, no," he said. In the back of his mind was the tenner he'd put on a horse in the one o'clock at Kempton races, which he'd rather fancied popping home to watch at lunchtime. "Now, what can I help you with today?"

"There's a hell of a lot to do here, isn't there?" Selby began. "All these run-down cottages and farmhouses. So much to renovate. The gardens, the orchards, Lady Maud's rose parterres—"

Selby noticed a look of alarm clouding William's visage. "Ah, well." He frowned and puffed. "That's the thing. It would be marvellous to do the estate up, but it's the funds."

Privately, William had been hoping that things were going to carry on under Mrs. Fairfax much as they had under Lady Maud: he would gather meagre rents from tenant farmers, make occasional improvements to walling or fencing if there were enough funds in the estate account, which usually there weren't, which meant, thankfully, that he couldn't do much actual work. This was not particularly distressing for a man with William's interests: little estate business left him oodles of time for rough shooting in the woods, following the hunt, or watching the afternoon's racing in his little sitting room at the Bothy, an ivy-strewn shooting lodge in the middle of the park where he'd lived with his wife, Shirley, for the past thirty years.

"Don't worry about the funds, William. Maud left plenty on that front."

At this, William jerked his head up, like a startled parrot, and stared at her. Finally he said, "You're having me on. She never wanted to spend a penny on the property."

"It turns out she was a very wealthy woman," Selby went on. "Not that I am interested in a profligate spending spree. Every penny counts. We'll start small."

"Quite. No point in spending unnecessarily," William said, nodding in agreement. Relieved the meeting seemed to be over, he started to tidy his desk.

"So the first thing on the list," Selby went on, completely oblivious to his cues, "is the girls' bathroom. The plumbing's medieval. The water comes out brown from the taps and the pressure's non-existent."

"Hmm. We'll need to get on to Historic England. It's getting to the pipes behind the sixteenth-century panelling. Can't touch it without permission," he said. "I don't want to put you off but—"

"You're not putting me off at all. If you could get started with that, it'd be great." Selby had begun to detect William's reluctance.

"Errr . . . yes, of course, Mrs. Fairfax," he replied. "Historic England takes three months to reply to each letter, and a bathroom usually requires at least two or three letters. It's a bureaucratic nightmare." *Surely*, he prayed, that would discourage her.

"Thank goodness you have so much experience dealing with them, then," she said, reaching for her tote.

"No problem," he said through gritted teeth, about to get up from his chair to leave.

But to his chagrin, Mrs. Fairfax then put a flashy iPad on the desk. "So, what I *really* wanted to discuss with you," she went on, as she tapped at the screen, "is the milking parlour, just beyond the stables."

She handed William the iPad, on whose screen was a photograph of the currently semi-derelict milking parlour and below it a rendering of the same building, beautifully renovated.

"I need a proper studio and office space for my work here. The parlour is absolutely perfect. I love the light in there."

"Er, well, ummm . . ." started William, aghast. "We're very short of builders round here, after Brexit."

When Selby saw the man's panic-stricken face, she attempted to reassure him. "Don't worry, William, I'm not going to put all this on you. I'll be around all summer, and I love a project."

William shivered slightly. There was nothing more terrifying, in his experience, than a rich woman in need of a project. Still, he didn't see another option. Grinning glumly at his new boss, he tried to put the one o'clock at Kempton out of his mind.

12

The valley of the shadow of death was not a place where Ian's thoughts often lurked, but towards mid-afternoon that day, our hero found himself unhappily inhabiting the moccasins of the Grim Reaper. Having dropped Tata back at home before lunch, and then delivered invitations to various recipients who acted as though he were Willy Wonka arriving with a Golden Ticket, Ian was now motoring up the drive to Middle Bottom Abbey, the estate boasting the Gothic mansion inhabited by Fernanda and Michael Ovington-Williams, their brood of children and oodles of staff.

It was here that only weeks ago Boris had met his tragic end. Ian and Boris had come up to the Abbey to visit Luca, and kick around a football with the little boy, but poor Boris had suffered a heart attack en route. One minute he had been sitting in the front seat enjoying the ride, the next he had collapsed, his body lifeless. Ian had known it was a possibility—Boris had suffered heart problems from a relatively young age—but still, it was a ghastly shock.

How Ian wished Tata with her chatter was still in the car with him now! Alone, as he wound through the acres of ancient oak forest, he was haunted by bleak images from that day. He could do little but pop a chewy Fruit Pastille in his mouth in an effort to distract himself from the memories that he would forever associate with the dark and forbidding woodlands that surrounded Middle Bottom Abbey.

It wasn't long before Ian reached an opening in the trees. A vista opened up ahead, revealing a view of the monumental medieval facade of the house. Grand as it was, with its towering stone arches, fortified skyline, and carved shields and gargoyles, the exterior of Middle Bottom Abbey was a bit too *Wuthering Heights* for a man of his aesthetics. He soon arrived at a pair of wrought-iron gates, set into the elegant park railing that enclosed a herd of twenty polo ponies, and rolled his window down to press the intercom button which read SECURITY.

"Middle Bottom Abbey. Guy speaking," said a voice through the speaker.

"Afternoon, Guy. It's Ian Palmer. I've got a delivery from Mrs. Hawkins for Mr. and Mrs. Ovington-Williams."

"They're in the old chapel. I'll buzz you in. Just drive on round."

A few minutes later Ian parked outside the old chapel and got out of the car with the invitation in his hand for the Ovington-Williamses, determined to compose himself enough for what would surely be a brief visit. He knocked at the studded door a couple of times. Ian noticed a crucifix carved in stone above the knocker, and as he waited said a little prayer for Boris, whom he missed so much.

The door opened and Fernanda appeared, dressed in a white boiler suit, plastic goggles, and white sneakers. Her only accessories were a turquoise headscarf and 1950s crescent-shaped gold earrings.

"Oh, Ian, am I glad to see you," she said, pushing the goggles up over the headscarf. "I'm having such a tricky time with Luca."

"I'm actually just here to drop off something from Mrs. Hawkins—" he started, but before he could continue, Fernanda had pulled him by one arm into the chapel and closed the door behind them. Like the main house, the building had been whitewashed from top to toe inside and was in complete contrast with its ancient exterior.

"What a wonderful space this is, Mrs. Ovington-Williams," Ian said, gazing around.

"Incredible, isn't it? It used to be the Benedictine monks' prayer room, around 1300. It's the most fabulous studio. It's got the north light, you see. It's perfect for The Work."

"Of course," said Ian politely.

Fernanda gestured at several trestle tables arranged along the middle of the room and piled high with organised heaps of feathers. There were pheasant feathers, black-and-white magpie feathers, spotted guinea fowl feathers, bright blue kingfisher feathers, and white goose feathers, to name but a few. A large canvas was positioned on an easel and had four emerald-green feathers adhered to its centre.

"I know, I know," went on Fernanda. "I can see you think I'm nuts—"

"Not at all—"

"But sometimes it can take me an *entire day* to place one feather."

She selected a yellow duckling feather from one of the trestles and walked over to the canvas-in-progress, holding it up between the feathers already *in situ*. "What do you think?" she asked Ian.

Ian had absolutely no opinion about what Mrs. Ovington-Williams should do with her duckling feather. So he just said, "I completely agree."

Fernanda picked up a little brush, loaded it with glue, and dabbed it onto the duckling feather. She then carefully positioned it on the canvas and surveyed her work.

"This is what I do, Ian, when I can take time out from—you know—*everything*. Speaking of which, Luca is in the vestry with Michael." She lowered her voice, looking troubled. "I couldn't even get him to school today. He's petrified of that Duffield kid now. Michael's completely jet-lagged, and honestly he's not helping the situation."

"Oh dear," Ian said. "Can I do anything?"

Her eyes lit up. "Sometimes I think you're the only person Luca will listen to. You *get* Luca."

"I can try talking to him," said Ian.

"I'd so appreciate it," said Fernanda. "Follow me."

As the pair walked along the old aisle of the chapel towards the vestry at the back of the building, Ian suddenly remembered why he was here. "I almost forgot," he said, handing Fernanda the invitation.

She opened the envelope and glanced at its contents. "Ooooh! A dinner for Selby Fairfax. Wow. Clever old Tats. Always first, isn't she? Except when I am! Ha-ha-ha-ha!" Fernanda giggled. "We're accepting. Obvs."

"Wonderful. I'll let Mrs. Hawkins know."

When they reached the entrance to the vestry, Fernanda tapped gently on the door. "Michael? Luca? There's someone special here."

After a moment, the door opened and Michael Ovington-Williams (forty-two, looked fifty-eight due to extraordinarily dehydrated skin, caused by chronic jet-lag) stepped out of the vestry. He was dressed in a rumpled black tracksuit emblazoned with the white Apple TV logo (the platform to whom he'd sold *Babyblood*, his tween vampire show, as well as the rights to every piece of related merchandise that currently existed or could exist in the future, in return for a big enough cheque to fund the Ovington-Williams clan's extravagant lifestyle at the Abbey for many more decades).

"Ian, good to see you," said Michael in a hoarse whisper as he took a drag from one of the weed pens he regularly smuggled in from LA. He had dark shadows under his eyes and the beginnings of a double chin was forming around his neck. "Luca's been refusing to go to school. Can you think of anything?"

"Michael!" Fernanda hissed back. "Put that fucking thing away." She glared at the pen, which he hastily stashed in a pocket.

"Sorry, sweetie."

"I mean, Luca's *eight*—" started Fernanda.

Ian could sense that things were fraught. Now was the time to draw on his Inner Mary Poppins.

"Do take me to Luca," he said in his calmest Nanny Knows Best tone. "I will do my utmost."

"He's over there," said Michael, pointing through the vestry door to the far corner of the room. Ian took in the sad sight: Luca was curled up on a white corner sofa cuddling a red-and-white Manchester United football.

"He's been like this all day," said Fernanda. "Says the other boys won't let him play football with them at break times any more. That Duffield kid's got it in for him and he's captain of the team."

"Sounds grim," said Ian. "I have an idea. If you'd give us five minutes?"

∽

"How about a drink?" said Michael a few moments later as he headed towards the refrigerator in Fernanda's studio that was stocked with everything from cold-pressed juices to champagne.

"I'm good," said Fernanda. "I'm just feeling upset for Luca. He's so sweet, and the other kids take advantage of that."

"Yeah." Michael sighed and cracked open a beer, and was about to take a sip when the door to the vestry opened and Ian breezed into the studio, leading Luca by the hand. The little boy had a happy grin on his face. Fernanda and Michael stared at each other in astonishment.

"Right. An announcement. Luca's going to school tomorrow," said Ian. "He's doing chess club at break times, and football when he gets home, on a roster. Tuesdays I'll play with him. Wednesdays, the twins, the next day the girls, then Michael, then you, Fernanda—don't look so surprised, you secret Lioness—"

"But—"

"No buts, Mom," Luca told Fernanda, laughing.

"Come on, it'll be good cardio," Ian encouraged her.

Fernanda smiled. "And fun. I'd love it, honey," she told Luca.

"Yaaa-aaa—aay! Ian, come and see my goalposts outside?"

With that, Luca dragged Ian from the room, leaving Michael and Fernanda amazed.

After a few seconds Michael said, "Who's going to take my slot on the roster when I'm on location? You know, Fernanda, we really need a new manny."

"I agree, but God knows where I'd even begin to find a good one."

"What about Ian?"

"Ian's not a manny, darling, he's a brilliant butler with some mannying talents."

"Two very good reasons to hire him."

"Michael, Ian is Tata's. He'd never leave her."

"Anyone will do anything for the right offer—"

"Not Ian. He's got a moral compass that makes Greta Thunberg look flaky."

Just then, a shout came from outside.

"Goal!!!" Luca's voice carried from the garden. Michael and Fernanda sauntered over to the window and looked out. Their son was dribbling a ball, and Ian was lying flat on his back in goal.

"Look at Luca now. Not a care in the world," said Michael with a smile. "He needs an Ian."

"Okay," said Fernanda, patting her husband on the shoulder. "You just go right along to the Ian shop and you buy an Ian."

"I do love you, darling," said Michael. "You have such good ideas."

13

"Do we have to have dog hair all over the front seats, Sophie?" whinged Hugh Thompson, holding up a single black Labrador hair from the driver's seat of Sophie's otherwise immaculate hybrid Hyundai. It was early afternoon on Saturday and the Thompsons were just about to set off for the Stow Hall sports day. "After I got you this *fantastically* expensive car?"

Sophie, in the passenger seat, recoiled from her husband's hand. Gosh, Hugh could be mean. He had known that what Sophie really wanted—actually, deserved—was a flashy black Range Rover Sport, the model with the white leather interior and heated steering wheel, just like Fernanda's and every other Rich Wife's round here. (Many of them felt obliged to own an electric car as well, but these vehicles mostly sat undriven outside big houses to advertise the owners' environmentally friendly credentials.) But Hugh had insisted on getting Sophie a used Hyundai in a nasty shade of maroon, a car Sophie equated with mummies of the horsey, rather than the yummy, variety. Sophie thought he was being cheap, but Hugh insisted the wife of a prominent politician such as himself couldn't be seen driving a gas-guzzler. (Sort of true.) Sometimes, Sophie thought to herself, Hugh should have been Secretary of State for Pettiness. He was clearly in one of his moods today. And when Hugh was in one of his moods, he picked at everything.

"What's the matter, darling?" said Sophie, trying to be understanding, as he turned on the engine. (Hugh hated Sophie driving him, even in her own car. Sophie hated Hugh driving her, but she'd put up with it for today.) "I'm so excited about Tata's Kitchen Supper for Selby," she continued in a jolly tone: Hugh would perk up when he remembered he'd finally be meeting Selby on Monday. "I think you'll really like her."

"As long as that Backhouse woman doesn't collar me again about hunting," he said, "I might just survive another of Tata's evenings."

Sophie winced but decided not to say anything. "Everything all right at Number Ten?" she ventured. Sometimes Hugh got like this when he had work difficulties.

"Dicey. Only just got the Health Reform Bill through its first reading," he said as he revved the engine and set off up the drive. "The PM's pleased but Davinia thinks there are problems to come. She's terrifically clever. Always ahead of the curve."

"Sounds rather like me," said Sophie, her laugh disguising a painful feeling in her gut.

As they motored through the gates of the Rectory, painted that same Edward Bulmer blue that Sophie had slathered the kitchen in and was now tired of, Hugh's frame of mind seemed to alter. He glanced at Sophie as he was driving and suddenly announced, "Darling, I've been thinking. I know you've always wanted a swimming pool—"

"Wouldn't it be divine? Beyond the orchard?"

"I rather agree."

"But pools are so expensive," said Sophie.

"Don't worry about the money. We're more than fine on that front."

Sophie couldn't believe it. She'd never thought they'd have the money to do a pool, and now Hugh was saying they did. There was something about her husband when he was being generous that she found so attractive. She leaned over and kissed him on the cheek.

"Golly," he said, stiffening. "Don't go overboard, sweetheart."

"I'm so thrilled."

"Good. That'll be a nice project for you." Hugh paused for a moment and then, looking miffed, said, "By the way, I think Eddie needs a private sports coach."

"A what?" Sophie was puzzled.

"When I dropped him at school early this morning, he said he's in the Cs for the rounders match today."

"He's always in the Cs," said Sophie. "I think it's brilliant. I was never even in a team at school." Considering Eddie could barely catch a ball, let alone hit one with a slim piece of wood, she was thrilled he had made it on to a team at all. And anyway, the Cs were now the place to be. "Hugh. The last thing we want is Eddie being moved up. Tess Fairfax is in the Cs too."

At this news, Hugh's expression softened. "Ah. That's different, then," he said. "For once the Cs are an opportunity."

Sophie was pleased that Hugh got the picture. The protocol at matches and sports days was always the same: the parents of the A team stood together to watch their children's games, likewise the parents of the Bs and Cs. Sophie had made some of her greatest friendships on the touchline, and why would her relationship with Selby be any different?

Fifteen minutes later, Hugh and Sophie drove beneath the Tudor bell tower that marked the entrance to Stow Hall, through the huge courtyard around which the school buildings were arranged, and out towards the playing fields. Once near the pitches, they were directed by various teachers to a large field that had been reserved for parking, where Hugh pulled up alongside banks of shiny Teslas, Range Rovers, Bentleys, and Porsches. Sophie noticed Hugh plastering a smile across his face as they got out of the car. As welcome as it was to see him making an effort, she couldn't help but wonder why her husband was so changeable at the moment. She couldn't put her finger on the reason, but something about him unnerved her.

14

There are times when even the most glamorous butler finds that his role doesn't involve delightful duties such as serving blinis and beluga to pop stars and *principessas* in a splendid chalet in Gstaad, but rather searching a cramped attic for an ugly stuffed toy. For Ian, the Saturday morning of sports day had been interrupted by the aforementioned task, which he performed, naturally, with his usual positive demeanour. After all, he well understood that the mental health of certain sections of the younger generation was largely dependent on access to their favourite teddy bears.

The fact was that while the Thompson, Fairfax, and Ovington-Williams families were dutifully attending sports day, the Hawkinses were not. The drama had started at breakfast, when Minty had had a meltdown after Charlene texted Tata to say that Bryan's plane from Munich, where he had been attending a trade summit, was cancelled late last night and he wasn't going to land at Heathrow until the afternoon.

"I'm not going to sports day without Dad," Minty wailed when she received the news that morning.

"I'll take you instead, darling," Tata reassured her. She didn't really have time—she had so much still to do for Selby's dinner on Monday—but she'd make it work.

"But I want Dada, and anyway I hate sports day." A tear fell from Minty's eye.

"It'll be fun—"

"I want to die." More tears. "Dad doesn't care about us, Mummy."

"He does, darling, he really does. Come on, you have to go to the matches today, sweetie—"

"I want cappuccino."

"What?" Tata was completely confused.

"C-c-c-appuccino will make it b-b-b-etter," hiccoughed Minty.

"Ian?" Tata called out.

Ian, ever the professional, swept lightly in from the staff kitchen, pretending not to have heard a word, and smiled suavely at his boss. "I'm here, Mrs. Hawkins," he said, taking in the scene. He was still not quite used to the vast scale and futuristic look of the front kitchen: it was almost forty feet long, had full-height plate-glass doors on two sides, a poured-concrete floor and walls, and a vaulted ceiling from the centre of which hung a massive silvery mobile.

"Could you make Minty a cappuccino, please?" she asked, then added sotto voce, "decaf, of course."

"I don't *want* a cappuccino!!!" Minty threw herself from her white leather stool at the marble breakfast bar and lay on the floor howling.

"But you just said you wanted cappuccino," Tata said, kneeling down beside her daughter.

"You don't understand anything about me, Mummy."

Tata looked up at Ian, desperately hoping he would have a solution. "Two minutes ago, she said a cappuccino would make everything okay. Her dad can't make sports day. I don't know what to do."

To Tata's relief, Ian said in his ever-relaxed tone, "Mrs. Hawkins, leave it to me."

The mysterious language of a child is a thing few understand, but Ian's childcare skills rivalled those of the finest Norland College nanny graduates. He knew perfectly well that when an eight-year-old girl screamed hysterically that she wanted cappuccino, caffeine was the last thing on her mind. What was on her mind was an oddly shaped stuffed toy, a "Beanie Boo," whose fur was printed with tiger stripes, whose paws were stitched with fluorescent green fleece, and whose pink, saucer-like, plastic eyes gave it the pathetic look of a lost dog. Every single Beanie Boo had a small label attached to its bottom which stated its name and birthday. Minty, like many of her school friends, collected Beanie Boos, and the bizarrely named Cappuccino was, Ian knew, the first that the girl had ever owned. Ian's experience had taught him that Beanie Boos solved almost any problem you could name, and were far less expensive and easier to come by than behavioural therapists.

Ian sprinted up to the attic playroom of the Old Coach House, retrieved Cappuccino from the vast pile of toys therein, and returned to the kitchen, all within the space of ten minutes. Minty was, by this point, shuddering in a heap on the giant white sheepskin sectional at the far end of the room and Tata was nervously peeling the gel polish off her nails, at a loss.

"Minty," said Ian kindly, as he went and sat beside her. "Here's Cappuccino."

The child lifted her head from her knees, took the toy from Ian and clutched it to her chest. The sobs slowed.

"Thank you, Ian," Minty said. "I feel a b-b-bit better. But I still don't want to go to sports day."

"Mrs. Hawkins?" asked Ian, looking at Tata.

"I defer to your far superior parenting skills, Ian," replied Tata sincerely. "You decide."

Ian smiled and put his arm around Minty's shoulders. "I think this little girl deserves an afternoon at home," he said.

"Phew," the girl said, giving Ian a hug. "The rounders captain is awful."

"Right, I'll call the school and let them know," Ian replied. "How about flumping around here while me and your mummy finish planning her dinner party?"

※

Tata had, for about a minute, thought that between them she, Ian, and Charlene could pull together a perfect Kitchen Sups. But after it had been ascertained that the Cat and Custard Pot caterers were fully booked for the next three months, and that Willow Corbett-Winder was too busy promoting her new line of carbon-neutral vases to help, and Charlene had presented her with one dire suggestion after the other for the table (no, jam jars filled with wild flowers were not cool at all. She'd already seen the look a million times, at Sophie Thompson's kitchen suppers, which were *actual* suppers in her *actual* kitchen), Tata had realised that the only way to present the impression of an effortless but insanely glam Kitchen Sups was to have someone else do the efforting. Nothing less than a one-stop dinner party shop was required.

So it was that after lunch on Saturday, party-planner extraordinaire Veronika Ward (thirty-six, looked twenty-three due to bang-on-trend London wardrobe and raw food diet) and *Vogue* stylist Lexi Longsdon (twenty-one, looked a decade older due to the stream of cigarettes she smoked while bored on fashion shoots) sloped into the foyer of the Old Coach House, where they were greeted by Ian and led through to the sprawling kitchen where Tata awaited them. (By now, Minty was fruitfully engaged in the creation of a Sylvanian Families tableau at the far end of the room.)

"The chicness, Tata! Party kitchen or what?" exclaimed Veronika. "Amazing to be here."

"Yay. Excited," added Lexi in the flat tone of a jaded fashionista.

After kisses had been exchanged, and espressos and juices produced by Ian, the foursome sat down at one end of the vast mirror-topped table (which could seat twenty-four). Tata was in awe of Veronika, who had come armed with mood boards, menus, cocktail suggestions, wine lists, look books, and samples of flatware, glassware, and stemware from all the parties she had organised; she could help Tata properly "express herself," she said. Anything Tata wanted for the dinner could be delivered the next day. They were soon discussing styles and themes.

"It's all about '*La Blanche*' right now," Veronika began.

"Which is . . . ?" asked Tata.

"White, white, white. White absolutely everything," Veronika replied. "White represents purity—"

"Calm," Lexi concurred.

"Hope."

"Innocence."

"Freshness. A *fresh start* . . . this is what this divorcée friend of yours will be searching for right now, Tata," Veronika told her authoritatively. "A palette of whites—that's what we're going for, with the flowers, the table settings. It will lift Selby's mood. Cancel out the negativity." (What Veronika did not note aloud was that one-colour schemes were always the most profitable for her. Plus, all those white hydrangea bushes and camellia trees she had left over from last week's Chanel event could be repurposed and re-billed for.)

"But you don't think people will think I'm not being creative enough if the flowers, china, and linens are all the same colour?" Tata asked, a little disappointed by the concept.

"It's quite the opposite now," Lexi informed her. "Everyone in London's *sick* of all those over-the-top multicoloured tablescapes."

"Totes, Tata," Veronika reassured Tata. "Just look out there," she went on, gesturing through the wall of glass that opened onto the garden. "Every blossom, every flower in your garden is white. This is more than just some tacky 'tablescape.' It's a concept, a vision of life. We need to complement your incredible planting. There must be flow, from inside to outdoors. Your guests will admire you for working with nature, for being organic in the truest sense."

"Mmmm," Tata replied. Veronika was going overboard on the flattery now, if Tata was being honest. But she rather liked that sort of thing.

"Wouldn't it be exciting," added Veronika, "to do a whole, you know, full-on nature thing, where you've got the most beautiful white birds outside—like doves."

Tata's eyes lit up. "Farmer Clarke next door has white bantams with feathery feet and pom-pom heads," she said.

"I'll pop in later and ask him if we can hire them for the night," said Ian.

"Great," said Veronika. "And no carbon footprint to bring in those birds. It's chic to be local now."

Tata was loving the flattery, but time was pressing on. "Okay, next up," she said. "Lexi, what are you thinking, clothes-wise?"

"A long, flowing, simple white dress will look genius on Instagram against the tablescape and the garden—" Lexi started.

"Tata, Lexi," Veronika interrupted, a grave expression on her face, "TikTok is just as, if not more, important. Only really old people go on Instagram now—"

"But all my friends are on Instagram—" began Tata.

"Exactly," said Veronika, then clapped her hand over her mouth. "Gosh, sorry, I mean, I didn't mean you're *old* or anything. It's just, it's like, now you've got to do Insta *and* TikTok *and* Reels if you want to be relevant."

"Course," said Tata, trying to sound relevant. "I want to build followers on every platform."

Lexi nodded. "Very sensible. So, Tata, the rail will be here later, you can try everything on. To give you an idea, there's an asymmetric tunic dress from Wiggy Kit, linen, floor-length. There's an Emilia Wickstead flared silk cocktail dress to the ankle, or a long Brandon Maxwell skirt and top in white eyelet cotton . . ."

Tata looked disappointed.

"Actually, I was thinking of something short and frilly and bright, from Zimmermann or Alaia. A piece that really shows my legs and cleavage. I'm not trying to look like the Angel Gabriel."

Lexi raised an eyebrow. If Tata's blingy style was not reined in, Lexi wouldn't feel comfortable having her handle hashtagged on Tata's Instagram. After all, she wanted clients who brought her more clients, not clients who made her look tacky. "Knee-length?" she said hopefully.

"I'll try a few things," said Tata, "but I haven't spent all that time contorting myself into a pretzel at Gyrotonics to cover my body in a shroud."

"I hear you, Tata. Don't worry, I'm not going to make you look anything but amazing. As soon as the clothes arrive, we'll start trying choices," Lexi said. "I'll photograph you in them, to see how they'll look on-screen."

"Ooh! Good idea!" Tata replied, thrilled. "About social media: the strategy is that we start posting on Monday morning, with the prep, the planning—people love seeing all that."

Tata was thinking of how annoyed Bryan would be when he saw how beautiful the supper he wasn't invited to was going to be. Her marriage would be back on track very shortly, she was sure of it.

"Course. What are the hashtags?" asked Lexi, pulling out her mobile. "I'll put them in my phone now."

"Just use #monktonbottommanor and then tag me at @tatahappycotswolds."

Lexi typed the hashtag in and then, as a film suddenly came up on her Reels, said, "God. Cute. Look," she continued, passing her phone to Tata.

Tata watched as a small, blond Teacup Pomeranian scampered around the rose garden at—*no!* Monkton Bottom Manor! It was soon apparent that the dog was being chased in some sort of game by an influencer-type person in a zebra-print thong bikini that left absolutely nothing to the imagination. The film was dotted with hashtags like #IloveyouPikachu! and #TallulahSwim and #ShopTallulahDeSanchezBikinis.

So that was Tallulah, "Daddy's friend," as Minty had put it at the fete, skipping round her grounds. Unbelievable. It looked like Bryan had a girlfriend, hence the radio silence from that department. Tata wanted to die, and simultaneously started wondering if there were any hit-men available in the Bottoms. She silently handed the phone to Ian, looking grave.

Summoning his Inner Jeeves to avoid revealing his true feelings on the subject of the twenty-something bikini designer, Ian perused the images and then, seemingly unruffled, simply replied, "Good information, thank you," before returning the phone to Lexi.

Tata meanwhile, stone-faced, said absolutely nothing: there was nothing like seeing a younger woman's toned butt-cheeks frolicking around one's rose bushes to galvanise a robust response. In the face of adversity, she was undaunted. Mrs. Hawkins was on the warpath.

15

The Stow Hall sports day, an annual fixture of athletic and social prowess, was just as much a competition for the parents as their dear children. There was a palpable rivalry between the families, with each couple praying their offspring would win their matches, the husbands praying that their wives would win the unspoken beauty pageant, and the wives praying that their husbands would win in the success stakes. (That prize was usually awarded to the dad who landed by helicopter on the rugby pitch.)

Like many of the other mothers, Sophie had spent a small fortune on a new outfit for the day. She was terribly proud of her pale yellow, glazed-cotton Ulla Johnson dress, with its intricately pleated skirt and the ruffles around the shoulders and cuffs. Hopefully no one would guess that it was last season, or that she'd got it 70 per cent off at Bicester Village (even discounted, it had cost hundreds of pounds). Her wedge-heeled espadrilles and wicker box bag added a summery air to her look, she hoped. As she and Hugh meandered towards the playing fields, Sophie felt as though she were in a Watts painting: in the distance, children in sparkling sports whites were dashing in and out of the cricket pavilion, teachers were blowing whistles and organising teams, and parents were spreading rugs and picnic teas at the side of the pitches. The azure sky and candyfloss clouds added a perfect backdrop to the blissful scene.

"Oh, Hugh, look, darling, there's Simon Hopeton," said Sophie, spotting the Richest Dad at School on the far side of the rounders pitch. He was chatting to Michael Ovington-Williams, a.k.a. the Coolest Dad at School who also happened to be the Second Richest.

"Would you mind terribly if I pop over and see him?" asked Hugh. "Haven't caught up with Si in ages. And, look, there's Michael O-W. Thought he was filming in LA."

"I think he got back a day or two ago." Sophie smiled sweetly at her husband, waving him off and adding, "I'll meet you in half an hour at the rounders match?"

"Yes. See you with the glamorous Cs. And don't forget to introduce me to your friend Selby this time."

As long as Hugh could hang with the Power Dads, Sophie knew he would be content. She started walking towards the cricket pavilion, hoping to find Eddie before his match, and, perhaps, oh-so-casually, run into Selby Fairfax again. But she hadn't gone more than a few yards when she heard her name and turned to see Fernanda waving excitedly at her, Luca at her side, clasping his mother's hand tightly. Drat, thought Sophie. The last thing she wanted to do was be outshone by Fernanda when she bumped into Selby. She painted on a smile, though, and kissed her friend hello.

Fernanda, radiant as ever, was dressed in an elaborate, belted Miguelina sundress of tangerine cotton that swept the ground. (Sophie had seen it on Net-A-Porter when she was searching for inspiration for the day, but had ruled it out upon seeing the ludicrous price tag.) White lace inserts ran around the bodice and hem, and lace bows sat on the shoulders, with long, dramatic ties that reached halfway down Fernanda's back. Her hair was swept up with tortoiseshell and diamanté clips, and her arms and wrists were dripping in gold and diamonds. A fringed leather bag hung from her left shoulder. She looked, Sophie had to admit, as original and alluring as ever.

"Heading to the pavilion?" Fernanda asked, linking her free arm with one of Sophie's. "Let's go together. Come on, Luca. Maybe we can find some of your friends, hey, poodle?"

"Mom, you said I could stay with you if I came today. Everyone at school hates me," Luca complained, standing stock-still. The remains of his black eye made him look rather vulnerable.

"That's not true," said Sophie. "Eddie thinks you're great. Let's see if we can find him."

Luca shook his head. "He doesn't."

"Come on, honey," said Fernanda, giving the boy's hand a little tug. "If you really can't face the matches, you can stay with me."

Luca huffed, and then reluctantly started walking.

As the three strode towards the pavilion, Sophie said to Fernanda, "Did you get Tata's invitation to the supper for Selby?"

"I did indeed," said Fernanda happily. "Should be fun. Luckily Michael's back from filming so he can't get out of it. Then he's off to Prague for a couple of weeks." She sighed. "He's barely home right now. Five kids!"

"I guess that's the price you pay for a hit TV show—"

Sophie's phone pinging interrupted her. "Sorry," she said, taking it from the box bag to see a text was waiting for her. "Oh, it's from Tata. Oh no, Minty's refusing to come as Bryan's delayed, so she and Ian are looking after her at home."

At this news, Luca emitted a squeal of disappointment.

Fernanda leaned down to her son. "What is it, sweetheart?!"

Luca had a tragic look on his face. "Mom, you *promised* Ian would be here. Ian's the *only* person who's nice to me."

"Oh, sweetie, I'm really sorry, I am," said Fernanda, giving the boy a cuddle. "But Ian works for Tata."

"Why can't Ian work at our house?" asked Luca sadly.

"Because . . . well . . . he can't."

"Can't you ask him?"

Out of desperation, Fernanda said, "No, honey. Look, he's promised to play football with you at least once a week. Okay?"

Luca nodded, his expression still miserable.

"Right, let's go find Eddie," Fernanda insisted, her patience running thin.

"Guess what?" said Sophie as they walked. "We're putting in a swimming pool."

"Hugh's agreed?" Fernanda looked surprised.

Sophie looked befuddled. "I know. I can't believe it either. He's really changed his tune."

"Take it while you can get it, Soph," said Fernanda with a laugh.

When Sophie, Fernanda, and Luca reached the cricket pavilion, they greeted various other parents and children. The men were mostly dressed in smart jeans and light sports jackets, and the women were wearing floaty, slightly hippie-ish dresses that had been picked up in one of those overpriced beach boutiques in Ibiza over the Easter break. Sophie's anguish at seeing Fernanda's divine dress only escalated when she realised that most of the other mummies were swinging a variation of her wicker basket and balancing on high-heeled espadrilles virtually identical to her own. Ugh. She was so unoriginal! She vowed to donate her shoes to that nice charity shop in Chipping Norton and go back to flat K-Jacques sandals henceforth.

Sophie scanned the sidelines for Eddie, not seeing him anywhere, but quickly spied her new neighbour and her two daughters sitting on a tartan picnic rug. Among the sea of bright dresses, Selby stood out for her simple look: faded tan-coloured denim pedal-pushers, a loose navy sweater, white baseball cap, expensive sunglasses and plain canvas Vans on her feet. And—OMG—was that the black Phoebe Philo tote, casually tossed to one side?

Sophie suddenly felt like an overdressed Easter egg in her frilly lemon frock—it was completely the wrong outfit for her second meeting with Selby. After the pyjamas Selby had seen her in during the Village Loon incident, she would think Sophie was some kind of desperate housewife—which these days didn't feel that far from the truth.

Fernanda soon spotted her as well. "Oh my God, Soph. Look. That's Selby Fairfax," she said. "On that rug. God, she's giving off a super-cool vibe in those preppie clothes, don't you think? Let's go and introduce ourselves now. No need to wait till Tata's party. Come on."

Before Sophie could protest, Fernanda had grabbed her arm and marched her over to Selby Fairfax. Praying that Selby wouldn't even recognise her in the awful Little Bo Peep number, Sophie was vowing to throw away *every single hateful thing in her wardrobe* that involved a frill, a ruffle, or a shade of pastel, when something completely heavenly happened. Just as they reached the vicinity of the Fairfax picnic rug, Selby glanced upwards, looked at Fernanda blankly and then, seeing Sophie, smiled warmly.

"Sophie! Hello! Such a relief to see a familiar face here," Selby said.

"Soph-ieeee," Fernanda started. "You didn't let on you already knew Selby Fairfax, you secret social butterfly—"

"We met in odd circumstances," Sophie interjected.

"Well, anyway," Fernanda went on, thrusting her hand towards Selby, who'd now stood up, "I'm Fernanda Ovington-Williams. I'll be at Tata's supper on Monday."

"Great to meet you," replied Selby, shaking her hand.

Selby's girls, Tess and Violet, rose from the ground and introduced themselves to the adults. Then Tess said shyly to Luca, "Hey, Luca. How are you?"

Luca shook his head sadly.

"Aww, no," Tess said to the little boy. "I'm glad to see you." Tess looked at her mother and said, "Mom, Luca's in my class at school. When I don't know where something is, he always shows me."

"Thank you for being so kind, Luca," Selby said. "It's tough starting a new school."

"One of my girls is in your year, Violet," Fernanda said. "Isabelli. Have you met her yet?"

"Yes, she's so cool," Violet replied. Then looked at Selby and added, "Mom, she's the most amazing dancer."

"We have a flamenco teacher come from London on Sunday mornings," Fernanda said. "I turned the old ballroom into a dance studio . . . Violet, perhaps you'd like to join in?"

Sophie couldn't believe it. Fernanda was already offering ultra-sophisticated playdates to Selby Fairfax's kids, literally seconds after *she* had introduced them.

"Please, Mom, can I?" begged Violet.

"Why not?" replied Selby. "Sounds fun. Thank you, Fernanda."

"Come tomorrow around eleven. Stay and watch the lesson if you like and we can have coffee. We're at Middle Bottom Abbey—just buzz Security from the gates and they'll let you in."

Behind her smile, Sophie was starting to feel resentful. Fernanda always mentioned "Security" (code from rich person to rich person that they were *really* rich). And casually dropping the fact that she had a ballroom. The closest thing Sophie had was the back barn with a disco ball and ping-pong table inside. She'd have to dream up her own fabulous playdate with Selby Fairfax, and fast, before the Fernandas of this world stole her away.

"I am so thrilled to meet you," Fernanda was saying. "Your gardens—well—I'm an enormous admirer."

Selby smiled. "Thank you."

"Actually, ever since I heard you were moving here, I've been thinking about our place in Uruguay—I want to redo the landscaping. I'd love to work on it with you."

Sophie noticed a glaze come over Selby's face. She sighed and said, "Hey, thank you, it sounds wonderful, but I know what the New York office is going to say—"

"Already?" replied Fernanda.

Selby shook her head apologetically. "They won't allow me to even think about taking on new clients. There's a two-year wait list, so I'm afraid it's a no."

Fernanda, unfamiliar with the word "no," stared at Selby for a few moments and then recovered herself. "Of course! *Of course* you've got a wait list. Anyways, I can't wait to see you at the Abbey tomorrow for the flamenco. Isabelli will be so excited. *Ciao.*"

With that, Fernanda turned on her heel and abruptly departed the Fairfax picnic rug, Luca trailing behind her.

Selby made a face at Sophie. "I hope you don't have a garden project too."

"I wish I had the acreage," Sophie said, giggling. "Oh, great, there's Eddie." Her son was grabbing a drink at the orange-squash station. "Eddie! I'm here, sweetie," she called out.

Her son waved back, took a swig of his drink and then sauntered over. "Hi, Mummy. Hi, Tess," he said.

Tess waved hello. "I'm scared about the match. I can't hit a ball with that rounders-bat thing. It's really hard."

"You'll be grand," said Eddie reassuringly. "And we're in the Cs. No one expects us to hit anything anyway."

Just then, a gravelly voice, which Sophie recognised as belonging to the headmaster, Mr. Pitman, came over the loudspeaker.

"C teams! Rounders matches begin in five minutes. Please assemble."

"Mummy, come and watch," said Eddie, grabbing Sophie's hand.

"Violet, Mom, let's go," said Tess and ran off ahead towards the pitch.

A few minutes later they all reached the edge of the rounders field, where the game was starting to cheers and shouts from the crowd of parents. Sophie scanned the faces for Hugh, but couldn't see him anywhere. Drat, she thought, he'll kill me if he misses Selby again, he'll kill me twice over if he misses Eddie batting, and Eddie will kill me if his dad isn't watching. She soon spotted Simon Hopeton on the far corner of the pitch, chatting with a group of parents, and sped over to him.

"Soph! Hiya!" said Simon. "Looking gorgeous, may I say."

"Thanks, Simon. You haven't seen Hugh, have you?"

"Had to go and make a call—he's over there," said Simon, pointing at a large, shady oak tree a few yards away, under which her husband was pacing back and forth, a serious expression on his face.

She walked over to him, but he simply carried on talking and waved at her to *ssshhhh*.

"... yes, I did mention it ... road tax ... but ... yes, yes ... Monday. Sounds ideal ... I'll be working from home ... I'll call the PM now, belt and braces... it'll be sorted... guaranteed. Right. Bye."

Hugh put his phone in his pocket, then realised Sophie was still standing there. "What are you doing?" he snapped.

Where had the nice, let's-get-a-swimming-pool Hugh disappeared to?

"Coming to get you," said Sophie.

"Can't you see I'm working?"

"It's Eddie's match now, Hugh. You need to come and join in," Sophie said, then added with a chuckle, "Anyway, what has road tax got to do with anything on a Saturday afternoon?"

"Who said anything about road tax?"

"You, just now."

"I did not," he said, flushing.

"You asked a question about it in Parliament as well. What's it got to do with the Health Department?"

Hugh coughed a little. Stuttered. It was very unlike him. "Er, um, yes... the vehicle tax. I see what you mean. Ambulances paying a fortune. Got to get tax down for those large vehicles in the health service, so we can have more emergency vehicles on the road."

"Oh. Right," said Sophie. "Come on, Eddie's going to be on in a minute."

Hugh looked panicked. "Sorry, Sophie. I've got to call the PM. It's urgent," he said, glancing at his watch.

Sophie didn't say a thing, just turned and walked back to the rounders pitch alone. She'd tell Eddie that Daddy had seen everything.

16

No room at Great Bottom Park was cosier or more inviting than Lady Maud's Parlour. Situated in a sheltered corner of the west front, the elegant little sitting room had last been decorated in the 1940s and had narrow French doors that opened out to a long-neglected knot garden. The walls were covered in pistachio-coloured shantung silk, sun-bleached in places, and the old sofas and armchairs were upholstered in faded floral-print slipcovers. An ornate George III gilt mirror hung above the marble fireplace, a collection of Indian miniatures decorated the walls, and the dust on the lampshades was so thick that Violet and Tess had cheekily written their initials on them.

It is here, sitting at Lady Maud's walnut writing desk, that Selby had ensconced herself on Sunday evening, sketching and writing notes for a garden design with an imminent deadline. The sunset outside had turned the sky lobster-pink and an atmosphere of peace had descended. At about eight o'clock, there was a tap on the door, and Doreen's quiff of lilac hair appeared first as she peeked around it.

"Sorry to disturb, Mrs. Fairfax," she said. "Just letting you know the girls have had tea and I'm going up to the flat."

"Doreen, thank you," replied Selby. "I couldn't have gotten any work done today without your help."

"No, love, you're welcome," she said.

"Are the girls doing their homework?"

Doreen shook her head. "Not likely! After tea Tess said she wanted to take Violet on an adventure. They ran off outside, I think."

"Really?" Selby was amazed. "They must be exhausted. They've been riding this afternoon with Josh and had a Spanish dancing lesson with the Ovington-Williams kids this morning."

"Do you want me to call them inside?"

"Don't worry," said Selby. "It's a gorgeous evening. I love it that the kids are outdoors, instead of stuck in an apartment glued to an iPad."

"If you're sure. See you tomorrow, Mrs. Fairfax."

Doreen withdrew and Selby built a small fire in the hearth and lit it. Even though it was early summer, the evenings were still chilly compared with New York. Soon the room was more cheerful than ever as flames danced in the fireplace. Selby had just sat down at her desk again to tackle a sectional drawing when she heard voices coming from outside, then footsteps dashing past.

"Oh my God, Tess. You've gone crazy. I'm freezing, quick, let's get towels," Violet cried between giggles.

"Wooooo! That was soooo fun!" Tess exclaimed. "I'm so cold, though."

Selby stepped out into the corridor to see a trail of sopping footprints on the old oak boards. At the other end, where the corridor opened into the entrance hall to the house, she spotted Tess and Violet, dressed in little more than their underwear, and soaking wet.

"Girls? What is going on?" Selby called out, walking towards them.

Tess turned to face her mother. Her lips were purple, her skin pallid, but she was grinning. "It's so exciting, Mom!" she shrieked.

"You won't believe it," added Violet.

"I'm sure I won't," said Selby, holding up both hands to calm her daughters. "But you both look as if you're on the verge of pneumonia. Grab a towel and meet me in the parlour. I've got the fire going in there. You can warm up and tell me everything."

"Ooh, that's sooo nice," said Violet, toasting her feet in front of the fire. She and Tess were wrapped in bathrobes, and the warmth of the flames was slowly transforming the girls' skin from a bluish shade back to their regular pink.

"Mom, we've had the bestest time tonight," Tess was saying. "The pool's awesome. But can we get it heated?"

"Pool—?" started Selby, frowning.

"It's hardly a pool," interrupted Violet, holding out her hands as close to the fire as she could. "More like a freezing-cold swamp."

Selby had to laugh. "What are you two talking about?"

"The pool. We just had a cold swim in it, Mom," replied Violet.

"It's just not like the pool we had in East Hampton," Tess added.

"When did you start swimming in this pool?" Selby asked.

"Today is the first day," Tess explained. "You see, it's taken us *so long* to fill it up."

Selby looked at her daughters sternly, an unpleasant thought forming in her mind. "Get some warm clothes on, then show me where this supposed pool is."

"Yay," squeaked Tess. "Are you going to swim now too, Mom?"

"No. Mom is very upset."

⁂

A few minutes later, Selby found herself following the girls, now clad in sweaters and jeans, through the old walled garden, past the semi-derelict Victorian glasshouses and along the edge of disused cutting beds that were thick with moss. The sun had virtually gone now, and the sky had faded to an other-worldly mauve, but Selby was feeling increasingly anxious.

"Where on earth is this pool?" she asked Tess.

"You'll see," her daughter replied.

Tess and Violet beckoned their mother to follow them along a tiny dirt path half-hidden in the undergrowth of an ancient apple orchard. The nettles were almost waist-height and the trees were choked with brambles. Selby ploughed her way through the prickly ground cover until the trio found themselves at the back of the old piggery, which was enclosed by stone walls thick with ivy. Tess soon located a semi-rotten door in the wall, and expertly slipped through a child-sized gap in the bottom of it.

"How am I supposed to get through that?" Selby asked.

"Fear not, Mother," Violet informed her melodramatically as she pulled back the curtain of ivy covering the top half of the door, revealing a rusty iron handle underneath.

As Selby took hold of the old handle, a loud cracking sound startled them. The door handle, along with a large plank of rotten wood, had come off in her hand.

"Ooooh! Mom!" yelled Violet.

"Drat!" exclaimed Selby.

There was now a large gap in the door, through which Selby could see Tess waving back at them. She could also see that the scene that awaited her was not particularly enticing.

"Come on, Mom, come look at the pool," cried Tess.

Selby stepped through the broken door, Violet following. Ahead of her was a large cement hole, overflowing with murky green water.

"Isn't it great, Mom?" Tess said, gesturing at the derelict yard behind her.

"Ummm . . . well," started Selby, glancing around.

It was hardly a pretty sight: a row of run-down pigsties along the back wall were now open to the elements, broken feed and water troughs had been left to rot, and the area around the "pool" consisted of cracked farmyard concrete sprouting with grass and weeds. Selby felt like she needed a tetanus shot just to look at it all.

"Girls, this is so dangerous," she scolded. "You've been swimming in a slurry pit."

"A what?" asked Tess.

"It's where they used to dump all the animal shit, literally," Selby said.

"Ugghhh, yuck!" Violet shrieked.

"Gross," Tess agreed.

"How did you fill it?" Selby asked.

Tess pointed to a bright blue hose that snaked from the pigsties across the yard and into the pit.

Selby was fuming, her worst suspicions confirmed. "Oh Christ, Tess. How long have you had the hose on for?"

"Ummm... maybe... Three days? A week?" Tess looked sheepish.

"Turn it off this minute," Selby ordered her. "You've stolen all the water from the farmer next door. His cows haven't got enough to drink, and they've got baby calves to feed. It's really serious."

Tess's face fell, and she dashed to the tap in the pigsty. The water soon stopped running and she reappeared, shamefaced.

"God, Mom, that's awful," said Violet. "I should've said something. I'm really sorry."

Selby had two words for her daughters: "You're grounded."

At this, Violet retorted, "I don't care, Mom. We're grounded here anyway. There's no one here and nothing to do. We *hate* it. I miss New York so much my heart aches."

17

When it comes to heartache, there are few in this tale who suffered it more keenly than Vere Osborne. In fact, double heartache was his deal—but we will return to that later. For now, we find him at nine o'clock on that Sunday evening in the calving barn at Great Bottom Home Farm, with his hand up the behind of a very large, very affectionate Gloucester cow named Buttercup, who had, over three years of producing calves, shown herself to be a brilliant mother but a slightly less brilliant birther.

Vere was an atypical example of that peculiarly British type, the "Gentleman Farmer." Not only was he a sensitive soul and very brainy, forty-six-year-old Vere was a Type-A dreamboat of the six-foot-two-inch, dark-haired variety. (The heartache only made him more attractive.) He'd been blessed with the good fortune to be able to divide his time between city and country, barn and boardroom, and when Vere was not farming, he was barristering in London. An expert in the complex realm of trust law, Vere hoped he was a rational being, whose judgement was based on a balanced assessment of the facts. But during calving, an invariably dramatic annual event which encompassed life, death, and sleepless nights, his coherent self would occasionally depart, to be replaced by a less prudent persona. Triggered by the life-and-death stakes of attempting to extract a distressed calf from its distressed mother, or feed an orphaned, malnourished offspring, he would, quite suddenly, find himself experiencing a violent and unjustified prejudice towards someone or something.

It's perhaps unsurprising that the object of Vere's prejudice tonight was his new neighbour. Even if that crotchety old estate manager, Mr. Ostler, had sworn to Arthur that Mrs. Fairfax was using no more water than usual, Vere was convinced that something suspicious was going on at Great Bottom Park. Perhaps the new chatelaine had commissioned a Japanese water garden? Or installed an American-style spa? Where else would the water have gone? Anyway, the infamous Mrs. Fairfax had been here for several weeks already and hadn't even bothered to come by and introduce herself. Vere had decided that she was an unfriendly, spoiled, jet-set interloper with no manners and no understanding of country ways, and now rather regretted accepting Tata Hawkins's invitation to supper tomorrow for this unpleasant woman. She was literally the last person he wanted to meet.

"Mooooooo!" groaned Buttercup, his beloved cow, shaking her head and puffing loudly, before stamping her front feet, as though in pain.

To Vere's dismay, Buttercup's calf's behind was pointing out, and it was going to be a breech birth, which could kill mother and baby. He swiftly removed his hand from her bottom, grabbed a calving rope, and then pushed both hands back inside the mother's womb along with the rope. He felt around for a leg to attach the rope to, regretting that he had decided to manage the calving alone that night. He could have used Arthur's help, but the farm lad had gone to the pub to drown his sorrows: he was as bereft as Vere about the problems they'd had with the herd this week.

"Sorry, darling," said Vere, eventually managing to loop the rope around one of the calf's legs. "But it's time to get that baby out."

∞

At that very moment, Selby was lurching up the rough, stony track that led to Great Bottom Home Farm in the old Land Rover. She felt terrible showing up so late and unannounced at Mr. Osborne's place: it was almost ten o'clock and darkness had fallen by the time she pulled up beside a dry stone wall, beyond which sat an austere stone farmhouse which looked like it had been there since medieval times. (It had.) Perched on a windswept hill, the house was dwarfed by the farmyard, which was covered in modern agricultural buildings.

As she alighted from the car, she noticed that the windows were dark, with only a solitary lamp above the front porch casting a weak glare. Although the place looked deserted, Selby felt obliged to check if anyone was home and she pushed a rusty gate in the wall which creaked open onto a path that led to the house. Even in the gloom, she could see that the building was, to all intents and purposes, situated in the middle of knee-deep grass. Walking towards the front door, Selby couldn't decide whether it was terrifically romantic or a bit too *Cold Comfort Farm* for her liking.

She reached the porch feeling nervous. She was angry with herself, upset with her children and anxious about admitting their crime to Mr. Osborne. If he was as high-powered a lawyer as she'd heard he was, that could make things even trickier. Regardless, she knocked. Nothing. Hopefully Mr. Osborne was in London for work. She felt herself relax a little. After a minute she knocked again, just to be on the safe side, and a cacophony of barks echoed around her and two enormous greyhound-like dogs bounded up, almost colliding with her in their enthusiasm. For a few seconds they were all affection, and then just as suddenly they disappeared, dashing off in the direction of the barns. There must be *someone* here, thought Selby, if dogs were around. Maybe Angry Arthur was in one of the sheds.

She picked her way from the house towards the farm buildings and soon found herself in a large concrete yard with a giant steaming muck pile, scruffy stable block, and rambling cattle byres. At the far end, she could see light glimmering from inside the largest barn, from which emanated a chorus of mooing. She walked towards it as a lone chicken scrambled across the yard. If Arthur was in the barn, at least she could apologise to him and leave a message for Mr. Osborne. She steeled herself for the (completely warranted) wrath of the farm lad.

Peering into the entrance to the largest cowshed, Selby came upon the sweet faces of about fifty cows, several with adorable calves. They were rustling among the straw in individual stalls which ran along each side of the barn. A few feet away, she spotted a man in a flat tweed cap and grubby blue farm overalls crouched behind a heaving, puffing cow so large that it looked as though it was about to burst. "Right . . . here we go . . . easy, girl," he was saying in a low voice.

Selby cleared her throat to try and attract the man's attention. He didn't notice, so she came a little closer and then said, "Erm . . . Excuse me?"

The man lifted his head and glanced at Selby. It wasn't Arthur, who she'd seen coming out of the estate office, but another farm-hand. Selby could barely see his face, camouflaged as it was in a mixture of grimy muck and flecks of blood, but his expression didn't indicate he was pleased to see her. He gazed at Selby for a few seconds, then frowned and quickly returned his attention to the cow without saying a word.

"I'm so sorry to bother you—" she began.

Before she could continue, the man shot her an irritated look and put his forefinger to his lips, miming, "Sssh-hhhh."

"Sorry," she whispered. "But I urgently need to leave a message for Mr. Osborne? The owner? I'm Mrs. Fairfax, his new neighbour."

"I see," replied the man curtly, just as she realised that he had both arms inside the cow.

"Is there any chance you're going to see him? That you could give him a message?"

The man didn't answer, just suddenly started pulling at something inside the cow, and eventually a rope appeared. He chucked the end of it at her, saying, "Grab this, please."

"Er . . . okay," said Selby, as she caught the rope. It was covered in blood, which was soon all over her hands and shirt.

"Right, when I say 'pull,' pull!"

"If you say so," Selby replied. She wasn't sure whether she felt terror, excitement, or a mixture of both—but regardless, she was about to see a calf being born.

"Easy, girl, easy," said the man as he started to inch the calf's head and two front feet, which had the rope looped around them, from inside the cow. "Right, a gentle tug, please," he directed her.

Selby gingerly gave the rope a soft pull, and slowly, slowly, out came the calf's forelegs and head. With much mooing and pushing, the cow eventually squeezed out the rest of her offspring's body, which landed with a soft plop on the straw beneath her. As soon as the calf was on the ground, the mother gently padded round and started licking off the sac. The little calf lifted its head for a few seconds, and then flopped it back down again, exhausted.

The man knelt down next to the newborn in the straw, took a handful of hay and started drying the calf off. "Well done, Buttercup. You have a beautiful little girl," he said, gazing at the cow while a blissful expression spread across his face.

"That was awesome," said Selby, quite overcome. She handed the rope back to the farmhand.

"Thanks," he said, starting to coil it up.

"So . . . um . . . I can tell you're really busy, but if there's any way you could give a message to the boss, that would be very kind."

"I can take care of that," he said, reverting to his brisk tone of earlier.

"If you could tell Mr. Osborne that Mrs. Fairfax owes him a huge apology," Selby said with a sigh, "about the water supply—"

At this, the man paused what he was doing and looked sternly at her, saying, "We need an explanation. It's been a terrible few days. Lost our best cow."

"Oh God," said Selby. "I didn't know."

"Bluebell. Wonderful girl. Loved her like . . . well . . . you should have tasted the double cream we got from her milk. Couldn't beat it."

"I am so, so sorry."

"Now her calf's an orphan. Right, I better get on," the man said, as he started to head out of the stall.

"I mustn't keep you. But, look, could you get this message to Mr. Osborne? I feel terrible, but, you see, it turns out that my eight-year-old daughter stole the water."

"What's she done with it? Made a lake for her teddy bears to paddle in?" The man looked unamused.

"I honestly don't know what possessed her," Selby replied. "But she filled up the pigs' old slurry pit—actually she's been filling it for days, it turns out—and went swimming in it. If you could pass on my sincerest apologies and do please tell Mr. Osborne I insist on paying him back for any losses incurred—"

The man shook his head. "Money won't bring Bluebell back." To Selby's astonishment, she saw the man's eyes well up. "But I'll pass the message on," he said quietly.

With that, he locked the gate to Buttercup's stall and started cutting open a bale of hay, his eyes averted from Selby's. She wished there was something she could do, but it didn't seem like the right moment to offer sympathy. Sensing the uncomfortable audience was over, she muttered an awkward "goodnight" and left the barn.

18

"Charlene? Whither art thou, *mon petit chou-fleur?*" Ian was fretting: it was already Monday morning—the day of the much-anticipated Kitchen Supper—and Charlene had not stepped up to the plate in terms of her mole role. He hadn't had any intel from her whatsoever since Friday, and except for the reels of Tallulah de Sanchez's dog roaming the rose gardens, the goings-on at the Manor were veiled in mystery. Now he'd finally managed to get her on the phone.

"I'm looking for Tallulah's Dior kimono," Charlene whispered back down the line. "She's taken over the guest suite in the west wing. The dressing room and landing are filled with racks of all her clothes. It's impossible to find anything."

"Alas!" Ian gasped. When a bikini influencer moves her entire wardrobe into a married man's house, things are grave. "What happened?"

"What happened when?" Charlene replied.

"When you mentioned very loudly, so that Bryan could hear, that Tata is having a dinner for Selby Fairfax tonight and he's not invited."

"Nothing."

"Nothing?" Ian was taken aback.

"That's what I said."

"Exactly what kind of nothing?"

"He told me to take Tallulah to the station—"

"Was he trying to get rid of her?"

"No, I took her to the station, and we picked up these two people she calls her Glam Squad, and brought them back here."

Ian was ever more confused. "What does she need a Glam Squad for when she's not invited to the dinner?"

"She doesn't know she's not invited."

"What? I told you specifically to make sure she knew she wasn't invited."

"Ian, I'm sorry." Charlene was starting to sound anxious. "But Mr. Hawkins said on no account was Tallulah to know anything about Tata's dinner because she'd be so furious she'd make him go out."

"I see," Ian said, well aware that Bryan would rather be dunked in a vat of boiling oil than made to leave the house on a Monday night. "So what is the Glam Squad there for?"

"The woman does her hair and make-up and the bloke takes pictures of her all day, then she posts them on social media—Ian, I've got to go," Charlene said. "She's calling me."

"Please report back."

"Copy that."

∽

Moments later, kimono in hand, Charlene trotted into the guest bedroom which Tallulah (twenty-six, looked thirty-six due to addiction to eyelash extensions and lip fillers) had annexed a fortnight ago and where she was luxuriously installed in a four-poster. Like the rest of the room, the bed was upholstered in pale blue silk embroidered with gold butterflies. On the pillow next to her, Pikachu was curled up in a little ball, sleeping soundly.

"Miss de Sanchez," said Charlene. "I found this."

"That's the one," said Tallulah, taking the scarlet kimono and draping it around her shoulders. "Thank you, Charlene. Now, the Glam Squad will be in shortly for a strategy meeting about the shoot tomorrow, and they'll need teas and coffees."

"No problem, Miss," replied Charlene.

Tallulah sighed and started scrolling through her phone. "It's non-stop, Charlene," she said. "Non-stop! Being a successful entrepreneur—I mean, honestly, you never stop working."

"I can tell." Charlene wondered how on earth lounging in a four-poster looking at TikTok counted as work. The more Charlene had seen of Miss de Sanchez, though, the more peculiar she found her. The bikini entrepreneur was so Other, so alien, in her skintight clothes, and with her solid-gold vape pens, and her high heels on the grass, that Charlene simply couldn't understand her.

"I get all my key business news this way," said Tallulah, tapping at her phone. "I can see how many new followers TallulahSwim has picked up overnight, how many profile visits I've had, how many clicks there's been on the website, and how many bikinis have been ordered while I was asleep. At least I get to do it all while I'm cuddling Pikachu." She stroked the little dog as he stretched his legs and slowly woke up. "*Ooh*, you adorable little thing, *oh yes*, you are," Tallulah cooed in a baby voice to the ball of fluff who was now scampering around the bed. "Who's starring in a photoshoot tomorrow? Yes, Peeks, *you are*. Such a clever little doggie-woggie, aren't we?"

"Your breakfast will be up in a moment," said Charlene, hoping she'd be dismissed.

"Yummy," Tallulah said. "You know, Charlene, that's the wonderful thing about Bryan. Doesn't skimp on household help. From the minute I arrived here, I haven't had to lift a finger."

Charlene smiled as benignly as she could. Indeed, this woman literally *never* lifted a finger, to the horror of the other staff at Monkton Bottom Manor. She began, "I should be going downstairs—"

But Tallulah was on a roll. "Honestly, Charlene, before I came here I thought living in the countryside would be dire, after being in my flat in Dawson Place. But I've just realised Soho Farmhouse is only down the road and if I'm missing London, I'll just go there and do barre and have a flat white. So," she went on, "being stuck out here in lonely old Oxfordshire is worth the sacrifices. I mean, Bryan's a brilliant man. He's already invested in my business, in *me*, you see."

At this point, Charlene realised that she'd have to put up with this egomaniac as long as she was spilling the beans. Ian would want to know all of it.

"So, how does that work, then?" she asked, trying to sound clueless.

Tallulah's eyes widened, and she put down her phone for a moment. "Bryan has injected a large chunk of cash into TallulahSwim.com. But there's far more to it than that. He'll probably introduce me to Jeff Bezos, fix me up with a TED talk, and . . ." She paused, then said, in a conspiratorial whisper, "And who knows what might happen next?"

"Sounds like you've got it all worked out, Miss de Sanchez," Charlene remarked.

Tallulah smiled confidently. "Bryan hasn't even tried to kiss me yet, which shows he's serious." She winked, batting her long eyelashes almost flirtatiously at Charlene. "You can go now. Thank you for listening."

"Very good, Miss de Sanchez."

With that, Tallulah picked up her phone again and started tapping on it. Just as Charlene reached the door, Tallulah let out a piercing screech.

"Fuck!" Tallulah shrieked, causing Pikachu to launch himself off the bed in fright. "*Selby Fairfax! She's* having a dinner for Selby Fairfax?! Charlene! You've got to look at this!"

Tallulah handed Charlene her phone, on whose screen an Instagram reel from @Tatahappycotswolds was playing. In it, a long table was being decorated with white linens and flowers by a uniformed team. Charlene glanced at the list of hashtags: #KitchenSups #joy #SelbyFairfaxwelcomedinner.

"Fancy that," said Charlene, playing dumb.

"Ugh." Tallulah shuddered. "Bloody Tata with her fake happy social media profile. Everyone knows she's miserable because her husband's crazy about me. It's completely obvious: she's excluded Bryan from a dinner party on his own estate to make him jealous."

"Would you like me to speak to Mr. Hawkins?" asked Charlene, her expression all innocence. "He's on his way to London in the car—why don't I call him?"

"No. Bryan must not know anything about this, Charlene. Not a word."

"Of course," Charlene said.

"As it happens, I don't want to meet all the ageing mommies round here anyway. All they talk about are disgusting things like the menopause and prolapsed vaginas. They're not exactly the target audience for my bikinis. And Selby Fairfax—I'll meet her soon enough and reel her in as a brand ambassador for TallulahSwim in no time. She's a little past it for the thongs, but she'll be great for the beach kaftans."

"Brilliant plan," said Charlene, warming to her role. If she was going to be a mole, she might as well really go for it.

"I've got a genius idea," Tallulah went on, getting out of bed and padding over to the dressing table. "I'll tell Bryan to get tickets to *La Traviata* tonight in London. Then he'll never know a thing about Tata's supper."

Charlene tried to be cunning: what would Ian do? she wondered.

"Mr. Hawkins loves that sort of thing," she said, thinking on her feet: Ian had briefed her when she started the job about Bryan's allergy to culture, but she sensed an opportunity here. "Why don't I book it for you?" she went on. "You can surprise him."

"That would be lovely, Charlene, thank you." Tallulah sat down on the upholstered stool in front of the dressing table, put her phone on it, and started pouting in the mirror and adjusting her mane of dark hair (and hair extensions) around her face. Just then, the iPhone rang. "Ooh, it's Bryan," she told Charlene. She pressed the loudspeaker button. "Good morning," she said brightly. "How's the Plugs'n'Stuff share price this morning?"

"Haven't checked yet, actually," he said. "I've got some bad news. My wife's having a dinner tonight at the Old Coach House and she hasn't included me."

"Really?" said Tallulah, plausibly feigning surprise.

"I didn't mention it because I've been trying to ignore it and pretend I don't care, but I do. It's for Selby Fairfax, of all people. Typical Tata. Always gets in everywhere, with everyone. People just . . . well, for all her quirks, they fall for her. You see, she's a fun person."

Tallulah stabbed at the powder puff on her dressing table with the end of an eyeshadow brush. "Why not invite Selby Fairfax here?"

"Women are just better at these things." Bryan sounded dejected. "I don't know, maybe I should speak to our butler, but he's with Tata now at the Old Coach House. He'd know what to do about this mess. Christ, I miss Ian. I think I miss him as much as I miss Minty and Ta—"

"Bryan," Tallulah interrupted. "You need to focus. You've got a huge board meeting today. And anyway, I've got a treat planned for you for tonight, to take your mind off it all."

"Ah, that's nice of you. Not necessary, though—"

"I insist. We're going to the opera."

"The opera." Bryan sounded underwhelmed.

"*La Traviata.*"

"Tallulah. It's a lovely thought but . . . I don't have time to go to the opera."

Tallulah looked quizzically at Charlene, who shrugged and tried to seem terribly surprised.

"*Of course* you don't," Tallulah said. "See you later." She hung up, turned round from her dressing table, and frowned at Charlene.

"He always *loved* the opera with Mrs. Hawkins," said Charlene, who was rather enjoying herself now. She shook her head sadly. "Don't know what's come over him."

Just then there was a knock, and one of the maids popped her head round the door.

"Miss de Sanchez, I've got your breakfast and Raymond the dog groomer's here," she said as she entered the room with a tray. "He wants to trim Pikachu's coat ready for the photoshoot tomorrow."

The entrepreneur smiled. "Great. Charlene, could you take Pikachu down to the mud room, please? Raymond can groom him in there."

Charlene nodded and scooped up the little dog. As she made her way down the back stairs, she dialled Ian. He needed to know absolutely everything that had just transpired.

19

With its gracious sash windows and exquisite view over the soft crowns of beech trees beyond the front of the house, Sophie and Hugh's bedroom at the Rectory was like something from a Jane Austen novel. Although it was years ago now, Sophie had wallpapered the room in a pale red *toile* of roses and ribbons from Nicholas Herbert, had oyster-pink striped chintz curtains made, and upholstered the antique French bed to match.

By late afternoon on the Monday of Tata's Kitchen Supper, she was happily ensconced in a terry robe at her make-up table, a cup of tea perched among the hairbrushes, scent bottles, cosmetics, and trinkets. She examined her eyebrows in the magnifying mirror. How she wished she'd had time to get them threaded. Oh well. She'd just flicked on her curling irons when she heard wheels crunching on the gravel outside. She stood up and peered out of the window. To her surprise, one of those flashy black Porsche 4x4s was entering the drive, tailed by a regular Porsche.

Must be something to do with Hugh, thought Sophie. After all the PM's office was always sending urgent papers whizzing down the M40 for Hugh to read at unexpected moments. They didn't usually do it in two Porsches—maybe a rich donor was swinging by.

Hugh was at the back of the house in his office working, and never heard the door, so Sophie padded down the staircase and along the front hall to open it. As soon as she did, she found herself confronted by two professional-looking men in their early thirties, both dressed in a uniform of dark trousers, white shirts, and navy quilted gilets with the Porsche shield and logo stitched on the top of their breast pockets.

"Can I help you?" said Sophie, rather confused.

"Hello, I'm Adrian, from Porsche," said the man on the left, who had a clipboard with him, "and this is my colleague Stuart. Just dropping off your brand-new, top-of-the-range, Porsche Taycan Turbo S Sport Turismo." He grinned at Sophie as if she'd won the lottery.

"The only fully electric high-performance sports car in the world," added Stuart proudly. "And it's four-wheel drive."

"Erm, but . . . we haven't bought an electric Porsche," Sophie insisted. "You must have the wrong house."

With a puzzled expression, Adrian looked at the clipboard and asked, "Is this the Rectory? Name of Mrs. Thompson?"

"Yes," said Sophie. "But really, I don't know anything about this. We could never afford this kind of car."

Adrian flicked through the paperwork. "It's all paid off," he said.

"What?" Sophie was flabbergasted. Hugh had just committed to a swimming pool. How could he afford a Porsche as well?

"Ooops! Naughty hubby's been car-shopping on his own! Oh dearie me!" Stuart chuckled. "Hope we haven't ruined a surprise birthday pressie."

She shook her head. "It's not my birthday."

"Maybe it doesn't need to be your birthday, Mrs. Thompson," said Adrian.

"Oh," Sophie said, and laughed. "You're so sweet."

She allowed herself to eye the car from the porch. It was stunning, a power car in every sense. Maybe, thought Sophie, trying to convince herself that she wasn't dreaming, *maybe* Hugh had realised about the Hyundai being so embarrassing. Maybe he'd realised he needed to get her something more ritzy. Maybe they had far more money than Hugh had let on?

"Okay, well . . . I guess it's mine." Sophie told the men. "I can't believe it. I'm so excited."

"You should be. You deserve it. Sign here and we'll leave you in peace."

Adrian offered her a pen and she signed the delivery note and took the key fob. He and Stuart then hopped into the other Porsche and had soon disappeared down the lane.

Sophie couldn't resist getting in the car before going to find Hugh. Giddy with anticipation, she unlocked the Porsche with the fob and slid into the front seat. A thrill coursed through her. She had never experienced such a luxurious vehicle. The front seats had thick sheepskins covering them—delicious. The steering wheel was padded and quilted with soft leather the colour of double cream. The dashboards were walnut, and a magnum of Bollinger was perched on the passenger seat, tied with a huge cream bow.

"Hugh? Darling!" she called a few moments later as she walked through the house to his office, a panelled room lined with books and hunting prints. Sophie tapped on the door and entered, dangling the key fob. "Sweetie. I love it! Thank you!"

Hugh looked startled. "What?" he said, swivelling round from his desk.

"The car. It's *stunning*. I'm so happy, sweetheart, thank you."

To Sophie's amazement, Hugh did not smile back, and instead got up and snatched the fob from her. "The car isn't for you, Sophie. It's for me. I'm the one who has to drive miles and miles back and forth to London and God knows where every week."

"But—I do all those school runs. It's hours of driving. The ministerial car takes you everywhere."

"I just got you a new car. The Hyundai."

"I know, but—"

"Sophie, please. You're being terribly spoiled."

She baulked. "But the delivery note. It said 'Mrs. Thompson.' The car's in my name."

Hugh shook his head. "Everything that gets delivered here for me is always in your name. I'm usually working or away. You're *always* here."

At times, including now, Sophie felt as though Hugh saw her as little more than a receptionist, but she wasn't going to have a row with him right before Tata's supper party. Instead she said, "But how can we afford it? Those cars cost a fortune."

At this, Hugh smiled reassuringly and said, "Great-Aunt Edith. The one in Aberdeenshire."

Sophie was disbelieving. "Great-Aunt Edith bought you a Porsche?"

"Not exactly. She died. Left me some money."

"What? When did she die? Why didn't you say anything before?"

"It was during the Covid lockdown. The family couldn't have a funeral, and didn't want anyone to know. You know how religious they all are up in that part of Scotland. It was all very sad, very hush-hush."

"But that was years ago now, Hugh. I'm your wife. You could have told me."

I wanted to," he said sorrowfully. "But I had to respect her children's wishes. Edith's will has taken forever to sort out."

"I suppose. But how sad for Great-Aunt Edith. Dying alone and then not even being buried."

Hugh looked gloomy. "Grisly end."

"Well, there's always a silver lining," Sophie said. "I'm looking forward to my trip in that car to Tata's party."

"No can do, darling," Hugh said. "I want to have a drink or two tonight. You'll have to drive me in your car."

"But—"

"Thanks, Soph," he said, checking his watch. "Right. I've got an interview now on Radio 4. I'll be ready by seven."

20

"Golly! Valet parking! How luxurious," Sir Reggie Backhouse roared enthusiastically as he pulled up the family's old Volvo estate car beside a team of young men in white dinner jackets, cream bow ties, and jeans, who were standing to attention in front of the Old Coach House.

"I think it's *frightfully common*," grumbled Lady Caroline from the passenger seat, taking in the tableau before her. "Staff in white tie! Good heavens. What is this? The Prince of Wales's Investiture? Oh well, I'm not surprised." She sniffed. "You know Mrs. Hawkins is from Sidcup originally?"

"Mummy, there are very decent people in the suburbs," came a determined voice from the back seat of the car. The Honourable Arabella Backhouse (forty, looked fifty due to numerous responsibilities as headmistress of grand London prep school) found her mother's snobbery almost as annoying as the way her poor daddy put up with it. "People are going to think you're going senile if you keep talking like that."

"Stop being so ageist, dear," retorted Lady Caroline, hauling herself from the car, while smiling graciously at the valet who opened the door for her. Tonight she was channelling "the Late Queen Dining Informally at Windsor" in an A-line navy frock to the knee, diamond brooch, tan stockings, and black pumps. She had set her hair the night before, and was carrying a red crocodile box bag that her mother had bought at Cartier in 1955.

Sir Reggie edged himself from the driver's seat and straightened out his moth-eaten Prince of Wales checked suit. (His Sunday best, inherited from his grandfather.) He handed the car keys to the valet, and offered Arabella his hand as she emerged from the back seat of the Volvo.

"Thanks, Dad," she said fondly, linking arms with him.

"Jolly sweet of you to come all the way down here on the train from London, Bels," said Reggie as the trio made their way towards the door across the freshly raked gravel. It was a clear night and the air was lightly scented with the perfume of the jasmine that climbed across the front of the house.

"Just wish I'd had a moment to change." Arabella, who was tall, with a powerful air about her, was in her usual headmistress garb of navy skirt suit, cream blouse with the collar turned up, and loafers. She had pearls at her neck and her greying hair was kept back by tortoiseshell combs on each side of her head.

"You look lovely," her mother said. "Anyway, Reggie, I said Bels *must* meet Mrs. Fairfax with us. For the good of the terrier breeds, mustn't she?" She winked surreptitiously at Reggie and then looked up at the facade of the Old Coach House in front of them, adding under her breath, "*Frightfully common* house."

"I think it's stonkingly nice," Arabella said.

"I'm rather confused," Sir Reggie said. "Why isn't Mrs. Hawkins at the Manor?"

"Family row," his wife told him. "Apparently a young woman who only wears bikinis has moved in there with Bryan. Terribly common."

"Ghastly," Reggie agreed.

"Parents, do stop judging." Arabella ordered. "Let's get inside. I need a glass of champagne."

∞

"What a *hideous* room," Lady Caroline hissed as she took a glass of Ruinart from a silver tray.

"Oh, Mummy," Arabella admonished her before taking a sip of her own drink. "This is what people want now. It's not 1925 any more."

Arabella looked around the whopping great foyer, which was already buzzing with the chatter of guests. The original Georgian entrance remained, with its broad double doorway and arched fanlight above, where carriages had once come in and out. But the space inside had been ruthlessly gutted and turned into a cavernous, double-height entrance hall that could easily hold thirty for drinks. It was decorated rather like a fashionable art gallery: one entire wall had been graffitied with a monochrome spray painting of an enormous bunny rabbit holding a pistol; life-sized plaster-of-Paris busts of Tata and Minty were perched facing each other on marble consoles, and a large oil painting of Bryan swinging a golf club hung above a reclaimed Provençal fireplace. At the far end, a cantilevered stone staircase floated up to a first-floor balcony and wide landing.

"Lovely flowers," said Arabella, taking in the sight of the mountains of white flora Veronika's team had installed. Creamy-flowered magnolia trees in oversized terracotta planters were stationed in each corner of the other room; groups of vases, cascading with white roses and peonies, were artfully arranged on side tables; the top of the white grand piano was crowded with tulips, and even the void beneath the instrument was thick with the fluffy camellias Veronika had used at the recent Chanel event.

Lady Caroline was less impressed. "In our day one just had a little posy on the hall table and that was it. Seems rather wasteful to put flowers on the floor," she said, peering disapprovingly at the camellias beneath the piano.

"I think it's a marvellous way to do a Kitchen Supper," guffawed Sir Reggie, glancing around him in amazement at the young, buff waiters stationed round the room with trays of cocktails and champagne. "Jolly good drinks," he added, draining his glass and reaching for a margarita.

Just then, Ian sailed in looking particularly elegant in a slim-cut dark suit, pink shirt, and black-and-white polka-dot tie, and bearing a silver tray laden with blinis and caviar. A plastic earpiece in his left ear, almost invisible, kept him in touch with Veronika and her team. Spotting the Backhouses, he went straight up to them.

"Good evening, Lady Caroline, Sir Reggie, Arabella," he said politely.

Everyone greeted him enthusiastically and then Caroline said, "Excellent turnout."

"Isn't it," Ian agreed. Then he added, "May I say you are looking as regal as ever, Lady Caroline."

"You *are* kind." She looked as tickled as a schoolgirl at the compliment, and then went on, with a hint of impatience in her voice, "But where is our wonderful hostess?"

Ian scanned the room. Almost everyone was here now and the party was already bubbling with atmosphere, but there was no sign of Tata. Despite his dismay at the aristocratic Backhouse family, and everyone else, not being greeted by their hostess upon their arrival, he did not, for a moment, betray his concern. After all, parties were the place where, professionally speaking, he was at the top of his (cashmere) socks.

"Mrs. Hawkins is just reading Minty a story before bed," Ian lied, offering Lady Caroline and her family the beluga. Good caviar could distract guests from most things, he'd found.

"Mmmm!" moaned Sir Reggie, gulping down the first of many blinis that night.

"How lovely that Tata is so committed to literacy," Arabella said.

"Indeed. She'll be down as soon as she can. Now, Miss Backhouse," Ian went on, "congratulations on your Independent Schools Headmistress of the Year Award."

Arabella blushed. "Crumbs. Didn't realise anyone kept track of those things. Thank you."

"It's hard not to, Miss Backhouse. Look, if you're all okay here, I've a few things to attend to," said Ian. At the very least he needed to get Tata downstairs before Selby Fairfax made her entrance.

Sir Reggie loaded another blini and popped it in his mouth. "As long as you come back with more of this," he said, as some caviar fell onto his tie.

"Course," said Ian, disappearing towards the back kitchen.

As soon as he'd gone, Lady Caroline glanced at her husband. "Reggie, dear, do eat with your mouth closed," she ordered him. "You're embarrassing Bels. Right, I'm going to talk to that *ghastly* Thompson man about the hospital crisis. Wish him luck."

As her mother made a beeline for Hugh, Arabella chuckled. "Rather him than me. And, Dad, I'm not embarrassed. I'm used to you spilling your food everywhere."

"Thank you, pet," Reggie said. "If only your mother was so forgiving."

―

Upstairs, Tata was eyeing a packet of Valium tablets in her bathroom cabinet. Our hostess adored throwing parties, but they tended to send her into a spiral of anxiety. The hours spent with Veronika and Lexi since Saturday had triggered a state of nervous exhaustion, in part because the planning of the event was as intense as the pressure to pretend there hadn't been any planning. Country Princesses were required to present as celestial beings who pulled off fabulous parties with no effort at all. (Their icon on this front was Jemima Khan, who would host gatherings for two hundred, including everyone from Mick Jagger to Lily James, with the insouciant air of a child hosting a teddy bears' picnic.)

There was no way that she could be the laid-back version of herself tonight without chemical help, Tata told herself as she popped half the blue diazepam tablet in her mouth and swallowed it, and that wouldn't be fun for anyone. She absolutely deserved to chill a bit after all the organising, she reasoned, as it began to take effect. Mmmm. It was nice to feel so . . . *woooshy* . . . suddenly. Carefree! Deliciously happy! Tata padded from her bathroom into the dressing room and changed into the outfit Lexi had (very reluctantly) approved for her: a cream, silk-linen Louis Vuitton shorts-onesie, with a wide belt of golden chain mail that cinched her waist.

She slid on the flat gold Aquazzura ballet pumps that Lexi had chosen, then regarded herself from every possible angle in the floor-to-ceiling bank of mirrors at the far end of her dressing room. Marnie had popped over from Soho Farmhouse that afternoon, and as a result Tata's skin glowed, her eyelash extensions were enough but not too much, and her Barbie-style caramel-hued ponytail hairpiece made her look at least ten years younger.

God, she had great legs, thought Tata, admiring her toned, tanned pins, but alas, those ballet flats Lexi liked so much didn't make the most of them. Feeling slightly reckless, she kicked them off and opened the door to her evening-shoe closet, which gleamed with row after row of footwear festooned with beads, feathers, and crystals. Tata grabbed a pair of Sophia Webster orange satin stilettos, which were studded with tiny gold rivets and had a glittering gold chain that fastened around the ankle. If Lexi was furious when she spotted them on Instagram, so be it, she mused, as she perched on a red velvet pouffe to put them on. After all, if her friends saw her wearing flats tonight it would seem so out of character for her that they would know she'd been professionally styled, which would have defeated the object of being professionally styled in the first place.

Tata pouted at herself in the mirror, satisfied that she looked sexy enough to annoy Bryan on Instagram but not so sexy that she'd scare off a new friend like Selby Fairfax. She tiptoed over to the chaise longue where she reclined lightly, so as not to crease the onesie. Lying down was nice. Maybe she could sneak in a disco nap before the evening's proceedings began, she thought . . . but just as she was about to drift off, there was a tap on the door.

"Mrs. Hawkins," came Ian's voice from outside, "everyone's arriving."

"What?" exclaimed Tata, sitting up and checking the time on her phone. "It's only seven-forty-five."

"You asked everyone for seven-thirty."

"That means show up at eight. Crumbs! Give me five?" Then she called out, "Is Selby here yet?"

"Not so far."

"Phew," said Tata.

"I'll hold the fort."

"I owe you one, Ian."

As Ian's footsteps receded, Tata wondered how she'd ever get up. She'd thought she'd have time for the Valium to wear off a bit before any guests arrived. Oh well, she reasoned, finally hauling herself off the chaise longue and making her way back into the bathroom, nothing like a good excuse for a line of coke for a quick pick-me-up.

21

While Tata dilly-dallied in her bedroom, Ian was deluged (as ever) by a tsunami of air kisses from the various glamorous couples downstairs. As he bustled among the throng, his primary concern was that the plague of ex-husbands he had hoped for tonight had not quite materialised. In fact, as several unattached men had declined Tata's invitation, Ian had started to feel that the plague of ex-husbands had metamorphosed into something of a famine. Charlie Holmes had got engaged; Wills Corrick had begun a scandalous relationship with his soon-to-be ex-wife's sister; Tom Meade-Featherstonehaugh had gone to work in France; and Wing Commander Freddie Naylor-Pitt had been sent to Afghanistan to rescue an American aid worker who'd been kidnapped by the Taliban.

But Ian had remained undaunted. With just a week's notice, a supply of "prestige" guests had been hard to come by and he had sensibly lowered his expectations: as long as Selby had a fascinating man on each side of her at dinner, the rest of the guest list was less of an issue. The only man attending tonight who was a serious candidate, Ian felt, for Selby Fairfax's fairy-tale ending was Antoni Grigorivich. Thankfully, a couple of other single men had accepted Tata's invitation—which was good for the mix—but none had the advantages of the dashing Polish billionaire.

Ian was relieved when, at about eight o'clock, the party guests heard an excited voice coming from the balcony above them.

"Hey! Hi-i-i-i!!! So happy to see you all!"

Heads swivelled upwards as one to see that Tata had appeared on the landing, waving at everyone. Hugh Thompson, desperate to escape Caroline Backhouse's bollocking about hospital closures, told her he'd absolutely ask the Prime Minister about reopening the minor injuries unit in Chipping Norton, and then, spotting an open-mouthed Sir Reggie gawping at Tata, said to her, "Looks like hubby's in need of some supervision."

"Honestly," grumbled Lady Caroline. "You'd think he'd never seen a beautiful woman in his life. Please excuse me, Hugh."

With that, she bulldozed her way back through the guests to her husband and daughter who were hovering with Ian near the bottom of the staircase. Sir Reggie, still taking in the delectable sight of Tata's teensy-weensy onesie as she tripped lightly down the staircase, remarked loudly, "Splendid the way the wives of Chipping Norton dress for parties as if they're at the *Playboy* mansion, isn't it?"

"Dad." Arabella looked mortified. "Are you trying to get yourself cancelled?"

"Do pull yourself together," Lady Caroline barked at him.

Before Reggie could respond, Tata had launched herself upon the man, hugging him excitedly. "Sir Reggie," she squeaked, enveloping him in a suffocating cloud of her Jo Loves White Rose & Lemon Leaves perfume. "So good to see you. Lady Caroline, Arabella—wow! You all look amazing." She glanced around the room at the crowd. "Oh, yay, there's Virgil Pitman."

"Here's your *piscine*," said Ian, handing Tata a glass of champagne packed with ice. "Yummy. *Merci*," said Tata, taking the drink.

She hadn't even taken a sip when Veronika Ward, clad in an upcycled 1993 silver lamé Versace cocktail dress and platform sneakers, sidled up to her.

"Mrs. Hawkins," she said. "I don't mean to interrupt, but I've just had word that Antoni Grigorivich's car has arrived. Would you like to greet him personally?"

Ian was on tenterhooks, praying that Antoni would live up to his expectations.

Tata nodded. "Yes, absolutely. Do excuse me, Sir Reg and Lady Caroline, but this is the first time I've met him face to face and he doesn't know a soul here. I'll be back in a moment."

She and Veronika headed away towards the door, hurriedly greeting guests on the way. As soon as Tata was out of sight, Lady Caroline turned to Arabella and said, "Well, that's marvellous news, dear."

"What is, Mummy?"

"Mr. Grigorivich is here. The tycoon who bought the Priory off Daddy and me. You can start to get to know him tonight."

Oh dear, thought Ian, an ear on the conversation, competition already. But Arabella simply looked bemused. "Why?" she asked her mother.

Lady Caroline cocked her head to one side and regarded her daughter fondly. "Darling. Don't be so obtuse. I mean, a flat in Fulham and a job as a headmistress at the age of forty can only lead to one thing."

"To what, Mummy?"

"A tragic, impoverished spinsterhood."

Arabella made a face. "Really. Mama. Have you not yet come across the phrase 'internalised misogyny?' "

Her mother ignored this. "Surely you want to settle down in the country and have children?"

"I've already got four hundred and fifty children at school."

Detecting a familial frisson brewing, Ian gestured at a waiter to top up the Backhouses' glasses.

"Bels. Mr. Grigorivich is a very eligible man, and he's on the prowl for a chatelaine," Lady Caroline intoned. "I've seen photographs of him in *Tatler* recently with entirely unsuitable girls on his arm."

"Caro," began Sir Reggie. "I'm not sure he's Arabella's sort. I can see you with an intellectual—an Oxford don, maybe."

"Dad, *shush*, I'm not sixteen," Arabella admonished him, reddening.

Moments later Tata reappeared with a distinguished-looking gentleman at her side. Ian was familiar with the billionaire type, and Antoni Grigorivich (sixty-six, looked fifty-six due to long stays at

La Prairie's dermatological centre in Switzerland) did not disappoint. Although he was not classically handsome, and his rather squat silhouette barely cleared five foot six inches, Antoni exuded the confidence and style of a highly successful man. His skin was burnished with the deep tan of a man in possession of his own megayacht; he still had a healthy head of slightly wavy salt-and-pepper hair; and tonight he was beautifully dressed, Gianni Agnelli-style, in eggshell-blue cotton trousers, a handmade shirt, and a butter-coloured cashmere sweater that was tied loosely around his neck. Ian approved.

"Good evening, Mr. Grigorivich," said Ian smoothly, darting forward and proffering a tray. "Caviar?"

"Thank you," said Antoni, helping himself and then taking a glass of champagne offered by a waiter.

"Lady Caroline, Sir Reg, I wanted to make sure Antoni gets to see you guys before anyone else," said Tata to the Backhouses.

"Mr. Grigorivich, good evening," Lady Caroline said as she shook his hand enthusiastically.

While Caroline and Antoni chatted, Tata, as though she were perhaps about to communicate a minor direction about a guest or a drink to her butler, tapped Ian's shoulder and drew him a few feet away from the group.

"I just had a lightbulb moment," she whispered to him, elated. "Antoni's *perfect* for Selby. As soon as I laid eyes on him it made me think they'd make the most brilliant couple."

"You're absolutely right, Mrs. H.," Ian replied in a low voice. He always liked to make sure a good idea appeared to have been generated by his employer. "I've seated them next to each other at dinner."

"Eek! So exciting," said Tata before she shimmied back over to Antoni and the Backhouses.

"Have you met my daughter, the Honourable Arabella Backhouse?" Lady Caroline was saying to him.

At the mention of her title, Arabella squirmed. "Mummy, must you?"

"Not yet," replied Antoni, smiling and shaking hands with Arabella before continuing, in his slightly accented English, "Pleasure to meet you, Honourable Arabella."

"Bels is fine," she chortled. "You deserve a thank you, Mr. Grigorivich."

"What for?" He looked surprised. "And, please, call me Antoni."

"Buying the family pile, of course. Never thought anyone would be rich enough and barmy enough to take it off Daddy's hands."

Lady Caroline glowered at Arabella, and an uncomfortable pause ensued until Tata said, "Are you enjoying being at the Priory?"

"It's wonderful," Antoni replied. "I hope to spend more time there in future."

"Isn't it lonely, coming back to a place of that size, *all by yourself*?" Tata asked.

Antoni contemplated this and dropped his eyes to the floor. "Indeed," he said, seemingly saddened. "A life alone is no life."

Lady Caroline snatched her opportunity. "Arabella knows the house like the back of her hand. What did you find most magical about it, darling, when you were young?"

"When you and Daddy installed central heating," she quipped.

"Why don't you tell Antoni about how you used to feed the robins on the lawn at sunset?" Lady Caroline continued, undaunted.

"Robins?" Arabella asked. "I don't recall those. There were masses of rats in the barns, though. Have you seen them yet, Antoni?"

"Rats?" Grigorivich wrinkled his nose as though there were a dead one beneath it.

"I'm sure there are no vermin there now," Lady Caroline tried to reassure her neighbour. "But really, the Priory would be such a special place for children, Antoni, don't you think?"

"A wife, children . . ." Tata added with a dreamy smile. "Imagine it Antoni—picnics on the lawn, games of Sardines in the attics, croquet matches in the summer—glorious."

Antoni seemed intoxicated by Tata's words. "I'd love to experience real family life," he mused. "It's time for me to devote myself to someone special now."

At this, Lady Caroline looked thrilled and Arabella simply frowned. She adored her work and the last thing she wanted was to be installed as a caretaker for the exhausting mansion her parents had finally rid themselves of.

"I'm going to the powder room," she said, escaping.

"Bels," Lady Caroline called after her daughter. " 'Powder room' is so common. Please say 'loo' in future."

At the very same moment that Arabella Backhouse was hiding from her parents in Tata Hawkins's silver-leafed downstairs bathroom, attempting to avoid asphyxiation from the smoky perfume of the giant three-wick Cire Trudon candle therein, Selby Fairfax was launching herself into the air in the riding arena at Great Bottom Park. She'd had a long afternoon of work Zooms and had treated herself to a riding lesson with Josh at the end of the day.

As Dublin, her chestnut sport horse with four white socks, landed the other side of the jump, Josh declared, "That was great."

"No, I was all over the place," Selby called out breathlessly as she cantered around the ring. "But thanks, you've been so helpful." She patted her horse's neck as she rode, cooing at him, "Nice work, Dublin. What a good jumper you are."

"Want to do the course again?"

Selby slowed to a trot. "Actually, I'm pretty exhausted," she said. "What time is it?"

Josh looked at his watch. "Just after eight."

Selby clapped her hand across her mouth.

"What is it?" he asked.

"Tata's Kitchen Supper. I've completely lost track of time today. Shit." Selby pulled up her horse. "We're late."

"Oh God!" exclaimed Josh. "Quick, let's put Dublin away. I'll drive. It's only a few minutes up the road. Hopefully they won't have started supper yet."

"I can't go in this," she protested as she dismounted and led her horse out of the arena. She was dressed in white breeches, a sleeveless cream top and black showjumping boots.

"Course you can. Tata said riding stuff was fine and it's only in her kitchen," Josh said, shutting the gate after them.

"It's all right for you—when you're young you can get away with wearing anything," said Selby as they walked quickly towards the stable block, the horse clip-clopping behind. Josh looked as cute as ever in brown breeches, tan boots and a pink shirt.

"Who's looking after the girls tonight?" Josh asked, leading Dublin into a stable and taking off the bridle.

"They're boarding at school, which is great," Selby replied as she undid the girth. "This past year, I've had them with me almost constantly. I love them and I can't complain, but there's no break." Then she giggled. "There, I complained."

"Sounds like you deserve a night off."

"Yup," Selby agreed as she removed the saddle. Then she asked, "What happened with the go-see, by the way?"

Josh grinned shyly. "Got a call-back."

"Not surprised," said Selby, just as her horse nuzzled her on her right hip, leaving a grass stain on the side of her breeches. "Dublin! No!" she wailed, trying to brush off the mark with her hand. "You've ruined my party outfit."

"You shouldn't worry, Mrs. Fairfax. You'd look gorgeous in a muddy old horse rug."

Selby stopped. She felt Josh's eyes on her suddenly. She couldn't help but be flattered by his words, but a flirtation with the stable lad? No. It wasn't an option, however ravishing the stable lad might be. She wasn't quite sure what to do. She didn't want to encourage him, but she didn't want him to feel embarrassed either. And, if truth be told, she liked the attention. It made her feel—*gasp*—attractive, something that had been sadly missing since the end of her marriage.

After an uneasy pause, Josh continued, "I'm sorry, I didn't mean—"

"Hey, don't worry," said Selby. "I'm used to men telling me I'm gorgeous. Happens all the time."

Relieved, he burst out laughing as they walked out of the stable. "I mean it. You look great in everything."

Ignoring the playfulness in Josh's voice, Selby simply raised an eyebrow at him, bolted the stable door behind them and said in a businesslike tone, "Let's put the tack away and go."

With that she strode off ahead, unable to stop smiling.

22

"You won't *believe* it . . . I was doing the Gong Cleanse with Aurelie Thurn und Taxis in her wild-flower paddock and the bikini person who's living with Bryan showed up—"

"I heard she was doing the splits in a jewelled thong—"

"She goes everywhere with that ridiculous dog in a car seat—"

"I've started Camilla Pettifer's Emotional Freedom dance workshop. Hope she doesn't show up there—"

"Maybe Tata and Bryan should go . . . Camilla's saved so many marriages—"

Almost an hour had passed since the party had started and the foyer was echoing to the sound of people mingling and chattering, mostly about Tata, Bryan, and Tallulah. Ian was not amused by this—gossiping about your host in their own home was tacky beyond belief—but nor was he surprised, as the Bottoms was the sort of place that lived and died on gossip. But he was starting to fret. He didn't want Tata overhearing something upsetting, and there was still no sign of the guest of honour or Josh Hall. Meanwhile, Maximilian d'Orleans-Ouzid, the heavily tattooed, twenty-three-year-old, Moroccan-French chef that Veronika had lured to the country from his Michelin-starred restaurant in Dalston, was determined to serve his famous lamb shank marinated in cumin and rose-water at the perfect temperature, guest of honour or no guest of honour.

"I don't care about this Selby woman, we are plating up," Maximilian grumpily informed Ian, who had been called into the back kitchen by Veronika, who was trying to reason with the chef while posting reels from the party on Instagram and TikTok. "The food will be ruined otherwise."

"If we seat everyone now, maybe she'll be here by the time the team have got all the food out," Ian suggested.

"*Oui.* Let's go," said Maximilian, gesturing at his staff to start putting food on the plates laid out on the countertop.

"Great," said Veronika. Then she held up her phone at Maximilian and said, "Smile! You're on every social media platform there is!"

The chef turned his back on her to get on with his work, and Veronika made a face at Ian. "She's nearly an hour late, what should—"

Veronika didn't get a chance to finish her sentence before her earpiece beeped. She listened for a second and then said, "They're here. The head valet says a Land Rover just drove onto the property. My team will seat the guests while you and Tata go and meet Selby and Josh at the door."

∞

A few minutes later, while the other guests flowed from the foyer to the party kitchen, Ian and Tata formed a mini-welcoming committee on the stone steps at the front of the house. Valets swooped to each side of the car and opened the doors, and Selby and Josh emerged.

"Sorry we're so late," Selby called out as she waved at Tata and went round to the trunk where she retrieved a large gardening basket which was overflowing with flowers.

"Completely my fault," added Josh.

Though Tata had told them that riding gear was fine, she couldn't quite believe it as the pair sauntered over to her in their breeches and boots and kissed her hello. They looked flushed and hot, and, well, *sexy* somehow. Tata took in every detail of Selby's appearance. The combination of her unruly dark bob, lean silhouette, riding boots that fit like a glove, a stack of three diamond bracelets on one wrist that looked like they could only be from Jar, even the grass stain on her dazzling white breeches—it was the kind of undone glamour Tata could only dream of. She suddenly rather regretted that she'd ignored Lexi's advice to wear that Wiggy Kit sack-dress tonight and vowed to herself that the next time she was anywhere near her new neighbour she'd be in nothing dressier than jeans and a T-shirt. (Fabulous ones.)

Meanwhile, when Selby saw Tata's outfit, her face fell. "Oh no, I'm so underdressed," she said. "Tata, you look amazing. Look at your legs! Those amazing shoes!" She handed her the basket of flowers, adding, "These are for you. Everything's from the old walled garden."

Tata regarded the pile of scarlet poppies, apple mint and tall daisies with polite curiosity. They looked like something that had been gathered from a derelict allotment and Veronika would go nuts if Tata attempted to bring them into the party kitchen: they'd wreck the white-on-white-on-white aesthetic that everyone had worked so hard to create.

"Wow . . . so, um, original," said Tata, taking the basket and handing it straight to Ian.

"Simply beautiful, Mrs. Fairfax," Ian declared, admiring the blooms.

"I love the way English wild flowers are so transient," replied Selby. "They remind me of the fragility of life."

"So true," he said. "Now, everyone, excuse me. I need to go and assist the team. I'll see you in a jiffy."

With that, Ian raced ahead of Tata, Josh, and Selby, dashed into the back kitchen again, updated Maximilian on the guest of honour's imminent arrival at the table and allowed himself a moment to arrange Selby's wild flowers in a large Victorian ironstone pitcher, which he left on the countertop. They might be required later, and Ian, as we know, liked to have every eventuality covered.

"Ta-da!" said Tata dramatically a few minutes later as she pushed open the vast door into the party kitchen.

"Very cool," Josh gulped, taking in the sight.

Selby grinned at Tata. "This is what you British ladies call 'camping' when you're in an argument with your husband?"

"I know, I know." Tata looked sheepish. "I'm completely overindulged."

It was such a balmy evening that Veronika had been able to throw open all the floor-to-ceiling glass doors so that the room seemed almost part of the garden, and she had conjured up an intricately layered tablescape for Tata: the tableau of embroidered white napkins, white porcelain candlesticks, Murano glass vases filled with divinely scented white gardenias, silver bowls of white sugared almonds from Ladurée, and rare white Meissen figurines, all set upon the sparkle of the mirrored dining table, was as lavish as it was chic.

"Are hens that match the table setting a British thing?" said Selby drolly, spotting the fluffy bantams Ian had borrowed from Farmer Clarke for the night scratching in the grass just outside.

"Aren't they cute?" replied Tata. One of them gingerly stepped over the threshold, clucking nervously, to the delight of the guests. "Right, grab a drink and come and meet everyone," she went on, leading Josh and Selby around the room as soon as they both had a glass of champagne in their hands.

Swiftly, Tata made sure that everyone at the table got to exchange a few brief words with Selby, but when they reached Fernanda, she sprung from her chair, saying, "*So* good to see you again, Selby." To Tata's amazement—and secret dismay—Fernanda embraced her as though they were old friends.

"Wonderful to see you as well. You look incredible," Selby said, unwrapping herself from Fernanda, who was clad in a strapless, lime-green dress, ruched at the bodice with deep tucks all the way down the skirt. Her luxurious dark hair was woven into a loose plait and tied with a large white satin bow.

Before Tata could register her astonishment at Fernanda's apparent familiarity with her star guest, Selby had tilted her head to one side with concern, saying, "How's little Luca?"

"He's doing okay—his eye's almost better. I'm trying to figure out some extra support for him," replied Fernanda. "Thank you for asking."

"Tess says he's the kindest boy she's ever met."

"Aww. He thinks she's super-sweet."

As if this display of intimacy between Fernanda and Selby were not irritating enough, Tata soon saw Sophie rising from her seat and making a beeline for Selby. Sophie looked unusually groovy tonight, Tata had to admit, in a vintage 1970s dress and Chanel ballet flats.

"Soph, I'm so glad you're here," Selby said. "It's great to see you."

Soph? Tata repeated to herself. Trying her best to seem thrilled that her two *old* best friends had already met her *new* best friend, she smiled at everyone and said, "It's so lovely that you already know each other. Amazing. Where did you all meet?"

Sophie smiled in her sweet, innocent, Sloaney way, and said, "We met a couple of times, actually. Once outside the Rectory in rather terrifying circumstances, and the second time at sports day."

"Such a shame you couldn't make it, Tats," added Fernanda. "Wasn't it fun, Selby?"

Her eyes lit up. "Gorgeous. That school, the grounds . . ."

As Selby, Sophie, and Fernanda waxed lyrical about the Stow Hall sports day she'd missed, Tata huffed inwardly. She couldn't believe that her two supposed best friends hadn't waited to pounce on the starry new neighbour before the starry old neighbour, so generously throwing a party for her, had time to throw it. But, Tata thought, she'd have to let it go. After all, Fernanda was too rich to have manners, and Sophie too desperate.

As Fernanda went to sit again, Selby said to her, "I wanted to apologise to you. I didn't mean to seem rude, turning down your offer of a garden project at your place in Uruguay . . ."

Uruguay garden project! Tata felt ready to expire. Friend poaching was a serious enough crime in itself, but trying to hire your old best friend's new best friend to design your garden? Fernanda was too brazen for words.

"No, no, I shouldn't have asked. You've had a lot on your plate."

"I know, but it is nice to be asked. I just wish I had more time," Selby replied.

"*Such* a shame you're so busy," Fernanda went on. "I've got a lovely mini-project at my place coming up that would only take someone a couple of days to do."

Selby looked intrigued. "Oh?"

"I'm throwing a trunk show the Friday after next for Shuang, that *incredible* pyjama line out of New York, in our orangerie. I want someone really fabulous to dress the space."

"*Ooh*," Selby said, her eyes lighting up. "I love doing that sort of thing, I'm sure I could squeeze it in. The old walled garden at home is literally overflowing with peonies and blossoms. Nothing's been pruned for years—we can just cut it and bring it over."

"Really?" said Fernanda.

"As long as you're okay with a mishmash of colours and species."

Fernanda looked thrilled. "You know I'm half-Venezuelan: colour makes me feel *completely* alive."

At this, Tata and Sophie caught each other's eyes for a moment and shared a look. Fernanda seemed to have conveniently forgotten she lived in a mansion whose interior had been completely whitewashed. Gazing at Tata's white tablescape, Fernanda went on, "That's not to say, Tata, that I don't *love* what you've done here tonight. It's so simple. So plain. Reminds me of that amazing

DKNY store on Madison that closed in, like, 1997. It was so original at the time."

Tata bestowed what she termed a "hard smile" on her so-called friend. Then, softening a little, she said, "Fernanda, you'll adore Selby's wild-flower look. Let me show you the bunch she brought for me tonight. Ia—" She started to call for the butler.

Ian, of course, was already by Tata's side, the pitcher of wild flowers in his hand. Every eventuality, he thought to himself, every eventuality.

A lifelong student of the art of the *placement*, Ian was chuffed with the way the seating arrangement had turned out. Selby's place was at the centre of the table, between Antoni Grigorivich and Vere Osborne, and Tata was opposite, with Michael Ovington-Williams on one side and Josh Hall on the other. The rest of the guests were seated around the table in a configuration that would allow everyone, Ian hoped, to meet someone new or at the very least enjoy an amusing conversation with a neighbour. Virgil Pitman, he noted happily to himself, seemed entranced by Arabella Backhouse, who was sitting on his right, and he noticed Sir Reggie giving his daughter an encouraging thumbs-up when Lady Caroline wasn't looking.

Subtly and unobtrusively, as was his way, Ian wafted around the party pouring Pellegrino, picking up fallen napkins, directing guests to the bathroom—and eavesdropping in the vicinity of the guest of honour as much as possible.

"Selby," said Antoni, extending his hand to her after she had sat down next to him, "an honour to meet you. Your reputation precedes you. You look stunning."

"Nice of you to lie," Selby said with a laugh, shaking hands. "I had no idea tonight would be so dressy." As soon as she was settled in, she took a bite of Maximilian's lamb, which was accompanied by a phantasmagoria of Moroccan salads. "Mmm. This is delicious, Tata."

"So glad," her hostess said from across the table.

"You see, I adore a woman in riding garments," Antoni went on. "They've always been an inspiration for my fashion line. They call me the Polish Ralph Lauren, you know."

"Well I hope the Polish Ralph Lauren likes grass stains, because my breeches are covered in them." Selby laughed again, looking relaxed and carefree.

Antoni looked across the table at Tata, then back at Selby, an expression of longing coming over his face. "I see nothing wrong. I see only perfection," he said. "Tata, what a wonderful choice of friend you have made in Selby."

"Thank you, Antoni," Tata replied, bemused. "Now, Selby, have you met Vere Osborne?" she asked, gesturing towards him on her other side. The gentleman farmer looked particularly dishy tonight, Ian noted, in a navy suit, his dark hair a little unruly. "He's your closest neighbour."

At this, Selby turned to her left and went to shake Vere's hand. But to everyone's surprise, he did not take it. Instead he said flatly, "Actually, we've already met."

"You have?" Tata asked.

"We have?" Selby echoed, scrutinising his face.

"You helped me deliver that lovely little calf last night at my farm."

"Oh, heavens." Selby clapped her hand across her mouth. "That was . . . *you?*"

"Yup. I was the man with his hand up a cow's bottom."

"Eeew," Tata squeaked.

"It's your happy place. Isn't it, Vere?" Michael teased Vere across the table, but he remained stone-faced.

Selby went on, "I am so sorry, I thought you were—I mean—that was—"

"A farmhand?" interjected Vere.

"Yes. I mean, no, I just got confused," she continued. "It was so dark. I really am truly sorry about the water situation. And the dead cow. I mean, if there is anything I can do . . ."

Alas, Ian thought. These two were already in some kind of petty neighbours' dispute. Why had he thought inviting Vere Osborne tonight was a good idea? He might have been single, handsome, and brainy but he was also tricky, permanently heartbroken, and rather too honest at times.

"There isn't," Vere replied, curt. "The cow is gone."

"Come on, Mr. Osborne, it's not her fault," said Josh.

"Really," Vere said, then abruptly turned his attention to the woman on his other side.

"Sorry," Tata whispered.

Selby shrugged and mouthed a "thank you" at Josh just as Ian floated round to Tata and asked her discreetly, "Would you like the staff to clear and then the loganberry sorbet and pistachio shortbreads can come out? The chef says—"

He hadn't finished his sentence before something in the garden caught Tata's eye, and she jumped up and pointed towards the terrace.

"Ian. *Ian!*" she gasped, a horrified expression on her face. "Look! It's Tallulah's dog!"

At this, the guests and staff watched as Pikachu trotted into the room from the garden, stopped at the first chair he found (which was occupied by Hugh Thompson), cocked his leg, and peed.

"Ugh!" Tata exclaimed.

"Christ," groaned Hugh, springing up to avoid the pool of yellow liquid on the floor. A waiter dashed to the site of the accident and started mopping it up with a cloth.

"*Frightfully* common, these 'toy' breeds," said Lady Caroline. "Too inbred to potty-train." She put out her arm to scoop up the little animal, but it immediately slipped under the table and soon appeared by Michael's feet. Ian leaned down and managed to pick it up with one hand and tuck it under his left elbow.

"Mrs. H., I'll drive it back up to the Manor now," Ian told her. As far as he was concerned, Tallulah's dog appearing at Mrs. Hawkins's dinner was almost as embarrassing as the girl appearing herself. It was clear that some of the guests knew exactly whose dog it was, and no one quite knew what to do or where to look.

"Ian, I can hardly spare you now," Tata said quietly as she sat back down. "Just let it out of the back door and it'll find its own way home across the fields. It's not very far and it's still light."

"If you're sure, Mrs. H." As an animal lover, Ian wasn't particularly keen on the idea of an innocent dog being left to its own devices this late. There were foxes and badgers in the fields between the Old Coach House and the Manor that could swallow the poor thing in one gulp.

"I am."

Rather reluctantly, Ian handed the dog to a waiter with instructions to let it wander home, and then sent another member of staff to tell Maximilian to send out the dessert. With the dog gone, the atmosphere in the room relaxed again.

"Antoni, Selby," said Tata a few minutes later, taking a tiny bite of the beautiful dark purple sorbet that had just been put in front of her, "sorry about that. How's everything going at the house, Selby?"

"It's chaos, mostly," she replied.

"I hear it's a magnificent example of Elizabethan architecture," said Antoni.

Selby smiled. "Magnificent and falling down."

"What are you going to do with it?" Michael asked.

"It's a balance between stopping the decay and keeping the beauty of what's there," said Selby. "I'm renovating a farm building as a studio to work in, and then I'll slowly restore the estate and gardens."

"Sounds like a lot of work," Michael said, taking a bite of his shortbread.

"True. But it's a great distraction from my recent divorce."

Antoni touched Selby's arm sympathetically. "I'm sorry to hear that. I am also alone. Failed marriages are heartbreaking." He looked wistful. "Don't let yourself get too isolated."

"Aww, that's sweet," said Selby. "Do you want to come over sometime? There's no point in both of us sitting at home like two lonely puppies."

Antoni looked terrifically pleased. "Is tomorrow too soon?"

"Course not. How about one of those proper English teas they do here?" she said.

Ian could hardly believe it. Antoni and Selby had only just met, and already they had a date. But he was rather surprised when Antoni looked across the table at Mrs. Hawkins and said, "Sounds wonderful. Tata, you must come too."

"Yes, please come too," Selby said to her hostess. "Bring Minty. Tess would love that."

"I wouldn't want to intrude—" Tata started, catching Ian's eye.

"But I insist," said Selby.

At this point, Ian mouthed the word "yes" at Tata who then said, "If you're sure, it sounds great. Now, let's go outside. We've got fresh-mint teas and coffee. And I need a cigarette after that dog fiasco."

∞

"Soph, you need to get Selby over to our place," said Hugh, as they wandered outside with the other guests into Tata's garden. "I wanted to talk to her about a donation to the goat sanctuary, but there's too many people here tonight to discuss it."

"I'll think of something," said Sophie. "Come on, let's go and sit with everyone."

The air couldn't have been lovelier, and Sophie and Hugh settled into the sofas on the terrace with Michael, Fernanda, Selby, Josh, and Tata. While sipping a mint tea, Sophie fretted about how on earth she could entice Selby over to the Rectory. She didn't have the space, staff, or budget of a Tata or Fernanda to pull off a fancy dinner or lunch, but maybe she should do that thing of getting someone over to teach something for the morning? There was that fab girl who taught lamb portraiture and you took home an adorable painting at the end. Or there was that class at Daylesford where you made your own espadrilles and then had lunch in the spa restaurant. Neither of them was cheap, exactly, but with the money from Great-Aunt Edith, it'd be easier to swing. Maybe a summer garland-making class in the garden? No, that sounded pathetic, like something her mother used to do with the Women's Institute c. 1974. Then it came to her: riding. Selby clearly loved horses and Sophie happened to be a rather good horsewoman herself.

Just then, Lady Caroline and Sir Reggie Backhouse came up to Tata to say goodbye.

"Awfully good supper," said Sir Reggie. "Thank you, Tata. We must be going. Got to get Bels back to the station in time for the last train to London. Where is she, by the way?"

"Push off and find her," his wife directed him in her inimitable style. "I need to ask Selby something."

As her husband sauntered off looking for their daughter, Lady Caroline said, "I hope you don't mind my raising this at our very first meeting, but there is a matter of some urgency that I must put to you."

Selby looked concerned. "How can I help?"

"It's an animal welfare issue." Lady Caroline pursed her lips with worry. "You see, dogs in Britain are under *enormous* threat nowadays."

Sophie saw Hugh start to yawn, and she jabbed him with her elbow.

"They are?" Selby asked, wrinkling her brow.

"Specifically the terrier type. The Patterdale, for example, and the Parson Jack Russell will both die out unless serious efforts are made to save them. Lady Maud was a great supporter of working dogs."

Selby nodded. "She loved her animals."

"And so she always gave her generous permission for the British Terrier Society to hold its annual summer pre-Crufts championship at Great Bottom Park. As the long-serving chairperson, I'm just wondering whether you will uphold this tradition? For the greater good of the terrier?"

"Absolutely, it'd be my pleasure," said Selby.

"Good. That is wonderful news. Little side note. We always have a full cooked breakfast for all the breeders in the formal dining room in the house."

"Right—"

"Then a seated three-course lunch on the south terrace for the judges, and a formal tea after the prizes have been awarded for the competitors. That takes place in a marquee on the lawn. It's the best dog show in the shires, you can imagine."

Before Selby could utter a word, Lady Caroline went on, "I can't thank you enough. Too generous for words. I'll be in touch with a schedule asap, but pencil in the seventeenth of July. Now, where's Bels?" She looked around and spotted Reggie returning from a shadowy corner of the garden. "Have you found her, dear?"

"She's under the orange blossoms, and appears to be having an intense discussion about Latin declensions with the headmaster of Stow Hall School," said Sir Reggie.

Lady Caroline looked annoyed. "She's going to jolly well miss her train."

"Virgil Pitman says he's going to drop her at the station."

"Right. How peculiar. Well. We'd better toddle off," said Lady Caroline. "Goodnight, everyone."

"Bye!" said Tata. "Love you!" she called, blowing a kiss. (The combination of half a Valium, a bump of coke, a gallon of rosé at dinner, and a few surreptitious drags on Michael's weed pen had unleashed her affectionate side.)

"You too!" called back Sir Reggie, eliciting a severe frown from his wife.

A moment or two later, Vere came over to say goodbye to Tata, after which Selby rose to speak to him.

"Look, I really am sorry," she said. "About the water, and . . . everything."

Vere simply replied with a curt "goodnight" and turned to leave.

Selby watched him walk off alone into the night. "Tata, I've seriously annoyed your friend Vere," she said.

"He was quite rude to you at dinner. I'm so sorry."

"No, I fully deserved it. Tess drained the spring we share with his farm, his cow Bluebell died—"

"Bluebell?" Tata repeated, a grave look crossing her face.

Selby nodded. "Yes. Why?"

"That cow was rather special to him."

"I know. I went around to apologise last night and Vere was delivering a calf and I just . . . well, *assumed*. I mistook him for the farmhand because he was in muddy overalls. So on top of being a cow killer, he thinks I'm a snobby American with no idea about the English countryside . . . both of which are true, I suppose."

"Look, I'm sure you two will make up," said Tata. "He's a decent person but he can be cranky. It's complicated. He's got history, like all of us."

∽

A little later, when the night had drawn in, Antoni came over to his hostess, saying, "Tata, what a marvellous evening it's been. I'd love to have a stroll before I leave. The moonlight is so beautiful. Shall we?" and offered her his arm.

"Sure," said Tata, getting up enthusiastically. "But wait a sec. Selby!" she called out. "Want to come and see the garden?"

Selby, who was happily chatting away to Josh, Hugh, and the Ovington-Williamses, waved at her host, saying, "You guys go. I like to see gardens in daylight."

As soon as Tata and Antoni were out of sight, round the back of a beech hedge, Sophie seized her moment. "Selby," she said, taking Tata's place next to her, "I was wondering. I'm thinking of arranging a really beautiful ride the weekend after next for a few friends. Would you like to come? And then, maybe, lunch afterwards at mine?"

To Sophie's delight, Selby's face lit up. "I've always wanted to ride out in the English countryside. That sounds wonderful."

"You'll really enjoy it," said Hugh, winking at Sophie. She felt as though finally she'd done something right.

"In her absence, may I add that Mrs. Hawkins would enjoy it as well," said Ian, who was gliding from guest to guest passing around a box of Charbonnel et Walker's chocolate-covered almonds.

"I hope I'm invited too, Soph," Fernanda teased.

"Of course, you all are," said Sophie. Then she turned to Selby and added, "We all keep our horses at Bunbury's Livery yard in Monkton Bottom. We could start there, if you can bring your horse over. It's only a few minutes' drive from you."

"Perfect," said Selby.

"Michael? How about it?" Sophie asked him.

"I'll be on location," he groaned. "Peril of the job."

"Well, I hope you're not on location tomorrow," said Selby. "Antoni and Tata are coming for tea, and I hope you can all join," she said, looking around at the group.

"Sounds great," said Fernanda.

"Choccy, Mrs. Ovington-Williams?" asked Ian who was hovering close by.

"Mmm. Yes." As he proffered the chocolates, she said lightly, "Oh, I almost forgot. Luca asked me to give you this card." She handed him an envelope on which his name was scrawled in childlike handwriting.

"Awww," cooed Ian, putting it in his top pocket.

Meanwhile Sophie, who couldn't quite believe she was about to turn down an invitation to Great Bottom Park, began, "Selby, it's such a lovely offer but on Tuesdays after school Eddie has cricket practice—"

"We'll make an exception tomorrow," Hugh interrupted, but before Sophie could say anything more, a scream came from beyond the beech hedge.

"What was that?" exclaimed Fernanda, leaping up from her seat.

"No idea," Sophie replied, grabbing Hugh's hand.

Ian hurriedly set down the chocolates and sprinted towards the hedge. As he did so, Pikachu scampered out from beneath it and over his feet. A scene of cartoon-like horror then unfolded before the party: as the dog raced away from Ian, it became apparent that one of the white bantams was clenched between its jaws. "Quick, catch it!" Ian called out to one of the waiters on the terrace, who raced after the dog.

The next minute, Tata appeared and staggered across the lawn on her vertiginous heels, with Antoni close behind. Her cream onesie was spotted with blood, her right hand was outstretched as far away from her body as she could reach it, and a limp hen dangled from her fingers. It was clearly dead.

"That bloody girl's dog," Tata yelled, furious, as she raced past her shocked guests and into the kitchen. Once inside, she dropped the murdered fowl on the table, pulled out a chair and collapsed onto it. Sophie and Fernanda rushed inside after their friend and watched as the hen's blood dripped onto the mirrored table and then seeped into the lace edge of a delicate napkin that had been left behind after the meal.

"That's *sooo* awful," whispered Sophie to Fernanda.

"Heartbreaking," Fernanda agreed, shaking her head sadly. "Ian will *never* get the bloodstains out of that linen."

23

Until tonight, Selby had barely had a drink or been to a party for months. She had pretty much given up on both of those things since Doug left. Going out on her own in New York had felt like a personal horror movie; a chance to receive pitying looks and a litany of seemingly concerned remarks that felt like backhanded insults. "How are you coping, ALONE?" would be followed by, "So hard, being a woman, managing everything ON YOUR OWN." Worst of all was, "I am *full of admiration* for SINGLE MOMS," followed by an unwanted hug or squeeze of the shoulder from someone she barely knew. There were the misguided attempts of the married to cheer her up: "You'll meet someone! This is a *wonderful* new beginning!" "*You* need to start getting out there." "Are you on all the apps?" Then there was the just plain vile: men who said things like, "I know someone who'll fuck you," or women who said things like, "The problem is, when you're single at your age, you just don't feel like doing *it* any more, do you?"

Selby's response had been to retreat into a self-imposed lockdown, staying home and focusing on work, the children, and an awful lot of television. Thank God for Netflix, Apple TV, Hulu, Disney Plus—she had every streaming service possible. On the occasions she had attempted to wash away her worries with a few glasses of wine, a hangover had made the next day painful, and near-abstinence had been her only option.

But Selby had made an exception for Tata's dinner tonight. The girls were staying over at school, and she could sleep in tomorrow morning if she felt weary. By the end of the night, Selby wasn't drunk, exactly, but the drinks flowing all evening had had a delightful effect. It was heavenly to feel so light, so merry, as Josh drove her home after the party, and it was such a balmy evening that she wound down her window and draped her arm outside to feel the air.

"That was a very, um . . . *interesting* night, Mrs. Fairfax," said Josh, grinning as he turned the Land Rover through the gates to Great Bottom Park and onto the drive.

"It sure was. The chicken drama! That dog! It was like *Beatrix Potter* gone mad. And call me Selby, please."

"Okay, Selby. I'm sorry Mr. Osborne was so hard on you."

"He's upset, I get it. But it was nice of you to stick up for me. Thank you."

"Anytime you need someone to back you up, I'm here," said Josh, pulling up in front of the house. As she undid her seat belt, he said hopefully, "Nightcap?"

Selby really should have made a polite excuse and declined. After all this boy—and he was a boy, frankly—was not only her employee, but the crush of her fourteen-year-old daughter.

"I guess the girls aren't here . . ." she started. "So we won't wake anyone up with one whisky. Sure. Come on in."

Josh tumbled sideways out of the car and followed her inside.

Somehow, a nightcap in the kitchen turned into a tequila shot in the drawing room which turned into a wander down to the rose garden which turned into a kiss under the stars which turned into . . . well . . . Suffice it to say that Great Bottom Park had not witnessed a night of such passion since 1947 when the young Lady Maud lost her virginity to her future husband in the airing cupboard in the East Attic. We'll say no more.

∞

A romantic face-licking was not something Selby had particularly anticipated, but on the morning after Tata's party her first experience of the day was the sensation of a wet tongue slithering across her cheek. Mmmmmm. It was kind of nice, actually. True, Josh was making an awful lot of snuffling noises, and delivering saliva on an industrial scale, but she was unperturbed.

It was dawn, and Selby was too sleepy to think about opening her eyes. Last night had been impassioned, ardent—and long. They'd barely slept. Maybe it was Josh defending her in front of grumpy Vere Osborne. Maybe it was the tequila. Maybe it was Josh's sweet, adoring personality, or maybe it was just that she hadn't had sex for ages. She wasn't quite sure. But it would not be an exaggeration to say that at this moment Selby was completely and utterly blissed out.

The licking continued, moving to her arms, her shoulders. Soon, even in her blissed-out state, it seemed a little weird.

"Josh, hey, stop," Selby cried with a giggle.

The response was even more licking, accompanied by snorting noises.

"Josh! What on earth?" said Selby, finally cracking her eyes open.

The sight that met her was not the stable lad's beautiful face and flop of brown hair. Instead, she was close up with a dog's snout.

"Oh my God!" she shrieked, sitting up in bed. She was even more startled when she recognised the blue-coated miniature dachshund that was now dashing around her bed wagging its tail.

"Pickle?" What the hell was Pickle doing here?

She didn't have a moment to think before a second dog leaped on top of her and started pawing at her arm.

"Peanut, oh, sweetie," cooed Selby, cuddling the other pooch, which was the same breed and colour.

What on earth was going on? Josh had vanished, and in his place were the two family dogs from New York. As cute as they were, it seemed like a lousy swap.

"Morning, Selby," came a familiar voice from the other side of the room.

She looked towards the doorway. There, standing on the threshold, was her ex-husband, a disapproving look on his face and an alarmingly large suitcase next to him.

"Doug?" Was she imagining things?

"Hi."

Was that it? *Hi?* He had trespassed his way into her house and her bedroom and led her to believe a hot young man was licking her all over as a precursor to another round of incredible sex, when in fact nothing of the kind had been taking place. He had humiliated her (as if he hadn't humiliated her enough already) and all he was going to do was say "Hi?"

The monosyllable was followed by a tense silence. Finally, Doug volunteered, "Nice . . . erm, place . . ." He sounded nervous, actually.

"I don't get it—"

"The dogs are thrilled to see you."

"What are you doing here?"

"It's a surprise."

Hell of a surprise, thought Selby, but resisted saying so. Instead, she just raised her eyebrows and said coolly, "Tell me more."

"You said I should visit."

"No. I said I'd send dates," she replied sternly, sitting up in bed and pulling the covers over herself.

"But you didn't send any—"

"Exactly. You've got no right to just show up here unannounced, Doug."

"Yeah . . . I know, I'm sorry. But . . . Vi's been texting saying how much she wanted me to bring the dogs over, and I've been missing the kids, and missing you—"

At this, Selby gave him an angry look. "That's rich. You left me. Us. You have a boyfriend—"

"I know, I know," said Doug, seeing her expression. "But it's true. And the dogs are *really* pining for the girls."

"I get that, but what are you doing in my bedroom?" Affronted by his casual manner, Selby was becoming more agitated by the minute.

"There are manners, and boundaries, and one of those boundaries is *my* bedroom."

"Sorry about that. The dogs led me up here." Typical Doug, thought Selby, always ready to blame someone else, even a pair of innocent dachshunds. "I took an overnight flight from JFK and arrived early this morning with the dogs, thinking I'd surprise the girls before they went to school, and I got here and there was no one around. Anyway, I came in through the back and the dogs got insanely excited the minute they were inside and ran off up the stairs. They must have picked up your scent. I followed them and, well, I guess, here I am."

"I guess you are." Selby was supremely unamused by now, and her hangover was starting to blossom. She was also worried about her ex-husband seeing the evidence of her night of passion: various items of clothing strewn around the room and an empty shot glass on her bedside table.

"Look, I'm interrupting," he said, as though reading her mind. "Point me in the direction of the girls' bedrooms and I'll take the dogs to go wake them up."

"The girls aren't here, Doug."

"What?" He looked ready to panic.

"They boarded at school last night because I was going out to dinner. They're coming home tonight."

"Right. Okay," said Doug, looking crestfallen. "It's just that I'm dying to see them." Then he went on, "So, who's Josh?"

Now it was Selby's turn to panic. "Josh?" she repeated. How the hell did Doug know about Josh?

"Josh. You said 'Josh' when the dogs jumped up on you just now."

"I did?" said Selby, playing for time.

"You did," her ex said knowingly.

Selby gathered herself somehow. Calmly, she replied, "You mean *Josh?*"

"Exactly. Josh."

"Josh is . . . the . . . dog."

"We don't have a dog called Josh."

"Doug. We've been apart for a while. Things change without you knowing about them. And we have a new dog. Josh the dog. I know we'll never replace Pickle and Peanut, but Josh kind of makes up for them."

Doug sniffed, looking unconvinced. "I can't wait to meet him."

"Great," said Selby. "Let's have some breakfast. Meet me downstairs in ten minutes? Then we can talk."

By seven, Selby found herself in the kitchen, introducing Doug to Doreen.

"Nice to meet you, Mr. Fairfax," said the housekeeper politely.

"Likewise," replied Doug. "Great hair, by the way."

"Ooh, thank you kindly, sir. I do like to change it up a bit now and again." For the record, Doreen's hair was fuchsia today. "Do you fancy a full English breakfast? Eggs, bacon, sausages, tomatoes, black pudding, fried bread?"

"Sounds awesome," said Doug.

Then, noticing his suitcase in the doorway, Doreen said, "The Chinese bedroom's all made up." She tossed eggs and bacon into a warm pan on the Aga which started sizzling. "I'll ask Alan to pop your case in there, ducky, all right?"

"Er . . ." Doug began, awkwardly turning to his ex-wife. "Is it okay if I stay here?"

Despite being furious with him for barging in on her, Selby reminded herself that her daughters came first. As Ian had counselled her, the girls needed to see their dad. A year ago, a situation like this would have ended in yet another miserable argument which got neither of them anywhere. But, today, Selby was determined to be grown up. She stayed calm (or fake-calm, if she was being frank) as she said, "Sure. The girls will be excited to see you after school."

"Can I pick them up?" suggested Doug.

"That would be great. I've got a ton of work to do today."

"Anything I can do to help you out let me know."

You could have helped me out, Doug, if you'd been honest with me when we got married, she wanted to say. But instead she said, "Thanks. There's a few neighbours coming for tea later, with some of their kids."

"Did I hear someone say 'tea?'" clucked Doreen as she started plating up the fried breakfast.

"Yes. Sorry for the short notice—I only invited them last night."

"No bother, love," replied Doreen. "Takes me two ticks to whip up some flapjacks. Ooh, and you'll be wanting scones with jam and clotted cream, and a Victoria sponge, crumpets, drop scones, melting moments, tiffin, madeleines . . . anything else?"

"Are you kidding?" Selby laughed. "We'll never eat all that."

"The English love their teas. It'll all go, I promise. Right, your fry-ups." Doreen set down two full platters on the table.

"Mmmmm, if this is what breakfast is like every morning, maybe I'll stay a couple of weeks," said Doug as he tucked in. Seeing Selby's face, he added, "Maybe not."

"Hey," Selby said. "Of course you can stay. Just—well, just be nice. No drama, okay?"

"Fair enough. And maybe I can design a new product while I'm here," he replied. "Honestly, I'm struggling. The office wants new lines all the time, and I haven't had a good idea in months now."

"There's a lovely footpath down to the church in the village that always inspires me. Why don't you go for a walk after breakfast, clear your head?" said Selby.

"Great idea," Doug replied, munching on his fried bread.

Once they'd finished their breakfast, Selby rose from the table and carried their plates over to the sink, finally feeling a little more relaxed.

"Take the dogs," she said.

"Sure. I can take Josh as well."

Selby froze as she was putting the plates in the dishwasher, grateful Doug couldn't see the alarm on her face. "What?"

"I can take Josh. On the walk with us."

"Nice idea, but you'll never get him out of the stable yard," interjected Doreen as she wiped the table.

"Really?" said Doug.

"Loves being around the horses," she carried on.

Doug looked confused. "Doesn't he get kicked?"

"Not so far. Josh is *very* intelligent," Doreen told him. "And what a pretty face—oh my!"

Doug stood up and stretched. "Okay. Well, I guess it's just me, Pickle and Peanut searching for inspiration in the churchyard, then."

Thank goodness for Doreen, thought Selby. Doug was none the wiser about Josh. Anyway, he would never know: Selby was already starting to feel that last night had been a terrible error of judgement and she couldn't let it happen again.

"Right, let me take you up to your room, Mr. Fairfax," said Doreen.

"Great," he replied, and followed Doreen out, the dogs trotting behind him.

Just after they had left, Selby's phone vibrated in her pocket. She took it out, saw the name "Josh" on the screen and tapped on the notification to read the message. *Hi, gorgeous! Fun night! Supper at the Great Bottom Arms this Saturday? XO J.*

Christ, Selby said to herself, he actually likes me. She quickly typed back: *Dear Josh, ex-husband appeared unexpectedly this a.m. I've told him you're the family pet. Yes, let's meet Saturday. In meantime, best to keep out of his way. Selby.*

Surely it was impossible for a message to sound less alluring, she thought, as she pressed "send." She'd tell Josh their brief entanglement had to end on Saturday, face to face, like a decent person. Let him down gently.

24

Charlene Potts was out of her depth. Bryan's chef had just handed her a mother-of-pearl tray on which was laid out a white porcelain pot of magnesium sulphate powder, a glass vial containing grapefruit extract, a fresh fennel juice, and a bottle of electrolyte water. Tallulah de Sanchez preferred to fast than to eat breakfast on photoshoot days, and these items were part of her "cleanse," as she put it. To Charlene, they resembled something the vet would give a sick piglet.

She climbed the stairs to the west wing at Monkton Bottom Manor and tapped on the bedroom door of the guest suite. "Knock knock," she called out.

"Come in," a sleepy voice said from inside.

Charlene entered to find the room in almost complete darkness. Very carefully she set the tray on a table close to the bed, and then went to the windows and opened the curtains. The milky morning light revealed a tangle of tanned limbs clad in silk animal-print pyjamas in the four-poster. Tallulah slowly emerged from her slumber and pushed a frilly eye mask up onto the top of her head. After stretching in the manner of a lithe panther, she eventually propped herself up against a pile of downy pillows behind her.

She yawned. "Morning, Charlene. What time is it?"

"Just after eight, Miss."

"Only an hour to get ready. It's going to be a hell of a long day shooting for TallulahSwim."

"Sounds very glamorous."

"You can't imagine how exhausting it is, standing around in bikinis all day having to look thin."

No, Charlene couldn't. "Dearie me."

"Oh no," Tallulah moaned, pointing at the windows.

"What?" asked Charlene.

"Look outside. I think it's raining."

"Only a little drizzle, and it's not cold." Charlene's sole concern was that her three-week-old piglets didn't catch a chill.

"The photographer is not going to be happy with the grey clouds. He's going to have to add blue sky on Photoshop."

"Very clever," said Charlene, turning to leave.

"Don't go, Charlene," said Tallulah, sucking the grapefruit extract from a dropper and making a face. "You see, I'm upset."

"Maybe the clouds will break later."

"No . . . it's not just the weather. The thing is, last night I took a painful executive decision." Tallulah stuck out her bottom lip in a pout. "It's agony, but I decided—in the best interests of my business—to forgo my scroll through my social media feeds today. I don't want to wreck my mood looking at all the pictures Tata will have posted of her dinner. But, God, it's depressing sitting in bed with nothing to look at."

"The park's a nice view for you, Miss."

Tallulah looked at Charlene blankly. "I guess." She stuck one arm out and patted at the bedclothes next to her. "Pikachu?" she called out.

The lapdog could normally be found first thing curled up on the pillow next to hers, but this morning the spot was empty. Charlene could not even detect the tennis-ball-sized dent that Pikachu usually left behind.

"Baby-waby? Darling doggie?" called Tallulah, tossing off the covers and standing up. She clicked her tongue against her teeth to make the noise that always brought the pup galloping towards her. Still nothing.

She whitened. "Oh my God. If something's happened to Peeks . . . Oh-my-God-oh-my-God—wait. He's got a tracker on his collar."

"Phew," said Charlene as Tallulah picked up her phone.

"You click on this app," went on Tallulah hopefully, her finger tapping on the screen, "and it locates your dog."

She waited a few moments, staring at the device.

"Miss?" asked Charlene, seeing Tallulah's face fall.

Tallulah sighed and tossed the phone on the bed. "Nothing. Those things only work if your dog's literally sitting underneath a satellite or Wi-Fi tower, which of course they never are. I'm so worried."

"Why don't I check downstairs? He sometimes sneaks into the breakfast room if he smells Mr. Hawkins's breakfast."

Tallulah nodded. "Okay. Okay. Good idea, Charlene." She inhaled several huge gulps of air through her mouth, then held her nose and let them out. "*Plooooo-ooooh*," came the sound as she exhaled. "Breathe, T, breathe. *Plooooo-ooooh*. I'll get dressed. Finding Pikachu will make a really good reel. Tell the Hair and Make-up girl to come up? We'll have to work on the run."

"Mr. Hawkins? Sorry to intrude," Charlene said as she popped her head around the door of the breakfast room. Bryan was greedily necking a bowl of porridge topped with blueberries, double cream, and soft brown sugar while scrolling through his phone with a pained expression on his face. To Charlene's dismay, there was no sign of the lapdog.

"No problem, Charlene," Bryan replied. "I'm trying to get into the home office, got an awful lot of work to do, but . . ." He trailed off. "You see, I'm quite upset."

Not him too. Charlene had thought being a PA meant opening the mail and booking travel, not having your employers dump their personal problems on you first thing in the morning. Still, they'd established a good rapport, and she worried about Mr. H. without his wife around. "Can I do anything?" she asked.

"Could you come in and shut the door?"

As Charlene timidly stepped into the room, he flashed his iPhone at her. "I'm on edge. All these pictures Tata's posted of her dinner last night. It's massively 'triggering,' as my therapist says."

"I am sorry, Mr. H., I don't want to overload you with problems, but I'm afraid that Miss de Sanchez is in a terrible state too."

Bryan grimaced. "When *isn't* she, Charlene? There's at least a drama an hour where Tallulah's concerned." He laughed joylessly. "Anyway, what's the latest with Miss Bikini?"

"It's Pikachu. He's disapp—"

Before Charlene could go on, Tallulah had flung open the door to the breakfast room. She'd changed into a palm-print bikini top, matching hot pants and green metallic slingbacks and was trailed by her social media crew which consisted of Peter, the photographer, and Peta, Hair and Make-up. Peta had already pulled Tallulah's hair into a high ponytail and was brandishing a mascara wand in one hand and a blusher brush in the other.

"Bry-Bry. You've heard the news? It's Peeky-Weeks. He's gone." She flopped dramatically onto a chair by the table and pouted at Bryan.

Peta saw her opportunity, saying, "Look up, babe, then I can get your eyes done."

Tallulah obliged, gazing solemnly at the ceiling, as Peta started loading mascara onto her lashes.

"Peter. Do you mind not filming while I'm eating?" Bryan looked put out. The photographer apologised, shuffled backwards, and waited outside. "Tallulah, please tell him not to film me *at all*. I'm a very private person."

"Sure," said Tallulah. "How do my eyes look?" She batted her newly coated lashes at Bryan as Peta started dabbing blusher on her cheeks.

"Er . . . very nice," he replied, sounding uncomfortable. "Have you looked for Pikachu by the lake?" he asked, changing the subject. "Dogs love it down there, lots of ducks to chase and—"

"The lake?" Tallulah interrupted. "He might have drowned. This is terrifying." She looked grief-stricken.

"I'm sure you'll find him pottering around somewhere there," Bryan said, his tone becoming increasingly irritated. "Don't worry so much."

"Okay. We'll look down there first."

"There, done. *Stunning*, babe," said Peta, finishing off Tallulah's cheeks and patting them with her fingers. She held up a small mirror for Tallulah to check the make-up.

"Looks fantastic," Tallulah told Peta, who left the room. As Tallulah got up to follow her out, she went on, "By the way, Bry, did you read the rough draft of my Miami Swim Week Female Entrepreneur of the Year Award speech yet? I need input, yah?"

"I'll get to it."

"Try to do it *today*, Bryan. I need to start the edit. One day, you'll be seeing me on that TED stage, I promise." With her hand on the doorknob, she turned to Charlene and said, "Please go and find Pikachu's lead and then meet me and the team at the lake."

"Of course," Charlene replied, then waited until the door had closed and Tallulah was out of earshot before she said, "Mr. Hawkins, have you got any idea where I'd find her dog's lead?"

"Obviously, no. I mean—!" He looked bewildered. "What does the girl think she's here for? To have you and I service her and her flaming dog? Christ. What was I thinking letting her stay here for the mentoring programme? Tata would never have allowed it. Give me a coder any day of the week."

"You weren't to know," Charlene said sympathetically. "She could have been really easy-going."

"Huh," puffed Bryan, screwing up his napkin until it was a little ball in his hand. "TallulahSwim.com is probably a good investment, but I've got lots of good investments and I don't have to have conversations with them at breakfast time about AWOL puppies or TED talks. Makes me miss Tata more than ever."

Charlene started clearing the breakfast things onto a tray. "Mrs. H. will come back. I'm sure of it," she said.

"You can't imagine what it's like," Bryan complained miserably. "Tallulah never stops talking. In the evenings she wants to discuss business models, or Google Analytics, or how I can engineer a meeting for her with Jeff Bezos. I don't bloody know Jeff Bezos."

"Who?" asked Charlene.

"Doesn't matter," Bryan said, and sighed. "All I want to do in the evenings is have a glass of vino and watch *Love Island* with my wife. I've got myself into an awful mess with Tata, you know. Tried to be too clever. Never works." He blew out his cheeks and frowned. "I do wish Ian was here. He'd know how to fix things."

"I better go and find that lead," said Charlene, picking up the tray.

"Thanks. Let me know if the dog comes back."

A few minutes later, Charlene arrived at the lake clutching a pale lilac £150 Mungo & Maud lead. She watched as Tallulah tottered about on her heels, Peter's camera on her, calling out, "Peeeee-kkkkkkeeeee!"

But it was only Tallulah's own voice that echoed back at her from the parklands of Monkton Bottom Manor. There wasn't a yap, a bark, a woof to be heard. Finally, she turned to the team and said, "Let's try the conservatory. It's really photogenic, and Pikachu sometimes hides in there."

Just as they started to head back towards the main house, a diminutive figure appeared on the terrace. It was one of the maids, waving frantically.

"Miss de Sanchez! Telephone! They've found Pikachu!" she called out.

"Yay," cried Tallulah, kicking off her heels and sprinting up the lawn, Peter and Peta in hot pursuit.

"Lulah, jump in the air for joy," the photographer directed her. "Your followers will love it."

Tallulah happily obliged, leaping and spinning as she ran. Finally reaching the terrace, she snatched the phone from the maid and put it on speaker. Breathlessly she cried, "Hi? Hello? You've got my dog?"

"Miss de Sanchez?" came a smooth voice on the other end. "This is Ian Palmer, Executive Butler to the Hawkins family. Mrs. Hawkins asked me to let you know that your dog was found here last night—"

"I'll be there," Tallulah interrupted sharply, pressing the red button on the phone to end the call.

She looked at Charlene and beckoned her over. Then she lowered her voice and said in a whisper, "Char, Tata Hawkins has kidnapped my dog—"

"She wouldn't—"

"She did. Pikachu is at the Old Coach House. Tata must have taken him to spite me. She's literally the Cruella de Vil of the Bottoms. Right," she said, eyeballing her crew. "Meet me at the car in five minutes. I need to change outfits for the next reel. Hashtag MissionPikachu starts now."

25

As soon as Tallulah had hung up on him, Ian began making a gooseberry pressé for Mrs. Hawkins in the back kitchen. She would have a frightful hangover after last night and the vitamin C would do wonders. As he started pushing the raw fruit into the juicer, he noticed an envelope lying on the countertop—the one Fernanda had given him from Luca, which he hadn't had time to read yet. He poured the drink into a glass for Tata, washed his hands, and opened the little envelope. Inside was a note in the large, wobbly hand of a child. Ian's heart sank as he read it.

Dear Ian,

My mom says she will pay you two times what Tata pays you if you come live at our house and hang out with me. Otherwise I will be very sad as I have no friends and the other boys at school are mean to me.

Love Luca

Ian's heart broke for the child. He knew what it was like to suffer taunts at school, and Luca was such a special, innocent boy. So he was torn. Ian was a loyal man, but he was human. He was not immune to a young boy's cry for help, or to a 100 per cent pay rise, and if he was being honest the Annexe was getting him down. But there was Minty to think of as well, and Mr. and Mrs. Hawkins. They needed him too. He was just resolving to speak to Fernanda on the q.t. and let her know why it was impossible for him to accept when he heard footsteps behind him.

"Morning, Ian."

Ian jumped, the note still in his hand, and turned to see Tata standing at the door in sweatpants and a T-shirt, looking washed out.

"Here's your juice, Mrs. H.," said Ian. He handed her the glass of pale green liquid, for which she thanked him, then he rummaged through the cereal cupboard so he could surreptitiously hide Luca's note under a box of granola.

"Christ. That murderous dog last night." Tata's expression was grim as she sipped her drink. "What on earth am I going to say to Farmer Clarke? Two dead chickens! His prize pedigree bantams! I couldn't sleep a wink. I stayed up all night watching *White Lotus* and drinking neat vodka. I feel awful. My Kitchen Supper was an utter disaster."

"Mrs. Hawkins, *quite* the contrary. Don't do yourself down. Last night was a *triumph*."

Tata was now perched on a high stool by the counter and stared at Ian with bloodshot eyes. "I think you've gone mad. I can't show my face around here for a while."

"You have nothing to worry about," Ian countered. "The locals will talk about your Kitchen Sups as the most eventful evening in years. What could be duller than a dinner where nothing happens and all anyone talks about is their children's schools?"

"True," Tata replied, starting to look a little less despondent.

"Everyone wants excitement and gossip—and you provided oodles of it last night. And you've got an invitation to tea at Great Bottom Park this afternoon."

"There is that. And we might have found Selby her dream boyfriend," said Tata, brightening up a little.

"Success all round, if you ask me."

Then, looking anxious, Tata said, "But what about Farmer Clarke's bantams? What on earth shall we tell him?"

"Nothing. He'll never know the difference between the chickens he dropped off and the ones he is collecting. Same breed, same colour—arriving any moment from Daylesford. A simple swap. It's all sorted."

She was visibly relieved. "You're a lifesaver."

"And I've arranged for Miss de Sanchez to collect the dog shortly. I suggest you are out when she arrives. Luckily your weekly infrared detox in the thermal cabins at Estelle Manor is in an hour."

"Ugh, nooooo," Tata groaned. "I'm too hungover to move."

Ian shook his head. "I am banning you from the house while Miss de Sanchez is here. So you've got to go," he told her. He didn't think catfights were particularly ladylike.

"Suppose so." Tata slid down from the stool and turned to face the cupboards at the back of the counter, saying, "I fancy a bowl of granola."

Before Ian could stop her, she'd started opening the doors and then, after she'd peered into the cupboard and put her hand in to reach the cereal, she suddenly froze, staring ahead of her. Ian realised she must have seen Luca's note. He blanched as she took it out and read it.

"Mrs. Hawkins—" he began.

"Fernanda has no shame. Never did. Never will."

"I honestly wouldn't have—"

"Ian. I'm not blaming you for wanting this job," Tata said, turning to look at him. "It's a lot of money—"

"Well, it is, but I'm not thinking of—"

"Ian. I will not be outdone by Mrs. Ovington-Williams. I will pay you twice what Fernanda is offering."

"Maybe you're being a bit hasty, Mrs. H.?" Ian was beginning to feel terribly guilty. He would never have accepted the Ovington-Williamses' offer. "I mean, if Fernanda wants to pay me two hundred per cent of what I get now, and you want to pay me twice that, that's . . . well, that's a four hundred per cent raise."

"Exactly."

"Mr. Hawkins may think that's a little above inflation."

"But Bryan would never forgive me if I let you go. That really would be the end of the marriage. Do you know how impossible it is to get good staff now?"

"You've got a point," Ian concurred. He'd had so much trouble finding maids for the Manor he couldn't disagree with Mrs. H.

"Ian. You are a special talent. That's why Fernanda wants you. But even she is not going to offer you an eight hundred per cent raise. I'm pricing her out of the market." Tata had a new grit about her now. "Right, I'm going to Estelle Manor. I'll take it up with her there if need be. See you later."

With that, Tata crumpled up the letter, threw it in the bin and waltzed out of the room.

There was nothing that had divided the rural community in Oxfordshire quite as brutally as the arrival of Estelle Manor, the faux-rural outpost of the Mayfair members' club Maison Estelle, which catered to London's glitzy media elite. Any locals who'd been refused membership, and who now found themselves stuck in traffic behind the Beckham or Cowell security convoys, were pitted violently against the smug members who consisted mainly of exercise-mad, coffee-mad, black-Range-Rover-mad yummy mummies homesick for London, who visited the sixty-acre Cotswold compound on a near-daily basis.

Sophie, like many of her friends, had been completely desperate to become a founding member of the club when rumours of its imminent arrival had swirled around the Oxfordshire dinner-party circuit. It was an upscale take on Soho Farmhouse, which had opened a few years before, and Sophie was ready for something more luxurious and sophisticated. She had spent months sucking up to the membership secretary and had felt validated when she'd finally been invited to spend thousands of pounds to enrol herself and Hugh. When the club opened, it had seemed like a dream. Set in the rolling grounds of Eynsham Park, not far from the Bottoms, it was centred around a palatial nineteenth-century mansion that had once been an aristocratic family home. There was a lavish brasserie in the main house, a

Chinese restaurant in the old billiards room, a tented sushi bar, and a state-of-the-art beauty salon. The jewel in the crown was the Eynsham Baths, a three-thousand-square-foot spa which included five pools, ten treatment rooms, and the vast "tepidarium," a columned bathing hall in which Julius Caesar wouldn't have felt out of place.

All of the above were fabulous until Sophie actually tried to use them: the hairdresser was booked solid three months in advance; a mani-pedi was rarely available when she called; and the thing that she'd most been looking forward to—the swimming pools—were members-only, meaning she couldn't even invite a friend. Despite this, Sophie wouldn't have dreamed of giving up her members' card holder embossed with the word "FOUNDER" for anything. The Manor, as regulars called it, had become a vital part of her routine and social life. She would go a couple of times a week after school drop-off for a class or treatment and would invariably bump into friends. Coffee would follow, which sometimes turned into lunch and a swim, and then, well, it was already pick-up time. The day would have drifted by in a delightful haze of exercise, caffeine, and gossip. Sophie sometimes felt a little guilty after such days, and chastised herself for taking so much time away from her chintzes—especially given that being a (Very) Part-Time Working Mother was *so* important to her—but the feeling didn't usually last long.

Despite the late night after Tata's Kitchen Supper, Sophie had arrived at the Manor early to meet Fernanda and Tata for their weekly thermal cabin session. (Block-booked by Ian months ago.) She had found a sunny spot on the outdoor seating in the spa courtyard and ordered a hibiscus infusion and a plate of power balls to keep her going. She was feeling rather thrilled with herself: after getting home last night she'd stayed up for ages creating an invitation with all the details for the hack, and while she awaited her friends she sent it out on Paperless Post to her guests from her phone.

Just then, Fernanda arrived clad in a cropped white vest and high-waisted white hot pants that showed off her toned, sporty arms and legs to perfection. She greeted Sophie, sat down opposite her, and put her phone on the table which immediately pinged with the Paperless Post invitation.

"Ooh, one from you," said Fernanda. As a waiter approached she said, "Just a matcha green tea, please."

Fernanda tapped her phone and the invite opened on the screen. Sophie had found an old sepia photograph depicting three young women dressed in old-fashioned breeches and tweed jackets astride beautiful horses, and over this, in pale pink lettering, she had superimposed the words:

Please Come for

Sophie's Hack

then

Lunch Under the Apple Trees

at

The Rectory, Great Bottom

Saturday 22 May, 11 a.m.

R.S.V.P.

"What a pretty invite, Soph. You're always so original," cooed Fernanda as she read. "Riding with friends is such a nice idea—it's good to do something constructive together rather than just socialising for socialising's sake."

"But wasn't last night fun?"

Fernanda laughed. "It was *insane*—"

"*Ssshhhh*," Sophie hissed. "Tata's coming."

Fernanda looked up and waved at their friend and then said in a low voice, "I thought there was no way she'd make it today. She must be so hungover."

"Hi, guys," Tata said wearily before flopping down in the chair next to Sophie.

"I had such a great time last night, Tata," said Fernanda.

Tata looked at her dubiously and shook her head. "It was a disaster. But it was good to have you and Michael there. There's nothing like really good, *loyal* friends."

"We just want you to feel supported right now," said Sophie.

"I do. I *do*," Tata said, then smiled at Fernanda for long enough to unnerve her friend, before turning back to Sophie. "I just saw your Paperless Post. I'd love to join the hack."

"Wonderful," said Sophie. "Tata, Selby is great. So low-key and cool. Can't wait to see her house today at the tea."

"Nor me," said Fernanda.

"Come on," said Sophie, getting up from her seat. "We can't miss our appointment."

Tata didn't budge. "You go. I'm going to have a coffee and croissant," she said. "I'm too hungover to boil myself alive today. I'm just avoiding the house while Tallulah collects her dog. Oh, and Fernanda, quick thing—"

"Sure." Fernanda stood and looked quizzically at her.

"I hope you're bringing Luca to Selby's tea today. I know Ian would just *love* to see him."

"Er . . . sure," said Fernanda. As she walked off with Sophie, she said in a low voice, "What's up with Tata? She's being weird."

"I wouldn't worry," Sophie replied. "She's probably just feeling fragile after last night."

"Okay," said Fernanda dubiously. "Okay."

26

Tallulah de Sanchez treated the lanes of the Bottoms as though they were the bends of the Monaco Grand Prix, and by the time her convertible Audi Q8 skidded into the driveway of the Old Coach House, Charlene was feeling both afraid and carsick. The Glam Squad, though, seemed unperturbed. From the front passenger seat, Peter had recorded every moment, punctuating the journey with compliments like, "Your hair is *incred*. Wind. Love."

As she drew up outside the house, Tallulah stopped and put on the handbrake, allowed Peta to comb her windswept ponytail, and then waved at Peter's iPhone. "Hi, everyone," she squeaked excitedly. "We're here in the gorgeous British Cotswolds, at the place where they found Pikachu. I just can't wait to see him again. Follow me. Charlene, can you bring the lead and the bag of organic ethical dog treats, please?"

"No problem, Miss de Sanchez," said Charlene, clambering out of the car with the items. Meanwhile, Tallulah, who was now wearing a beaded minidress and high-heeled booties, beckoned the crew (and her followers) along as she tottered towards the front door. Before she got a chance to knock, though, it swung open and Ian appeared on the front steps.

"Miss de Sanchez? I'm Ian Palmer, Mrs. Hawkins's butler. Please, follow me."

Tallulah went to take a step towards the house, but Ian rapidly closed the door behind him, led her and her party to the other side of the driveway, and then through a narrow gap in the hedge. A few yards beyond it, they came to an enclosure fenced in with rabbit wire which had a wooden dog kennel at the far end.

"We had to put your dog in here," said Ian. "I'm afraid, Miss de Sanchez, that last night he killed two hens—"

"No!" gasped Tallulah. "That's simply not true. I don't believe it."

"I'm terrifically sorry, but there was no mistake. The dog was found with a dead chicken in its jaws. You'll have to do something. Once they've tasted blood, dogs keep killing."

"Peter, can you stop filming?" she ordered, putting her hand up.

"Yeah, sure," he said, lowering his phone.

Tallulah looked genuinely distraught. "Ian, you're not saying—saying—that, well, that he'll have to be put down?"

"Good lord, no. I'm sure it won't come to that," he reassured her. "Retrain, rehome, there are all sorts of other options."

Tallulah looked like she was about to faint, but Charlene intervened. "That dodgy vet in Chipping Norton will pull out all a dog's teeth for fifty quid so they can never kill anything again. Works a treat."

"*Ugh.*" Tallulah grimaced. "But I'd do anything to stop my dog being put to sleep. Anything."

"Right, let me open up," said Ian, unbolting the tall wooden gate into the grassy run.

Tallulah walked in, calling out, "Pikachu? Darling?"

Nothing.

"Peeks?" she called again. "Are you hiding from me, Peeks-Weeks?" she said, tapping the roof of the kennel.

Nothing.

Charlene looked at Ian, and he looked back at her, mystified. They followed Tallulah into the run and started pushing the grass to one side, hunting for the dog.

"Oh, dear," Charlene's face fell as she pointed at the corner of the fence. "Look."

Tallulah and Ian came closer and saw that a Pikachu-sized hole had been gnawed through the wire. Ian instinctively fished in his pocket and produced a freshly starched cotton handkerchief which he offered to Tallulah. She grabbed it and dashed out of the run, Peter and Peta disappearing with her through the gap in the hedge.

"I sense Miss de Sanchez is on the verge of a weep-a-thon," Ian told Charlene. "She must be heartbroken about her dog. It's really sad."

Moments later they heard the sound of Tallulah's car revving up and screeching out of the drive.

"What a mess, Ian," said Charlene, realising, among other things, that she had lost her ride back to the main house. "It's all been so difficult for Mr. Hawkins. He's very upset about Tata's dinner last night—"

"Marvellous result," interjected Ian.

"And Miss de Sanchez has been driving him batty."

"Excellent," said Ian coolly, strolling out of the run and closing the gate behind them.

Charlene looked at him. Sometimes he made no sense at all.

"The more trouble Tallulah is for Bryan the better," Ian said by way of explanation, sounding rather more confident about that than he really felt.

"Oh, Ian," Charlene cried, more mystified than ever. "Send me back to the pigsty."

"Get this right, Charlene, and Mrs. Hawkins will build your pigs a palace to rival Versailles. Trust me. Now, get yourself back up to the Manor and keep your eyes and ears about you. I'll call later."

※

Beneath his composed exterior, Ian had an emotional core that could wobble like jelly if provoked. Though he had seemed calm earlier, the truth was that the butler, as we know, was an animal lover and he hated the idea of a dog coming to grief even if it did belong to someone as aggravating as Tallulah de Sanchez. The thought of tiny, terrified Pikachu roaming the estate alone was almost more than he could bear. Things were starting to seem a bit of a strain and Ian's wits were rather closer to their end than he would have liked that morning.

On such occasions, Ian always sought the same solace: spending time with Boris. That Boris was dead and gone mattered less, dear reader, than you might imagine. Ian was a spiritual man, and he felt Boris's eternal presence deeply. A visit to St. Mary's of All the Angels in Great Bottom, and Boris's grand grave, would, he was sure, lift him. After all, he wanted to be on top form when he drove Mrs. H. up to Great Bottom Park this afternoon.

Having gathered a posy of lilacs and laurel from the kitchen garden at the Old Coach House, Ian departed mid-morning in his off-duty "mufti." This consisted of a chic combination of dark jeans, toffee-hued V-neck sweater, starched white shirt, and, of course, a pair of velvety soft, putty-coloured Gucci loafers. And so while Tata was torturing herself with thoughts of Fernanda's disloyalty, and Sophie and Fernanda were torturing themselves in the furnace-like heat of the infrared cabin at Estelle Manor, Ian was ambling beneath the medieval timber lychgate at the entrance to the churchyard and along the path to Boris's final resting place. Having solemnly laid his posy on Boris's grave, he soon found an Elysian spot under the ancient chestnut tree that shaded it and then spread out a chocolate-brown plaid rug next to it.

Sitting cross-legged on the rug, bathed in dappled light, Ian slowly closed his eyes, waiting for Boris to get in touch from above. He felt a gentle wind float across his face. Heard the delicate song of blue tits perched in the trees. But from Boris, there was nothing. A lone tear travelled down Ian's cheek. Heartache was never far away where Boris was concerned.

Ian sighed, feeling bleak: Boris was gone; Mrs. H. seemed to be crashing from one drama to another; his accommodations were far from ideal. He could only put on a brave face for so long.

"Oh, Boris," he said quietly. "If only you were still here, everything would be all right. You'd know what to do—"

Except! What was that? Something brushed against Ian's hand. He cracked open his left eye and was met by a glorious sight: the noble yet diminutively proportioned head of a blue-coated miniature dachshund, nuzzling him enthusiastically. The blue-grey coat, the satin-like texture—Ian gasped. Was this a miracle? Was the ghost of Boris here with him in the churchyard in his hour of need?

Now, Ian was generally a level-headed type. But on this occasion, he *almost* believed that Boris had come back from the dead—until he gingerly stretched out one hand to pat the ghost, and it jumped up on him and started licking his face. By the time Ian's peachy complexion was completely slathered with saliva, our hero knew this dachshund was *not* the ghost of Boris: Ian had trained his dog never to jump up on people and face-licking was an absolute no-no. Boris would never behave so badly.

"Pickle! Peanut! Hey, come here," a voice called out in an American accent, and Ian looked up to see a man jogging towards him, chasing another blue-coated miniature dachshund.

"Hey, I'm so sorry," he said as soon as he reached Ian. "Pickle can be a bit forward at times. Sorry to intrude."

"Not at all," said Ian, taking in every detail of the rather attractive man before him. He was tanned and tawny-haired, with hazel eyes. He was dressed in luxurious-looking jogging bottoms and a matching zip-up sweater of fine navy cashmere (which Ian immediately clocked as being Loro Piana, loungewear of the super-rich). His feet were clad in neon sneakers, which wouldn't have been Ian's first choice, but they worked. Kind of. "Actually, I thought your dog was my dog for a moment," he went on.

The man's face lit up. "You're not telling me you have a blue-coated miniature dachshund too? They're so rare."

"Did. He's buried there," Ian replied, pointing at Boris's grave.

"I'm sorry," said the American. "Splendid headstone, though."

"He deserved it," said Ian, getting up from the rug. "Boris was my life until a few weeks ago. I'm still devastated. But I come and visit him whenever I can."

"Might you get another?"

Ian shook his head. "I can't imagine it yet. I still can't even believe he's really gone."

"I get it," said the American kindly.

"Thanks. Cute doggie names," Ian went on.

"I wanted to call them Calvin and Kelly after the Kleins but my daughters wouldn't let me. Said it was too pretentious."

"They're not wrong," Ian laughed, his mood lifting. How unexpected to meet a cashmere-clad fashion maven in the churchyard. Perhaps he'd found a *simpatico* new friend today.

"Sorry," said the man, "I should have introduced myself. I'm Doug. Douglas Fairfax."

Ian could barely contain himself—but he did, of course. *This* was Selby's former husband? He should have guessed from the accent, but the near-Boris experience had disoriented him.

"I'm Ian Palmer. Nice to meet you," he said. "So, what brings you to our lovely church?"

"I just came out for a walk. I'm staying with my ex-wife Selby for a few days, visiting my daughters. They all live at the big old house up the road."

"I know it," Ian said. "I work for a friend of Mrs. Fairfax, Mrs. Hawkins. I'm driving her up there for tea later."

"Great—it'll be nice to see a friendly face. Rescue me if my ex is giving me an earful, will you?" said Doug. "I'm terrified of her right now. She's furious with me."

"In my experience, most husbands are terrified of their wives and most wives are furious with their husbands, whatever their legal status."

Doug chuckled. "So true. I've just got to focus on my daughters while I'm here, and ignore everything else. Although . . ." He trailed off, looking suddenly downcast.

"Are you all right?" asked Ian.

"Yup. Sure. It's just . . . I have a feeling Selby might have met someone over here."

Ian was startled. Selby had fallen for Antoni *already*? That was a turn-up for the books. Mrs. H. would be thrilled when he reported the news back to her.

"Commiserations," he replied.

"No, it's absurd that I'm upset. I mean, I've had other partners since we broke up. Why shouldn't she?"

"I'm not surprised her having a boyfriend is getting to you. Marriage seems so complicated. That's why I stick with dogs."

"Hey, stop it. There's someone for everyone. You're cute," said Doug, blushing just a bit as he added, "Has anyone ever told you, you look just like Colin Firth in *A Single Man*?"

Crumbs, thought Ian, was Doug flirting with him? He was not the sort of butler who overstepped staff–client boundaries, and Doug Fairfax was definitely client-level. Despite his charms, Ian was certainly not going to flirt back.

"I'll take your word for it," he replied politely.

There was a long pause and then Doug ventured, "Very nice pair of shoes you've got there."

"I collect them," Ian said, happy for the change in topic. "I've got pairs going back to the 1960s. In fact, I'm lending all of them to the Savannah College of Art and Design for their Gucci retrospective next year."

"Nice," said Doug. "I'm in the shoe business."

"Sounds glamorous," Ian remarked.

"It isn't. It used to be fun and now it just feels like a lot of pressure. I haven't had a good idea in months and the New York office is going nuts. I promised I'd sketch new lines on the plane and all I did was watch some horrible true-crime series." Doug shook his head, downcast. "SneakersDirect was visionary once, but everyone's copying it. Can't think of anything cool now."

"LoafersDirect?" quipped Ian, clicking his heels together jauntily and cocking his head to one side.

"What?" said Doug.

"LoafersDirect," he repeated.

Doug looked intrigued. "That's . . . an idea . . . at least a germ of an idea. Our technology could be modified to deliver a loafer that's as comfy as a sneaker . . ." He began pacing excitedly under the chestnut tree. "I'm going to go back to the house, I'll start doodling, see if there's anything there."

And with that, Doug, Pickle, and Peanut took their leave of Ian, who had—just for a moment—forgotten about Boris.

27

Charlene wasn't one to judge, but the more she'd seen of Tallulah de Sanchez, the surer she felt that the girl would never, ever have made it in the agricultural world. For a start, her nails were too long to milk a cow without piercing an udder, and secondly, she simply didn't possess a work ethic in the conventional sense. As if further proof of the latter were needed, when Charlene arrived back at the Manor from the Old Coach House, she found Tallulah slumped tearfully on a bench in the hall, with Peter and Peta looking on helplessly.

As she attempted to tiptoe past to reach the office and get on with some filing, a lean arm emerged from the sobbing heap and grabbed her leg. The grip, enhanced by Tallulah's trapeze classes, was vice-like. She was not going to let Charlene get away now.

"Char. We've got to enlist Bryan in the search for Pikachu." Tallulah sat up, snivelling. "Peter and Peta, I think we should call it a day. I can't be filmed like this."

Looking relieved, the pair disappeared off to pack up their things and go.

"Mr. H. is working, Miss," Charlene explained. "He can't be disturbed."

She didn't know what to do. When she had first started her job at the Manor, Ian had directed her to a sign on Bryan's office door which read DO NOT DISTURB UNLESS YOU ARE DEAD. He'd made it quite clear this was to be taken literally, unless it involved his beloved Minty, who could break every rule in the book as far as her dad was concerned.

"I only need two minutes with him, Charlene. Please?" Tallulah pleaded, dabbing her cheek with the handkerchief Ian had given her.

Charlene felt some pity for the girl, imagining that if it had been one of her precious piglets in Pikachu's place, she would have felt exactly the same. She gestured at Tallulah to follow her to Bryan's office. "Just let me talk to him first," she warned as they walked.

When Charlene knocked on Bryan's door, she heard him call, "Yup," and she popped her head into the room.

"Miss de Sanchez would like to see you."

"Is she dead?"

"In her heart," Charlene said.

"Oh Christ," Bryan said, and sighed. "Can it wait till tonight? I'm about to get on a Zoom with Beijing and then I've got a pile of P and L reports to deal with."

"Of course—" started Charlene. But she was soon interrupted.

"Bry! Bry!" called Tallulah from behind her.

Bryan rolled his eyes at his PA, then mouthed, "I'm too bloody busy."

Charlene could do nothing as Tallulah pushed past her and threw herself onto the high-gloss leather chesterfield at the far end of the office.

"It's Peeks. He wasn't at the Old Coach House. He's run away."

"Tallulah, I've got a lot to get through today," Bryan replied, glancing at his daunting in-tray. "Can we discuss this later?"

"Later?" Tallulah blurted. "Peeks could have been run over by then. Or stolen. Do you know how much they get for lemon-coated Teacups on the black market?"

His eyes glazed over and his voice took on a sceptical tone. "The people round here have got better things to do than steal your dog. Has he got a tag on his collar with your number on it?"

"Of course," replied Tallulah.

"Then someone will find him, they'll call you, it will all be fine. Won't it, Charlene?"

Charlene nodded. "Yes. Now, why don't we go and put a notice in the village shop? Maybe one of the locals has seen him," she said. Anything to get the girl out of the house and away from Mr. H.

Tallulah ignored her. "You're really hurting me, you know, Bryan."

Charlene noticed Bryan was starting to look uneasy. "Tallulah, no one is trying to hurt you, least of all me. I just want a return on my investment."

"If you'd read my Miami Swim Week talk, you wouldn't say things like that," said Tallulah defensively, her face reddening. "You just don't understand the insane pressure of being a highly successful female entrepreneur."

"Tallulah, if you'd calm down a bit about yourself, you'd do great in business," Bryan said, his patience waning. "Your talk is on my list to read tonight. I promise. And don't worry, Charlene will find your dog."

"Pinkie promise me, Bryan," ordered Tallulah, getting up from the chesterfield and offering him her little finger. Bryan reached over his desk and reluctantly linked his pinkie with hers, rolling his eyes at Charlene.

Tallulah finally smiled. "Okay. I'm going for a soak in the hot tub. I get all my best ideas in there."

***

Once Tallulah was out of earshot, Bryan beckoned Charlene into the office and gestured for her to close the door.

"Why is she behaving like a wounded girlfriend? Saying she's 'hurt'? Charlene, deliver me from this purgatory."

"Let's get a second opinion," she said. She knew about pigs, not temperamental bikini designers. She put the office phone on speaker and dialled.

Ian's sing-song tones soon rippled down the line. "Mr. Hawkins. How may I assist?"

"I can't go on," Bryan said desperately.

"With what?"

"With*out* Tata and Minty."

"Of course you can't," replied Ian.

"Nor can I," added Charlene.

"And nor can she," Ian told them. "Sir, I do not think I would be speaking out of turn if I were to tell you that Mrs. Hawkins is very keen to be reinstalled at the Manor."

"Really?" Bryan said. "Well, why doesn't she beg me to take her back, then?"

"She's thinking the same thing, as far as I can gather."

"I don't follow."

"She thinks you're the one who needs to do the begging."

"But she was the one who left!" exclaimed Bryan.

"True. But she seems to think there was a good reason for her to leave. Something to do with a piece of jewellery?"

"Oh, that," sighed Bryan. "Those diamonds cost me a fortune, and my marriage, by the looks of things. Ian, I need your help. You understand Tata better than anyone."

"My gut instinct is that it will require a bended knee, sir, both literally and metaphorically," Ian told him.

Bryan frowned at Charlene and then at the phone. "Really?"

"And the diamonds . . ."

He looked sheepish. "Ah, those . . ."

"If I don't know the truth about this mysterious jewellery situation, I can't help you. Spill the beans, sir."

Bryan reddened as he said, "Look, it's Tata's birthday coming up in a few weeks. Don't tell anyone but it's the big four-oh."

Ian nodded. "I am aware."

"Of course you are. Anyway, you know and I know that Tata wouldn't want anyone to know that she's going to be forty." Bryan paused and looked at Charlene. "Don't tell a soul."

"My lips are sealed, Mr. H.," she reassured him.

"At the same time, I know she'd be devastated if she didn't receive a present of . . . significance. I secretly ordered her a suite of emeralds and diamonds from Bulgari on Bond Street. Very blingy, just how she likes things. Anyway, it was a special commission, not ready for months. So I paid for it, then Tata saw the invoice, and started asking me what it was, and I wanted to keep the jewels a secret till her fortieth, not even *mention* forty, so I told her it was a little present for Gertrude, my accountant, who's retiring."

"Oh dear," lamented Ian.

"I've been a fool," whimpered Bryan. "Tata said that Gertrude wouldn't have anyplace to wear diamonds—which is true—and that she could tell I was lying—also true. She thought I was lying about an affair. Me! An affair! We had a row and, as you well know, she left. And you left too, Ian, which is just as bad, frankly."

"I take that as a great compliment," Ian replied.

"And Minty. I miss her so much, bothering me in the office or wanting to play Scrabble after school. It's awful only seeing her now and again."

"Where is the jewellery now?"

"In the Bulgari workshops being finished in time for Tata's birthday. I'm still going to give it to her, come what may. I love her as much now as I did the first time I saw her dancing on the bar at Matthew Freud's New Year's Eve party all those years ago!"

"May I make a suggestion?"

"This is what I've been praying for. Please do, Ian."

"Collect the suite as soon as it is ready. Keep it safe at the Manor. Do not mention our conversation to a soul."

"Roger that."

"Meanwhile, you and I and Charlene will secretly arrange a *fabulous* surprise birthday party for Mrs. Hawkins at the Manor, to which I will safely deliver her on the night, and at which, having practised your lunges, you will athletically go down on bended knee—"

"My orthopaedist will kill me—"

"Nothing less will do, I'm afraid. As I said, you must at least attempt to go down on bended knee, offer Tata the wonderful gift, declare undying love, and implore her to come home, in front of all your friends and neighbours."

"Sounds like a lot of begging to me," Bryan protested.

"Just the medicine required," Ian told him. "And, Charlene, it's your job to keep Miss de Sanchez out of the way and in the dark about all of this."

"Shouldn't be too difficult," said Charlene. "Tallulah doesn't think about anyone except herself anyway."

28

"Why aren't we going home, Mummy?" Minty asked her mother from the back seat of the car.

It was half past four, and Ian and Tata had just picked Minty up from school. Instead of going back to the Old Coach House, Ian had just driven them through the unfamiliar gates of Great Bottom Park.

"We're going to a lovely tea party at Selby's," Tata replied, a newly jovial air about her after a lymphatic drainage massage that afternoon had finally rid her of the prior night's toxins.

"Can't we go and see Daddy instead?" Minty asked. "I haven't seen him for days."

"How about tomorrow?" suggested Tata. "I can't cancel Selby now."

"I'm *so tired* from sport, Mummy," complained Minty, who was using her bag of games kit as a makeshift pillow on which to rest her head.

"You won't feel tired when we get there," Tata assured her. "There's some really nice kids to play with. Eddie Thompson's coming."

"He's weird."

"Well, guess who lives there? That cool new girl in your class, Tess Fairfax."

"She's not cool."

"Fine," said Tata, giving up. Minty was clearly not interested in helping her mother to restore her position as Queen of the Bottoms. And why should she be? Tata had to ask herself.

Ever the diplomat, Ian was keen to bring a speedy halt to the mother–daughter dispute. "There's a lollipop in the armrest for you, Minty," he said.

"Yummy," said the little girl, finally placated once she'd found it.

As they drove he remarked, "I have some *very* interesting news to impart, Mrs. H."

"Oh?" Tata asked.

"I have it on good authority that Mrs. Fairfax and Mr. Grigorivich have fallen for each other."

Tata was amazed. "Already?"

"It sounds like something happened last night," he said.

"What?" asked Minty from behind them, suddenly all ears.

"Nothing, darling," said Tata. Then she whispered to Ian, "How do you know all this?"

"Sources at the church, is all I can say," he replied mysteriously.

"Don't think I'm getting carried away," Tata continued, her excitement palpable, "but I can imagine them married, can't you?"

"Oh yes," said Ian.

"And guess who will get all the credit for finding Selby the most incredible husband?" Tata smiled. "*Moi*—"

Before she could go on, there was a yelp from the back of the Bentley.

"Owwww," Minty squealed as the car lurched from side to side as Ian tried to avoid a deep pothole in the drive. "It's so bumpy."

"Sorry," said Ian. "Look, we're just coming up to the house. I promise you'll like it."

As the silvered stone facade came into view, Minty clambered up between the front seats and gazed through the windscreen with an "oooooh." Even she was not immune to the grandeur and beauty of Great Bottom Park: a ramble of lilac-hued roses were just starting to flower among the branches of white wisteria on the stonework, and in the broad, old beds below the windows, drifts of creamy peonies and foxgloves peeked from between woody thickets of rosemary and lavender, and clematis crawled, jungle-like, up and around clouds of overgrown box hedge. Ian soon pulled up on the gravel driveway and whizzed round to the passenger side of the car to open Mrs. Hawkins's door.

"Why is their garden so messy, Mummy?" asked Minty as she clambered out of the back seat and looked around.

"Sssshhhh," Tata scolded her daughter. "They probably haven't had time to prune it yet."

"Actually, Minty, this was Lady Maud's design. She's the lady who used to live here," Ian said. "She was a really talented gardener. It's very posh to let your garden run riot. Only bourgeois people like me prefer everything neat and tidy."

Tata winced. Her garden at the Manor was arranged in neat squares and straight lines, not a leaf or blade of grass out of place, and the knot garden resembled a pie chart from one of Bryan's PowerPoints. But Ian seemed to be implying that it was bourgeois. That *she* was bourgeois. Tata made her mind up there and then that when she finally moved back to the Manor, the whole horrible "neat" scheme would be ripped out. It was so out of date. *She* was so out of date. Tata wanted to be posh, and she could be—if she had the correct level of aesthetically pleasing mess in her garden. If only Selby Fairfax didn't have a two-year waiting list, she rued, Tata could be posh *now*.

At least she was correctly dressed for today, she consoled herself. Guided by Selby's casual appearance at supper last night, Tata had resisted the daytime bling in her wardrobe and chosen a simple white cotton smocked top, fringed denim shorts frayed at the cuffs and plain gold hoop earrings. The only logo she'd succumbed to was the gold F on the side of her Fendi sneakers, which were the most understated option in her daytime shoe collection.

Just then, Sophie pulled into the driveway in—what was that? The brand-new, electric *Porsche Taycan*? Tata couldn't believe her eyes. Where was the grotty Hyundai she always drove? She spotted Fernanda in the front passenger seat. Luca and Eddie were in the back together.

"I think Fernanda knows that I know," Tata said to Ian, eyebrows raised.

"Knows what, Mummy?" asked Minty.

"Nothing, darling," Tata said brightly, then whispered to Ian, "I could tell when I was talking to her at Estelle Manor this morning. She had guilt written all over her face. But she's *acting* as if she doesn't know that I know."

"In my professional opinion," said Ian, speaking very quietly, "I suggest the simplest thing is to play along for now. Act as if you know that she's acting as if she doesn't know that you know, and she will know that you know and admire you for not saying that you know."

Tata gave him a blank look.

"Trust me. All's well that ends well if one resists the temptation for a teatime brawl. Meantime, I will find a private moment to discuss Luca's letter with Fernanda and tell her that I must politely decline 'his' offer. I will, indirectly, leave her in no doubt that I know that the letter was designed by her, if written in Luca's innocent hand. After all, what eight-year-old would take the initiative to poach an employee?"

"Hi, Tata," called Sophie, stepping out of the huge, shiny Porsche.

Tata walked over to her, grinning. "What the hell happened? I *never* thought Hugh would buy you a nice car."

"He didn't," Sophie replied wryly. Clearly inspired by Selby too, she was dressed as though she had come from a riding lesson in plaid jodhpurs, Schnieder boots, and a navy T-shirt. "But he's in London today, so I decided to take *his* new car out for a spin. He'll never know."

"It's so cool inside," said Eddie, emerging from the back seat with Luca.

Meanwhile Fernanda got out of the car and strolled round to Tata. Like her friends, she had dressed informally, in pale grey cotton dungarees, a Liberty print blouse and Greek sandals. She kissed Tata on both cheeks, and following Ian's instructions, Tata received her embrace with a level of warmth and graciousness she did not feel.

"Hi, Minty," Eddie said.

"Why don't we explore the house?" Minty asked, conveniently forgetting she had dissed Eddie as "weird" a few minutes before. "Luca, come too?"

"I don't want to, I'll get lost," he whined anxiously, grabbing his mother's hand and holding it so tight his knuckles went white. Then, spotting Ian and the Bentayga, he said, "Unless Ian will come."

"He's working, honey," Fernanda told her son firmly. "Just stay with me."

"I'm sure Ian wouldn't mind—" started Tata.

Fernanda shook her head. "Luca's fine with me," she snapped, which left Tata feeling more confused than ever about her friend's devious intentions.

Minty and Eddie ran off together towards the house, where they were seemingly swallowed up by the enormous stone porch. Moments later, Antoni Grigorivich arrived in the driveway at the wheel of a sporty blue Tesla.

"Good afternoon, Sophie, Fernanda," said Antoni, approaching them after he'd parked. "Marvellous seeing you again." Then to Tata's surprise, he strolled up to her, took her hand in his, and brushed his lips across the tops of her fingers. "What a stunning dinner yesterday! What a spectacular woman you are!"

Tata laughed, taken aback. "My Kitchen Supper was a mess and I'm in my beach-bum clothes today, but if you're offering a compliment, Antoni, who am I to turn it down? Come on, let's go inside and see Selby."

"Ah, Selby," echoed Antoni. "What an impressive character. So fascinating, so beautiful—like you, Tata."

"Hey, what about us?" said Fernanda, pulling a sad face and pointing at herself and Sophie.

"You are all remarkable if you are friends of Tata," Antoni told them obligingly.

A figure soon appeared in the shadow of the porch. It was Goodsen, the elderly butler, who had, upon hearing that a tea party was being thrown at the Park for the first time in fifteen years, deigned to don his black coat and pinstripe trousers and help Doreen serve the tea. The little group drifted towards the doorway and when they reached him, Goodsen said in the solemn tones of one delivering a eulogy,

"Ladies and gentlemen, welcome to the seat of the Earls of Bottom. Please, come with me and I will escort you to the drawing room."

Tata had never seen a drawing room quite as grand, or as threadbare, as the one at Great Bottom Park. As she and the other guests followed Goodsen in, her eyes drifted up to the intricate strapwork on the ceiling and the two chandeliers which hung from it, glinting in the afternoon light. She shuddered when she noticed that they were laced with cobwebs. The panelled walls, painted decades ago in a dusky rose colour that was sun-bleached in parts, were dense with oil paintings, most of them dark with age, and the room was so sprawling that it fit both large sofas and small sofas, occasional chairs and armchairs, side chairs and side tables, cabinets, writing desks, and even an old rocking horse. There was a grand piano at the far end, crowded with black-and-white family photographs and piles of sheet music, and an elaborate marble fireplace at the other, dancing with crackling flames, above which hung a portrait of the First Earl of Bottom on a splendid chestnut horse. Tall, arched windows, framed with heavy, fringed ivory curtains, looked out onto a balustraded stone terrace, and a pair of double doors had been thrown open to it. Maybe, Tata thought to herself, this was what that Manderley place was like. She'd ask Ian later.

Selby, somewhat dwarfed by her surroundings, was tending to a vase of flowers when her guests arrived and as she heard them coming in, turned to wave hello and walked over to greet everyone. Tata quickly registered, to her dismay, that Selby was not kitted out in some kind of ultra-casual sports gear, but in a long flowing djellaba of paisley silk. Her feet were clad in jewelled sliders, she had an amethyst cocktail ring on her left hand, and she looked somehow insouciant and outrageously glamorous at the same time. No wonder Antoni had already fallen for her. Tata felt like she wanted to shrivel up and die, sartorially speaking. Why-oh-why had she come in these revolting shorts? She had closets rammed with £3,000 floaty silk garments and here she was looking like she'd shopped at the Gap. *Quel* disaster. Still, she had to show a fighting spirit, so as Selby kissed her hello, she said, "You look incredible, Selby."

"After my wardrobe error last night, I thought I'd better up my game," she replied with a grin. "Come on, let's grab something to eat."

Selby led the party to the end of the room near the piano where Doreen had laid on a tea of such magnificence that it would have put the head chef at the Ritz to shame. A large, round table had been laid up with a heavily embroidered white linen tablecloth, white napkins, and a tall, cut-glass vase tumbling with orange blossom from the garden. The Bottom family's Victorian tea service, which consisted of a forty-piece set of porcelain intricately painted with the Earl's crest encircled with honeysuckle, was arranged to one side. There were little silver toast racks filled with wafer-thin slices of white toast with the crusts cut off, platters of shortbread, piles of hot-buttered crumpets, silver dishes of jam tarts, gingerbread, flapjacks, rock cakes, sausage rolls, and cucumber sandwiches. Positioned on various cake stands were a Swiss roll dusted with icing sugar, a Victoria sponge topped with strawberries and whipped cream, and Doreen's speciality, the peculiarly named Dundee mincemeat cake. A trolley laden with pots of China tea, kept warm with old-fashioned quilted tea cosies, was Goodsen's territory and from here he poured cup after cup for the guests from a great height, to aerate the drink correctly.

The children were soon enthusiastically digging into the feast— even Luca managed to let go of his mother's hand to indulge—while the grown-ups took their tea and went to sit by the fire. Cup in hand, Tata moseyed around the room, gawping at every delicious detail, and eventually headed towards the fireplace to join the others. She decided to settle herself on one of the inviting-looking chintz armchairs close to it but as she sank onto its down cushion, she was quickly submerged in a cloud of dust. She felt a tickle in her throat. She coughed to try and clear it. More tickling. She coughed again.

Then again. At this point Antoni put his teacup on the mantelpiece and came over.

"Let me get you some water," he said, looking down at her, concerned.

"Ugg-ggg-uuuggg—I'm-fff-fine-uggh," Tata croaked.

"I insist." He went and fetched her a glass of water, which she gratefully sipped when he returned. Antoni was so considerate, mused Tata. Such nice manners. He was perfect husband material for Selby. Lucky her.

Next Selby came over. "Are you okay?" she asked.

Tata's cough had abated. "I'll survive," she said, getting up from the lethal chair.

"I'm sorry about the dust," Selby went on. "It's out of control. I'm on major antihistamines until we get it taken care of."

"But that's what makes it so special here, Selby," said Sophie, glancing at the particles twinkling in the shafts of afternoon light. "The untouched grandeur. It reminds me of my parents' drawing room in Yorkshire. It was just like this."

Typical Sophie, thought Tata, pulling an aristo flex on Selby.

"It's a very romantic room," agreed Selby, plopping down onto the sofa next to Sophie.

"Romance," declared Antoni, "is all, is it not?"

"Absolutely." Tata winked at Antoni, whose expression was blissful. He was clearly besotted.

"Speaking of 'romance,'" Selby interjected drily, "my ex-husband showed up here this morning, completely unannounced."

"What?" said Tata. An ex-husband was not part of the plan.

Fernanda, who had found herself a spot on a cushioned stool by the fireplace, and had Luca sitting cross-legged at her feet with a plate of cake in front of him, asked, "Absolutely no warning at all?"

"Total surprise. Doug's actually on his way back here now with the girls—he's picking them up from school today."

Tata thought fast. The last thing she wanted was Selby's ex-husband wrecking this blossoming love story before it got a chance.

"Why don't you take Antoni on a tour of the house, Selby, and we'll wait here for Doug and the girls?" she suggested.

"That sounds fun—" started Selby.

Before she could continue, Pickle and Peanut had scampered into the room, prompting *oohs* and *aahhhs* from the assembled crowd. Violet and Tess pottered after the dogs, and behind them, Doug appeared.

"Mom! It's so cool, Dad's here," Tess squealed, grinning from ear to ear. "And the doggies!"

Tata noticed that Violet seemed less impressed. Frowning, she gave her mother a look as if to say, "You could have warned us." Selby raised both hands in the air to telegraph, "I didn't know either."

"Girls, Doreen's made a massive tea. Grab some treats and then go outside and play with the other kids."

"'Kay," said Tess, then noticed Luca sitting with his mom. "Want to come too?" she asked him.

The little boy smiled and got up and followed Tess, to Fernanda's happy surprise. Violet, meanwhile, gave her mother another look. "I'm a bit old to 'play,' Mom. I'm going to read on the terrace."

Selby nodded and introduced Doug to her guests, after which a tricky pause ensued where no one quite knew what to say. It was broken only when Sophie said, "Adorable dogs you've got." She held out her hand to Peanut, who came and licked her fingers enthusiastically.

"I love 'the Sausages,' as the girls call them," said Doug. "They've really missed having the kids to play with." Goodsen handed him a cup of tea and he sat down. "Such loyal animals, dogs. I am looking forward to meeting Josh."

"Swoon!" said Fernanda, dramatically drawing her hand across her brow.

"He's so handsome," Sophie confirmed.

Doug looked enquiringly at Selby. "Where is he?"

"Oh, um . . . Josh . . ." Selby began. Her voice seemed strained. "He's, you know, around, somewhere . . . Now, how about that tour of the house, Antoni?" she asked, quickly standing up.

"Yes, please," he replied. "I'm so curious."

Selby seemed extremely keen to be alone with Antoni, Tata noticed. It was adorable.

"May I join in?" asked Sophie. "I've heard so much about the interior architecture here but never visited—"

"No!" Tata nearly shouted, giving Sophie a look. "You and I and Fernanda need to watch the kids. And Doug."

"Oh. Yes, sure. Don't worry," Sophie said, but seemed disappointed.

"Thanks," said Doug. "I'm so jet-lagged I'm not sure I'm much good for childcare today."

"Shall we go out and find them?" said Tata. She looked at Fernanda and added pointedly, "I do want to make sure little Luca's okay, don't you?"

Before anyone could leave the drawing room, a fearful scrabbling noise came from beneath an armchair by the fireplace and Pickle and Peanut started barking.

Doug looked startled. "What was that?"

"Ugh," Tata gulped, pointing. "There's something under there."

The assembled party watched in horror as a furry tail poked out from under the frilled loose cover on the chair and then suddenly disappeared. The sausage dogs, yapping wildly, attempted to go after it but Doug grabbed their collars and stopped them.

"Is that a rat?" hollered Fernanda, climbing up onto the sofa.

"I am so sorry, everyone," said Selby, mortified, but sensibly hopping up next to Fernanda.

Next, the group heard a snuffling sound and a small, black, wet nose appeared from beneath the frill. Then the body of a tiny dog followed: a fluffy, lemon-coated Teacup Pomeranian.

"What on earth—?" said Tata, recognising Pikachu. What was the hen-killing machine from last night doing in Selby's drawing room?

"Selby," Doug exclaimed, bursting out laughing. He released the sausage dogs, who started sniffing at the canine interloper, who snarled at them warily. "I cannot believe you got a Teacup. Josh! Josh-ie! Here, boy," he said, making a kissing sound with his lips and holding out his hand. The little dog ran up to Doug, who began fussing over it.

"Erm, well . . . he's so . . . cute," began Selby. "Josh," she said, picking up Pikachu. "You should be . . . um . . . in the kitchen. Come on, I'll take you back."

Selby started for the door, leaving Tata, Sophie, and Fernanda completely confused about what was going on. But, just as she did so, Josh dashed into the room. He looked concerned.

"Josh?" blurted Selby, without thinking.

"Josh?" repeated Doug, looking at the stable lad, and then back at the dog in Selby's arms.

"Um . . ." stuttered Selby.

"Why is everyone around here named Josh?" Doug went on.

"They're not," said Tata.

"They're not?" repeated Doug.

Looking baffled, Josh said, "Sorry to interrupt, Mrs. Fairfax, but one of the girls' competition horses is looking very poorly. Maple's covered in bumps all over her hindquarters. Looks like we may need to call the vet."

"Let me look at her first," said Selby, clearly keen to extricate herself.

"Good idea," Doug said. Then, extending a hand towards Josh, he went on, "Hey, sorry. Let me introduce myself. I'm Doug Fairfax, Violet and Tess's dad."

Josh visibly whitened. He looked at Selby, who avoided his eye, and then mumbled, "Doug—Mr. Fairfax. Excellent to meet you. I'm Josh Hall."

"I gathered," said Doug curtly.

"Right, let's go and see the horse," said Selby to Josh. "Here, take *Josh*," she added, handing Doug the Pomeranian.

"Aw, Josh," said Doug, cuddling the little canine.

"Josh?" asked Tata, ever more confused.
"Yes," said Josh.
"Not you," said Tata.
"Who——?" Josh started.
"Josh, we need to go," Selby interrupted brusquely. "Everyone, enjoy the tea. I'll be back as soon as I can."

A few miles away at Monkton Bottom Manor, Charlene was delivering a late-afternoon snack to Tallulah in the suede-lined "snug." A bowl of watery cabbage broth and sliver of hazelnut bread had to be brought religiously every day to wherever she was "designing" to keep her going. "Designing," as far as Charlene could tell, meant cutting and pasting cool pictures of cool people in cool bikinis off cool websites and sending them to the factory in China to copy.

But today even Tallulah's version of designing was not happening: the girl was languishing miserably on the enormous chaise that Tata had bought Bryan as their tenth wedding anniversary gift from Soane, still in her robe from the hot tub earlier. She was oblivious to the "Jingle Bells" melody coming from the phone which had been tossed on the floor.

"Your phone's going, Miss," said Charlene.
"I can't talk to anyone. I'm too upset about Peeks."
"Why don't I get it?" Charlene asked, putting the broth on a side table.
"It's some notification. Just switch it off, please." Tallulah sat up and scowled at the bowl of broth.
"Of course," Charlene said.
Picking up the phone, she glanced at the screen. The "Find My" icon was flashing. She tapped on it, the "Jingle Bells" melody stopped, and Charlene let out a whoop of joy.
"Miss! 'Find My' has found Pikachu."

Tallulah snatched the phone from Charlene. Her dog's photograph had pinged up on the "Find My" app.

"No way! My phone's picked up the tracker. It's saying it's at Great Bottom Park," she cried, staring at the live map that had appeared on the screen. "Charlene. I'm going to change. Meet you outside Bryan's office in fifteen minutes and make sure your phone's fully charged. I need you to film everything. Wish I hadn't sent the Glam Squad home."

Charlene stood at the entrance to Bryan's office praying he wouldn't ask her why Tallulah was interrupting him yet again today if she wasn't dead.

"Hey, Boobie," Tallulah called out to Bryan, leaning seductively against the doorframe.

Bryan glanced up from his desk. He seemed relieved that the distraught Tallulah from earlier had vanished, although the sultry siren that she had morphed into was almost as alarming: Tallulah was now dressed as though she was going to Loulou's for a night out, in a ruched red tubedress and high-heeled, open-toed black "sock-boots." Her long dark hair slunk around her left shoulder, and she had three large TALLULAHSWIM shopping bags with her.

"You look very, er . . . dressy," Bryan told her. "Going somewhere?"

"Brand Tallulah is ready," declared the self-styled entrepreneur.

"And where is Brand Tallulah off to this afternoon, may I ask?"

"Great Bottom Park."

He seemed surprised. "I didn't know you'd met the new lady of the manor?"

"I haven't yet. But I've got the perfect in: I think Pikachu's there. I'm going to pick him up, have a snoop around the place, introduce myself to that rich American woman, and do some product placement," Tallulah said, tapping the shopping bags. "You know me, Bry," she added as she turned to go, "always working, always working."

"Maple's going to be fine," said Selby, coming back into the drawing room a bit later, looking more relaxed. "It's a skin infection but we've got some antibiotics that will take care of it."

"That's a relief," said Doug. Tallulah's dog was now snoozing peacefully in his arms.

"All right, puppy?" asked Selby, stroking Pikachu affectionately.

"He's a real cutie," said Doug.

Tata watched from a little way away. She'd had quite enough of Tallulah's dog by this point and wished it would disappear. Just as she was thinking that perhaps it was time for her and Minty to leave, a voice could be heard calling from the corridor beyond, "Peeks! Peeeekie-Weeekie!"

The dog awoke, startled, and leaped from Doug's arms. Moments later, Tallulah de Sanchez waltzed into the drawing room, carrying three TALLULAHSWIM bags like the one Minty had been given at the fete. Tata felt herself freeze. Here, finally, was the woman she dreaded. She might have been tacky but she exuded a youthful sexiness that Tata found threatening. The little dog sprinted up to her and started biting at her heels and jumping up on her. Charlene came in behind the entrepreneur, looking mortified when she saw that the roomful of people included Tata. "Sorry," she mouthed at her apologetically. Tata simply shrugged her shoulders back at her.

"Oh, honey," cooed Tallulah, dropping the bags on the floor and scooping up the dog to give him a kiss. "I thought you were dead. Charlene, quick, photo!" she went on, flashing a huge smile. Seeming embarrassed, Charlene obliged.

Next, Tallulah looked at Selby and the other guests and said, "I am so sorry to interrupt your party. I'm Tallulah de Sanchez—"

"I love your bikinis," blurted out an excited Violet who had just strolled back into the room for a second helping of Doreen's cake. "I'm Violet, by the way."

Tallulah smiled at her. "Well, Violet, it's your lucky day, because I brought some swag for you," she said, tucking her dog under one arm and handing the teen one of the shopping bags. She offered the other two to Selby.

"Thank you but—" started Selby.

"No, I *insist*," said Tallulah. "One for you and one for your youngest. I'm just so grateful the tracker brought me here, to my doggie-woggie. Oh, I love Pikachu you, yes, I do. *I do, I do, I do do do*," she went on to the furball in her hands. "I owe you, Selby, I really do, for looking after him while he was lost."

At this, Doug glared at his ex-wife and then, to the party's surprise (but not to hers), stalked out of the room followed by Pickle and Peanut. Selby, meanwhile, sensing how uncomfortable Tata was, turned to her and said, "Poor Antoni's been waiting forever for his tour. Can I impose on you, Tata, and ask you to take him around while I give Tallulah some tea?"

"Why not," said Tata, jumping at the chance to escape Tallulah. "But I don't know the house at all."

"Just wander," said Selby. "It's more fun that way."

Even the best-laid plans, Ian thought to himself with a sigh. He had just watched Charlene gallop after Tallulah into Great Bottom Park, and he dreaded to think what was going on in there. There was nothing for it, he decided, but to indulge in a contemplative cigarette. Just a few moments later, lolling elegantly against the side of the Bentley, a curl of smoke twisting upwards into the sunset, Ian briefly forgot his troubles. The light was soft, and the only sounds were the occasional call of a pheasant and the moo-ing of cattle grazing in the park.

It wasn't long before his reverie was broken, though, by someone emerging from the shadow of the house: the American from the churchyard, Doug Fairfax. He was wandering out from the porch, dogs in tow, hands plunged in his pockets, head down.

"Afternoon," Ian called out.

Doug looked up and walked over, a despondent air about him. "Hey, Ian," he said, gazing longingly at the butler's cigarette.

Ian offered him the packet. "Fancy one?" Doug gratefully accepted and Ian lit his cigarette with the platinum lighter that the Von Preussen family had bestowed on him after he'd worked a Christmas for them in St. Barth's.

"Thanks. Boy, am I glad to see you."

"Terrifying wife, I presume?"

Doug nodded and took a deep drag, then exhaled a skinny plume of smoke before he spoke. "Yeah. Come on, let's go and sit down. I need to talk to someone."

Ian followed, intrigued, as Doug walked over to a lichen-covered stone bench which had a far-reaching view of the park. They sat down side by side.

"Gorgeous, isn't it?" Doug remarked glumly, staring ahead.

"Heavenly," Ian agreed. "Everyone enjoying the tea party?"

"Everyone except me," Doug said. "It was all going great. I'd just picked up the girls from school, and I was so happy to be with them again. They were so cute, so glad to see me and the Sausages. That's what they call Pickle and Peanut. Then things went downhill at teatime." He looked at Ian, his face drawn. "I was right. Selby *does* have a boyfriend."

"I feel for you, really," Ian said, although at the same time he couldn't help but feel excited that the plan for Selby was on track.

"Thanks, Ian. I know I sound ridiculous. We're divorced. But, still, I never thought Selby would be like one of *those* ex-wives . . ." Doug ran his fingers through his hair, agitated. "You know, the kind who goes and gets themselves a boyfriend. It's painful."

"What do you think of him?"

"I only met him for a few minutes at tea. Nice-looking. Polite. Bit of an age difference. Just Selby's type."

"Agony," Ian groaned, clutching his chest melodramatically.

"I guess she had to find someone eventually. But, God I feel like a fool, coming over here expecting a warm welcome." Doug shook his head and stubbed out his cigarette on the ground. "I should probably go back to New York."

"May I give you some unsolicited advice?" Ian asked politely.

"Sounds like you're going to anyway," Doug said.

"Stick around," Ian said. He had warmed to this man. "The girls need to spend time with you. Suck up the pain, and the agony, and the pride, and be their father. It's worth it."

Doug's grim mood seemed to break a little. "You're right. I know you're right. It's just—well, it's hard."

"How did the sketching go?" asked Ian. "Any bursts of creativity after our meeting among the gravestones?"

"Actually, yes," Doug replied. "I spent the rest of the morning in some falling-down dairy barn that Selby told me is going to be her studio, sketching my first-ever collection of loafers."

"Oh, the glamour," Ian declared, with an ironic look at Doug.

"Came up with a nice tag line for the campaign, though: *Saving the planet, one loafer at a time.*"

Ian chuckled.

"No, I'm serious," said Doug. "No one takes a brand seriously these days unless it's going to 'change the world.' For every pair that's bought, we'll give a pair of shoes to a disadvantaged child."

"That's lovely," said Ian. "I can't wait to hear more about the project."

"Look," said Doug, regarding Ian a little tentatively. "Why don't we meet up for a drink? Then I can tell you all about our charitable foundation and we can really get into some detail about shoe design."

"Right up my *straza*." Ian couldn't think of anything more inspiring. And surely, he told himself, an innocent drink in public wasn't crossing the staff–client boundary.

"This Saturday? Do you know anywhere around here?"

"The Great Bottom Arms is wonderful."

"It's a date," said Doug, getting up from the bench. "See you there. I'll bring the Sausages."

29

From: The Office of Virgil Pitman, Headmaster, Stow Hall School
To: Mr. and Mrs. Bryan Hawkins
Re: Incident at school
Date: Friday 14 May

Dear Mr. and Mrs. Hawkins,
I must trouble you both to meet me in my office this morning at 11 a.m. Forgive the short notice but there has been a report of a serious complaint from another parent regarding your daughter Minty, and I'd prefer to discuss this with you in person. Unless I hear otherwise, I will see you later today.
Best wishes,
Virgil A. Pitman

"Ian!" called out Tata, dashing into the back kitchen on Friday morning brandishing her phone. "I need to be at school in an hour. Look at this."

Ian put aside the candlesticks he was cleaning and read the headmaster's email, keeping his countenance calm.

"Don't panic, Mrs. H. Just get yourself ready and I'll drive you up there shortly."

"Okay, give me a few minutes," said Tata, and disappeared upstairs to do her make-up. There was no way she was seeing Bryan for the first time in weeks without putting on her Charlotte Tilbury Pillow Talk lip gloss and eyeshadow.

An hour later, Tata found herself face to face with Bryan in Virgil Pitman's office, a rambling room overflowing with books which gave it the air of an untidy library. The headmaster was running behind, so the pair were left to their own devices for a few minutes. It was odd to see her husband again after so long, and Tata found herself desperately wishing they'd never had that argument: she missed him.

"What on earth could Minty have done?" Bryan asked Tata, a frown clouding his brow.

"She's such a good child, I honestly don't know," she replied.

There were a few moments of quiet and then Bryan looked at his wife with the expression of an orphaned teddy bear. This usually meant he was about to apologise for something.

"Look, Tata, before Mr. Pitman comes in, I just wanted to tell you that, well, I—"

"Mummy and Daddy? Coffee? Tea? Biccies?" came a jolly voice from the doorway. It was Mr. Pitman's secretary, Karen Grant, a woman who wore a lot of bright make-up and specialised in calming anxious parents.

"I'm fine," said Tata.

"Just a black tea," said Bryan. "Please."

"Okey-dokey. The headmaster's on his way," she said and disappeared.

Meanwhile Tata wondered if Bryan might be on the verge of begging her to come home. "You wanted to tell me something," she said, a smile playing at her lips.

"Ah, yes," said Bryan, shifting to the edge of his seat. "You see, I didn't know how to say this but—"

He got no further.

"Apols, parents," Mr. Pitman called out to them, blowing energetically into the room and plopping his large frame down into the leather chair at the mahogany desk in front of the window.

"Tea for Daddy," said Karen, bringing Bryan a pot on a tray.

"Thank you."

"Right. I always say no point in dithering, let's get to the point," said Pitman, eyeballing the Hawkinses.

They nodded, both rather terrified of what was to come.

"Well," said Pitman, "let's call a spade a spade, shall we?"

The Hawkinses nodded again, mute.

"Or rather a diamond a diamond? Ha!"

Bryan and Tata looked at each other.

"Er—" started Bryan.

At this, Pitman pulled a small black velvet pouch from his pocket and tipped the contents onto his desk: a pair of glittery rhinestone clip-on earrings.

"The earrings from the Fortnum's Christmas crackers last year," said Tata, surprised. "But, Mr. Pitman, why do you have them?"

"I have them because Minty sold them to another child here—"

"That's my girl," chuckled Bryan proudly, provoking a crushing look from Tata.

"And the parents of that child," Pitman went on, "have lodged a formal complaint."

"Why?" asked Bryan.

"Because Minty claimed they were a pair of her mother's real diamond earrings, and sold them for two hundred and fifty pounds cash, which the child in question stole from her parents' safe."

"That's just good marketing on Minty's part," Bryan replied, looking rather pleased.

Pitman narrowed his eyes disapprovingly. "That may or may not be, but we cannot have young children conducting business deals in the playground."

"Are you sure this is true?" asked Tata. "I haven't seen Minty with any money at home."

"I don't think the parents are the type to lie."

"Who are they?" asked Bryan.

The headmaster cleared his throat. "It's Lettice Duffield's mother, the Lady Anne."

Tata's face started to burn. "I'm telling you this is not true. That woman's got it in for my family."

"What are you talking about?" said Bryan. "They're all right."

"Bryan, if you don't back me up on this—"

Pitman, clearly uninterested in witnessing a domestic spat, carried on, "I'm afraid I'm going to have to give Minty a debit."

"Please don't do that," begged Tata. "Minty's never had one. This is so unfair."

"And she needs to pay back the money to Lettice."

"I can deal with that," said Bryan, taking his wallet from his pocket, pulling out a wad of notes and slapping them onto the headmaster's desk.

"Bryan, no. That's completely inappropriate," said Tata.

"I thought you said you wanted me to back you up," he retorted.

"Not like this."

Mr. Pitman pushed the cash back across the table to Bryan.

"Minty needs to give Lettice the money herself, Mr. Hawkins. Learn her lesson."

"Well, at least let me give a donation to the school to get rid of the debit," replied Bryan, pushing the money back again to Pitman's side of the desk.

"Bryan, stop." Tata was aghast. Bribing the headmaster! She wanted to die.

"Mr. Hawkins, Minty can get rid of the debit herself," replied Pitman reassuringly.

Bryan looked relieved. "Oh, okay. That's all right, then. How does she do that?"

"The children here work off their debits," Pitman explained.

"Huh?"

"She can sharpen colouring pencils in the art department after school. Once she's done a hundred, the debit's gone. Now, Mr. Hawkins, Mrs. Hawkins, please excuse me. I'm due to teach a Greek lesson. Oh, and, Mrs. Hawkins," he added, as he picked up his books, "thank you for the Kitchen Supper. Thoroughly enjoyed it."

At this, Bryan's complexion, usually on the red side, turned almost purple. "Huh," he grunted, and rose abruptly to leave.

"You've completely corrupted Minty already, Bryan, and she's only eight," said Tata furiously as they left the headmaster's office and walked out into the school courtyard.

"What do you mean?" asked Bryan.

"Setting up a business in the playground? It's so tacky."

"Well, she's not going to make her fortune playing tag, is she? I'm really impressed with her."

"That's not the point. I just don't want her turning into a money-grabbing nouveau riche when she grows up."

"Would you rather she ends up as an entitled aristo like those Duffield kids? One of them's so useless he just got kicked out of Eton."

"I just want Minty to be a nice girl, Bryan," said Tata, her voice rising. What she secretly meant was, she wanted her to grow up posh and marry Prince George, and Prince George was not going to marry a brash nouveau riche.

"Oh, Tata," said Bryan, finally exasperated. "You need a reality check."

With that, to Tata's amazement, her husband walked off without another word and left her standing alone outside the school. How on earth, she wondered to herself, could things have come to this?

30

Like his peers, Josh was the sort of twenty-something who communicated almost exclusively by text. As the week had drifted by, he had stayed away from the house and stuck to the stable yard as requested, but this had not stopped him from bombarding Selby with a stream of flirty messages which consisted mostly of corny emojis, the most recent of which was a GIF of two pink unicorns, dancing nose to nose, with purple hearts exploding between them. Selby didn't know whether to be flattered, giggle, or weep—but she became more and more determined that she had to be frank with him.

And so it was that on the aforementioned Saturday night, Selby was almost ready to go and meet Josh at the pub to deliver the bad news when Doug tapped on her bedroom door.

"Come in," she said, as she squirted a splash of scent on her wrists.

Doug popped his head in, seeming to be in a hurry. "I'm heading out. See you in the morning?"

"What?" said Selby.

"I'm going out."

"But you're staying with the girls."

"Why?" Doug asked.

"Because *I'm* going out."

"You never told me that."

"Didn't think I needed to."

"You need to tell me if you want me to stay here and take care of the girls, Selby. It's common courtesy."

"They're your kids too," Selby said. "And I've been with them every night for months now. It's definitely your turn. Anyway, you don't know anyone here. How can you be going out?"

"I've made a friend."

"Already?"

"Is it that hard to imagine?"

"Who is this friend?"

"You know him. Ian."

"*Ian* Ian? The Colin Firth lookalike who works for Tata?"

"Exactly."

"But you've got Kirk back in New York."

Doug blushed. "It's not like *that*."

Selby raised her eyebrows. "Why have you turned the colour of a tomato, then?"

"We're just friends. Ian's very inspiring. Style-wise. Shoe-wise. Have you seen how elegant his footwear is?"

"It hadn't escaped my notice."

"Look, I'm sorry but I'm going to be late. I'll have to go. I thought you'd watch the girls."

Why was Doug assuming that she was always the fallback? No one ever changes, Selby fumed internally, and they get even worse after a divorce.

"Well, I was assuming *you* would." Selby's voice was rising.

"Stop getting resentful."

"I wouldn't be resentful if you weren't so selfish."

"I wouldn't be being selfish if you'd asked me in advance."

"You haven't changed."

"*You* haven't changed."

There was a bitter pause, during which Selby somehow regained her emotional equilibrium. "There is only one solution," she declared.

"What?"

"Flip a coin."

He shrugged. "Sure."

With that, Selby tossed a pound coin in the air and caught it on the back of her left hand, covering it with her right.

"Your call," she told him gallantly.

"Heads."

Selby removed her right hand and looked: it was heads. She showed Doug and before she could say anything, he was gone.

Selby sat down at her dressing table, took out her phone, and texted Josh to cancel. She had to smile when a cartoon heart pouring with tears appeared moments later, with the words, *Gutted. Next Saturday instead? X J.*

He was sweet. Selby sent back a thumbs-up. She'd have to wait until then to tell Josh that the fling was over.

~~~

The Great Bottom Arms was a picture-postcard version of an old-fashioned English pub. Located at the edge of the village, the historic coaching inn had been *in situ* since the late sixteenth century. It was built of local stone, had low, beamed windows, and an old panelled front door, above which a portrait of the sixth Earl of Bottom hung in an iron frame. A sprawling yellow rose had taken over the front of the building, and a group of lead planters brimming with irises were arranged by the entrance.

Thank goodness, Ian thought, as he pulled up outside the pub in his convertible Mini, for Tuggy Drummond, the posh new landlord who'd made the place over. Until Tuggy, who also owned a glamorous caviar bar in Mayfair, had acquired it, the Great Bottom Arms hadn't been exactly Ian's thing. In its prior incarnation, it had been a pongy dive that offered football on a dodgy flat-screen TV, warm beer and crisps, both of which were consumed from sticky tables set upon a swirly red carpet—hardly the sort of place that Ian would suggest to someone as sophisticated as Douglas Fairfax for a drink.

"Ian, old boy!" Tuggy called out from behind the bar as soon as he walked through the door. The thirty-five-year-old landlord, nicknamed at birth for his similarity to a tugboat at that young age, rather enjoyed bartending on the odd Saturday night. "Your usual, sir?"

"Sounds good." Ian perched on one of the bar stools, which had been painted yellow and had just the right amount of colour sanded off for a vintage effect, and leaned an elbow on the marble-topped counter while Tuggy put together his "usual" in an old-school highball glass. This consisted of a Franklin & Sons rosemary tonic water, a splash of Ceder's Classic juniper, coriander and rose-geranium botanical spirit, a stem of fresh mint, and a generous heap of ice.

"A gin and tonic minus the gin, darling," said Tuggy, putting the appetising creation in front of Ian, then offering him a blue-and-white Wedgwood dish piled with nuts. "Try these. Salted almonds from the Newt in Somerset. Wildly overpriced, wildly moreish."

"Delicious," said Ian, nibbling one. "Thank you."

"Looking very dapper tonight," Tuggy teased.

Ian blushed a little. Was it so obvious he'd made an extra effort? Alas. Maybe the lilac trousers were a bit dressy? And the cream shirt—was it a little too formal?

"The renovation looks fabulous," he said, swiftly changing the subject. Tuggy had class—the whitewashed walls and pale furniture were the perfect foil for a staggering collection of oils that he had borrowed from the Drummond family vaults.

"Praying Granny's forgotten about the paintings," Tuggy said with a chuckle. "Want to see the bar menu while you wait?"

"Sure," said Ian.

He hadn't got more than a few lines in when he heard his name being called from behind him and turned to see Doug walking across the room, with the dogs on leads. He was dressed in chinos, a blue shirt, pale grey linen jacket, and the neon sneakers. He was well put together, Ian thought to himself. It was just the footwear that Ian couldn't quite get past.

"Hey! Hello!" said Doug.

"Wonderful to see you," said Ian, getting up from his stool and putting his hand out, but Doug went straight in for a kiss on both cheeks. Sensing Ian's discomfort, Doug apologised. "Oops. Being all New York. Sorry. Keep forgetting England's different."

"No, no, not at all. Hello, doggies," Ian went on, giving them both a pat. "Now, what would you like to drink?"

"Nice cold lager?" said Doug.

"Coming up," said Tuggy. "Snack at all?"

Doug looked at the menu. "Caviar? Lobster rolls? Feel like I'm at the Palm in East Hampton."

"I take that as a compliment," said Tuggy as he poured the lager into a tall frosted glass and handed it to Doug.

"I'll get a lobster roll. Anything for you, Ian?"

He shook his head. "I'm good."

"You know," went on Doug, taking in the scene, the gorgeous clientele drifting in and out, "I could really get to like it here. Not that my ex-wife would like it if I got to like it here."

"How are the loafers coming along?" asked Ian, not too keen to get involved in a conversation about the Fairfaxes' relationship woes.

"Let me show you." Doug took a small sketchbook from his inside jacket pocket and started showing Ian various drawings of shoes, heels, soles, and so on.

"Those are nice," said Ian, stopping him on a sketch of a loafer with a crêpe sole. "Very summery. But . . . maybe . . ." He held up the drawing and examined it more closely. "Maybe a little shorter on the toe? Squarer on the heel?"

Doug handed Ian a mechanical pencil. "Have a go," he said, as Tuggy set down a lobster roll in front of him, which he tucked into with gusto. "God, this is delicious."

"The lobster's from the coldest waters off the Cornwall coast," said Tuggy, looking pleased.

While Doug was finishing his food, Ian drew a line here and there, shaded, doodled, adjusted.

"I always have this ridiculous dream," said Ian while he drew, "where my Prince Charming comes and puts a sparkly loafer on my foot."

Doug burst out laughing.

"And we live happily ever after in a fairy-tale castle," said Ian as he handed the sketchbook back.

Doug examined Ian's adjustments to his design with great concentration. Eventually he looked up and said, "That's it, Ian. That's *the* look for LoafersDirect. It's a winner. Seriously."

"It's nothing. Happy to help," Ian said modestly.

"Has anyone ever told you that you have a great eye for proportion?" said Doug.

Ian blushed a little. "Not in so many words."

"Well, you do. What is a *gorgeous*, talented guy like you doing being a butler, anyway?"

Ian coloured a little. It was nice to receive compliments but the staff–client boundary was there for a reason, and he wasn't sure if he was very keen on Doug's dismissive attitude to butlering anyway.

Sensing that it was time to extricate himself, Ian looked at his watch, feigning concern. "Oh goodness, look at the hour. I'm afraid I've got to go. Mrs. Hawkins will be needing her bedtime hot chocolate and sleeping pill soon."

"Oh. Okay," said Doug. "Sounds like she's Liz Taylor or something."

"You're not wrong there," quipped Ian, getting up from the stool. "Goodnight."

31

Sophie Thompson had not had a moment to herself over the weekend. She'd spent both days ferrying Eddie between sports matches and playdates, cooking family meals, and endlessly clearing up after Hugh and the dogs. By Monday morning she was shattered, and wished that, like some of her friends, she could take the day off as they did, to "recover" from the physical and emotional labour weekends entailed. But this was impossible if she was to keep what was left of her career going, and she had vowed that, however exhausted she felt, she would devote Monday morning to the hideously dull chore of updating her company database. Still, by the time she'd seen Hugh off to London in that flashy new car, dropped Eddie at school, done the grocery shopping, got back home, and made herself some breakfast, Sophie's mind had drifted from work: creating a menu and tablescape for the luncheon she'd be hosting after the hack she'd arranged for Selby suddenly seemed far more pressing than going over the dreaded company database. After all, she only had a few days to get everything organised, and she was determined to make a success of this event.

And so it was that at mid-morning on Monday Sophie was to be found perched at a garden table which was situated in a shady corner of the lawn at the Rectory, joyfully scribbling in her treasured leather-bound Smythson "hostess" book. From where she was sitting, she had a beautiful view of the apple orchard at the far end of the garden which was bursting with white blossoms; there was a grassy glade between the trees which could be mown and would make an idyllic spot for a summer luncheon if the weather held up; the long garden table would seat everyone comfortably, and she'd dress it with that frilled, pink-and-white striped seersucker tablecloth that she'd got on sale at Cutter Brooks last year. With the coordinating frilled napkins, green hessian place mats, that trendy pearl-handled cutlery she'd found on Etsy, pretty vases and jugs full of cornflowers and bluebells, terracotta bowls brimming with those Sicilian lemons with the huge waxy leaves, and vintage crystal glasses, the tableau would be the most charming Selby Fairfax had ever encountered. And the food would match. Sophie jotted down a menu—they'd have goat's cheese soufflés, followed by Devon crab with a pomegranate salad, and pudding would be an apple and blackberry sorbet.

She happily sipped a coffee while imagining the day: she would plan a scenic route for the ride, include a pit-stop for a drink on the way, and on arrival back at the Rectory afterwards, she'd swiftly change from her horsey clothes into a vintage Chanel dress embroidered with daisies that she'd just paid a fortune for on The RealReal. The lunch would be spent sucking up round after round of compliments about Sophie's "incredible talent" for table decoration and gardening. There would be endless praise expressed for her organisational and equine skills, followed by congratulations on the lightness of the soufflés and the surprising Asian notes in the salad dressing, then screams of delight at the "insane" home-made sorbet. Sophie would repeatedly be told how "clever" she was for transforming the traditional concept of a leaden apple and blackberry crumble into something as light and clean as an ice. There would be polite enquiries about who had done the cooking and when Sophie revealed that she had a "new person," a local girl who was "very good value" (really cheap) because she'd only just graduated from the two-week course at the Orchards Cookery School, the other women would say, "But you're *so* brilliant at finding people," and then quickly demand the new person's contact details, block-booking her so that she was never, ever available again to cook for the Thompsons. (A less happy part of the fantasy.)

Sophie's bubble was burst by her phone ringing, Tata's name on the screen.

"Sophie, sweet pea. It's Tats. Where are you?"

"At home. I'm, um . . . working." She wasn't keen to let on to Tata how much energy she was putting into the ride and lunch for Selby.

"God, you're *so* good, keeping your career going. Look, Soph, I'm feeling really anxious."

"Can I help?"

"Mr. Pitman called Bryan and me into school on Friday, and he gave poor Minty a debit—"

"But she's always so well behaved."

"Lettice Duffield got her into trouble."

"No surprises there."

"That's exactly what Ian said. The worst thing is, Bryan and I ended up having a fight outside the school."

"Oh dear."

"And as if that isn't awful enough, Fernanda's tried to steal Ian."

"All your friends have tried to steal Ian," Sophie reminded Tata.

"But Fernanda's in the inner circle."

"True."

"People don't understand. I *rely* on Ian." Tata sounded hurt. "It's the way she tried to do it that I'm more upset about than anything."

"What did she do?"

"She got *Luca* to write a letter asking him to come and work with them."

Sophie thought this sounded unlike their friend. "Are you sure Fernanda was behind it?"

"This sad little letter offered Ian a giant raise."

"Oh, I see," said Sophie. "That's so unfair on Luca."

"Fernanda thinks she can buy whatever she wants. Well, it turns out she can't buy an Ian. I would never have got Ian if that crypto guy he was working for in Patmos hadn't gone broke. Ians are not available willy-nilly: Ians are rarer than golden pheasants. They are precious things that have to be nurtured. As a result of Fernanda's scheme, I gave my Ian an enormous pay increase."

"Very sensible."

"Anyway, the reason I'm calling is because I need a favour from Fernanda, but things feel too weird right now for me to ask her myself."

"What can I do?"

"Can you ask her to invite Antoni to the trunk show she's doing on Friday?"

Sophie was surprised. "Isn't it all ladies' pyjamas?"

"Yes, but the thing is, I think a romance is blossoming between Selby and Antoni," Tata said. "The problem is that Ian says her ex-husband is still staying at Great Bottom Park, so we can't get Antoni to her place. Selby's doing the flowers for the trunk show, so she'll be there all day and we just need to get him to come by."

"Won't Fernanda think it's odd if I ask her? Men never go to those things."

"Tell her Antoni's looking for fashion brands to fund or something. Fernanda would love the idea that she's introducing her protégé to a potential investor. Don't let on to her about Selby and Antoni, though. She's so gossipy."

"I won't," said Sophie. "I'll take care of everything, don't worry."

Now she really did need to get off the phone and get down to her company database, however dull it seemed.

"Sweetie, I need to go—" she started.

But Tata hadn't finished. "And can you invite him to your hack?"

"Consider it done," said Sophie. "I'll organise a horse for him from Bunbury's yard."

"'Kay. Thanks so much. Bye, sweetie."

As Sophie rang off, she felt worried for Tata. What she hadn't mentioned was that early that morning her gardener had told her that he'd heard from his daughter, who was a barmaid at the Great Bottom Arms, that Tata's beloved Ian had been spotted at the pub on Saturday night deep in conversation with Douglas Fairfax. If Ian was fielding offers from the SneakersDirect tycoon as well as Fernanda, what chance did Tata stand of hanging on to him?

32

"Can't believe it's Wednesday already," Selby said to Doug as she dashed into the kitchen back from the school run. He was sitting at the table tucking into one of Doreen's famous breakfasts, dogs at his feet awaiting tidbits of food. The week had flown, even with her ex lurking around, and she had so much to do over the next few days.

"Coffee?" asked Doug.

"No time," she replied. "I'm meeting Alan in a minute down at the walled garden to figure out the flowers for the trunk show."

"Can I help?"

Selby was rather amazed by the offer, which felt like something of a rapprochement from Doug after his irritation over Josh. She paused a moment, then said, "That would be great. Thank you."

"Okay," said Doug, hurriedly finishing his food. "Let's go."

"I think you'll like the walled garden," she said as they walked away from the house a few minutes later, Selby swinging her old canvas gardening tote in one hand. "It's so wild and overgrown."

"Sounds charming," said Doug, his eyes dancing merrily.

"What have you got to be so pleased about?" she went on. She'd noticed that her ex had had a new jauntiness over the last few days.

"Oh, you know, just enjoying life, the girls, being here . . ." Doug mused.

"You look like the cat that got the canary to me," Selby said jokily to him. "Did Cupid strike on Saturday?"

"Ian's a talent, Selby," replied Doug.

"You've fallen for him!" Selby laughed. "Keep in mind, everyone around here does, man, woman, child, or pet."

Doug shook his head. "It's not that. We only had time for a quick drink, but he redrew my latest design, rather brilliantly, before he had to go—his boss sounds pretty demanding. But I think he should come to America, he'd be a hit in the fashion world."

"Doug," Selby retorted, disbelieving. "I'll be in deep trouble with Tata if Ian runs off with my ex-husband. Anyway, you're devoted to Kirk and Ian's devoted to Tata—there's no way he'd leave her. Follow me through this gate and we'll be there in a sec."

※

It was the most beautiful animal—a dapple-grey horse with four white socks and a silver mane and tail. But what on earth, Selby asked herself, was it doing standing in the middle of the walled garden, munching on a mouthful of peonies? She had no idea who the horse belonged to, but she quickly ascertained how it had gotten in: the old walls had mostly collapsed and were easily low enough for it to have stepped over.

To Selby's utter dismay, she also realised that barely a bloom remained in the old beds, and the wild poppies, lilacs, and hollyhocks were gone: the horse had eaten Fernanda's trunk-show flowers for breakfast. The only thing it hadn't consumed were great mounds of stinging nettles and docks.

"Shit," she said. "Shit. Shit. Shit."

"Not good," said Doug, staring at the devastation.

Just then the sound of whistling came from behind them and they turned to see Alan arriving, pushing a wheelbarrow piled with buckets and cutting tools. His whistling abruptly stopped when he saw what had happened.

"Well, well, well," was all he said, as he parked the wheelbarrow and walked up to Doug and Selby. "Horses. Trouble all round."

Alan made a clicking sound with his tongue at which the horse startled, raised its head high into the air and eyed the trio suspiciously. It then stamped a hind hoof as if irritated to be interrupted, swished its tail back and forth, and flared its nostrils, snorting loudly. After a few moments it lost interest in them, dropped its head down and carried on grazing.

"Any idea who owns it?" Selby asked Alan.

He shook his head. "I couldn't say, Mrs. Fairfax. But Josh will know. Keeps tabs on all those things."

With one eye on the horse, Selby put down her gardening tote and took her phone from her pocket to call Josh.

"Good morning, *gorgeous*," he said as soon as he picked up.

"Josh, don't," Selby whispered. This was the last thing she needed, especially with Alan and Doug right there.

"Sorry, *beautiful*," Josh said, laughing. "Missed you on Saturday—"

"Josh ," she said, cutting him off and reverting to her most professional tones. "Doug and Alan and I are in the walled garden. There is a very pretty dapple-grey horse in here, but it's eaten *everything*. Do you have any idea who it might belong to?"

"Silver mane and tail, four perfect white socks?"

"That's the one."

"I know that gelding. He's a wild one. Belongs to Mr. Osborne."

Selby huffed audibly. "Vere Osborne? That horse is Vere Osborne's? You don't think he could have done it on purpose?"

"Done what?"

"Let it get out and eat all my flowers. To get back at me for the water and the poor dead cow."

"He's not like that."

"Right. Well, this is a disaster. I don't know what I'm going to say to Fernanda. Can you send me Vere's number? I'll call him."

~~~

Half an hour later, Selby, Doug, and Alan watched helplessly as Vere, in his farm overalls, tried to catch the horse, who was having such a delicious meal that no sugar lumps, Polos, or pony nuts would tempt him anywhere near a human being. Whenever his owner got a few feet away, he simply flicked up his tail and spun around in the opposite direction, adding a buck for good measure.

"Maybe the stable lad can help," Doug suggested as Vere eventually gave up after twenty minutes and walked back towards them, sweating and out of breath.

"I'd be very grateful," Vere replied, looking defeated.

"I'll get Josh," Alan offered, pulling out his phone and walking off to make the call.

The last thing Selby wanted was to be around Doug and Josh together, but she didn't have much choice. She just hoped they'd behave themselves.

"I'm sure Josh'll be able to catch him," said Selby.

"Thanks," said Vere. "I'm certainly no use." He sat down on an old wooden bench that had seen better days, wiped his forehead with the back of his sleeve, and then looked up at Selby. "I guess we're even now."

"A cow dying does not equal a trampled garden," Selby insisted. "You lost an animal, I've just lost a few buds."

"You're being very generous." Vere looked a little ashamed. "Especially after I was so rude to you at Tata's supper."

"It was fair enough after I was a total bitch to you in your barn."

"I wouldn't put it quite like that. Horrible snob is closer to the truth."

Selby couldn't help but burst out laughing and was soon joined by Vere. Doug, meanwhile, looked at the two of them, utterly confused.

"Like I said, we're even," Vere went on. "Let bygones be bygones?"

Selby nodded. "Sure."

"Handsome horse you've got there," said Doug.

"If I could only catch him. Thing is, he doesn't like me much." Vere paused for a moment and his expression altered. "He belonged to Anjelica. My late fiancée."

"I'm sorry," Selby said.

Eventually Vere continued, "She named him Paris, after her favourite city, because he's so beautiful."

"He's literally a painting—"

Before she could go on, Selby was interrupted by the sound of a quad bike and moments later Josh appeared, halter and rope in his hand.

"Morning, Mrs. Fairfax, Mr. Fairfax," said Josh politely. He was looking Adonis-like in cream breeches, white top, and worn-in boots.

"Hello," said Doug curtly, bristling at this heavenly vision of youth.

Josh ignored Doug's terse response. "Mr. Osborne, may I?" He gestured at Paris, who had now moved on to a bramble thicket in the far corner of the garden.

"It's certainly more your area of expertise than mine," Vere said, looking relieved.

The group watched as Josh hid the halter and rope behind his back and slowly, slowly stole across the garden towards Paris. He was soon rubbing the horse on the wither and eventually, after gently placing the rope over its neck, managed to slide the halter over its head.

"Brilliantly done," said Vere, getting up and strolling over to them.

"Righto, I'll go and get the trailer sorted so we can drive the horse home," said Alan.

"Thanks," Selby replied.

While Josh and Vere were out of earshot, Doug asked Selby, "So, who exactly is Vere?"

"He owns the farm next door. We were in a terrible fight until today," Selby said, and laughed. "But I think we've made up."

"He's perfect for you," said Doug. "Much better than Harry Styles over there."

At this, she rolled her eyes. "Please stop, Doug. I'm past that, but even if I wasn't, it's none of your business."

"All right, all right. I'll never mention your sex life again."

"Ugggh! Doug!" Exasperated, Selby poked her ex-husband in the ribs and shook her head at him.

"All right, all right, no need to get touchy."

The last thing she wanted was to get into a childish spat with Doug, so she ignored this remark and was relieved when Josh and Vere walked over, Paris ambling along behind them at the end of the lead rope.

"Right," said Josh. "I'll get this horse back to your farm, Mr. Osborne."

"That's very helpful, thank you," Vere replied as Josh led the horse away. He turned to Selby. "Look, if there's anything I can do to help repair the damage to the garden . . ."

"The immediate problem is the flowers for Fernanda's trunk show on Friday," Selby said. "We've got to fill that huge orangerie at Middle Bottom Abbey—but I'll figure it out. I've still got time."

"Let me help," said Vere.

Selby shook her head. "No. Honestly. This event, it's really just a rich lady showing off her table settings and dresses to other rich ladies," she said. "I can order more flowers from Holland."

"Don't do that," insisted Vere. "Come back to the farm with me. I've got something there that might fix things."

"She'd love it," Doug said before Selby could answer.

"Great," said Vere. "My car's in the drive."

―≫―

When Selby and Vere arrived at Great Bottom Home Farm, he led her through the farmhouse and out to a grassy paddock beyond it, then down a path that led to an iron gate in an overgrown hedge. Behind the hedge was a large, ugly greenhouse constructed of breeze blocks and glass.

"Voila!" said Vere, standing outside. "Hideous, isn't it? But it does the job."

He showed Selby into the warm greenhouse, where she was immediately overwhelmed by the most delicious green, lemony scent.

"Mmmmm," she sighed. "Pelargoniums!"

Selby looked around. The slatted wooden counters on each side of a narrow walkway were crowded with terracotta pots spilling with rare varieties of geraniums. She reached out and rubbed a leaf between her thumb and forefinger to release the scent.

"It's the freshest smell," she said, drinking it in. "Unlike anything else."

"Isn't it?" agreed Vere. He had a satisfied air about him now.

"Looking at you," she said, "I'd never have guessed that you're a secret geranium fiend."

"Anjelica collected them. She used to bring them into the house, admire them, feed them, and cut them back," Vere said, wandering a little further into the greenhouse. He picked a sprig of parsley from a pot and chewed on it. "Then out they went again, for sunlight, then in they came again the minute they looked the faintest bit miserable. She treated them like children."

"Quite right," Selby said. "They're very sensitive plants."

Vere looked nostalgic. "It's nice, still having them. I bring them indoors like she used to and I come out here and muck around with them, and it feels a bit like Anjelica's still here. A bit."

"I'm sorry she's gone."

"Yup," he said sadly. "But, anyway, the point I am trying very hard to get to, is that Anjelica, like your ex-husband, would not have wanted the rich ladies' lunch table to be bare of blooms. So, please, borrow anything."

"Thank you, Vere," said Selby. "That's really generous."

"Not at all," he said.

He stopped speaking for a moment and his eyes suddenly welled up.

"Are you okay?" asked Selby.

"Yup, yup." He drew the back of his hand under his eyes quickly and smiled. "Sorry. Right. I'll leave you to it. Got to get back to the cows."

With that, he turned on his heel and hurriedly departed the greenhouse, leaving Selby in the company of the geraniums and the ghost of his late fiancée. She was there, in every single stem.

33

In recent years, the midweek trunk show, previously an institution exclusive to suites at the Carlyle Hotel in New York, or the languid mansion of an heiress in Houston, had become a crucial part of the Country Princesses' social calendar. Where once these events had involved humble sample racks bulging with luxurious bargains that a designer bestowed on a privileged, well-connected few, they were now a major aesthetic, social, and branding event. They usually entailed attending a breakfast or luncheon at the home of the hostess, as well as the compulsory dropping of several thousand pounds on exquisite custom items such as quilted silk cushions trimmed with sustainable pom-poms, organic sweaters hand-knitted by Nepalese monks using the hair of Himalayan goats, or ethical curtain tassels woven by a women's collective in Marrakesh. They were also an opportunity for rich women to dress competitively, gossip discreetly and gawk at someone else's house, garden, and guest loo, and often spilled, deliciously, into the next day, which would be taken up by a dissection of the hostess's taste, either over coffee or via a group WhatsApp. Whether it was her tablescape or her tree planting, her wallpaper or her wisteria, every creative decision was complimented or crucified, the whole affair permitting a free-flowing outpouring of envy, judgement, jealousy, and resentment from the hostess's closest friends and distant acquaintances who had so recently enjoyed her generous hospitality.

The English summer is an unpredictable animal, and as Selby motored up the drive to Middle Bottom Abbey, clouds drew in, the heavens opened, and the forest of oaks was swiftly cloaked by sheets of monsoon-like rain.

"Drat," she said out loud, peering through the windscreen, the old-fashioned wipers barely able to keep it clear. It was hard not to feel discouraged by the fat raindrops thundering down onto the trees and whooshing down the drive. At least she'd installed all the flowers yesterday. Between Doug, Josh, and the Hunnigans, they'd somehow transported everything from Vere's greenhouse and into Fernanda's orangerie in a very short space of time.

The inclement weather barely affected the Country Princesses, though, who mostly arrived with drivers armed with broad umbrellas to escort them from their cars to the door of the Abbey. If not, one of Fernanda's multitude of staff members helped them inside without a spot of rain ever touching their being. As a result, their attire adhered to the agreed-upon dress code for a country-house trunk show on a beautiful summer's day: ankle-grazing, flowing print dresses worn with floppy straw hats, ballet flats or embroidered sandals. Their arms were piled with bracelets, their necks draped in diamond-studded lockets and fine necklaces, and their shoulders weighed down by "serious" handbags clinking with logo-ed gold or silver hardware. Selby, who was in her work uniform of navy cropped trousers and a crisp white top, hoped that she would be able to dart around moving vases or perking up arrangements virtually unnoticed.

She alighted from her car and dashed through the rain and into the Great Hall of Middle Bottom Abbey. Like the rest of the property, the cavernous Gothic room had been whitewashed and transformed into an avant-garde space: the walls were hung with large charcoal nudes, two curved white sofas faced each other in the centre, and between these sat a Perspex cube containing a sculpture of decaying flowers. The stone fireplace, richly carved with branches and gargoyles, was dominated by a Tracey Emin piece hanging above it, a light sculpture which read FUCK OFF in neon letters. (Fernanda liked to call it her "welcome mat.")

As Selby walked on and out to the orangerie, her phone buzzed. She stopped momentarily, took it out of her bag, and tapped on the screen. It was yet another text from Josh: *Good luck today, you hottie! Can't wait for tomorrow night.* Selby couldn't help but cringe as she read it: Josh was like a besotted teenager. How was he going to react when she told him their little fling couldn't continue?

Moments later, Fernanda greeted Selby at the entrance to the orangerie. She was barefoot, dressed in a floor-length, turquoise silk dress, and sipping at a herbal tea in a delicate glass cup. With her olive skin, dazzling smile, and waves of dark hair, she seemed goddess-like.

"Wow," said Selby, genuinely awed. "What an original dress."

Her friend looked thrilled. "Perk of the job," she said. "Eric Shuang made it for me as a thank-you gift for hosting the trunk show. Goodness knows how I'm ever going to thank *you* for what you've done here. It's amazing."

Selby gazed around the orangerie. It did look wonderful, thanks to Vere's greenhouse, which had contained far more than a few potted pelargoniums. The long, elegant room now felt like a Victorian conservatory that had been filled with plants for generations. The flat, glossy leaves of fig and apricot trees disguised the entire back wall, and the ceiling was criss-crossed with vines. Tall potted palms anchored each corner and pretty wicker sofas and chairs were dotted around. The lunch table was covered with vintage striped Provençal tablecloths, upon which Selby had arranged terracotta pots brimming with geraniums, Japanese Imari vases flopping with ranunculi and ox-eye daisies, blue-and-white planters tumbling with dark pink roses, and solid majolica-ware jugs bursting with blue delphiniums. A bubbly atmosphere was starting to grow as the room filled with women letting out squeals of excitement every time they found a friend, and Fernanda soon disappeared off to greet them.

As Selby went to get a drink, she spotted Tata and Sophie heading towards her. Tata was clad in a white dress embroidered with poppies at the neck and waist, while Sophie had chosen a cream sundress trimmed with lace. They kissed Selby hello, and then drenched her in a sea of compliments about the room.

"I can't believe you grew all this," said Tata, impressed.

"Actually," said Selby in a whisper, "I didn't. Anjelica did."

"Vere's Anjelica?" asked Sophie, looking surprised.

Selby nodded. "Her old horse got into the walled garden and literally ate every single bud and blossom in it."

"What?!" gasped Tata, half-horrified, half-laughing.

"When Vere came to get the horse and saw the damage, he offered me these flowers from Anjelica's old greenhouse," Selby explained. "He's kept all her plants going."

"That's so sweet," said Sophie. "He's a decent man, under the heartache. Anjelica was only thirty-eight when she died, he's been through a lot."

"That's awful. Thank goodness we've made up," Selby replied.

"Yes. You don't want to be enemies with the neighbouring farmer. You never know when you might need him," said Sophie.

"Totes," said Tata. "Right, shall we go and try some PJs?"

∞

For an hour before luncheon was served, the orangerie echoed with the sound of twenty or so women experiencing a group hysteria about Shuang New York's line of hand-painted, silk-satin, day-to-night pyjamas. The glorious space soon took on the appearance of a Broadway dressing room, with ladies wantonly tossing off their summer dresses and flinging on the garments. The Shuang team soon procured matching dressing gowns, sending the ladies into a crazed fever of fashion lust which was exacerbated by the lashings of icy Pimm's and lemonade that Fernanda's team of Portuguese staff were sloshing into everyone's tumblers. The guests didn't seem to care a jot that they were only half-dressed in front of their most glamorous friends. There were far more interesting things to worry about: could clients monogram the pyjamas as gifts? (Yes.) Would the pyjamas work for the New Year's Eve party at the Peponi Hotel in Lamu? (Totally.) Were the pyjamas suitable for sleeping in? (Absolutely not.)

Centre stage today was, of course, the designer himself. Eric Shuang, a striking young man in his early thirties, had the angular face and lanky build that was so desirable in the New York fashion world. He was dressed in a pair of ripped plaid trousers and a Free Britney tee, over which he'd thrown one of his billowing kingfisher-blue dressing gowns decorated with a swirling pattern of ivy leaves.

Just as Selby was making sure the arrangements along the centre of the table were looking their best, Tata sidled up to her and said in a low voice, "I'm really happy for you, Selby."

"What?" said Selby, not totally sure if this was another compliment on the flowers.

Tata had a coy expression on her face. "You know, about you-know-who."

At this, Selby felt her face redden. How on earth had Tata learned about her and Josh? She hadn't told anyone. Had *Doug* been spreading the word? What if the girls found out?

"Um—" Selby started, wanting to die.

"I know. It must be so fun," Tata interrupted in a whisper. "Having someone new."

"Tata. *Ssshhh*. Don't say a thing to anyone, please," Selby begged. She'd been *so* stupid. It was bad enough that Doug knew, but far more embarrassing that her lovely new friend did too.

"Wouldn't mention it to a soul," Tata said, regretting that she'd let the news slip to Sophie already.

Just then, Sophie bounded up to them, a pair of pyjamas in each hand. "What do you think?" she asked, holding them both up by her face. "The cerise or the violet?"

"Love the violet," said Tata.

"I'd go with the cerise," said Fernanda from behind them, and before Sophie could reply, she'd whipped the violet pyjamas out of her hands.

"Selby, these would look great on you," Fernanda told her. "My gift to you, a thank you—"

"Absolutely not," said Selby. "I'll get them myself."

"My treat," insisted Fernanda. "Right, better go and pay."

She was just about to walk away when she stopped and said, "Soph, I almost forgot. I ran into Doug yesterday at drop-off and tomorrow's ride came up in conversation. He wants to come. I said I was sure he's invited."

"Um, well . . ." Sophie stuttered, seeing Selby's face fall.

Selby's heart sank. Really? Was her ex going to tag along on every outing now? She'd been looking forward to a break from him. His visit had seemed to go on for a very long time already.

"Oh, shit, sorry," said Fernanda. "Was that not a good idea?"

"No," Tata replied on Selby's behalf, thinking of Antoni.

"Er . . . no, no, it's fine," Selby said. "I've got a horse he can ride." There was nothing she could do about it now.

"I'll keep Doug with me and out of your way," said Sophie. "Don't worry, it'll be okay. Right, let's go and pay, Fernanda."

She took her arm and they walked away together to purchase their goodies. As they did, Selby simply shrugged her shoulders helplessly.

"How annoying," said Tata.

"Very," agreed Selby. "Oh well. Lunchtime."

A little later, Selby was helping herself from the buffet table, which was full of platters laid out with everything from grilled halloumi and Thai roasted fennel to rare steak and Lebanese chicken skewers, when a voice came from beside her.

"Selby, my dear."

To her surprise she turned to see Antoni standing next to her, plate in hand.

"Antoni, hi. What are you doing here? Don't tell me you're pyjama shopping too?" she said, passing him the salad spoons.

He grinned at her. "Designer shopping, actually. I might invest in Shuang. A label like this would bring a lot to my business."

"The designer seems quite talented."

"I agree. Shall we sit?" asked Antoni.

"Delighted," said Selby.

She led the way to a pretty corner of the orangerie, where she and Antoni settled in two wicker armchairs and talked about the tea party the week before.

"I so enjoyed going round your house with Tata. She makes everything fun."

"She's very entertaining, that's for sure."

"And Great Bottom Park is a treasure," Antoni said, taking a bite of salad.

"Isn't it? I'm loving being there so much."

※

Unbeknownst to Selby and Antoni as they chatted merrily away, eyes were on them—specifically Tata's and Sophie's. The pair, who were sitting at the main table, were far less focused on their own conversation than the love story they imagined was playing out in the corner of the room.

"Look at her, flicking her hair like that," Tata whispered, making sure none of the other ladies could hear. She didn't want anyone else finding out about Selby's love life after their conversation this morning. "She's being so sexy and flirtatious."

"She *really* likes him," Sophie replied in a low voice. "And look at him, touching her arm like that. He's bewitched."

"I googled his yacht last night, the *Galina*, which he named after one of his wives who won Miss Russia 2008," whispered Tata excitedly. "The boat sleeps twenty, so Selby can easily invite all of us on it."

"How many wives has he had?" asked Sophie, sounding concerned.

"I wasn't really concentrating on that. A few, I think."

"I hope he's genuine," Sophie went on. "I think Selby's more vulnerable than she looks."

"Antoni's a keeper. When we went round Great Bottom Park at the tea that day, he never stopped talking about her. You look great by the way, Sophie," Tata said, changing the subject. "Let me guess. Last season Marni?"

"Actually, Tata," Sophie replied, "it's brand-new Gabriela Hearst."

Tata looked rather taken aback. "But Hugh never lets you buy current season."

"Hugh just got that Porsche. So I bought myself a dress. He's been left a bit of money by one of his nutty old aunts up in Scotland."

"Buy yourself an entire wardrobe, Soph, you deserve it."

"Don't worry, I'm on it," Sophie said with a giggle. "He's even offered to take me and Eddie to Lamu for my birthday at New Year's."

"Lamu?" repeated Tata, feeling miffed. "He's taking you to Lamu for your birthday?"

"Yes," replied Sophie. "Why?"

"I've always said *I* wanted to go to Lamu."

"That's why Hugh's taking us," Sophie continued. "Because you always said it's so cool."

"I've *heard* it's cool. I haven't actually *been*," said Tata huffily. How on earth could it be that Sophie Thompson was going to hit Lamu before Tata Hawkins? Why hadn't Bryan ever thought of taking her there for a holiday? He knew she was desperate to go. Mind you, after the scene outside school the other day, a holiday with Bryan seemed like an impossible dream.

"I'll tell you if it's as nice as everyone says," said Sophie, trying to be helpful.

"I'm going for a walk," said Tata, getting up from the table.

God, why is Sophie so lucky and why is Fernanda so fucking chic? Tata asked herself, as she sat nursing her third Pimm's inside a lavishly upholstered Bedouin tent situated at the far end of the vast croquet lawn while the rain continued. A gorgeous Bedouin tent in the garden for the summer! Why don't I have a fucking gorgeous Bedouin tent in the garden right now? Why had she told Sophie that Lamu was a cool place? Why had Bryan been so mean to her at the school that day? She was even beginning to wonder if he had forgotten about her fortieth birthday. She started tearing up, and before she knew it, her cheeks were wet.

Suddenly she heard a voice from outside the tent. "Are you okay?"

Tata looked up to see Antoni peering in at her, concerned.

"Is it that obvious?" asked Tata through her tears.

He came in and sat on the paisley rocking sofa next to her. "What's happened?" he asked.

"Oh . . ." Tata hiccoughed. "It's just. Everything. My best friends are cooler than me—"

"Never," he insisted. "You're beautiful. Smart. Funny. Caring—"

"My daughter's in trouble at school—"

"I'm sorry."

"Fernanda's always impossibly original and Sophie's going to Lamu for New Year's."

"Ah. Lamu. Wonderful place."

Did *everyone* have to rub it in?

"I've heard," said Tata, patting away her tears with her fingers. "I'm sorry . . . I feel so alone and I'm in a terrible fight with my husband. We're not really even speaking. It's awful, and it's my birthday coming up, and I'm not doing anything. He hasn't even *mentioned* it, and it's only two weeks away."

"What a foolish husband," said Antoni, looking pensive. "Tata, it's perfectly simple. *I* will host a birthday party for you, at the Priory.

You deserve it. I am alone. You are alone. I don't know anyone here and I need friends. You need a party. Makes sense for us both."

"No, Antoni, I couldn't accept. That's far too generous."

"Don't be ridiculous. A wonderful woman like you deserves a wonderful birthday."

"Goodness, well . . . I'd love a party at yours, if you really mean it?" she said, her bleak mood starting to lift.

"It will be beautiful, Tata, I promise," Antoni declared sweetly. "Now, I must go, but I am hoping I see you on this hack with Sophie tomorrow. I am a poor equestrian, but Sophie is saying a safe horse will be there for me."

Antoni kissed Tata on both cheeks and departed, leaving her to enjoy a few minutes alone in the tent, dreams of a fantastically glamorous party at the Priory swirling in her head. Eventually, she got up, strolled back through the garden, and went to find Ian, who was waiting for her in the driveway, feeling as though she was floating on a cloud. Life was suddenly grand.

∽

"Things are looking up," Tata told Ian as he chauffeured her back down the tree-lined drive from Middle Bottom Abbey. The rain had eased and Mrs. Hawkins was in a buoyant mood.

"Glad to hear it, Mrs. H. Well deserved."

"It's about my birthday. There's going to be a phenomenal party."

As soon as the words were out, Ian swerved halfway across the drive.

"Ian!" Tata shrieked, grabbing the side of the door. "What on earth?!"

"Apologies, Mrs. Hawkins. I was surprised to hear that you've arranged a birthday party."

"Why?" she asked.

"Historically you have stated that you hate your birthday."

"I do," she said. "Doesn't mean I'm not upset when people ignore it."

"But, Mrs. Hawkins, do you recall our recent conversation in which you told me that if Bryan doesn't get to organise a fabulous surprise birthday party for you, he'll never forgive you and it will be the end of the marriage?"

"Of course. But he hasn't done anything about the surprise birthday party."

Ian was feeling under strain. "But you wouldn't know if he'd not done anything about, or had done anything about it, if it's a surprise."

"I always know when Bryan's organising a surprise party for me." Her jolly mood quickly deteriorating, she went on, "I mean, Hugh Thompson is taking Sophie to *Lamu* for her birthday at New Year! *LAMU!*"

"Doesn't sound like standard Hugh Thompson behaviour," Ian observed.

"I know. Ian, I'm so jealous. You know I've wanted to go forever."

"I do."

"Bryan always wants to go to those yucky golf resorts. Honestly, if he'd already taken me to Lamu, our marriage would be in great shape now."

"No doubt," Ian concurred.

"Anyway, Antoni has come to the rescue."

Ian gulped. "He has?"

"I was having a lonely little cry in a tent on the croquet lawn—"

"I'm sorry—"

"Thanks. Anyway, he saw me and asked what was wrong, and I told him how sad I was about my birthday and he offered to throw me a party at Little Bottom Priory. I'm so thrilled. Bryan will come running back when he hears about it, but I'm not sure I'll have him now."

"Indeed," was all Ian said.

Alas, Ian's plans for Tata, Bryan, Minty, and his beloved Guccis seemed suddenly to be in disarray. Nevertheless, he remained calm. It was simply time for Plan B. Because a man like Ian *always* had a Plan B.

Charlene was at her desk in Bryan's office typing up a letter to a supplier of non-carcinogenic cables as fast as her little fingers would go. She could barely wait for the weekend, when she'd be down in the sty with the piglets, having a romp in the straw. Charlene checked her watch. Four o'clock. Maybe Bryan would let her off at half past, as he occasionally did on a Friday.

Bryan ambled over to her desk, a frown plastered across his forehead. "Blast. That new factory in Hong Kong is two weeks behind with the pins, Charlene."

"Do you want me to send an email?" Charlene rather liked typing up Bryan's *I'm very cross* letters to his underlings when she got the opportunity.

He pushed his glasses up on his head and rubbed his eyes. "I don't think there's much else that can be achieved today. Why don't you take an early—"

Before he could finish his sentence, Tallulah blew into the room. She was dressed in an orange terry trapeze dress trimmed with sequins at the collar and cuffs and fluffy Ugg slippers on her feet, and she was cuddling herself as though she had just found herself adrift in the Antarctic.

"It's *so* cold. I hate the English summer," she said sulkily before flopping onto the chesterfield. "It's just rain, rain, rain. If I wasn't working so hard, I'd be at the Cala di Volpe for all of May. It's twenty-nine degrees in Sardinia right now."

Charlene didn't have a clue what Tallulah was talking about, but nodded politely.

"I'm feeling really crummy, Bry," whined Tallulah.

"Just got some things to finish up with Charlene," Bryan said, looking tense. "Haven't we, Charlene?"

Charlene nodded, all hopes of leaving early gone. "Shall I write to the Hong Kong factory manager about the—"

With a pout on her face, Tallulah interrupted, "It's all over

Instagram. There was a fabulous Shuang New York trunk show earlier today, round the corner at Middle Bottom Abbey, and I wasn't invited—"

"Why don't you just delete Instagram, if it stresses you out so much?" Bryan snapped.

Tallulah looked at him as though he were a brainless tortoise. "Bry, I can't. Or at least not until we sell tallulahswim.com. Social media is at the heart of my work."

"All right, so don't delete it," Bryan agreed. "Now, I've got a few things to finish—"

"Bry-Bry, you know what would cheer me up?"

"Just tell me, it's yours," said Bryan hurriedly, keen to placate Tallulah.

"There's an opening at Gagosian tonight, why don't we pop up to London for the evening?"

He shook his head. "I'm teeing off from the lawn after cocktail hour tonight with my coach. Why would I go schlepping up to London to see some bits of art that are completely unfathomable?"

"It's far too wet for golf, Bry," Tallulah continued, undaunted. "We could go for dinner at Dorian afterwards. I've got the secret number."

"Tallulah, I like playing golf at the weekends."

"*Every* weekend?"

"Yes."

"But art improves the right side of the brain—"

Tallulah, thank God, was interrupted by Bryan's phone ringing. It was sitting on the arm of the chesterfield sofa.

"Could you pass my phone, please, Tallulah?" asked Bryan.

"Sure."

As she picked up the device, Tallulah glanced at the screen and the contact name that had appeared.

" 'My One and Only?' " she said accusingly to Bryan, jumping up from the sofa. "I get it." She slapped the phone down on Bryan's desk and flounced out of the room.

"Er . . . thanks," he mumbled, looking dumbfounded. He finally answered the call and put the phone on speaker so Charlene could hear. "The One and Only Ian!" he cried, relieved. "How are you getting on?"

"I'm afraid I have bad news, sir."

"What kind of bad news?" Bryan looked gloomier than ever.

"Mr. Hawkins, I'm sorry to say that our plan is in a state of disarray."

"Ian, your plans are never in a state of disarray," Bryan protested.

"Rarely, I agree. But sometimes even I fall foul of fate. The fact is, we did not act quickly enough regarding Mrs. Hawkins's fortieth birthday."

"What do you mean?"

"Someone else got there first."

"What?"

"Antoni Grigorivich is hosting a party for her."

"He's richer than me! Christ. He's not after her, is he?"

"No, not to worry. Mr. Grigorivich is madly in love with Selby Fairfax."

"Then why is he throwing a party for Tata?"

"He found her weeping in a tent at the Ovington-Williamses' earlier today and took pity on her. He's offered to throw her a party at Little Bottom Priory. She's extraordinarily chuffed."

"But she hates her birthday."

"It's emerged she hates it being forgotten even more, Mr. Hawkins."

"But I didn't forget it," Bryan said impatiently. "She knows I always throw her a surprise birthday party. I tried to talk to her when we were at the school last week but . . . well, it all went wrong."

"I heard."

"What am I going to do now?"

"Plan B," Ian said. "The bended-knee strategy remains in place. But it must occur at a different venue. Instead of going down on bended knee, with the diamond necklace, at a surprise party at Monkton Bottom Manor, you'll go down on bended knee, with the diamond necklace, at the not-surprise party at Little Bottom Priory."

Bryan swallowed. "Must I?" His tone suggested he would rather be dunked head first in a vat of boiling oil.

"I'm afraid so. I'll make sure that *you* are the surprise that night," Ian declared. "In addition, there is another gift to be acquired asap."

"Ian, this is getting tiring. And expensive."

"If you want Tata back, there is no other option, sir. Tickets to Lamu."

34

English riding chic was an area in which Sophie Thompson felt she comfortably excelled. But then she should. After all, it was a topic she'd studied so conscientiously since she'd moved to the Cotswolds that she could have turned in a PhD on the subject.

Regrettably, Sophie had learned the hard way that in Oxfordshire one's riding clothes are judged as ruthlessly as one's party dresses. She'd never forget the sartorial shame of her first ride with friends, innocently billed as a "girls' hack." Sophie had shown up for the ride in jeans, the scuffed jodhpur boots she'd had for Pony Club when she was fifteen, and an old sweatshirt, to find everyone else turned out immaculately in spotless white or cream breeches, custom riding shirts, and expertly polished black boots. As if that hadn't been bad enough, her friends' glistening sport horses, groomed and bathed and pulled for the occasion, had made her own mount—a grubby, furry, 14.2 cob pony with a short neck and thick tail—look like an old nag from a downmarket riding school. Since that fateful ride, Sophie had upped her game. Better horses, better horsey clothes, better riding teachers, better tack.

As hostess of today's ride, Sophie was not going to let herself down. She had worked very, very hard at her look. This had involved many stolen hours studying @jodphursandsons, one of her favourite Instagram accounts, which was full of sepia-toned photographs of women like Jackie Onassis or Lady Astor astride wonderful horses in retro outfits. Then there was @sitwellandwhippet, which documented the equestrian looks of Lady Martha Sitwell, a horse-mad young aristocrat who posted pictures of herself riding side-saddle and clad in bespoke riding habits which she paired with an old-fashioned bowler hat, her cat-like eyes veiled by black net.

Early that Saturday morning—which was sunny, thank goodness—Sophie rose alone because Hugh had unexpectedly departed the night before for what he called a "jolly"—a government tour of Central Asia, though what benefits it would bring to the Health Department Sophie was unable to fathom. (Nor, it seemed, was Hugh when she'd buttonholed him about it.) But Sophie was not very jolly about the "jolly": as she'd pointed out to Hugh before he left, he was going to miss Selby's visit to the Rectory, which she'd arranged for his—and the goat sanctuary's—benefit. "Look, if you could bother her for five grand," Hugh had said, without any apology, "that's all I'm really after." Sophie hadn't even deigned to answer. Hugh was selfish, did what he wanted when he wanted, and there was no use trying to talk him round: that usually just made things worse for her.

She put such matters out of her mind as she slid off her lace nightdress and donned her riding clothes which consisted of a pair of corduroy "elephant" breeches that had belonged to Hugh's mother, a cream silk blouse tied with a wide black grosgrain bow beneath its Peter Pan collar, and a pale yellow moleskin waistcoat. The finishing touch was a pair of brown knee-high, buckled boots that she had bought at a country horse show. Sophie regarded herself in her bedroom mirror with a satisfied air and then went to wake Eddie and give him some breakfast before he was picked up to go to Saturday school.

It was just after eight when there was a rap at the door and Sophie said, "I think Wonky's here, darling. Let's go."

Eddie grabbed his backpack and followed his mother to the front of the house where Stuart, a.k.a. Wonky, the wizened proprietor of the aptly named Wonky's Wheels, the cheapest taxi service in the area, was standing in the driveway with his red people carrier.

"Mornin', Mrs. T.," he said, opening the passenger door for Eddie. "Here you go, lad."

"Thanks," said the boy, hopping inside.

"So kind of you to drive Eddie today," said Sophie. "My husband's suddenly disappeared to the other side of the world with the government and I'm going out riding this morning."

"That why you're dressed like that lady from *National Velvet*?" he chuckled. "You look lovely, dear."

"Thank you." Sophie felt flattered. If Wonky thought she looked as glorious as Elizabeth Taylor had in that movie—well, her look was a success. "Bring Eddie back at four after his cricket?"

"All right, Mrs. T. By the way, I saw that old drunk in the village last night."

Sophie's heart sank. "Oh gosh."

"He was ranting and raving about the Tories outside the pub. Tuggy Drummond had to threaten to call the police to stop him harassing the customers. Just you watch your back, Mrs. T., won't you?"

"Course, Wonks, thank you. As long as he doesn't show up today for my lunch party, I'll be fine," she said with a laugh. The last thing she wanted was Jacko frightening her guests or scaring off Annabel Slingsly-Leland, that lovely girl she'd found on the Radio H-P website to do the table and cook lunch today. "Right, you better go or you'll be late."

A few minutes after they left, Sophie was making herself avocado toast in the kitchen when a message popped up on her phone. *See you at yard at 10 a.m. Ballistic will be looking his best. X Betty.*

Good old Betty Bunbury, thought Sophie, getting her horse ready for her today. The luxury of keeping her beloved gelding at a livery yard meant that Sophie had oodles of time to have a leisurely breakfast and fiddle around with her outfit before she needed to leave. When they'd moved to the Cotswolds all those years ago, she'd been amazed that Hugh had readily agreed to pay for horse livery, though over time she suspected that he hadn't done it to help *her* out, he paid up to make *him* look good. Horses are the simplest *entrée* into local society, but red-faced, hay-strewn wives who show up to the hunt or a dressage lesson on a horse that they have mucked out and tacked up with their own bare hands do not make it into the charmed inner circle of glitzy females in the Cotswolds, because the glitzy females all have grooms, or keep their horses in the same place: Bunbury's Livery Yard in Monkton Bottom. Hugh did not want his wife to be "left out"—because that would mean he would be left out—so he had all-but-begged Sophie to bag a stable at Bunbury's within weeks of their arrival at the Rectory.

Hmmm, Sophie thought, observing her reflection in the kitchen mirror. Maybe she looked a bit too *National Velvet?* Perhaps the old-fashioned hairnet she'd swept her locks into was too dated? She pulled it out and tied her hair into a short ponytail instead. Yes, that was better, she thought, looking in the mirror again. Then she had another idea. She took one of her vintage Hermès scarves from the side of the mirror, and tied it around the ponytail. Perfect, she thought to herself happily, and bounced out of the house.

Sophie pulled Hugh's Porsche (which he now grudgingly allowed her to drive when he was away) into the large concreted parking area at Bunbury's Livery a few minutes before ten o'clock. The yard, situated on the edge of rolling farmland, consisted of two huge American barns that housed around twenty horses in five-star comfort, and a one-storey mobile home that housed Betty Bunbury and her family in far less luxurious conditions.

Sophie alighted from the vehicle to see Betty approaching her at a quick march. The sight of her brought a smile to Sophie's face. Betty (forty, looked fifty-two due to refusal to cover grey roots, or wax chin, plus steady diet of Red Bull, white bread sandwiches, and Mars Bars purchased at the village shop in Monkton Bottom every lunchtime) was one of those stalwarts upon whom British country life depends to run smoothly, the type who can sort out everything from a lame horse to a broken tractor. Today, Betty was dressed in her usual attire, which she dubbed "Barn Hag": a hay-strewn

Joules polo top with thick purple-and-white stripes across the chest, slightly too-tight, manure-stained maroon jodhpurs, orange-and-green knee-high argyle socks, and well-worn moccasins. The huge benefit of the Barn Hag aesthetic was that it meant that Betty was never mistaken for her nemesis—a horse owner or a Pony Club mother. For, although the survival of the Bettys of this world depended on these women, Betty and her ilk held them in disdain. It was not their oodles of money, their absurd clothes, or their braying entitlement that annoyed her and her peers. No, their crime was their *complete* ignorance about horses. If you didn't know the difference between a snaffle and a Cheltenham gag, Betty had zero respect for you. (Unless you decided to employ her to unravel that particular mystery, at exorbitant rates.)

"Morning, Mrs. Thompson," said Betty, beckoning Sophie into the barn and towards a stable near the front. "It's very grand you've got that Mrs. Fairfax from the big house riding out with you today." She opened the stable door to where Ballistic was waiting. "He's all ready for you. Should be good over those jumps at the end of the hack onto Mr. Osborne's farm."

"He's looking so well, Betty. Thank you." Sophie ran her hand over her handsome mount. Ballistic was a quality black 16.2 Irish sport horse whose only marking was a single white star on his forehead, and Betty turned him out for every hack or lesson as though he was attending the Horse of the Year Show. Sophie led him out of the stable and into the yard, where she mounted from the block.

It wasn't long before the yard was full of cars from which Sophie's friends soon emerged. Among the guests, there were, of course, two unspoken contests in progress: who had the best horse, and who looked the best on said horse. Tata had arrived chauffeured by Ian and dressed in a new riding ensemble from Holland Cooper, who did by far the blingiest, sexiest riding stuff you could buy. Today, she'd chosen skintight riding "tights" with a black-and-white houndstooth stripe down the side of each leg, and a matching top emblazoned with an oversized gold logo on the back.

Her matching crash hat was black with a gold trim, and she carried a long schooling whip in one hand. Tata was not one for puffy riding breeches and old-fashioned blouses: she liked riding things that had a hint of S&M. Naturally she was wearing three diamond bracelets, inspired by Selby.

"Soph, such a gorgeous day," Tata called out to her as she sashayed across the yard and looked up at her hostess on Ballistic.

"I know," said Sophie. "Aren't we lucky?"

"God, you're brave being on such a huge horse," Tata went on. She had started riding two years ago, when Minty took it up, and had only recently begun to feel confident on horseback.

"He's very mannerly, which helps," laughed Sophie.

Betty appeared from the shadow of the barn, leading a small palomino mare. "Good morning, Mrs. Hawkins," she said, virtually curtseying to Tata, who was one of her best-paying customers. "Jewel's all set. Can I help you on?"

"Jewel, baby, oh, my baby-baby-baby," said Tata, rubbing the mare's forehead and ears enthusiastically. "God, she is cute."

As soon as Tata was on, Jewel started jogging a little, ready to go, but Tata, who was fit and sporty, simply stood up in her stirrups without losing her balance.

"Betty, can Ian borrow a quad to follow?" she asked. "In case we need someone to come back for something."

"Good idea, Tats," Sophie said.

"Of course, Mrs. Hawkins."

"Here's the key, Ian love, the bike's just behind the farm office," said Betty, pointing across the yard. "Looking very country today, if I may say," she added, regarding him admiringly.

"Thank you," replied Ian as he took the key. He was dressed in a safari shirt, a light-brown quilted Schöffel gilet, and green moleskin trousers tucked neatly into a pair of green Le Chameau wellies, the kind favoured by the royal family. On his head was a lightweight flat cap from Purdey and he had chosen tinted tortoiseshell-framed sunglasses for today.

"Ian looks *so* chic, Tata," said Sophie, looking after him as he headed across the yard towards the farm office. She couldn't quite imagine what it must be like to be accompanied everywhere by a butler who dressed better than any other man in the area.

"He should. He spends even more time than I do on his outfits," laughed Tata. Then, seeing Fernanda's car turning into the yard, she said, "Here comes the woman he'll never leave me for."

"Tata, stop," Sophie shushed her.

Fernanda was soon approaching Sophie and Tata, who were now side by side on their horses in a corner of the yard that was out of the way of the cars. She was dressed like an equestrian Georgia O'Keeffe in denim jodhpurs, cream cowboy boots, a Mexican belt beaded with chunks of turquoise, and a flowing cotton shirt. She greeted the two of them and then said to Tata, "God, *really* love your outfit. You look so sexy like that. Incredible."

"Thanks." Tata's tone was rather cold, and Fernanda looked unsettled.

Sophie diplomatically broke the tension by saying, "Right . . . Fernanda. Why don't you get on? The others will be here soon, then we can all set off."

"I don't trust her an inch any more," said Tata as she and Sophie watched Fernanda stride off towards the barn just as Ian was returning from the other side of the yard on a rather battered green quad bike.

"I'm sure she didn't mean to upset you," said Sophie, trying to placate her. "She's just a mother trying to do the best for her kid. I mean, Luca's had a horrid time—"

Before Sophie could go on, Tata was saying, "I *don't* believe it! Look! Talking to him! In front of me!" Tata pointed towards the entrance to the barn, where Fernanda was chatting with Ian, who had stopped the quad bike next to her. "Shameless," Tata added sniffily.

Sophie watched the exchange closely. Ian said something to Fernanda, who then started gesticulating, as if she was confused. Next, Fernanda glanced over at Tata, then shook her head and carried on talking. It was strange. After a little while Betty appeared with Fernanda's horse—an Appaloosa with extraordinary spotted markings—and she got on.

"She's a total phoney. But she looks amazing on that animal," Tata had to admit.

"Look, Ian's never going to leave you, so can you try and forget this tiff and enjoy the day?" Sophie beseeched her friend.

Thankfully, before Tata could continue whingeing, Antoni had arrived in the yard and parked. Dressed in jeans, sneakers, and a shirt, he sauntered over to them, smiling broadly. "Sophie. Good morning. I am sorry I don't have the correct clothing. As you can tell, I am not a rider. I am praying I don't fall off today."

"You'll be fine, I promise," she reassured him.

He turned to Tata. "My dear, you are looking tremendous, and this golden horse you are on—what a beauty."

"Aw, thank you, Antoni," said Tata, her distress vanishing. "That's why I bought her. As a girl I always wanted a princess pony, something that looked like it was out of a Disney movie."

Betty marshalled Antoni over to the mounting block, where she somehow loaded him onto an enormous cob named Winston who had a hogged mane, fluffy white fetlocks, and hooves the size of dinner plates. He looked like he should have been pulling a cart on a Victorian farm.

Antoni appeared to be petrified. "It's very high up here."

"Winston's safe as houses. If in doubt grab this strap," Betty told him, and pointed at a thick leather band that was buckled around the horse's neck as she led him over to Sophie and Tata. "In any case, I'll be riding next to you to catch you. Ha-ha-ha! Just don't look at the ground and you'll be grand."

At this, Antoni tittered nervously and fixed his eye rigidly on the skyline.

"Where's the guest of honour? I don't know how much longer I can keep Cherokee calm," said Fernanda, who'd just joined the group on horseback. Her horse was fussing and pawing at the ground.

"Looks like she's just arrived. We'll set off as soon as she and Doug are on." Sophie pointed her whip at Selby's Land Rover turning through the gates, pulling a trailer behind it. Josh was at the wheel, with Doug in the front passenger seat, and Selby waved at the group from the back window.

"No one else would have the balls to show up in an old banger like that," remarked Tata.

"You know that old saying," Betty said, a look of approval on her face as Josh lowered the front ramp and led out two stunning chestnut warmblood showjumpers, one after the other. "Don't drive a Rolls-Royce and bring out an old banger of a horse. Drive an old banger and bring out a Rolls-Royce of a horse."

"Too true," Sophie laughed.

Doug got out of the car and Selby followed, dressed in a white figure-hugging, all-in-one stretch riding catsuit and black knee-high boots. The outfit, which zipped all the way up the back, was sleeveless, showing off Selby's lean arms and making her look like a cross between a downhill skier and Jennifer Lawrence in *The Hunger Games*.

"I am *so* jealous," said Sophie, seeing Selby's outfit. "She's in the Yagya equestrian onesie. They're from Sweden."

"Very cool," agreed Tata, making a mental note to buy one online tonight.

Doug and Selby greeted everyone while Josh brought their horses over to the mounting block.

"Hey, everyone, sorry we're a bit late," said Selby, swinging herself athletically onto Dublin's saddle.

"Don't laugh when I get on, guys," said Doug as he hauled himself up. "I haven't ridden in a year."

As he thudded down onto the horse's back, Selby flinched. "Hey there, light seat. Remember that Violet usually rides Maple. If you're not careful, she'll buck you straight off."

Doug batted away her concern. "I'm good. We love each other, don't we, Maple?" he went on, patting the horse on its rump. At this the horse spooked sideways and started jogging on the spot.

"Doug," tutted Selby, shaking her head.

"Ssssh, I'm fine."

Once Betty had heaved herself onto her old hunter, a sturdy strawberry roan named Paddy, Sophie called out, "Okay, everyone, follow me." She jogged ahead on Ballistic and rode towards a farm gate in the far corner of the yard that opened straight out onto pastureland. As the mounted party trotted through the gate, Ian revved up the quad bike and Josh hopped onto the seat next to him.

"Horses look smart, Josh," Ian told him as they zoomed off. "Well done."

"Thanks. Just trying to keep the boss happy. All part of the service."

"She looks very happy to me. But then, she's in love, why wouldn't she look happy?"

"She is?" Josh almost choked.

"That's the rumour."

"Ah, um, right . . ." Josh said nervously. Then he went on, "Where did you hear that?"

"A butler can never reveal his sources. But trust me, it's true."

35

As they rode up onto the hills above the village of Monkton Bottom, Sophie couldn't have been more pleased with the way things were going. Her guests didn't stop oohing at the idyllic views or cooing about how all they *really* wanted was to live in one of the adorable little thatched cottages they occasionally passed en route.

"I feel like I'm in *The Wind in the Willows*," said Doug, jogging along on Maple next to Sophie as they followed the path beside a gurgling stream whose banks were dotted with yellow kingcups and pink cuckoo flowers. "It's paradise. I can't thank you enough for including me."

"Not at all," said Sophie. "It's nice to get to know you. I'm really glad you came."

"Not sure Selby is," he said. "Think I might be getting in the way of some kind of romance she's got going on."

Sophie turned and looked behind her for a moment. Selby and Antoni were sauntering along on their horses, with Tata at their side, the three of them gossipping non-stop. She wasn't quite sure what to say to Doug, so she grasped around for a platitude. "I'm sure there's nothing to it," she said.

"Maybe," Doug replied, sounding unconvinced. "Thanks, though. So, any chance of popping a jump on the way?"

"Actually, yes," said Sophie. "There are some wooden fences and a nice hedge into Great Bottom Home Farm, Vere Osborne's place."

"A hedge? Really?" Doug's eyes lit up. "That would make my year, to jump an English hedge."

"Great. But before that, there's a treat in store."

About an hour into the hack, Sophie turned off a rough, stony bridleway and beckoned the group to follow her along the edge of a field swaying with the green ears of early wheat.

"Where are we going?" asked Doug.

Sophie pointed towards a woody copse situated at the top of a gentle hill in the distance. "Surprise," she said coyly.

It wasn't enough, you see, in the competitive world of the Oxfordshire riding scene, to provide a spectacular hack and a Claridge's-level lunch. No. An equestrian event had to be far more unique than that—there had to be the aforementioned "treat" along the way. Something whimsical. Magical. Something that everyone could post on Instagram that minute. Sophie knew that a hack with friends was not just a social exercise, it was a social media exercise. It was about who *wasn't* on the ride just as much as who was. She wanted to make damn sure that all those grand girls round and about, like those Pennybacker-Hoare sisters, the ones who hadn't invited her on their hacks, would be well aware that she'd not invited them on her hack, the first of which that had included Selby Fairfax, and thus the most prestigious one of the summer.

"Anyone fancy a cold drink?" she called out to the other riders.

"Mmmm! Lovely!" came the chorus from behind her.

"This way," Sophie replied, kicking her horse on and heading deep into the wood, while retrieving her phone from the pocket of her breeches and somehow managing to dial a number without losing the reins.

"We're two minutes away," she said briskly. "Is everything ready?"

"Yes, Mrs. Thompson, all set. Just ride up," said the voice at the other end.

The group meandered along a leaf-strewn track beneath a green canopy of beech trees. After a few minutes, the riders came upon a castellated stone folly situated in a sunlit glade.

"Is this for real?" asked Doug. "Soph, I could really get to like this English riding thing," he went on, as four staff dressed in monogrammed tops and safari trousers stepped forward to help the riders from their various mounts, aided by Ian and Josh, who had climbed off the quad.

The scene was dreamy. Sophie's pit-stop in paradise centred around a rustic outdoor table temptingly arranged with drinks and eats: there were chilled jugs of home-made lemonade; decanters of iced sloe gin; cold-pressed fresh-mint extract and silver goblets with gleaming gold insides to drink it all from; as well as wooden bowls of herbed walnuts and homemade truffle crisps to snack on.

"I'm impressed," said Tata to Sophie, as the group wandered over to the table, their horses' reins looped over their arms. "How the hell did you find this place?"

"Oh, just, you know, one of Hugh's business friends," replied Sophie, trying to sound casual. She didn't want anyone knowing how hard she'd had to work to pull this one off. "Some Kazakh oil guy owns it. It's his 'shooting hut' so he only uses it in season. So pretty, isn't it?" Sophie didn't let on that the four staff were also the Kazakh oil guy's, or that Hugh had been in a fearful huff about having to list "loan of shooting lodge" in the members' Register of Interests in the House of Commons.

While her friends sipped drinks from the Kazakh oil guy's silver goblets, Sophie made it her business to snap as many joyful images of the table, the guests, and the folly as she could, though she'd wait to post them until she was at home. There was a particularly gorgeous shot of Selby chatting to Antoni, the horses behind them, and she loved a photograph she'd taken of Tata and Doug, laughing together, with the folly in view.

After a while, Tata came up to Sophie and whispered to her, "Don't they seem perfect together?" She gestured towards Antoni and Selby, who were still deep in conversation, a few feet apart from everyone else. "You can see it in their body language, can't you?"

"Totally," agreed Sophie, sneaking a sideways glance at Selby and Antoni, who did seem very taken with each other.

Just then, Ian sidled up to his boss. "Sorry to interrupt. May I have a quiet word, Mrs. H.?"

Tata looked, for once, a little annoyed with her butler. "Does it have to be this minute, Ian?"

"Apologies. But it's about the—ahem—situation vis-à-vis Luca, Mrs. Ovington-Williams. I feel I must inform you of a development."

Tata pinged to attention. "In that case, spill the beans."

Sophie made to leave the pair, but Tata said, "Sophie. Stay." She looked at Ian. "Sophie knows. So come on," she said impatiently. "What's happened?"

"Well, this morning, when Mrs. Ovington-Williams arrived," said Ian, in his most discreet tones, "I told her that I could not possibly accept her generous offer."

"What did she say?" Tata was on tenterhooks.

"She said, 'What offer?'"

"'What offer?'" Tata repeated, agape.

"So I said, 'Mrs. Ovington-Williams, I am talking about your offer to double my salary to come and be Luca's manny.'"

"What did she say?" asked Tata.

"She said she had no idea what I was talking about," Ian replied. "She was terribly offended."

"But didn't she give you the letter from Luca herself?" Sophie asked.

"Indeed she did. So when I asked her what she had thought was in the envelope, she said that Luca had told her it was my birthday card."

Tata's face fell. "Oh, Ian, don't tell me I've missed your birthday."

"You have certainly not. It isn't my birthday for many months and I will be making you aware, as ever."

"Phew. But then why did Luca say it was your birthday?"

"To get his mother to give me his letter without suspicion, I'd imagine."

"I feel sorry for that little boy," Sophie said. "I mean, the whole thing is so sad."

Ian nodded sympathetically. "The upshot is, Mrs. Hawkins, that I can't possibly accept your four hundred per cent pay rise."

"No, Ian, I insist."

"*I* insist, Mrs. Hawkins, and that is the end of it."

"What on earth do I say to Fernanda now?" said Tata.

"Nothing," Ian told her.

"What?"

"She doesn't know that you know."

"But I was so offish to her the last few times we met. She *must* suspect that I suspected her."

"I hope you don't mind, Mrs. Hawkins, but when she mentioned a worrying cooling of relations between you, I invented a problem with your health. Nothing life-threatening."

Tata sighed in relief. "Very sensible," she said.

"I explained your 'irrational' behaviour by saying you had run out of your De-Liver-Ance liver cleanse supplement and it had temporarily affected your usually upbeat mood."

"Ian," said Tata, pressing her hands together gratefully, "you really are an angel."

∽

Sophie looked at her watch. It was a quarter past twelve already and still an hour's ride to the Rectory. Everyone needed to get back on their horses and go, or the lunch would be ruined. Soufflés waited for no man.

"Hey, guys, let's be off," she called out to the group, who were still by the table chatting, drinking, and snacking, oblivious to the time. "There are a few jumps at the end. But Betty will take anyone who'd prefer not to do them through the gates."

"That would be me," said Antoni, his hand aloft.

"Can't say I'm an expert at leaving the ground either," Tata admitted. "Antoni, I'll stick with you and Betty."

"Wonderful," said Antoni, smiling warmly at her. "And then we can discuss your birthday party. I want it to be perfect for you."

A few minutes later, after a round of girth-tightening and stirrup-shortening, the riders left the woodland and were soon flying across open fields bordered by broad hedges and stone walls, Antoni hanging on for dear life by the neck strap. As they headed towards an open gate, the horses eventually slowed to a trot and Sophie signalled for everyone to stop. Once the horses had calmed and their riders had their breath back, she said, "Okay, now for the fun part. Jumpers, follow me; the non-jumpers go with Betty. Then it's a shortcut over Vere's farm across the fields to the Rectory and lunch."

With that, the party divided into two. Betty, Antoni, and Tata walked their horses briskly towards the next gate, followed by Ian and Josh on the quad, while Sophie, Doug, Selby, and Fernanda set off at a canter towards the hedge line in the distance.

***

As Sophie rode ahead, Selby started to wonder if this eccentric British tradition of "hedge-hopping," as her hostess had described it, was an entirely sensible idea. Selby was a confident rider, not usually prone to nerves, but the hedge they were approaching, which had looked manageable from a distance, now appeared enormous.

"It's massive!" Selby yelled at Doug, who was cantering next to her.

"It's fine, I'll give you a lead over it," Doug shouted back, as fearless as ever.

"Okay," said Selby, slowing up her horse so that Doug could go in front of her and get in line behind Fernanda, who was following Sophie. She wanted to leave plenty of space between them.

Moments later, Selby watched as Sophie leaned forward, tickled Ballistic's flank with her whip, and sailed over the hedge as though she was in full flight. She was quickly tailed by Fernanda, who cleared the jump confidently.

Maple, a few paces behind, pricked up her ears, locked onto the jump, and took off boldly. Selby saw Doug and the horse land on the other side of the hedge, but in a split second, Maple tripped, throwing Doug head first onto the ground and crashing down on top of him. Somehow, Selby managed to halt Dublin in front of the hedge before he took off, and looked on horrified, as Maple writhed on the grass for a few seconds, Doug half underneath her, before she eventually struggled onto her feet.

"Doug!" Selby shouted. "Doug!"

But Doug didn't move. He lay motionless on the ground, exactly where he had fallen.

―――

The non-jumping party had seen the accident unfold, aghast, from the adjacent field. "Christ," said Ian to Josh. "We need to get over there now."

"Step on it, Ian," Josh replied.

"Betty, Antoni, Tata, follow us. We're going to need all the help we can get," Ian shouted behind him as he sped towards the scene of the accident. "Mr. Fairfax could be seriously injured."

As the riders followed behind the quad, Betty tutted, "Always the Americans. They say they can ride, but they never can."

"Mrs. Fairfax is a wonderful rider," said Antoni defensively.

"She's an exception," was Betty's curt response.

"Will Doug be okay?" Antoni asked Tata, bumping awkwardly up and down on the saddle as he cantered next to her.

"We just have to pray," she replied.

Ian, no surprise, excelled in an emergency. He raced the quad across the terrain towards the side of the hedge where Doug had fallen off, Josh hanging onto the seat of the vehicle for dear life as it lurched up and down. Selby, who had had to go around the hedge and through the gate, galloped on and soon caught up with them.

When they arrived, they were confronted by a ghastly spectacle. Doug was lying on the ground just beyond the hedge, splayed out and motionless, with Sophie kneeling down next to him while Fernanda stood a few feet away holding both their horses, her expression wan. Doug's face was half-blackened with earth and spattered with blood, and the glimpses of his skin that were visible were either ashen-white or starting to turn a bluish-purple where there was bruising. His clothes were torn where the horse had landed on him, and Maple was limping away, blood coursing from a gash at the top of her near leg. The scene was mayhem, with everyone talking at once, getting off their horses, then hanging on to them by the reins from the ground and panicking about what to do next. Selby threw her horse's reins at Tata and rushed over to Doug, dropping onto the grass beside him.

"Ian, can you deal with the patient?" said Josh, leaping off the quad. "I need to save Maple."

"No problem," Ian replied as he dashed towards Doug and crouched next to him. He had, naturally, graduated with a Distinction in the Greycoats' Advanced First-Aider module and considered himself as well qualified as any NHS paramedic. He looked at Selby with a sympathetic expression on his face. "Mrs. Fairfax," he said as reassuringly as he could. "Let me check him over before we decide what to do."

"He's not responding to anything," said Sophie, looking scared.

"I'm so worried," said Selby, as Ian set to work.

"Doug? It's Ian. You're going to be all right," he said as he gently squeezed Doug's right wrist. "We have a pulse. Great." Next he put one ear close to Doug's face and listened intently. "Breathing, but laboured and he's very cold." He took off his prized Schöffel gilet and laid it over Doug's chest, while Sophie removed her waistcoat and carefully placed it over his legs.

"Ian, is he concussed?" asked Sophie.

"I think so, Mrs. Thompson," said Ian.

"I feel so awful," said Sophie, a helpless expression on her face. "Selby, I'm sorry. I'm incredibly sorry."

"It's not your fault," Selby replied.

"He looks like he's shaking," Tata said from where she was standing.

"It's the shock. Right, we need to get him to hospital," said Ian, looking up at the others. "Before his temperature drops even further."

"The only way out of here is the air ambulance," said Betty. "I'm calling now." She grabbed her phone from her pocket and started tapping at the screen but soon gave up. "Oh, Lord. No signal."

"If I'd known, I would have brought my helicopter," said Antoni, trying to be helpful.

"It's too dangerous to take him on the quad," Ian said, wracking his brain.

"Wait! Look!" said Fernanda, pointing to the fence line at the bottom of the field. "There's someone coming."

The whole party turned to see an ancient red tractor-trailer chugging slowly along the edge of the field, a flurry of smoke puffing from the chimney on the front.

"Dreamboat to the rescue," said Betty, suddenly all aquiver.

"Who?" asked Antoni.

"Vere Osborne. Only the posh gentleman farmers from London drive those old-fashioned tractors."

"Betty, quick, go and intercept him on the quad," said Ian. "He can help us get Doug to the hospital."

"Okay," she replied, handing her horse's reins to Tata. She climbed onto the quad and was soon speeding across the field, waving down Vere.

Josh, meanwhile, had managed to catch Maple but her leg looked awful.

"Mrs. Thompson," he called out as he walked towards her leading the horse, "I need to make a tourniquet. Did you bring any bandages with you?"

"No—God—I just didn't think," said Sophie. "I feel so stupid. How on earth could I have left for a long hack without bandages?"

"Don't worry. This'll do," replied Josh.

Before she knew it, Josh had reached around to the back of her head, whipped the vintage Hermès scarf off her ponytail, and started to bind it around the horse's wound.

"Wait—" she began.

"What?" Josh asked. "Do you think it's tight enough to stop the bleeding?"

"Probably," said Sophie, resigned.

It wasn't long before Betty was heading back on the quad, the red tractor-trailer lurching slowly across the field behind her. They soon pulled up as close to Doug as they could safely get. Vere, a grave look on his face, jumped down from the cab and dashed to Doug's side, where he squatted opposite Selby and peered at the victim.

The party fell silent as Vere spoke. "Josh, Ian—everyone—use anything we can to make a stretcher. There are old sacks, fence posts and rope in the back of the trailer that'll do. Selby, stay here, keep talking to him."

As Vere got everyone working together on the stretcher, Selby tried desperately to think of things to say to Doug, rambling something about the children and the dogs. Suddenly his eyes flickered open for a moment.

"Vere! Quick. I think he's coming around," Selby called out.

He and Ian rushed from the trailer and bent over Doug, who very slowly opened and closed his eyes a few times, but they were completely bloodshot, unseeing.

Vere said, "Let's ask him questions, try and keep him awake."

"Doug?" whispered Selby, leaning closer to him. "Can you hear me?"

Gingerly, painfully, Doug slid his eyes towards Selby and fixed them on her. "Who—are—you?"

"Oh no," Selby said, trying her hardest not to cry.

"Who is the President of the United States?" asked Vere.

Doug whispered hoarsely, "Ban-an-a-milk-sh-shake."

"What's he talking about?" said Selby. "If he's got a head injury . . . oh, God—Doug? Doug!"

But Doug didn't reply. His eyelids gradually shut and his head lolled heavily to one side. He was unconscious.

"Ian, Josh, let's get him out of here," said Vere, sounding perturbed. "There's not a moment to lose."

36

The uneaten soufflés were the saddest thing Sophie had ever seen. She had never imagined that a human being could mourn a flan so intensely, but that afternoon, as she sat gloomily in her kitchen with Fernanda and watched Annabel pack up the food she'd made to take it to the local shelter, Sophie realised how much those tragic little puffs of egg and goat cheese had meant to her. The soufflés, you see, were not just food. They were a symbol of Sophie's dreams, her aspirations for herself—part of a performance that had been meant to happen at lunchtime today. Had Douglas Fairfax not fallen off his horse, she would now be sitting at the long garden table under the apple trees with her friends, with not a care in the world. There was nothing Fernanda could say to mitigate the situation: the hack had been a disaster, Selby Fairfax would blame her forever, and Hugh would probably make her get rid of Ballistic to punish her for being so stupid. Now, she was rather grateful he was away after all.

She and Fernanda had even failed to do the one task they'd been given by Selby—getting in touch with Kirk Somers, Doug's boyfriend, and giving him the news. His phone kept going to voicemail.

"Why don't we send him a WhatsApp?" suggested Fernanda eventually.

"You can't text with news like that," Sophie said. "What if he doesn't get it until it's the middle of the night here, with the time difference, and then he can't get hold of anyone?"

"What about Doug's parents? Has anyone talked to them?"

"They passed away years ago."

"That's sad," said Fernanda. Then, seemingly out of nowhere, she said, "I had the weirdest conversation with Ian earlier."

"You did?"

"He said Luca had asked him to be his manny."

Sophie played dumb. "No!"

"Yup. Luca asked me to give a birthday card to Ian but it turned out to be a note containing a job offer. Can you imagine the drama if Tata had found out?"

Sophie raised her eyebrows in mock horror. "Dread to think."

"There's no way Luca would have done this by himself. Michael put him up to it, I'm sure of it."

"What?" said Sophie, disbelieving. "Why would he do that?"

"A couple of weeks ago he suggested we hire Ian. Of course I said no, but I never thought he'd go behind my back. He worries about Luca a lot, but it's no excuse. Anyway," she went on, looking put out, "my husband will have a lot of explaining to do to yours truly when he gets back from location—"

Before Fernanda could say any more, the sound of shouting came from outside the house. She leaped up from her seat. "What the hell was that?"

"Probably that poor old drunk from the village," said Sophie. She was so emotionally exhausted by the day's events that she didn't have the energy to go to the door.

"Burn the Tories!" came the refrain.

"Let's call the cops," said Fernanda, looking suddenly pale.

Sophie simply raised her arm and batted the air, dismissing Fernanda's concern. "He'll go. Honestly, don't worry."

"Michael would *freak* if someone came anywhere near our property and behaved like that. At least call Hugh."

"He's in Kazakhstan on some work trip. Anyway, Hugh always says he's harmless," said Sophie, getting up and putting on the kettle. "I mean, burn the Tories? Really? It's ridiculous."

The airless, windowless waiting room at Banbury General Hospital was the kind of place you wanted to spend five minutes, not five hours. For Selby, Tata, and Vere, who had been there since lunchtime, the wait for news seemed endless.

"I'm going to get a drink and something to eat," said Tata, standing up from the orange plastic bench. "Can I grab you both something?"

"If they've got a chicken sandwich, that would suit me down to the ground," said Vere. "I'm starving."

"I'll come with you. Stretch my legs," said Selby, getting up too.

She and Tata walked out into the busy corridor. It was noisy, clattering with the sounds of trolleys and wheelchairs and staff stalking up and down, too busy to even make eye contact. Eventually they found a lone vending machine.

"I'll have a Coca-Cola," Selby said, looking into the window.

Tata pushed her card into the slot and bought two Cokes and two sandwiches in packets which clanked into the tray at the bottom.

"Mmmm, sugar," said Selby, taking a glug of soda. "Listen, you don't need to stay here any longer, Tata. You've been so kind."

"Don't be silly. Ian's looking after Minty."

"But—"

"And she much prefers him to me anyway."

Selby smiled gratefully. "I appreciate it."

"Course," said Tata, popping open her Coke and sipping it.

They wandered along the corridor for a few yards towards a newspaper stand which gleamed like a beacon in the dreary environs. When they reached it, they started listlessly flicking through the sparse selection of magazines and books for sale.

"Dreamboat's a bit of a hero, isn't he?" said Tata, perusing a copy of *Vogue*.

"I keep thinking Doug could have died if Vere hadn't shown up," said Selby. "He was amazing today."

"Betty says he gives her a 'fanny flutter' if he even looks at her."

Tata giggled naughtily and Selby burst out laughing at this. "He's much more sensitive than he seems from the outside," she said.

"Hmmm," Tata mused, putting back the magazine. "Sounds like I need to set him up with someone."

"I don't think he's ready," Selby replied. "I mean, he's still got Anjelica's horse, and his greenhouse is full of her plant collection. He's grieving her."

"But she died three years ago." Tata looked at Selby, bemused. "If you weren't already taken by you-know-who, I think he'd be your perfect man."

Selby blushed. "Honestly, it's not going anywhere with you-know-who."

"He adores you."

Selby grimaced. "That's the problem."

"What?"

"It's just . . . there's a few things. I mean, our ages, for one—"

"You're not *so* far apart," Tata said, puzzled. Did Antoni's age really matter?

"Then, he sends me these silly texts, *all* the time, like a teenager."

"Awww. So sweet," Tata replied. "Just enjoy it, Selby. Especially now. You need someone who's got your back. Come on, let's take this revolting-looking sandwich to Vere."

∞

Selby checked her watch, feeling strung out. "It's nearly nine o'clock. Why hasn't anyone told us anything?"

As the afternoon had started to fade and the evening had drawn in, Tata had finally gone home and Selby and Vere had sunk into an exhausted silence, as though saving their energy for the crisis that must inevitably come.

Suddenly the door to the waiting room opened and a nurse put her head around it. "Fairfax family?"

"Sort of," said Selby.

The woman entered the room. She was dressed in a blue uniform with a badge reading NURSE BEATTY pinned to her lapel and was holding a clipboard in front of her. A stout female with a meaty chin and strong hands, she looked like the sort of person who was capable of lifting a sick patient into a bath single-handed.

"Evening," she said. "Are you Mr. Fairfax's wife?" she asked Selby.

"Was. We used to be married but he doesn't have any other family except our daughters, who are at home."

"Right. Mr. Granby's on his way."

"Who?" asked Selby.

"The top doctor here," she said.

At this news, Vere and Selby exchanged worried looks but before they could ask anything, the aforementioned Mr. Granby blew in from behind Nurse Beatty. Kitted out in blue scrubs, he had an authoritative air about him and a grave expression on his face.

"Apologies to you both for such a long wait," he said politely. "I've been in theatre all afternoon with patients. Mrs. Fairfax?" he asked, looking at Selby.

"Yes," she replied.

"I'm sorry to tell you . . ." Mr. Granby began, but seeing the fear on Selby's face he paused. As though trying to find the right words, he finally went on, "The thing is, very unexpectedly, when Doug was admitted this afternoon he fell into a coma."

Selby gasped, speechless. Her face whitened and she instinctively clutched Vere's arm.

"We're doing everything we can."

"How long will this last?" Vere asked, putting his hand on Selby's to comfort her.

"Head injuries are unpredictable," Mr. Granby replied, pursing his lips. "It can be a few hours, days, or sometimes weeks. All we can do is keep him comfortable and pray he wakes soon."

"And when he does, he'll be okay?" asked Vere.

"There are a lot of unknowns." Mr. Granby spoke in a deadly serious tone. "We need to do scans, then I'll be able to tell you more."

"What am I going to tell our daughters?" said Selby. "I don't know how they'll cope."

At this, Nurse Beatty went towards Selby and gave her a reassuring pat on the shoulder, saying, "Tell them the truth, Mrs. Fairfax, and that their dad is going to be okay. He will be. I promise. Just make sure they're going to school and are around their friends. Stick to your normal routine, that's the best thing for them."

"Okay, yup," Selby mumbled.

Mr. Granby's pager soon started beeping and he glanced at it and then said, "Nurse, we need to get back to our ward rounds. Mrs. Fairfax, we will be doing the scans later, just as soon as the machine is free. We'll let you know."

"Thanks," she said, sitting down on the bench, resigned.

"But in the meantime I suggest you both go home, get some rest, and we'll see you in the morning," he went on.

With that, Mr. Granby and Nurse Beatty left the room, leaving the duo stunned.

"You get back to your girls," said Vere. "I'll stay."

"If you're sure."

"I am," said Vere. "There's no one waiting for me at home. I'll ring you if there's any news."

∞

Selby was just emerging from the hospital when she heard someone call her name.

It was Josh, walking towards her up the wheelchair-friendly ramp from the car park. He looked worn out, still in his bloodstained breeches.

Selby was surprised to see him. "What are you doing here so late?"

"I wanted to see if you were okay."

"Doug's so ill," she said, shaking her head. "He's in a coma."

Shock registered on Josh's face. "I am truly sorry, Selby. Truly."

"I honestly can't believe it," she said. "The girls will be devastated."

"I know it's not much comfort, but Maple's okay. The vet put some stitches in her leg—she's going to be fine."

"That's good news. I really appreciate you coming here to tell me."

"Of course." He smiled kindly at Selby and went on, "And, we did have a date tonight . . . not that I was expecting it after the day we've had."

Shit shit shit, said Selby to herself. The break-up dinner. What was she going to do about Josh now? She could hardly break up with him outside a hospital while her ex-husband was in a coma inside, and when what she really wanted and needed to do now was get back to her daughters and reassure them that Dad was going to be all right. Her heart sank when she realised that Josh was holding a bunch of red carnations wrapped in cellophane in one hand.

"Maybe . . . er . . . another time?" Selby said non-committally. Surely the flirtation would die a natural death now without the need for any kind of explanation.

"Um, the thing is—" Josh went on, an anxious expression on his face.

"What?" asked Selby. "Are you okay?"

"Yeah. It's just . . ." He shifted awkwardly from one foot to another as he spoke. "What I was going to say was, that go-see I did recently, well, I got the job."

"I knew you would," Selby said, wondering why he was telling her about this now.

"It's the new Hermès men's fragrance campaign."

"That's great," she said, making to leave.

But Josh didn't take the hint and continued, "They wanted someone who can ride for the photographs, and . . . this is the hard part . . . my agent thinks I should move to Paris. They think I'll get a lot more work out there after this job."

Phew, thought Selby, but tried her best to look disappointed. "We'll all miss you," she told him.

"Look, I knew you'd be really upset. I wanted to tell you tonight, at dinner, but with the accident and everything . . ." he went on.

"Oh." Selby was surprised to feel a little annoyed. *She* was going to have been the one to break it off over dinner tonight.

"That's why I got you these flowers, at the petrol station on the way." He handed her the bunch of carnations.

"Thanks." Selby took the flowers and sniffed them. They had no fragrance at all. "Very sweet of you."

"I wanted to try and cheer you up. I know how awful it is, being dumped—"

Dumped? Selby was too furious to speak. Seeing the look on her face, Josh then garbled, "You know . . . what happened the other night—it was a mistake, I see that now. But, Selby, I don't want to make you feel bad about yourself over this. You are an incredibly attractive woman. This has got nothing to do with your age. Nothing."

If she hadn't been quite so exhausted, Selby would have swung a right hook in the general direction of Josh's stunning face and wrecked his modelling career for the foreseeable future.

"It's just," he mumbled, "you see, much as I like you, I don't think you and I feel the same way about each other."

Selby couldn't help her sarcastic tone. "Perhaps not," she said.

"I mean, I'm not in love with you—"

"What?" she started.

"Please, I apologise for leading you on. I didn't mean to break your heart like this. I can stay on for a few weeks, until you find someone to take over the stables. The campaign starts shooting early July."

"Sure," said Selby, too tired to do anything but try to end the conversation.

"Friends?" said Josh.

"Friends," Selby replied.

"Can I give you a ride?"

"Nope, I'm good," said Selby. "Alan's on his way to pick me up."

With that, Josh pecked her on the cheek and strolled back to the car park, leaving Selby standing outside the hospital. As if the accident hadn't been bad enough, being dumped by a younger man on the same day was just about all she could take. The second Josh was out of sight, Selby burst into tears.

37

Tata had no appetite at all. The beautiful pear and papaya fruit plate that Ian had prepared for her breakfast sat untouched on the table in front of her.

"I can't believe what's happened," she said to him as he set down a little pot of coffee and a jug of hot oat milk. "Selby rang me last night in the most awful state. Doug's in a coma."

"Goodness, Mrs. Hawkins, what horrible news," said Ian, unnerved. "Very worrying."

Tata regarded the cup in front of her, and poured herself some coffee, thinking intently. "Ian," she suddenly said, looking up at him, "do you think I need a 'reality check?' "

Ian was rather surprised. Tata was not usually one for reflection, but examination of the self was hardly something to be discouraged. "It's never a bad idea to remind oneself of the state of things in the real world," he said.

Tata looked pensive. "You're right," she said, finally starting to pick at her fruit salad.

Just then a car horn honked in the driveway. Tata put down her fork, got up, and grabbed her handbag.

"That's Sophie. We're going to meet Selby at the hospital together. Moral support."

"I'm sure she'll appreciate it," Ian said. "I'll get Minty up in a bit and drop her at the stables for her lesson. Shall I collect you from the hospital after that?"

"Perfect. See you later."

"Soph, are you all right?"

As soon as she'd got into the car, Tata could tell all was not well with her friend. She looked unusually drawn and tired.

"It's Hugh," she said as they drove away from the Old Coach House.

"What's happened?"

"There's been huge anti-government protests in Kazakhstan and everything's shut down. He's stuck in the embassy and no one's allowed to go anywhere and there are no flights in or out."

"Christ," said Tata.

"I haven't said anything to Eddie," Sophie went on. "I mean, I'm sure it'll be fine, the Foreign Office will get them out eventually, but . . . it's a worry."

"Of course. Look, anything I can do."

"Thanks," said Sophie. "Anyway, that's enough about me and my problems. Let's focus on Doug now. I mean, a coma—it doesn't get any worse, does it?"

When Tata and Sophie walked into the waiting room at Banbury General a little later, they were surprised to be met by the sight of Vere Osborne sprawled on a bench, fast asleep, still in his farm overalls from the day before.

"What's Sleeping Beauty doing here?" Tata whispered, hoping not to wake him.

Sophie shrugged. "Search me."

Just then, the door opened behind them. They turned to see Selby enter the room, looking tired and pale. When she saw Vere asleep on the bench, she smiled.

"He stayed all night," she said in a low voice. "To make sure there was someone here for Doug. He doesn't even *know* Doug."

"How sweet," said Sophie.

"He is officially the nicest man IN THE WORLD," Tata whispered, her mind whirring.

"So kind of you both to come," said Selby.

"Of course," said Tata. "We want to be here."

On the bench, Vere was starting to stir. He soon opened his eyes and looked, blankly, at the three women who were now staring at him from above, as though he were an alien species.

"Oh," he said, gradually sitting up. "Sorry! Morning! Must have fallen asleep. Hi, Selby . . . Tata. Sophie." He rubbed his eyes and yawned, ruffling his hair.

"I stopped at Daylesford and got *croissants aux amandes* on the way for everyone," said Sophie, offering up a thick paper carrier-bag printed with a photograph of a handsome cow.

Vere eyed the bag hungrily. "May I?" he asked.

"Of course," replied Sophie and handed him a croissant.

"Mmmm," said Vere, biting into it.

"Any news overnight?" Tata asked.

He stopped eating for a moment and said, "A nurse came in about two a.m. and told me Doug was 'stable.' That's it."

"In other words, they don't know anything," Selby said, her tone pessimistic.

Vere sighed. "All we can do is wait."

Resignedly, Selby sat down on the bench, took a croissant from the bag and nibbled listlessly at it. "Tell me your news, girls. Anything to distract me."

Before anyone could offer anything up, the door opened and Nurse Beatty had marched into the room.

"Good morning, everyone," she said. She had a fixed expression on her face this morning, as if she were trying not to give anything away. "Mr. Granby is just coming."

"What is it?" asked Selby, getting up.

"Let's just see what the consultant says."

The minutes ticked by but Nurse Beatty was adept with distraught relatives and she soon got some chat going, asking everyone about work and where they lived.

"I'm in a flat in Chipping Norton," she said when they mentioned the Bottoms. "But I do enjoy a trip out to the Great Bottom Arms now and again. Lovely pub now it's all been redone, just lovely."

Eventually Mr. Granby arrived, looking no less serious than the day before. Short of time as ever, he got straight to the point.

"There's no easy way to put this, Mrs. Fairfax," he said, "but the scans show a swelling on the brain—"

"What?" Selby started.

"When he fell, he hit his head hard, and the tissues around that blow are inflamed."

"But what does that mean for Doug?" Tata asked.

"The injury has to heal now and sometimes a coma is the body's way of allowing the brain to rest and have the chance to get better," Mr. Granby explained.

"How long will that be?" Selby asked.

"I can't say precisely, but at least a few days, maybe even a few weeks."

"And when he comes round, he'll be okay?" asked Vere.

"I hope," was all that Mr. Granby would say.

Nurse Beatty checked her watch and then said, "Mr. Granby, you're due in theatre in an hour. We'd best be getting on."

"Right. Yup." The consultant gave Selby as hopeful a look as he could and then said, "Mrs. Fairfax, I will be in touch if anything changes."

∞

A few minutes after the medics had left, Ian arrived to collect Tata.

"What a shock," he said when he heard the latest news. "I am sorry, Mrs. Fairfax. If there's anything I can do to help, you know I'm here."

"That's very thoughtful, thank you," said Selby. "But I get the sense it's just a waiting game now."

"Right, yes," he replied.

"Ian, I think we should call Antoni," said Tata. "Tell him what's happened and that we need to cancel my birthday party."

"Cancel," Ian repeated. He was perturbed: what about Bryan, and the diamonds, and the bended knee? He'd thought Plan B was foolproof but if there was no party, there was no move back to Monkton Bottom Manor for Tata, Minty, or Ian.

"It doesn't feel right planning a party when Doug's so ill," Tata went on.

Ian didn't want the strategy to fall apart, but Tata had a point. Parties and comas didn't exactly go together like strawberries and cream. You can imagine his relief when Selby said, "Don't do that."

"But it's less than two weeks away," Tata replied.

"Tata, you *must* celebrate your birthday," Selby insisted firmly. "I'm sure Doug will be up and about by then."

"Really?" Tata looked hopeful.

"Please don't call it off," Selby said. "The last thing Doug would want is everyone moping around because of him. We could be waiting weeks for him to regain consciousness. And if we're not, even better, he's got a party to look forward to."

"Only if you're sure," Tata said.

"Of course I am." Selby managed a smile. "Let me do the flowers? It'll take my mind off everything."

"That would be a real treat," Tata said, a warm feeling enveloping her. Selby was more than just a glamorous acquaintance now. She was a true friend.

38

Charlene Potts was a bit miffed, if she was being honest, and Charlene was someone who liked to be honest. The reason for her aggravated state was that she had planned to attend one of the great annual events of the Bottoms that Sunday evening— the Young Farmers' Ferreting Fest, which was, right this minute, taking place on a steep bank beneath Potts' Piggery. But instead of getting blotto on cheap local cider with a group of twenty-something farm lads and lasses tonight, she found herself in Bryan's office at Monkton Bottom Manor, wordlessly examining a glittering emerald and diamond necklace and a pair of matching earrings.

Charlene couldn't quite believe her eyes, or her boss: Mr. Hawkins had telephoned her just a few hours earlier from the airport in Frankfurt and informed her that she needed to get up to the Manor pdq to receive a package from a company called Bulgari on his behalf, wrap the contents beautifully and then store it safely until Tata's birthday. Her protestations about the upcoming ferreting fest had done nothing to sway him, which is why she now found herself struggling with reams of tissue paper and ribbons on Bryan's desk. Gift-wrapping was not part of her skill set.

Still, Charlene had somehow managed to make the box look presentable and was about to put it in a drawer when she heard a sound coming from outside.

"Hello?" she called.

"Only me." Tallulah was standing at the door, draped in a canary-yellow silk dressing gown and not much else. "What are you doing in Bryan's office on a Sunday?" Her voice was accusatory, and her eye soon fixed on the large Bulgari bag on the desk and the gift-wrapped box sitting next to it.

"Just catching up," said Charlene unconvincingly, hurriedly tidying away the tissue and ribbons.

Tallulah clutched at her heart in a melodramatic fashion. "Bryan! So sweet! Oh my God, I *knew* this was going to happen."

"What?" said Charlene.

"Nothing. Just—don't tell Bryan you saw me in here, please. I was worried there was, you know, a burglar or something."

"Won't say a thing," said Charlene.

"*Merci*," said Tallulah. A dreamy look came over her face. "It's worked, hasn't it?"

"What has?" asked Charlene.

"Not having sex with him. I think Bryan's about to propose."

Late that night, while Tallulah was dreaming of her (first) white wedding, and exactly what sort of bikinis she would design for the honeymoon, a few miles away at Great Bottom Park, Selby tossed and turned in bed, worrying as much about the children, who were shocked and upset, as about Doug. Her conversation late that night with Kirk, Doug's erstwhile boyfriend, had not helped things: he'd told Selby that he'd been royally chucked by Doug a few days after Doug had arrived in England, and, despite some lingering fondness, he was not in the mood to cross the pond to play Florence Nightingale.

Eventually, she had managed to drift off but she'd only been asleep for an hour or so when she was suddenly woken by something. She sat bolt upright in bed and listened for a few moments. Nothing. She was about to try to go back to sleep when she heard a sound from downstairs, a banging noise. Her heart started racing and she quickly switched on her bedside light, glancing at the time. Midnight.

"Mommy," came Tess's voice from the landing outside her room. Selby threw back the covers and sprinted out to her daughter in her sweatpants and T-shirt. Tess was standing there, looking afraid.

"Mom, Lady Maud's ghost has come to get us. I'm scared. I wish Dad was here."

Violet soon appeared from her bedroom, looking sleepy, saying, "What's happening?"

"I'm not sure. Just stay here, okay," Selby said, about to check out the ground floor, when the Hunnigans descended from their attic flat in pyjamas and dressing gowns with startled looks on their faces.

"Dreadful racket from outside," Doreen remarked. "What on earth—"

"Mrs. Fairfax, Dor, stay here with the girls," said Alan, heading for the stairs.

"I'm coming," said Selby. "Two's better than one."

※

That night there was a full moon and as Selby and Alan descended the grand staircase into the hall, the gleam of silver slanting through the glass dome above the stairwell lit their way. It was soon clear that the banging sound was coming from the front door—someone was knocking on it—and Selby and Alan half-ran towards it, alarmed.

When they reached the entrance, Selby called out, "Who's there?"

"Selby," came a desperate voice. "I'm so sorry—I tried to call—it's us, Sophie, and Eddie."

As she ushered Sophie and her son inside, Selby couldn't believe her eyes. Sophie was in a dressing gown and nightdress and had a hand clenched round her phone. Her face and clothes were dusty and she looked traumatised. Eddie, flanked by the two family Labradors, was in pyjamas with a school tracksuit jacket over the top. He was trembling and gulping down big, panicked breaths of air. Selby grabbed Eddie's hand and he squeezed hers as though his life depended on it.

"What happened?" Alan asked when he saw the pair.

"It-it's the Rectory—" Sophie stuttered. "There's been a fire."

"No!" said Selby.

"Christ alive," exclaimed Alan. "Let's get you two to the kitchen," he said, offering Sophie his arm. "Thank goodness you are both all right, that's the main thing. Bring the dogs."

Tess and Violet raced down the stairs, followed by Doreen at a slightly slower clip.

"Lorks above! Whatever now?" cried Doreen, seeing Sophie and Eddie.

"Fire at the Rectory," said Alan, as the party made their way to the kitchen.

Doreen soon had the lights on and pulled out some chairs while the Sausages sniffed curiously at the Labradors, who simply ignored them, heading straight to the warmth of the Aga and lying down in front of it.

"Here, Mrs. Thompson, Eddie, sit down. I'll put the kettle on."

"Eddie," said Tess, "are you okay?"

"No," he said miserably.

"What happened?" Selby asked.

Sophie put her head in her hands on the table, looking broken. Finally, she spoke. "I was woken up by the fire alarm going off," she said. "There was smoke everywhere, it was terrifying, I could barely see or breathe. Somehow Eddie and I escaped from the house and I called the fire service once we were outside, but they took so long to get to us, half the kitchen was gone by the time they arrived. Thank God the dogs were in the kennel."

"What a fright," said Alan sympathetically.

"How did the fire start?" Selby asked.

Sophie's face crumpled. "It's so awful. The police think it might be arson—"

"Don't say Jacko Whisky was up to no good—" Doreen began.

"No. The police found Edgar Duffield stoned in a lane near the house with an empty petrol can."

"Who?" asked Selby.

"He's a posh local kid who's been expelled from school," Sophie explained. "He's only fifteen. What was he thinking? We could have been killed."

"Why on earth would Edgar do something like that?" asked Doreen, bewildered.

"God knows," said Sophie.

Eddie soon whispered, in cracked little tones, "I'm hungry, Mummy."

"We've got snacks," said Tess, dashing about finding him cookies and chocolate and bringing them to him on a plate.

"Thanks, Tess," Eddie said. "Where are we going to go, Mummy?"

"You'll stay here, of course," Selby said immediately.

"You've got enough on your hands with everything that's going on with Doug—"

"I insist. It isn't like we haven't got six thousand bedrooms." Selby looked hopefully at Sophie.

"We'd like it," Violet chimed in.

"Please, Mrs. Thompson?" said Tess. "Then I can play with Eddie after school."

"Well, if you're absolutely sure, just temporarily," said Sophie. "That would be incredibly helpful. Thank you."

"Where's hubby, Mrs. Thompson?" asked Alan, pouring her a cup of tea from the pot Doreen had put on the table. "Down there still sorting it all out?"

Sophie turned from Eddie as she answered, making sure that he couldn't see her, and said, "He's away on business and I haven't been able to get hold of him yet."

"I'm sure he'll get on the first plane tomorrow," Alan replied, trying to reassure her.

Sophie shook her head. "He's in Kazakhstan, where there's some kind of coup going on. No one can get in or out."

At this news, the grown-ups' faces collectively fell. "You poor love," said Alan.

Sophie sighed. "It's okay. It's almost easier if he's not here. He's going to go nuts about this. Honestly, he'll be so angry—" She broke off and wiped a tear from her eye.

"Oh, dearie, dearie, dearie me," tutted Doreen, bustling about refilling cups of tea and making toast.

Just then, Sophie's phone, still in her hand, started ringing. She looked at the screen. "It's him," she said, picking up. "Hugh? Hugh!"

A hush descended on everyone in the room as Sophie recounted the evening's events to him. Eventually, a serious look on her face, she said goodbye and put the phone down.

"When's Daddy coming home?" asked Eddie.

"Just as soon as he can, darling," she said, stroking her son's hair. "Just as soon as he can."

39

When she heard the tale of her son's alleged crime from the police, Anne Duffield—who simply couldn't believe her darling Edgar would do such a thing—speed-dialled the best legal team in London. A grand solicitor reassured her that Edgar's story—that he had simply been drunk after going to the pub, got lost on his walk home, and come across an empty petrol can—was totally plausible. In any case, he was a minor, so there was very little point in the police charging him and the press couldn't reveal his identity. Clearly, the grand solicitor told her, a disgruntled local was responsible for the crime, and after digesting this new narrative, Anne and her sister started to wonder, loudly and to absolutely everyone they knew, whether that weird old drunk in the village could have been behind the fire. They hoped that the Thompsons and their ilk would now feel so threatened that they'd get out of the Bottoms before they ruined it for decent people like the Pennybacker-Hoare clan forever.

Within twenty-four hours, the story was in the hands of the national media, and by the middle of the week Sophie couldn't go into the village shop without seeing her husband, herself, or her home splashed across the front pages. The headlines ranged from *The Times*'s dour "No Arrests After Attack on Health Minister's Family" to the *Sun*'s sensationalist "Arson Terror in Cotswolds," while an article buried in the *Guardian*'s foreign section reported that the Health Minister was stranded in Kazakhstan leaving his wife to clear up the mess alone. But the story that everyone read was in the *Daily Mail*. "Fire and Loathing at the Rectory" was a gossipy article illustrated with a charming pre-fire photograph of the house filched off Sophie's Instagram which was juxtaposed against a dismal image of the charred remains of it. There were glamorous party snaps of Sophie and Hugh clad in black tie, and a shot of Hugh with the ever-present Davinia at his side as he entered 10 Downing Street.

The fire was an excuse for the newspapers to run reams of column inches comparing the lives of "ordinary" rural locals with the rarefied existences of the country elite. It was as though the lifestyle of the Thompsons had become a morality tale to be dissected by the press and public, with Sophie painted as a Marie Antoinette figure to Hugh's Louis XVI. Sophie was devastated. She had always known she had a "nice" life, but she had never felt it was particularly remarkable, or lavish, certainly not compared with those of her friends. But the newspaper stories, with their focus on the "extortionate" costs of her horse, her tea parties, her flower arrangements, her pretty tablescapes, her son's picturesque prep school with its eye-watering fees, her husband's ministerial car, his Porsche (how she hated that car now), her lovely clothes—now that her home was half-ruined, she knew these things were utter luxuries that she had taken for granted. The negative press sent her into a fight with her conscience that left her languishing in that painful hinterland that occupies the space between spoiled and woke. It was not a happy place to be.

It didn't help that Sophie felt as though she was coping with all this alone. Hugh was barely contactable, and on the few occasions she could reach him by phone or he rang her, the line was so poor they could hardly make out each other's words. There was still no certainty about when he and Davinia would be able to leave the British Embassy, let alone Kazakhstan.

On Thursday morning, after she had dropped Eddie and the Fairfax girls at school, Sophie had arranged to meet Selby in Doug's room at the hospital. She figured she'd feel better if she spent a bit of time cheering someone else up instead of focusing on her own problems.

"So sweet of you to come, Soph," said Selby when she arrived just after nine.

"It's the least I can do. It's so kind of you to let me and Eddie stay. If my house wasn't in ruins, this would be the best week of our lives, what with all Doreen's cakes."

"I'm grateful to have you and Eddie around. It's distracting me and Tess from worrying about Dad twenty-four-seven."

Sophie pulled up a chair to the side of the bed where Selby was sitting. Doug lay there, eyes closed, his breathing light. His peaceful expression belied the Spaghetti Junction of tubes weaving from drips and machines into his arms and nose. She noticed that Selby was holding Doug's hand.

"It's shocking," said Selby, peering at Doug. "People keep asking me for 'updates' or progress reports and there's nothing to give them. Have you had any more news from Hugh?"

Sophie shook her head. "It's so hard to get any information. The Foreign Office won't tell me anything and I've only managed to speak to him a few times."

"I'm so sorry," said Selby. "What a nightmare."

"At least he's safe and well," said Sophie, regarding Doug sadly. "But sometimes I wish he'd leave politics altogether. It doesn't seem worth it any more." She sighed. "Shall I get us a coffee?"

She'd started to stand up when there was a light tap on the door. To her surprise, she saw Vere Osborne peering through the square of window in it. He opened the door a crack and whispered, "Shall I come in?"

"Please," said Selby.

His farm overalls gone, Vere was looking smart in a dark suit and tie. "I'm on my way to London for a meeting, but I wanted to drop by and see how Doug is."

"He's the same," Selby replied.

"Whatever I can do," he said. "Very draining for you, Selby."

"It's worse for the girls," said Selby miserably.

"I can imagine," said Vere, a kind expression in his eyes.

Sophie's phone pinged. "Sorry," she said, taking it from her handbag. She wandered over to the corner of the room, tapped on the screen and gasped audibly.

"As if things could get any worse," she said out loud, dashing back over to the bed. "Selby, Vere, look what Tata's just sent me."

They looked at Sophie's phone, on which she'd pulled up a story in the *Financial Times*. The headline, "Was Minister Bribed by Kazakh Oilman?," was followed by an article in which a Mr. Jack O'Malley was quoted at length, alleging that "Health Minister Hugh Thompson has received considerable funds from an oil company owned by a Mr. Ainar Ulzhjalgas, in return for 'political favours.'"

"I don't get it," said Selby.

"Jack O'Malley is Jacko Whisky," Sophie replied. "And Ainar . . . he's a friend of Hugh's . . . owns the folly we stopped at on the hack. But this thing about bribes *can't* be true. I mean, how would Jacko know stuff like this?"

"Doesn't really matter," said Vere. "Screenshot the article and send it to Hugh."

Sophie whitened. "I can't. He's under so much stress already, stranded out there."

"You don't have a choice," Vere told her.

"Guess not," Sophie replied. She screenshot the story and texted it to Hugh with a message saying, *Have you seen this?*

Two minutes later, Sophie's phone was ringing. "I'll take it outside," she said grimly.

Once she was in the corridor and out of the others' earshot, Sophie said, "Hugh? Hugh? What on earth—"

"Soph. Don't worry *at all*, darling," Hugh reassured her from the end of a crackly line. "No one will take this seriously. Jacko Whisky is a nut-job. God knows why a decent broadsheet like the *Financial Times* is printing things someone like him says. It's outrageous. Outrageous. I'd sue them if I could be bothered but Davinia's handling it. It'll go away."

"Really? Everything's really okay?" Sophie asked desperately.

"Ainar's a friend, that's all. I mentioned borrowing the folly in the Register of Interests, everything's above board, and Davinia says I've followed the rules correctly. There's nothing to be concerned about."

"Phew," sighed Sophie. "When do you think you'll get home?"

"The ambassador here thinks they might be able to get us to the border in the next few days, then hopefully onto a plane out of Uzbekistan."

"I'm so worried about you, Hugh, and Eddie's really traumatised by the fire."

"Poor boy. Send him a big hug and tell him Daddy will be home soon, all right?"

"Okay. Take care." With that, Sophie hung up and went back into Doug's room.

"What's the story?" asked Vere.

Sophie paced back and forth as she told them what Hugh had just said.

"Do you trust him?" asked Vere.

Sophie laughed nervously. "You go straight for the jugular, don't you, Vere?"

"Well?" he went on, scrutinising her.

She didn't answer straight away: the thing was, Sophie wasn't always sure if she did trust Hugh. He had never actually lied to her, as far as she knew, but sometimes she experienced an unnerving sense that he wasn't telling her everything. But she couldn't face admitting this to Vere and Selby now. After all, she could barely admit it to herself. Eventually she just said, "I suppose so."

"Good," said Vere and stood up. "I need to get going, but I'll be back in a day or two. Keep me posted, Selby?"

"Of course," she replied. "And thank you."

"You're a great hospital visitor," added Sophie.

"I'm used to it," said Vere, a wistful expression on his face. "Bye."

A few minutes after he had gone, Sophie said, "No wonder Anjelica was so in love with Vere. Honestly. They were the best couple."

"Must have been devastating for him."

"Yup. But that's why he's so good at this," said Sophie, looking around the hospital room and at Doug.

"You're not a bad visitor yourself, Soph," said Selby. "Thank you for the company. Otherwise it would just be me here, ranting at my ex."

"They say talking to people while they're in a coma can help them."

Eyebrows raised, Selby turned and spoke directly to the unconscious figure in the bed. "Honey, you were always a *complete* hypochondriac, but this is taking it too far, Douglas, okay?"

There was no response. Doug just lay there.

"See. Milking it for all it's worth, as usual," Selby said wryly.

"I hope he can hear you. I bet he knows you're here."

"Soph, all I want is for him to wake up and be healthy. For the girls. For me." Selby looked fondly at Doug. "I mean, I hate him but I love him too. Now, did you say something about a coffee?"

∞

Like a latter-day Rip Van Winkle, Douglas Fairfax snoozed away the days at Banbury General Hospital, oblivious to the swirl of worry circulating around him. Somehow the weekend passed, and Selby's new friends stepped up and helped out unasked. Fernanda scooped up the girls and distracted them with fun treats at the Abbey, Sophie and Eddie provided company at the house despite their own woes, and Vere was a stalwart presence, checking in by phone or dropping by the hospital when he could.

On Monday morning, Ian and Tata picked up Selby to go and meet Antoni at Little Bottom Priory to discuss the flowers for Tata's birthday party. With no change in Doug's condition, an alarming level of anxiety had started to invade Selby's every waking moment. She had, foolishly she now realised, spent too many hours down the

Google rabbit hole and had become convinced that the longer the coma lasted, the worse his chances were of coming around safely.

"I have no idea what to do," she told Tata, as Ian drove. "I just go to the hospital, sit there—and, nothing. The doctors don't tell you anything. It's awful."

"God," said Tata. "Do you want to forget the flowers? Maybe it's too much—"

"No way," Selby interrupted. "I'm not going to let you down and I need to stop thinking about hospitals and comas. We can plan everything today and you'll have a wonderful evening on Friday. It's so helpful, thinking about something nice, seeing you and seeing Antoni."

Tata seized the opportunity. "He's *such* a lovely guy, isn't he?"

"He is."

Ian eventually pulled up in front of Little Bottom Priory, a decorative rococo mansion which overlooked formal gardens. The building was immaculate—Antoni had had the place renovated and repointed as soon as the Backhouses moved out, and the pockets of disrepair they had left behind them had vanished. He soon appeared at the front door, a huge smile lighting his face, followed by two uniformed butlers who immediately swept into action and opened the car doors for Selby and Tata.

"My dear," he said, enveloping Tata in a warm hug and kissing her on both cheeks. "I am getting very excited about your birthday celebrations." Next, he embraced Selby, saying, with a concerned look, "Selby. Welcome. How is poor Douglas?"

"Thank you for asking. No change."

Sounding solemn, Antoni said, "I have sent the family priest to the Basilica of St. Mary in Krakow to light a candle for Douglas every single day—"

"Awww," said Tata, cocking her head to one side and regarding him as they all walked into the house. "That is the dearest thing, Antoni, that someone could do, for another person."

"It is, thank you," said Selby, smiling at him. He meant well, he really did.

~

A few minutes later, Selby and Tata found themselves in the ornate Octagonal Room, where the party would be held. With its graceful arched windows, *trompe l'oeil* walls, mirrored panelling, silver-gilt mouldings, glistening chandeliers, and chequerboard marble floor, the room was as intricate as a piece of Fabergé. A large door was open to the velvet lawn beyond.

"It's incredible," said Selby, walking through the room and taking in the view ahead. "What a place for a party."

"It's one of the most romantic rooms in the house," Antoni said.

"It just says love, love, love," agreed Tata, directing a coy smile at their host.

A maid soon arrived with a tray of iced water, tea, coffees, fresh fruit, and delicate pastries and set it down on a little table. Tata, Antoni, and Selby sat down on plump needlepoint chairs and helped themselves.

"Something to eat, Selby, Tata? A lychee? *Macaron?*" asked Antoni, before the maid left.

"God, how delicious," Selby replied, taking a tiny cheese puff from the tray.

"Who makes these?" asked Tata, impressed, as she bit into a miniature choux pastry.

"Roland, my chef. He will do the most exquisite canapés and petits fours for your party—lobster, foie gras, handmade chocolates—anything you want, Tata. Anything."

"Antoni, you are *so sweet*," she said.

"Right, can we stop talking about how *wonderful* you are, Antoni," said Selby as lightly as she could, "and move on to the flowers? We've got to finalise everything now so I can install it on Friday morning."

"Yes. Sorry," said Tata.

"Apologies, I'm rather distracted," Antoni added.

"I can tell." Tata winked at Antoni, and then gave Selby a knowing look.

"Okay, so, Tata, we've got this exquisite space," said Selby, gazing around her, noticing the elegant sofas and chairs dotting the room. "It's already pretty magical. What do you want me to do with the flowers?"

"I want something that is . . ." Tata paused for moment, pondering ". . . all about passion."

"Oh. Okay, that's fun," said Selby. She started scribbling on her notepad.

"The heart," added Antoni, a dreamy look on his face.

"Moonlight . . ." started Tata.

". . . and roses?" said Antoni, finishing her sentence.

"Say no more," said Selby. "I can't guarantee the moonlight, but Maud's old rose beds are literally brimming. I can dig them up this week, replant them in pots and bring them up here over a few days."

"I can send workers to help you," insisted Antoni. "Or I'll help with my bare hands."

"Honestly, a few guys to lift things is all I need, but thank you," Selby told him gratefully.

"If you're sure—"

Antoni was interrupted by the maid returning to the room.

"Excuse me, Mr. Grigorivich, I am sorry to interrupt you all, but Mrs. Hawkins's butler needs to confer with her urgently."

"Send him in, please," said Antoni.

"He said it's a private matter. He's waiting in the hall."

"Excuse me a moment," said Tata, looking surprised and getting up. She followed the maid out of the room.

"How are the lovebirds doing?" asked Ian jovially as soon as Tata entered the hall.

"All they're talking about is moonlight and roses. It's adorable. Did you pull me out of there to give them some alone time?"

At this, Ian coughed momentarily, looking uncharacteristically flustered. "Mrs. H., a little news."

"Yes," said Tata, slightly apprehensive.

"I've had a Mr. Guy Cooper-Keel on the phone."

"Who?"

"Guy Cooper-Keel. Writes the gossip column at MailOnline."

She grinned. "*Love* that website. Does he want to come to my birthday?"

"No."

"Oh," Tata said. "What does he want, then?"

"He's digging for dirt about the Thompsons."

Tata frowned and sank onto an upholstered bench. "I feel so bad for Sophie."

"Mrs. H., do not be alarmed."

"You have a plan?"

"Always. Cooper-Keel needs an alternative story to take to his editors and I suggest giving him an exclusive about your birthday party. Not only will this distract him from chasing crumbs of grubby gossip about the Thompsons, but it will also remind Mr. Hawkins of your impending birthday."

"Hmmm," mused Tata. "I like it. But how are we going to pull it off?"

"Your press office will handle all the details."

"But I don't have a press office."

"Yes, you do," he said. "You're looking at it."

"Ian, promise you'll never leave me."

"I promise," vowed Ian. "Now, details, please, about the flowers, the food, and the guests. Cooper-Keel wants to run something today."

Later that evening, when he had finished work and was back at the Annexe, Ian slipped off his loafers, put his feet up on the miserable little sofa that was squashed into the tiny slice of real estate he now called home and read Guy's article on his iPad:

TATA'S TOP OF THE BOTTOMS

Despite the woes of their friend MP Hugh Thompson, who faces allegations of bribery the same week his home was the target of an arson attack, Oxfordshire's Country Princesses are not letting a local scandal get in the way of a good party. They are readying themselves for the lavish cocktail being thrown by Polish apparel tycoon Antoni Grigorivich at his mansion, Little Bottom Priory, this Friday for the thirty-ninth birthday of his close friend, socialite and former publicist Tata Hawkins. Mr. Grigorivich, whose net worth is thought to be over £2 billion, purchased the house and estate for an undisclosed sum from the Backhouse family. He is said to have persuaded another very close friend, American garden designer Selby Fairfax, to create the flowers for the event. Local glitterati including the Beckhams and the Delevingnes are rumoured to be among those attending but no one knows whether Thompson, stranded in Kazakhstan after a military coup, will appear.

Thank goodness Cooper-Keel hadn't caught a whiff of gossip about Bryan, Tallulah, or the situation at Monkton Bottom Manor. Ian retired to his freezing-cold bedroom that night, pulled on his warmest pyjamas, sank into his pillow, and was soon asleep, dreaming of life back at the Dovecot.

40

Tata had spent most of the week obsessively tweaking the details of her party, as was her habit in the run-up to any event. Noting her elevated anxiety, Ian had booked her an entire day of treatments at The Club by Bamford on Thursday. And so, while Tata was engaged in an indulgent programme of healing activities ranging from a sound bath to a skin-plumping, red-light therapy session, her friends were, to put it simply, labouring hard.

That morning, Selby and Sophie had started at nine in Lady Maud's overgrown rose garden and were pushing heavy steel spades deep into the earth beneath the root balls of the old "Albertine" rose bushes.

"Give me a hand with this one?" Selby called out to Alan Hunnigan, who was on standby.

"I'll lift it, Mrs. Fairfax," he said, hauling the weighty plant and its pale pink buds into his large wheelbarrow.

"Antoni's guys are waiting in the old greenhouses," said Selby. "They'll replant them in the pots and drive them up to the Priory."

"Right you are," said Alan. "Let's load up as many as we can on this." He trundled the barrow over to Sophie, who was working a few yards away, and lifted another bush into it.

"Thanks," said Sophie, wiping her brow. The sun wasn't high yet, but it was hot work. Still, she was enjoying herself. Just then, her phone rang. She took it from the pocket of her jeans and regarded the number, which she didn't recognise. Probably the house insurance people about the fire—they'd been ringing non-stop. She left her spade on the ground and picked up the call.

"Sophie Thompson speaking," she said.

"Is Hugh there?" came a weak, watery woman's voice from the other end of the line.

The voice didn't seem familiar. "I'm sorry, this is Hugh's wife, Sophie. Hugh's abroad on work."

"Ah. Well. Can he ring me when he's back?"

"May I take a number?"

"Yes. It's 01750 322 101." Sophie punched the number into her contacts. As she did so, she noticed Vere slip into the rose garden, walk up to Selby and start discussing something intently with her.

The woman continued: "I telephoned to say I read about the house fire and I'm so sorry."

"Thank you. Who may I tell him is calling?"

"It's his Great-Aunt Edith—"

Sophie was flabbergasted. "What?"

"I said 'Great-Aunt Edith.'"

"I know."

"Why did you say 'What?,' then?"

Sophie didn't have an answer. She could hardly tell Great-Aunt Edith that she was supposed to be dead, and to have left pots of cash to her husband, who'd spent it on a flashy electric Porsche.

"Er . . . I . . . I don't know. I have to go," said Sophie, ending the call.

Fighting back nausea, she tossed the phone onto the ground and sank onto the grass.

"Are you okay?" asked Selby, coming over with Vere.

"You look like you've seen a ghost," he said.

"I might as well have," Sophie replied, putting her head in her hands. "I've been played by my own husband."

"What's happened?" said Selby.

"Remember the newspaper story about bribes? It's true. He told me his Great-Aunt Edith died of Covid and there was an inheritance—but she's just called! He *must* have taken money from that Kazakh oil guy. He'd never have been able to afford the Porsche otherwise, as well as the house upgrades he's been promising me." Everything started to click into place. "All those questions he asked in Parliament about fuel prices had nothing to do with ambulances. He must have been paid by the oil company to ask them. There's no other explanation. What on earth am I going to do?"

Vere bent down and put a hand on her shoulder. "You need to protect yourself, and Eddie," he said calmly. "Let's start by getting you an extremely good lawyer."

Sophie looked even more distraught. "But I haven't done anything wrong."

"Doesn't matter," said Vere. "Hugh could implicate you, so you need to get your legal team together now."

"He's right," said Selby.

"I don't have the money for lawyers," Sophie wailed. "Christ."

Vere smiled at Sophie. "Forget about the money. I'll do it for nothing."

"But, Vere, no, that's too much—"

"Sophie, we've been neighbours for years. It's the least I can do and anyway I've always secretly thought Hugh was an arrogant tosser."

Somehow Sophie managed a laugh.

"Wish I'd had a neighbour like you, Vere, when my husband walked out on me," Selby said, and sighed.

"Luck of the draw," Vere replied. "Sophie, I'm going up to London later and I'll instruct my office to start on it today. Don't worry, it'll be okay—"

Before he could finish, Selby's phone began ringing and she grabbed it, looking at the screen. "It's Banbury General," she said, picking up.

"Mrs. Fairfax?" said Nurse Beatty. "The patient is conscious. Can you come to the hospital as soon as possible?"

Shortly after that, Selby, Sophie, and Vere were standing beside Doug's hospital bed, accompanied by a beaming Nurse Beatty.

"Mr. Fairfax has fallen asleep again, but that's not unusual," she said, smiling benevolently at him. "Coming round from a coma is like surviving the Battle of Waterloo. The patient is shattered from the fight. He'll be very tired. He won't know what's happened and will seem very confused. But he's not in a coma any longer, that's all that matters."

"I think he's trying to open his eyes," whispered Selby, noticing that Doug's eyelids were starting to flicker. She took his hand and held it in hers.

The little group stood silently now, watching and waiting for any other signs. After what seemed like ages, Doug's lips moved, ever so slightly forming words.

"Where . . . is . . . he . . . ?" The words came out painfully slowly.

"Kirk?" Selby whispered to the others. "He broke up with him . . . maybe he's forgotten . . ."

"No . . . not . . ." was all Doug managed to say, his voice hoarse.

"I'm not sure what he means," Selby said, looking perplexed.

"He probably isn't sure either. His brain will still be organising itself in there. Don't worry, Mrs. Fairfax, it will come," Nurse Beatty reassured her as she smoothed Doug's blankets and gently plumped the edges of his pillows.

"Ooooh . . . owww . . ." he whimpered.

"Is he in pain?" asked Sophie.

"He'll have a cracking headache," Nurse Beatty said. "And his throat will be really sore after the tube was removed. He's still very poorly."

"Look, his left eye just opened a little," said Vere. "There!"

The party could see that Doug's eyes were opening the tiniest bit.

"Doug? Doug?" Selby said, almost in tears. "It's me, Selby."

"Hurting." Doug winced, then stared blankly at the faces surrounding him, as though he didn't recognise anyone or anything.

"Do you need more painkillers, Doug?" asked Vere.

"Eeeeee-aaa-nnn," was all Doug managed to say in response.

Everyone looked at each other blankly and eventually Sophie said, "Tata will be so happy Doug's awake. She can really enjoy her party tomorrow now. I'll text her the good news."

There was a faint rustle of sheets as Doug tapped his finger weakly on the bed, then managed to work his face into a hint of a smile. His voice raspy, he said, "I . . . go . . . to . . . party."

At this, Nurse Beatty sternly wagged a finger at her patient. "Mr. Fairfax. You are not well enough to go to any party. You need to walk across this room first."

She then addressed the assembled group in a whisper, saying, "I don't think he realises what's happened yet. It's unrealistic for him to think he's going to be up and about tomorrow." Doug blinked a couple of times, but the effort seemed to deplete him, and his eyes soon closed again.

"He'll drift in and out of sleep this afternoon," the nurse went on. "The physio will try and get him out of bed later, see if he can stand, or at least get him sitting up in a wheelchair."

"I hope he manages that," Selby replied.

"Meantime, I suggest you all go and get on with your day," Nurse Beatty continued. "You should *all* plan to go out to this party tomorrow, as Mr. Fairfax is going to make a full recovery."

Vere looked at his watch. "Selby, Sophie, I've got to go—I've got meetings today. I'll see you tomorrow at the party."

Selby gave him a hug. "Thanks. You've been so kind."

"It's nothing," said Vere, hugging her back. "I'm just happy Doug's on the mend. Sophie, I'll ring you later when I've spoken to the team."

"Thank you," she said.

As soon as he'd left the room, a Vere Appreciation Society started to form.

"I get a hot flush every time that dish walks in here," said Nurse Beatty, her face perspiring as the door swung closed after him.

"He's so decent," said Sophie.

"A real one-off," Selby said.

"Kind," Sophie added.

"Sensitive," Selby said.

"Amusing," Sophie went on.

"Thoughtful," Selby replied.

"No wonder that Pennybacker-Hoare girl's got her eye on him," said Nurse Beatty. "Saw them in the Great Bottom Arms a few nights back having a drink. They'd make a lovely couple, wouldn't they?"

41

Ian lived for flower arranging, which he viewed as the most civilised of all the domestic arts. It also, conveniently, allowed him to eavesdrop on his boss and her friends at critical moments. The flower room at the Old Coach House, located off the pantry, had a little window that looked onto the terrace by the lavender garden and he'd learned from experience that the breeze, and all conversation taking place outside, flowed through this opening and into the room.

Sophie had arrived after the school run on Friday morning, laden with birthday gifts for Tata. Tata and Ian had, of course, already been briefed about the latest horrid development in the Thompson drama and of Doug's happy awakening. Ian escorted Sophie out to the terrace, brought her a coffee, and then retreated to arrange vases for the bedrooms. He could hear every word of the ladies' discussion:

". . . I am *so* sorry, Sophie," Tata was saying. "What a *nightmare*."

"It's the shock of your own husband lying to you like that. It's devastating."

"What are you going to do?"

"I don't know . . . What am I supposed to do? Leave, I think."

"You're going to have to," Tata said. "He is the most entitled prat I've ever met."

"I know. I always knew. I was literally trying to keep it together for Eddie. But I can't any more, after this. Vere's been wonderful. He's going to do the legal work for me for nothing."

"Wow. That guy is a saint. I've been dying to set him up with someone," said Tata. "I mean, he's gorgeous. Single. Brainy."

"I hear Cecily Pennybacker-Hoare's after him."

"What?"

"Nurse Beatty said she saw them in the pub together—"

"There is no way that vile Pennybacker-Hoare sister is having Vere Osborne. I simply won't allow it, especially after her nephew destroyed your house."

Ian couldn't resist peering surreptitiously through the open window and observing the two friends.

"You can hardly stop them getting together," said Sophie, shaking her head and managing a laugh.

"Wait . . ." Tata paused for a moment. "That's it! You! Hugh's going to be out of the picture. You're perfect for Vere."

"No, I mean—" started Sophie.

"He's obviously nuts about you already, if he's doing all that work for free."

Ian saw Sophie give Tata a dubious look.

"It's Selby he's nuts about, Tata," she said. "And if you ask me, she's nuts about him."

"No, Selby's nuts about Antoni," Tata corrected her.

"I think she might have moved on."

"That can't be right," said Tata. "You should have seen how sweet they were together planning the flowers for my party. They kept talking about moonlight, and roses, and romance . . . it was adorable."

"Well, maybe you're right."

"So you see, Vere *is* available. He's coming tonight. Honestly, Soph, you and he would be so happy together—"

"Tata," Sophie snapped at her. "Please stop. My marriage is over. My husband might go to jail. He's awful, but he's the father of my child and I did love him once. It's very sad. The last thing I'm thinking about is meeting someone new. I've just got to survive this now. Please, open your gifts and let's not talk about it any more."

Sophie didn't deserve any of it, poor dear, thought Ian as he popped a final anemone stem in a tall vase. But she was an alluring woman and Tata was spot-on: Vere was ideal for her. They just needed to make sure of one thing—that Cecily Pennybacker-Hoare was kept far, far away from him until Sophie was completely ready for love.

※

Sophie was relieved to return to Great Bottom Park later that morning, where she found Selby bustling about in the kitchen after coming back from a visit to the hospital.

"How's the patient?" asked Sophie.

"He was sitting up in bed, eating breakfast," said Selby, smiling. "I couldn't believe it. He seems a bit confused, but I'm relieved."

"That's great. How long till he can come home?"

"I think it'll only be a few days."

Just then they both heard a voice from outside the kitchen. "Morning, all!"

They were surprised to see Vere wander in, a parcel under one arm.

"Sorry to interrupt," he said, putting the package on the table. "No idea how the FedEx man mistook my shack for this palace, but he's delivered it to the wrong address."

Selby looked at the label on the package. It was addressed to Doug.

"Oh, shoot," said Selby. She checked her watch, agitated. "I just got back from the hospital and now I need to get over to the Priory to finish up the flowers."

"I'll take it for him," said Vere.

"Really?" said Selby. "Aren't you busy?"

"You've got way too much to do," Vere insisted. "I'm going to Banbury now, I can easily drop it at the hospital."

"Well, if you're sure," she relented.

"I am. Sophie, I have an update for you," Vere said, turning to her. "I briefed everyone in the London office yesterday, and we're going to need to speak to you next week, if that's okay, to go over absolutely everything. We need to accelerate this because it may quickly become very public, and we don't want the other side getting ahead."

Sophie gulped. "Whatever you say."

"Right, I'm off," said Vere, picking up the parcel. "Oh, and why don't I collect you ladies tonight and drive you both to the party?"

∾

A few minutes after he had left, Sophie said, "Nice of Vere to offer to drive us."

"Very," Selby agreed.

"Tata started saying some crazy stuff earlier about setting me up with him if I end up without Hugh—"

"What?" Selby sounded piqued.

"Setting us up. Vere and I."

"It's too early," said Selby defensively. Vere was *her* friend. He was her ally.

"That's what I told her."

"If you leave Hugh, it'll be, honestly, at least, I don't know, *at least* a couple of years before you can get into a healthy new relationship."

Sophie's face fell. "That's a long time to be on my own," she said despondently. "But I have to leave Hugh, Selby. I can't stay after this."

"I think you're probably doing the right thing," said Selby. "It's hard, though."

"I can't believe Vere hasn't been snapped up already," Sophie went on.

"Right, I'm going to go up to the Priory to get everything ready," said Selby rather abruptly, and hurriedly gathered her things to leave.

"Want me to come and help?" offered Sophie.

"No," Selby said sharply, then regretted it. "Sorry. I'm just a bit overwhelmed with everything."

"I totally get it. I'll collect the kids from school this afternoon."

"Thanks."

Just then Sophie's phone vibrated in her bag. She took it out and blanched when she saw the screen. "Oh, no. It's a text from Hugh."

"Want me to wait while you read it?"

Sophie nodded and tapped on the screen, and showed Selby the message. *Finally getting out*, it read. *I'll be at Heathrow this evening at eight. Ministerial car not available—meet me at Arrivals. H.*

"So rude," Sophie remarked.

"He really has no manners, does he?" Selby said.

"None. He just takes it for granted that I'll show up for him wherever, whenever, without a please or a thank you. Well, guess what, Hugh?" she spat at the phone. "I've got a wonderful party to go to tonight and I'm not going to let you ruin one more day of my life."

With that, Sophie simply typed back, *GREAT-AUNT EDITH CALLED FOR YOU* and pressed "send."

42

Ian's fairy-tale ending felt so close he could almost touch it. The scent of roses that evening in the Octagonal Room was heavenly, and as he escorted Tata in, he could hardly believe the beauty of the flowers. Tumbling from terracotta pots, trailing from stone urns, clambering up corners, the roses, a Pantone of pinks ranging from the palest oyster to the darkest damask, looked as though they had been growing here forever.

Not that he was feeling relaxed, though. For a butler orchestrating a complex détente between the members of an estranged couple, a détente in which his future was inextricably bound up, he couldn't afford to miss a beat. Behind the scenes, Bryan was on nervous standby while Charlene was fretting like an orphaned piglet, and both were texting him ceaselessly. Happily, Tata, having been dosed up with one of Ian's margaritas while getting dressed, had stopped asking why on earth Bryan hadn't appeared with a birthday present yet, and was in a state of unadulterated bliss.

"Oh, Ian," she cooed as she looked around, "it's a dream. Antoni! What a poppet to do this for me!"

"He's very generous," agreed Ian.

"Stick close to me, Ian, tonight," she went on. "I need you."

"Of course." Ian had planned to be nothing less than limpet-like on this auspicious night.

Tata was soon deluged by a tsunami of birthday wishes, compliments, and pressies. At least thirty of her friends were already in the room, more were trickling in, and Antoni's attentive staff never let a guest go for more than a few seconds without a fresh drink or a canapé. With a pianist tinkling in the background near the dance floor, it felt as though the swirl of a fabulous party was already under way.

"My dear," said Antoni, who had appeared at Tata's side dressed in a white tuxedo, a gleam in his eyes, "you look like a goddess."

Indeed she did, thought Ian proudly. Tata was the belle of the ball, dazzling in a silver lamé cocktail dress and pale pink satin heels. She had a delicate diamanté Alice band threaded through her hair, and her only other jewellery was a pair of low-key diamond studs. She looked chic, she looked sexy, she looked classy. This wasn't just bling, it was actual glamour.

"Oh, Antoni, it's just glorious in here, glorious," she told him.

"All thanks to your wonderful friend Selby."

He then took Tata's right hand, kissed it, and proceeded to kiss her extravagantly all the way up her right arm.

"Very European," she said with an embarrassed giggle.

"Happy birthday, princess. Enjoy your bash. I have a very special gift to give you later."

"Ooh, I do love presents," Tata squeaked excitedly.

Ian soon spotted Fernanda and Michael making their way towards them. Fernanda was attired in a 1980s-inspired orange taffeta gown with an oversized black velvet bow at the waist and she handed Tata a vast, beribboned Asprey bag, which Tata handed to Ian, which Ian handed to a waitress, which the waitress handed to a runner to put with the ever-growing stash of gifts in the hall.

Standing a little behind her, Ian looked on as Fernanda greeted Antoni and then hugged Tata warmly, saying sincerely, "Happy birthday, darling. I'm *so* sorry about Luca, and the note—"

"No, *I'm* sorry," interrupted Tata. "How I could ever have thought a good friend like you would do something like that—"

"She wouldn't," said Michael, looking sheepish. "Tata, I've got a confession to make. It wasn't Fernanda or Luca who tried to steal Ian. It was my idea. I suggested to Luca that he write the note."

At this, Antoni looked bemused and Fernanda simply tossed her hands in the air in a sort of "I give up" motion.

"I hope you can forgive me," Michael went on.

"If Ian wasn't mine, I'd try and steal him too," Tata said, and smiled graciously. "All is forgiven."

"Still, I feel terrible," he insisted.

"Don't. Ian would *never* leave me for you." Then she turned around and called out to him, "Would you, Ian?"

"Certainly not, Mrs. Hawkins," Ian concurred.

"Antoni, it's extraordinary in here," said Fernanda, changing the subject.

"Selby worked so hard," he said, "even while her ex-husband was so ill."

"Thank God he's on the mend," said Michael, taking a drink from a tray.

Just at that moment, Ian noticed Selby coming into the room. He discreetly tapped Tata on the arm.

"She's here," he whispered to her.

Tata immediately turned to Antoni and said, "Look, there's Selby. Doesn't she look amazing?"

"Very pretty," he mumbled, not paying much attention.

Pretty? Ian was underwhelmed. Iconic was a more appropriate word for the way Selby looked tonight, swathed as she was in a column dress of white silk crêpe, her dark hair loose. Just behind her were Vere and Sophie, he in a dark suit and Sophie in a black 1950s-style party dress.

"Don't you think Sophie and Dreamboat would make the perfect couple?" Tata said to Ian, as the three of them made their way over to her.

"Yes, superb," Ian agreed, acting as though he was hearing this for the first time.

"That's my next project," Tata said. Then with a giggle she put her hand up to Ian's ear and whispered, "After Selby and Antoni's wedding."

Selby and Vere stopped to greet Ian, and Sophie enveloped Tata in a hug. "Happy birthday, sweetie," she said. "You deserve this stunning party. You're a brilliant friend."

"Aw, thanks, Soph," said Tata. Then she stood back and regarded Sophie's dress. "Never see you in black usually but you look *so sexy* . . ." Then she said to her in a low voice, "Completely irresistible to Vere."

"Tata, ssshhhuussshhh," said Sophie, turning puce.

Vere and Selby were soon chatting away to Antoni, who congratulated Selby on the flowers. "I love what you did in here today," he said. "Thank you."

"It wasn't hard," Selby replied. "It's an impeccable space."

"How is Douglas?" he asked her.

"So much better. The nurse called earlier to say that he's out of bed, looking at samples that arrived today from the New York office."

"A miracle," said Antoni.

"That's Doug," said Selby, rolling her eyes. "Nearly dead one minute, back to work the next. You never, ever know what to expect with him."

The evening passed in a delicious whirl of champagne, chatter, and beautiful frocks, and when Ian checked his watch a little later he was amazed to see that it was already half past eight. The sun was lowering, and broad shafts of golden light poured through the windows, glancing off the silvered mouldings and mirroring and giving the room a magical atmosphere: the moment for Bryan to make his entrance, per the plan, seemed opportune.

"Two ticks, Mrs. Hawkins," he said to Tata, raising his eyebrows mysteriously at her, "and I'll be back with a very special surprise."

As soon as Ian had slipped into the hall and away from the hubbub of the party, he WhatsApped Bryan: *Ready now. Meet me at the entrance to the Octagonal Room.* In a nanosecond a reply pinged back: *On way.*

Ian dashed to the meeting spot and waited. Everything, finally, was coming together, he thought, as he rested for a moment against the gilded doorframe. As he observed the scene, he noticed Antoni whisper in Tata's ear, take her by the hand, lead her past the other guests and then onto a small stage that had been installed for the evening at the other side of the room. She seemed rather surprised when the beam of a powerful spotlight suddenly lit it up. Looking unusually nervous, Antoni tapped on his champagne glass a few times and the chit-chat started to die down. A hush eventually descended and all faces turned towards the host and guest of honour.

Antoni pulled a thick stack of notecards from his inside jacket pocket. Oh dear, Ian thought to himself, his heart sinking, a half-hour speech loomed. It wasn't ideal timing for Bryan's imminent appearance, but there was nothing he could do now.

"Welcome, all," said Antoni. "This is the first party in the Octagonal Room since I took over this house from Lord and Lady Backhouse—"

"It's *Sir* Reggie," Lady Caroline corrected him from the crowd. "He's a baronet, not a peer."

"Humble apologies," replied Antoni.

"Jolly good champers, though," Lady Caroline told Antoni.

"Jolly pricey champers," pointed out Sir Reggie jovially, draining his third glass of Cristal.

Smiling affably, Antoni went on, "It is an honour to have a woman of the calibre of Tata Hawkins in my home. To be able to throw a party for a lady of such charisma—"

Before Antoni could continue, Tata had stopped him and the crowd saw her whisper something in his ear.

"Ah, yes," he stuttered. "My dear Selby, please join us up here."

Selby, seeming bemused, went and stood on the other side of Antoni who picked up where he'd left off. "Selby, you are such a talent. Thank you for these roses. They are so . . ." He looked longingly at Tata on his left and then back at Selby on his right.

"So . . . *romantic*. Perfect for this occasion, a day on which I feel so much excitement for the future . . ."

Antoni appeared to be besotted. He went on and on, and, watching from the doorway, Ian found himself carried away by the moment, almost tearing up. Selby had her future husband, and Tata had her new best friend. She just needed her spouse back, and that would happen soon enough. He felt a tap on his shoulder and turned to see Bryan had arrived, the Bulgari bag in his hand.

"Ian, I'm feeling so embarrassed," he whispered. His complexion had already turned the shade of smoked salmon, and beads of perspiration were starting to bubble on his forehead. Ian even noticed a couple of visible sweat patches on his shirt. "I hate grovelling and there are so many people here."

"No choice, Mr. Hawkins," Ian told him firmly. "Have you been practising your lunges?"

"My trainer can't believe the work I've been putting in—my knees are like new. Tata looks incredible," Bryan said, gazing at his wife at the other end of the room, her dress twinkling in the beam of the spotlight. "How I ever let her go . . ."

"Exactly," Ian concurred.

Antoni's lengthy speech was continuing, his eyes shining. ". . . Tata, your beauty lights up the room. Your character inspires fun, happiness, and I have something for you," he said, fumbling in his jacket pocket.

"Someone's got a crush on my wife, huh," Bryan said to Ian, looking perplexed.

"Antoni's got a crush on Mrs. Fairfax, actually," Ian informed him calmly. "They're seeing each other, on the q.t."

"Phew," said Bryan. "Wait, what is he doing?"

They watched as Antoni took hold of Tata's left hand with what Ian could only describe as a lovestruck expression on his face.

"My dear, this is a very special birthday gift for you. Here," Antoni continued, handing Tata a small red leather box.

She opened the box and gasped when she saw the contents. "Isn't it a bit much for my *thirty-ninth* birthday? You've only known me a few weeks."

Before either of them had a chance to react, Ian and Bryan heard steps coming from behind them. They turned to see an elegant woman gliding across the hall towards the Octagonal Room. Her willowy frame was clad in a simple navy dress that floated around her calves, and her hair, which had the odd grey streak, was caught up in a French pleat at the back of her head. That was odd, thought Ian; he knew everyone on the guest list but didn't recognise her, and her restrained elegance was not typical of Tata's circle. When she reached the doorway, she stopped, smiled graciously at Ian and Bryan, and then eyeballed Antoni on the stage.

"Antoni-*v-ich*," she said under her breath in a strong Eastern European accent and then furiously added the word "bastard."

Bryan seemed shocked for a moment, and then said, "Quite agree."

The woman in navy gave him a knowing look and then marched towards the stage. Bryan, meanwhile, turned to Ian, said, "Come on," and without waiting started to weave his way behind the mysterious guest through the throng. Ian had no choice but to follow: Plan B was not going to plan at all, but they could hardly dither any longer away from the action.

As they got closer to the stage, Antoni was still talking and becoming ever more ardent. "You see, nothing is too much for you, Tata." He solemnly took a large diamond ring from the red leather box and placed it on the fourth finger of Tata's left hand.

"Antoni!" Tata shook her head. "What are you doing?"

"Isn't it obvious?"

There was a collective gasp from the assembled guests. Murmurs of surprise bounced around the room, and Bryan turned and looked at Ian as if to say, *I told you so*. At a loss, the butler simply threw his hands in the air in a gesture of frustration.

"Fool," the woman in the navy dress declared coolly from in front of them.

Tata, meanwhile, seemed stunned by the turn of events. "But, Antoni, I'm already married, and what about Selby?" she stammered, gesturing to her friend, who was still standing next to her, looking half-amused and half-confused.

"What about Selby?" repeated Antoni.

"Selby's the one you like."

"Yes, I like Selby very much."

"Exactly."

"Exactly," he repeated.

"I don't understand, Antoni." Tata was starting to get frustrated. "You are in love with Selby."

"What?" said Selby, astonished.

"I am?" exclaimed Antoni, looking flabbergasted.

"He is?" Selby asked.

"Yes. And she's nuts about you," Tata replied, taking off the ring and handing it back to Antoni.

"I think there's a mistake," said Antoni. "Selby and I are not in love."

Selby nodded in agreement.

"But . . . but . . ." started Tata. "Every time I mention Selby you say how fabulous she is, how beautiful, how talented . . ."

"If she is your friend, she is fabulous, beautiful, and talented. I only want to please *you* . . ."

Ian, Bryan, and the mystery woman were now close to the stage, but, blinded by the glare of the spotlight, the actors therewith couldn't see them.

"But you spent the night with her," Tata went on.

"What? When?" Antoni and Selby exclaimed simultaneously. They stared at each other with faint horror.

"After my Kitchen Supper."

Antoni shook his head. "I did not."

"Why would she say you did, then?"

"I never said I spent the night with Antoni," Selby replied, looking mortified.

Tata was crushed. "Oh."

"Ian!" Bryan seethed under his breath. "What on earth is going on—"

"Ah . . ." said Ian. "Ah . . ." he said again, buying a little time and feeling himself starting to perspire rather more than usual. The truth was that for once in his life he didn't have a clue what was going on. Plan B was a shambles and it seemed as though Antoni Grigorivich was attempting to poach Tata from Bryan. Before Ian had a moment to think further, the woman in navy had climbed up onto the stage.

"Antonivich. You are *dupa*," she said furiously as she strode towards him.

Ian, who had picked up a basic vocabulary of slurs from his time as under-butler to the exiled Polish royal family in Vienna, translated for Bryan. "*Dupa* is Polish for ass."

"Right," said Bryan, ever more confused. "Who is that woman?"

"I have my suspicions," said Ian, observing closely.

The second Antoni had laid eyes on the mysterious guest, his lovestruck expression vanished. He looked as though he would rather be drowning in quicksand than remain in the delightful surroundings of the Octagonal Room at Little Bottom Priory at that very moment.

"Oh, Jesus. Galina—" he started, holding up his hands, as if to shield himself.

"*Wieprz!!!*" she shrieked in response.

"That's the Polish word for swine," Ian informed Bryan.

"Galina—" Antoni repeated.

"The boat?" asked Tata.

"Yes, exactly," Antoni nodded.

The woman planted herself in front of Antoni, who seemed to shrink in her presence.

"Boat?" she said sternly to Antoni. Her tone was so menacing that he flinched. "Wife. I still you wife."

"What?" Tata looked aghast.

"I'm completely confused," said Selby, with a baffled look.

"Galina, we have been separated for many years now," said Antoni, a sheepish look on his face. "Anyway, I'm not actually getting married, just engaged—"

"I know!" Galina spat. Then she turned to Tata. "Antonivich never marry any of girlfriend."

"I'm not his girlfriend," insisted Tata.

"They all say they are not girlfriend," Galina retorted.

"*She's* meant to be his girlfriend," Tata said, and gestured at Selby.

"I'm *definitely* not his girlfriend," Selby declared.

"He always have two girlfriend." Galina's tone was matter-of-fact. "Antonivich get engage to *all* girlfriend. Every single one. Then they find out he can't marry because he *married* to *me*. A lot convenient for him. Seventeen year. He too mean to get divorce. This time I find out before you two hearts broked, from *MailOnline*. I read *MailOnline* every day. Best newspaper in world. I read about party, I travel here from Krakow. I save you both."

With that, Bryan, Ian, and the rest of the party watched as Tata glared at Antoni, smiled sympathetically at Galina and Selby, and then stalked off the stage. But Ian, undaunted, unthwarted and at this point only slightly undone, turned to Bryan.

"Buckle up, Mr. Hawkins," he said. "It's time for a happy ending."

43

May we pause game, dear reader, for a few moments, and abandon the party in order to whizz over to Monkton Bottom Manor? The house was quiet as a tomb that night. Charlene, to her intense irritation, had been ordered by Ian to hang around in the office late in order to "keep an eye on things"—specifically Tallulah, lest she get any ideas about crashing any local birthday parties. Still, Charlene had fallen so behind with Bryan's travel itinerary for next week that she decided to use the time wisely and was still printing out boarding passes and tickets at this late hour. But then, she'd never been good with computers, and everything took her three times as long as it should have. By quarter past nine, she was tidying up Bryan's desk when she heard a familiar voice.

"Where's Bry, Charlene?"

Tallulah was standing at the door to the office, clad in a black sequin ra-ra dress and sky-high heels.

"Said he was going to the pub, Miss de Sanchez," lied Charlene, exactly as she had been instructed to by Ian if questioned. (He was convinced that Tallulah would consider herself too glamorous to follow Bryan to a pub, even one as posh as Tuggy Drummond's.)

Tallulah's face hardened. "I think he's gone to the party Antoni Grigorivich's having for Tata."

"Don't know about that, Miss de Sanchez," said Charlene. "I don't know nothing about high society in the Bottoms."

"It was all over the *MailOnline* . . . I can't believe I got all ready for dinner with Bry," she huffed. "He *promised* he'd listen to me practise my speech for the Miami Swim Week Female Entrepreneur of the Year Award this week."

"Dear me, Miss—"

"I did think he was in a funny mood today, didn't you?"

Charlene, knowing perfectly well that Bryan's "funny mood" had been triggered by the threat of Tallulah rehearsing her fifty-minute speech for him *again*, combined with the hurdle of luring Tata back home in front of all her friends, said innocently, "I think he's a bit preoccupied with the cabling contracts from the French."

"Phew," said Tallulah. "I was starting to think it was something I did. Okay, I guess it's just me and Pikachu in the cinema room for dinner— Wait!" She jumped up and rapped her hand on Bryan's desk.

"What is it, Miss?" asked Charlene.

"Where's the bag?" Tallulah asked.

"What bag?" said Charlene.

"The Bulgari bag. It's been on Bryan's desk all week. I checked every day. And now it's gone."

"Has it?" said Charlene, a blank look on her face.

Tallulah turned to Charlene, a thunderous expression clouding her visage.

"Charlene, have a good weekend," she said. Then she added in a cold voice, "I'm going to that party. I bet Antoni Grigorivich knows Jeff Bezos."

44

There are those of us who wobble like blancmange in a crisis, and then there are those lucky souls who rise magnificently to the occasion, like a perfectly baked truffle soufflé. Ian was the latter type.

He patted down his navy-and-white silk herringbone Charvet tie, dusted off the shoulders of his navy suit jacket, tweaked his tortoiseshell glasses, and smoothed his dark hair into place. He reminded himself that he was the sort of butler who could handle any eventuality. My point is that despite the shambles into which Plan B had descended, despite the high emotions in the Octagonal Room at Little Bottom Priory that night, Ian somehow collected himself and remained cooler than a strawberry sorbet.

A quick recap of the complicated scenario in which Ian now found himself: he had, incorrectly it now turned out, assumed that Mr. Grigorivich was romancing the starriest new neighbour in the area, Selby Fairfax; but Antoni's infatuation was not with Mrs. Fairfax at all, but with Mrs. Hawkins, to whom he had just unexpectedly proposed marriage; Selby Fairfax *had* spent the night after Tata's Kitchen Sups with a man, but that man had not been Antoni Grigorivich, which is where the misunderstanding lay; and in any case, as they had all discovered that night, the Polish billionaire was secretly married all along. The upshot was that Ian's plot to set up Selby with Antoni, in order to restore Tata's social standing, as well as her marriage, had unravelled spectacularly.

But Ian Palmer was not the truffle soufflé of butlers for nothing. There was no situation that could not be salvaged. A disaster, he always said, was simply an opportunity dressed in poor man's clothes.

"Ian. Ian!" Bryan said as Tata raced past the two of them without even a glance. "We should call it off. This is barmy."

"Mr. Hawkins," said Ian, thinking wistfully of his comfy digs at the Dovecot. "There are some minor circumstantial disruptions, but the mission remains the same. You have the jewellery. Mrs. Hawkins wants to come home. She just needs to know that *you* want her to come home and she wants to know that in front of all her friends. The moment is perfect: we couldn't have organised this better if we'd planned it."

"We did plan it, remember?" retorted Bryan crossly. "Look, Ian, I'm sorry—"

But Bryan was interrupted that very second.

"There you are! Bry-yyyy!" Tallulah was suddenly standing next to him, all legs, sequins and hair extensions. "I've been looking for you *everywhere*," she said, her eyes fixed beadily on the Bulgari bag in his left hand. "I couldn't find you at the house. What's going on? Don't you remember? Tonight we were going to practise my speech for the Miami Swim Week Female Entrepreneur of the Year Award?"

At the mention of the dreaded speech, a fresh look of agony crossed Bryan's face. "Tallulah, I'm, um, busy," he said. Then he turned to Ian and continued, "Come on."

"Right-ho, Mr. Hawkins," said Ian, as Bryan dashed ahead of him towards Tata, who was now huddled with Sophie, Vere, and the Ovington-Williamses by the door that opened to the lawns.

"Wait!" yelled Tallulah, chasing behind Ian, who was now chasing behind Bryan, who was soon followed by Antoni, who was followed by Galina, who was followed by Selby. The rear was brought up by the Backhouses. Lady Caroline never liked to miss out on a local drama.

"Tata! Tata!" Bryan called out as he approached her.

His wife turned at the sound of her name. When she saw him, she stopped stock-still for a moment and then, after a few seconds, breathed a long sigh, and said, "Oh, Bryan, thank goodness you're here."

"I wouldn't miss your surprise birthday for the world, sweetheart," he said.

"I thought you'd completely forgotten—"

"Never."

"You'd love the boat, Tata," said Antoni in a pleading tone.

"Give up," Galina ordered her estranged husband.

"We're partial to yachting," chimed in Sir Reggie hopefully.

At this, Galina looked approvingly at the Backhouses, smiled and said, "It's an open invitation."

Ignoring all of them, Bryan took Tata's left hand in his, and then plunged down onto one knee, wincing as he did so.

"Bryan, what are you doing?" Tata looked down at him, as incredulous as the other guests in the room. "You're going to wreck your knee after the operation."

"My darling Tata," said Bryan from the floor. "I have been a fool. I told you a stupid lie about this." He delved into the Bulgari bag and handed Tata the box which Charlene had wrapped, not very well as it turned out. The tissue paper was crinkled, Sellotape was visible, and the bow on the top had come undone. But Tata was oblivious to these details as she unwrapped the gift, handed the tissue paper to Ian, and found herself holding a square suede box of papal purple. Slowly, excitedly, she opened it and lifted out the diamond and emerald necklace. A chorus of *oohs* and *aahs* rippled around the room.

"Oh my God, Bryan," she gasped. "It's incredible."

"Allow me," said Ian, stepping forward and carefully fastening the glittering jewel around Tata's neck.

"That's one hell of a necklace," said Selby.

"Michael darling, you've got a lot to live up to for my next birthday," Fernanda teased her husband.

"Hugh never gave me jewellery," Sophie said, looking pained.

"Someone much better will come along who will," Vere told her.

At this, Sophie batted her eyelashes at him, then said, "You sound very sure of that."

Bryan, meanwhile, was still on bended knee trying to explain himself to Tata. "I wanted to surprise you. On your fort—"

"Thirty-ninth, honey," Tata snappily corrected him.

"Sorry. Thirty-ninth. It took me months to organise this necklace with the jeweller, and then it backfired when you found the receipt. I was furious that you doubted me."

"I'm sorry, Bryan," Tata cried.

"No, *I'm* sorry. I was too proud to explain."

"No, I was spoiled and silly," went on Tata. "You were right the other day. I do need a reality check."

"But, Tata—my lovely wife, Minty's wonderful mother—I now realise that this has been good for me, for us. Because the time at Monkton Bottom Manor without you has been . . . the bottom. And, I've got you something else," he continued, hauling himself up from the floor and retrieving an envelope from his jacket pocket. "Here."

Tata took the envelope, opened it and threw her arms around Bryan's neck. "Lamu for New Year. Bryan, you're *the best*. We're going at the same time as Sophie and Hugh—"

"Not any more," Sophie interrupted sadly.

"Oh, God, I'm sorry, Soph," said Tata. "Forgive me."

"You should come with us anyway," said Bryan.

"You're sweet, but . . . I don't want to be a third wheel," she replied.

"If the man of your dreams happens to come along between now and then . . ." said Tata, her eyes alighting on Vere Osborne, "I'll insist."

Sophie smiled coyly at Vere, who looked bemused.

"Ian," said Bryan. "I'm going to drive my wife home. Please stay on and enjoy yourself."

"If you're sure, Mr. Hawkins."

"I am. And thank you, Ian," said Bryan, shaking his hand as he passed him.

"My pleasure," the butler replied. "Always."

Ian smiled to himself and loosened his tie. He was on his way back to the Dovecot. The dance floor beckoned.

Ian, you can imagine, had the moves of a pro on *Strictly Come Dancing*.

"May I have the pleasure of this dance?" he asked Sophie. She was sitting at a table alone now, looking lonely and vulnerable, and Ian felt for her.

She seemed relieved. "I'd love it."

"Come on." Ian took Sophie's hand and was soon twirling her under his arm to an old rock-and-roll piano tune.

"You are one hell of a dancer, Mrs. Thompson," Ian complimented her.

"Coming from you, that's flattering," Sophie replied. "Congratulations for sorting out Tata and Bryan. What a relief. Though I do feel a little bad for Antoni."

"It's worse for his wife. Anyway, I can't wait to get back to the Manor," replied Ian. "And it looks like Mr. Grigorivich has found something to distract him already."

Ian glanced to his left, where Tallulah was dancing, if you could call it that, around a rhythmless Antoni, as if he were a pole. Galina didn't notice: Sir Reggie Backhouse was waltzing her around the dance floor, oblivious to his wife's disapproval.

"DO YOU KNOW JEFF BEZOS?" Tallulah shouted over the music as she gyrated around the evening's host.

"GOOD FRIEND," Antoni said and nodded dizzily, mesmerised by the vision swirling around him.

"WOULD YOU LIKE TO HEAR MY MIAMI SWIM WEEK FEMALE ENTREPRENEUR OF THE YEAR AWARD ACCEPTANCE SPEECH?"

"Oh my God," Sophie said, laughing genuinely for the first time since her house had burned.

"They're perfect for each other," declared Ian, wondering how quickly Charlene could have Tallulah's clothes packed and sent up to the Priory.

Something caught Sophie's eye as the song ended. "True. Right, I need to go and flirt with someone, and I reckon you've got a full dance card waiting," she said, then wandered off.

As the opening notes of a new tune played, Ian glanced to the edge of the dance floor where, as usual, an audience of ladies were looking longingly at him, including Selby Fairfax. He made a beeline for her—trying to put off the moment for as long as possible when he would have to take on Lady Backhouse—when his phone rang. That familiar *Psycho* ringtone screeched from his pocket. What had happened to Mrs. H. now? he wondered.

"Excuse me, Mrs. Fairfax," he said, reaching for his phone. "It's the boss."

"Of course," said Selby.

"Good evening, Mrs. Hawkins," said Ian, picking up.

"Bryan's left his jacket there. His wallet and everything's in the pocket. He thinks it's in the hall. We're coming back up now. Can you meet us on the drive with it? We can't face coming back inside and seeing Antoni."

"Of course," said Ian. "Two minutes." He then turned to Selby and said, "I'm sorry, Mrs. Fairfax, but I have to go."

"Oh, but I *love* this one," said Selby, already swaying to the melody.

"How about him?" said Ian. "I know for a fact he's a great dancer. Keeps very quiet about it."

Ian grabbed Selby's hand and spun her straight into the arms of Vere Osborne, who was looking, as you can imagine, absolutely gorgeous. And talking to Sophie Thompson.

But more of that later.

45

Ian trotted swiftly into the entrance hall and cast an eye along the large Empire sofa. No sign of Bryan's jacket. He glanced at the ornate gilt stools on each side of the marble rococo fireplace. Nothing. As he lifted a tapestried cushion off an armchair to look underneath it, Sophie wandered into the hall, alone.

"Lost something?" she asked him.

"Trying to find Mr. Hawkins's jacket," he replied. "He and Mrs. H. are coming back to get it but it's not here."

They heard a vehicle pull up outside and the doors opening and closing.

"I'll go out and let them know," he said.

"I'll come too. I could do with a breath of air," said Sophie, looking wan.

"Are you all right, Mrs. Thompson?" Ian asked.

"Heartbroken, actually. Twice over."

"Welcome to the club you never wanted to join. I'll send you a badge. I'm sorry about everything you're going through."

"I thought there might be someone for me but . . ." Sophie paused and Ian saw sadness in her eyes as they walked through the long hall. "Well, there isn't," she finished.

"I'm sorry," said Ian.

When they got out to the porch at the front of the house, they were greeted not by the sight of Bryan's two-seater Mercedes, but by the peculiar spectacle of Douglas Fairfax being pushed across the gravel in a wheelchair, Nurse Beatty's opulent being at the helm. A hospital van was parked behind them.

"Doug?" Sophie said.

"What on earth is he doing here?" said Ian.

Doug was in pyjamas and a dressing gown, and had a parcel on his knee. The wheelchair didn't really like the gravel and kept getting stuck, jerking its occupant forward, who would then cry out with discomfort, only to be scolded by Nurse Beatty. "I did warn you, Mr. Fairfax. No one's fault but your own."

Before Doug could complain again, Bryan's convertible pulled up and he and Tata emerged and walked towards Ian.

"Mr. Hawkins," said Ian, stepping out onto the gravel. "I'm afraid I can't find the jacket."

"Drat. Maybe it's been taken away by a maid," said Tata. Then she went over to Doug and said, "What are you doing out here, in your pyjamas?"

"I wasn't going to miss your birthday party for the world," said Doug.

"That's so sweet but really, you shouldn't have."

"He insisted," said Nurse Beatty, sucking her cheeks together, unamused.

"Ooh, a birthday pressie," said Tata, greedily eyeing the parcel on Doug's lap.

Doug slapped an arm protectively across it. "Actually, it's for someone else."

"Sorry, of course. Selby's inside," Tata said, a little embarrassed.

"It's not for her," said Doug.

Tata frowned. "Who is it for, then?"

A dreamy air came over Doug. "Ian," he said slowly. "It's for Ian."

"Ian?" Tata went on.

"Ian?" repeated Bryan, looking confused.

Ian was rather startled. "Oh," was all he managed.

"I said Ian and I mean the wonderful Ian," Doug said firmly. He tapped the package on his knee and looked at him. "This is for you."

"Thank you," said Ian, feeling somewhat bashful as he took the gift.
"Come on, open it," said Doug.
"Now?"
"I'm curious," said Tata. "Come on, Ian."
"Chop-chop," Nurse Beatty chimed in, checking her watch. "My shift ends in an hour."
"Okay," he said, and started removing the brown paper wrapping to reveal a cream shoebox, the top of which was emblazoned with the words "LoafersDirect.com" in coffee-coloured lettering. Ian couldn't help but utter a squeak of delight as he took off the lid: inside, wrapped in several layers of cream tissue paper, was the most beautiful pair of shoes he had ever seen—a pair of silken loafers in a putty tone. They were embroidered with tiny pearlescent sequins.
"Doug, these are heavenly," he said, lifting the shoes to show everyone. They glimmered in the evening light. "Thank you."
"No. Thank *you*, Ian," said Doug. Then he paused for what seemed like a long while before taking a deep breath and saying, "You've inspired me, since I've met you, since I've arrived in this lovely part of England. In fact, Ian, and I might not be saying this if I hadn't had this terrible accident, but life's too short not to be real, isn't it?"
"Er—" started Ian.
"What I am saying is that here we are, on this beautiful night, and we must snatch happiness when we can." Doug paused, and then went on rather nervously, "You see, Ian, I'd like to be your Prince Charming."
"Excuse me?" said Ian, taking a step backwards.
"I think it's the medication that's muddling him," said Nurse Beatty, putting a hand on Doug's shoulder. "Mr. Fairfax, come on, time to get back to the hospital, dear."
"Nurse Beatty, there is no muddle," Doug snapped at her. Then he turned back to Ian. "The last thing I remember before the accident is our conversation at the pub, when you talked about how your Prince Charming would come, one summer's night, with a beautiful pair of glass loafers—"

Tata took a fairly aggressive step towards the wheelchair-bound Doug. "Ian is *mine*," she announced definitively. No one was going to poach her most prized staff member, head injury or not.

"Actually, he's *ours*," Bryan corrected her.

"Why don't I come back to the hospital with you?" asked Sophie.

"No," said Doug. "I'm staying here. With Ian."

Ian felt terrible. He went up to Doug and crouched down at the side of the wheelchair. "That night in the pub, I was telling you about a dream I sometimes have. The Prince Charming, the sparkly loafers—it's just a dream, Doug. It's not real. You've been really unwell, your mind's playing tricks, that's all."

Doug was crestfallen. "What about the fairy-tale castle?"

Slowly, sadly, Ian returned the shoes to the box, placed the tissue paper over them and pressed the lid on, before handing it back to Doug.

"The Dovecot's my castle," he replied.

"If you came to America, you could be a superstar with my help—"

"But—"

"I can see it now. This gorgeous English butler-turned-shoe-designer. It's the dream backstory for a marketing team." Doug was on a roll. "You wouldn't have to be anyone's butler any more. Hell, you'll make so much money you could have your own great big house and your own butler."

Ian smiled at Doug. He looked at Tata. He looked at Sophie. These Rich Wives, with their huge houses—he wouldn't swap with them for the world. His happy ending was being tucked up in front of the fire at the Dovecot, perhaps with a new Boris at his side one day. "Thank you for the offer, Mr. Fairfax," said Ian in his most respectful tones. "But you can't sway me. You see, there's nothing in the world I'd rather do than be Mr. and Mrs. Hawkins's Executive Butler."

"Nurse Beatty," said Doug. "Painkiller, please."

There are Prince Charmings, it seems, everywhere, if only you are prepared to look.

Let us return to the dance floor, where Vere had been whirling Selby around the room with such panache it quite took her breath away. In fact, she was soon so tired out that she had to beg him to stop.

"Breather?" she said, laughing.

"Okay, as long as you promise me another dance later," he replied. "I haven't had fun like that in ages."

They wandered out to the terrace beyond the Octagonal Room, champagne saucers in hand, leaving the hubbub of the party behind them. It was the most gorgeous summer's evening: the moon was opalescent; the scent of roses hung deliciously in the still night air; the lake below the house, blanketed with water lilies, rippled like molten silver.

Selby strolled over to the low stone balustrade at the edge of the terrace and perched against it, and Vere joined her. They looked back at the house and the glittering Octagonal Room, now lit by candles, seemed to twinkle in the night sky.

"You made it very special here tonight, Selby," said Vere.

"Thank you. Tata asked for moonlight and roses—"

"And she got love and romance—"

"Just from the wrong man!" Selby broke into giggles. "I can't believe she thought that Antoni and I would *ever* . . . I mean, there's no way . . ."

Vere shook his head, seeming bemused. "Not quite your type, in my opinion."

"Definitely not," said Selby.

"Who was the mystery man, by the way?"

"There's something in my life called the vault of vaults and that information is staying in the vault inside the vault of vaults." She tried to keep an enigmatic expression on her face.

"Fair enough," said Vere. Then he added a little shyly, "Can I ask if he's still, you know, around?"

Selby's lips started to form a playful smile. "You can. And he's not."

Vere moved a little closer to her on the balustrade. Their legs were almost touching. "Good," he said.

Silence followed: it was the electrifying sort that can only be described as full of romantic promise. It seemed to go on, and on, and on. And on, and on, and on. Selby sipped her champagne and looked longingly at Vere. Vere sipped his champagne and looked longingly back. An owl tooted. A dragonfly dipped over the lake. A soft wind stirred the leaves on the trees. She moved a little closer to him, so that their arms were touching.

"Oh," said Vere, grinning at her.

"Oh, what?" she replied flirtatiously.

Vere looked straight into her eyes, a pensiveness about him. "You know, I never thought I'd not feel heartbroken after Anjelica, but these last few weeks, after meeting you . . . I'm not as sad."

"Same," Selby said.

She put down her champagne and looked at Vere again. Wasn't he at least going to try and kiss her, or something, after all that?

Just then, they heard the sounds of a jazzy melody starting in the house.

"May I have this dance?" said Vere, standing up.

"You may." Selby put her hand in his as the tinkling of piano chords drifted outside.

And there, dear reader, let us leave the two of them, dancing together, on the terrace, under the moonlight, the intoxicating perfume of roses—and love—in the air.

The End . . . almost . . .

POSTSCRIPT

Selby and **Vere** *did* kiss, on the terrace, under the moonlight. This kiss, as I am sure you can imagine, was the kiss to end all kisses and the beginning of a beautiful love story.

Tata took the credit for Selby's happy ending, obvs. (She'd *always* known in her gut that Vere was The One.) Joyfully reinstated at Monkton Bottom Manor, she is once again Queen of all the Bottoms, as reported by Guy Cooper-Keel in the *MailOnline*.

The Pennybacker-Hoare sisters, displeased by this turn of events, are licking their wounds at Castle Hoare, the freezing-cold family pile in the Outer Hebrides, and trying to keep Anne's violent sons out of trouble.

Bryan is buying a new set of clubs for Lamu. (Ian has taken the executive decision not to mention, until Bryan has a cocktail in his hand on the terrace at the Peponi Hotel, that Lamu is not a golf resort, rather a tiny Kenyan island favoured by the fashion crowd.)

Doug spends half of every month in England with **Tess** and Violet, and any spare time designing sparkly loafers with Ian, which are so popular the website crashes with every drop. **The Sausages** have got jet-lag.

Sophie is rebuilding her house and has become the tireless patroness of the Royal Society for Hospital Visitors. (The bonus, she has happily discovered, is that hospitals are overflowing with potential Prince Charmings in white coats.)

POSTSCRIPT

Hugh is serving a twelve-month prison sentence for bribery. He's softening up his contacts in the Justice Department to obtain an early release.

Davinia is restoring her reputation by doing unpaid work in an adult education centre in Basingstoke. She isn't taking Hugh's calls.

Fernanda has hired a manny who was captain of the Inter Milan junior soccer team in his youth: **Luca** is now the star striker at Stow Hall School.

Galina and **Antoni** are on a six-week, two-person vacation on the yacht in the Ionian islands. (Her idea.)

Sir Reggie and Lady Backhouse are thrilled that **Arabella** has taken the job as deputy head of Stow Hall School. Arabella is thrilled because she has a huge crush on **Virgil Pitman**. (Reciprocated.) They are joining the Grigorivich's on the *Galina* in August.

Tallulah still hasn't met Jeff Bezos.

Josh has bought himself a top-class showjumper with the earnings from his modelling jobs. It is luxuriously stabled at the Hermès yard outside Paris.

Charlene entered Cheyanne into the Great Yorkshire Show and has won Sow of the Year. Tata paid for the manicure, shampoo, and haircut (for the pig).

Ian has won the Greycoats' Magazine Platinum Award for Outstanding Executive Butler of the Year. He plans to spend his winnings on a puppy sired by the champion of the Crufts miniature blue dachshund section and a small antique Ziegler rug for the sitting room at the Dovecot where—as they say in all the best fairy tales—he intends to live happily ever after.

That's All Folks!

ACKNOWLEDGEMENTS

I have had a lot of fun writing this book, thanks to amazing support from my publishers, friends, and family. Thank you to the incredible team at Harper: Jonathan Burnham for spurring me on to write a fourth novel, and always being at the end of the phone; Emily Griffin for the beautiful and tireless editing job, always there day, night, or weekend; Robin Bilardello for the delicious cover design (featuring Maizie Clarke's glorious illustrations); Rachel Elinsky for organizing an amazing publicity campaign; and Katie O'Callaghan and her marketing team for the work on the promotional side. My agent Luke Janklow never fails me, and thank you to Hope Coke for designing my social media. Thank you to Alexandra Pringle and the team at Bloomsbury in London.

Writing a novel can be lonely at times, and my friends and family took the edge off this. I am ever grateful to those of you whose houses I stayed at and wrote in, in particular I'd like to thank Tree Sherriff (lovely log burner, brilliant editorial notes), Miranda Taylor and Colin Dunsmuir (gorgeous armchair by the fire); Alice Sykes (great sitting room) and Claudia Rothermere (heavenly guest room for finishing an edit). There are so many others who have offered support: Frances Osborne; Gela Taylor; Whitney Bromberg and Peter Hawkings; Jemma Mornington; Arki Busson; Helen James; Georgia Beaufort; Jo Allison; my other Sykes siblings, Tom, Fred, Josh, and Lucy; Louise Galvin; Catherine Ostler and Albert Read; and my daughters Tess and Ursula.

Finally, of course, I must acknowledge the people and places who inspired the characters and the settings for this book—I literally couldn't have made them up. On that front, I won't reveal too much, but there is one person I must thank who really inspired me: Graeme—the real Ian. You know who you are. *Merci!*

ABOUT THE AUTHOR

PLUM SYKES was born in London and educated at Oxford. She is the author of the novels *Bergdorf Blondes*, *The Debutante Divorcée*, and *Party Girls Die in Pearls*. She is a contributing editor at *World of Interiors* and *Vogue*. She lives in the English countryside with her daughters.

A NOTE ON THE TYPE

The text of this book is set in Fournier. Fournier is derived from the *romain du roi*, which was created towards the end of the seventeenth century from designs made by a committee of the Académie of Sciences for the exclusive use of the Imprimerie Royale. The original Fournier types were cut by the famous Paris founder Pierre Simon Fournier in about 1742. These types were some of the most influential designs of the eight and are counted among the earliest examples of the "transitional" style of typeface. This Monotype version dates from 1924. Fournier is a light, clear face whose distinctive features are capital letters that are quite tall and bold in relation to the lower-case letters, and *decorative italics, which show the influence of the calligraphy of Fournier's time.*

READ MORE BY
PLUM SYKES

"Take one posh university, mix in a queen bee, throw in a murder, and you've got a mystery that makes *Heathers* look almost snoozy."
—*Cosmopolitan*

"Into the blender go Bridget Jones, Anita Loos, *Sex and the City*, and *Clueless*; out comes a diabolically amusing concoction."
—**Janet Maslin**, *New York Times*

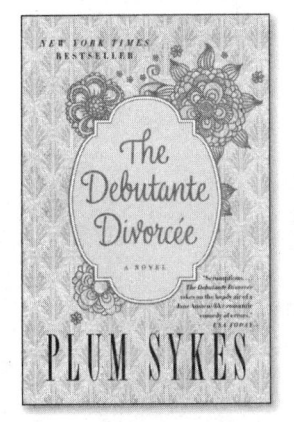

"Scrumptious . . . *The Debutante Divorcée* takes on the heady air of a Jane Austen–like romantic comedy of errors."
—*USA Today*

HARPER

DISCOVER GREAT AUTHORS, EXCLUSIVE OFFERS, AND MORE AT HC.COM